A Provincial Newspaper
and Other Stories

Judaic Traditions in Literature, Music, and Art
Ken Freiden, *Series Editor*

Select Titles in Judaic Traditions in Literature, Music, and Art

The People of the Book and the Camera:
Photography in the Hebrew Novel
Ofra Amihay

Jewish Identity in American Art: A Golden Age since the 1970s
Matthew Baigell

From a Distant Relation
Mikhah Yosef Berdichevsky; James Adam Redfield, ed. and trans.

Café Shira: A Novel
David Ehrlich; Michael Swirsky, trans.

Diary of a Lonely Girl, or The Battle against Free Love
Miriam Karpilove; Jessica Kirzane, trans.

The Rivals and Other Stories
Jonah Rosenfeld; Rachel Mines, trans.

The Odyssey of an Apple Thief
Moishe Rozenbaumas; Isabelle Rozenbaumas, ed., Jonathan Layton, trans.

Paul Celan: The Romanian Dimension
Petre Solomon; Emanuela Tegla, trans.

For a full list of titles in this series,
visit: https://press.syr.edu/supressbook-series
/judaic-traditions-in-literature-music-and-art/.

A Provincial Newspaper and Other Stories

Miriam Karpilove

Translated from the Yiddish
and with an Introduction by

Jessica Kirzane

Syracuse University Press

A Provincial Newspaper was originally published
in Yiddish as *A provints tsaytung* (New York: 1926).

All short stories in part three were published in the Yiddish daily *Forverts* in the 1930s.

First Edition 2023

23 24 25 26 27 28   6 5 4 3 2 1

For a listing of books published and distributed by Syracuse University Press,
visit https://press.syr.edu.

∞ The paper used in this publication meets the minimum requirements
of the American National Standard for Information Sciences—Permanence
of Paper for Printed Library Materials, ANSI Z39.48-1992.

ISBN: 978-0-8156-1158-5 (paperback)   978-0-8156-5687-6 (e-book)

Library of Congress Cataloging-in-Publication Data

Names: Karpilove, Miriam, 1888–1956, author. | Kirzane, Jessica,
translator, writer of introduction.
Title: A provincial newspaper and other stories / Miriam Karpilove ;
translated from the Yiddish and with an introduction by Jessica Kirzane.
Description: First edition. | Syracuse : Syracuse University Press, 2023. |
Series: Judaic traditions in literature, music, and art | "A provincial newspaper
was originally published in Yiddish as A provints tsaytung (New York : 1926),
All short stories in part three were published in the Yiddish daily Forverts
in the 1930s" —Title page verso. | Includes bibliographical references.
Identifiers: LCCN 2023007568 (print) | LCCN 2023007569 (ebook) |
ISBN 9780815611585 (paperback) | ISBN 9780815656876 (ebook)
Subjects: LCGFT: Poetry.
Classification: LCC PJ5129.K3 P69 2023 (print) |
LCC PJ5129.K3 (ebook) | DDC 839/.133—dc23
LC record available at https://lccn.loc.gov/2023007568
LC ebook record available at https://lccn.loc.gov/2023007569

Manufactured in the United States of America

publication supported by

Jewish Historical Society of Greater Hartford

*In memory of my great-grandmothers: Dora Kirzner,
Becky Mont, Claire Simon, and especially my Nanny,
Gussie Cheshansky Kaminsky, who I imagine may
have read Miriam Karpilove with delight.*

*And in honor of my grandmothers, Joan Mont,
of blessed memory, and Joan Kirzner, may she live to 120,
and especially my mother, Debbie Kirzner, the very best
mother and friend I could possibly imagine.*

Contents

Acknowledgments

I owe an extraordinary debt to my research assistant and student Eyshe Beirich, with whom I first read Miriam Karpilove's memoir about her time in Palestine during an independent study. Eyshe expertly pored over these translations and offered editorial suggestions, as well as contributed to the footnotes. This work is substantially improved under his careful readership.

Thank you to Rachel Beth Gross, Ayelet Brinn, Sasha Senderovich, Liora Halpern, Mindl Cohen, and Josh Lambert for generously reading and offering suggestions to improve the introduction. Thank you also to the Oak Park Yiddish Book Club—Deborah Spector, Cindy Barnard, Michael Bass, Jon Marcus, Sheri Gilley, Skye Lavin, Franette Liebow, Aaron Burnstein, Florence Braum, Ofra Peled, Liz Simon, Leonard Grossman, Heidi Kieselstein, Melvin Loeb, Kathy Bezinovich, Roberta Baruch, Deborah Holdstein and Doris Angell—for your unending support and for reading this book in manuscript. I am enormously grateful also to the students in my Women Who Wrote in Yiddish courses at the University of Chicago for their insights and their creativity. I would especially like to acknowledge Elena Hoffenberg for providing a model of gracefully integrating historical research into the study of literature.

To my colleagues at In geveb—Casandra Euphrat Weston, Sandra Chiritescu, Dalia Wolfson, Miranda Cooper, Sandy Fox, Josh Lambert, Mindl Cohen, Matthew Johnson, Aya Elyada, Elena Hoffenberg, LeiAnna Hamel, Jeremy Sarna, Eyshe Beirich and Alexander Stern—I hope working with me is nothing like working for Mr. Rat! Thank you for all you do.

Thank you also to Daniel Kennedy, David Mazower, Sean Sidky, Saul Noam Zaritt, Sonia Gollance, Sunny Yudkoff, Karen Underhill, Sebastian Schulman, Sarah Biskowitz, Ri Turner, Asya Schulman, Justin Cammy, Barbara Mann, Jessica Carr, Caroline Rody, Hannah Pollin-Galay, Sheera Talpaz, Allison Schachter, Agnieszka Legutko, Samuel Spinner, Jeremy Dauber, Lori Harrison-Kahan, Miriam Udel, Sasha Senderovich, Alona Bach, Sarah Biskowitz, Joel Berkowitz, and to many others as well who have listened to me speak about Karpilove over the years, and to my colleagues at the University of Chicago, especially Matthew Johnson, Na'ama Rokem, Anna Torres, Kenneth Moss, James Adam Redfield, Faith Hillis, Anne Moss, Nicole Burgoyne, Colin Benart, Maeve Hooper, Kimberly Kenny, Frederic Kopp, Sophie Salvo, David Wellbery, Eric Santner, and Shiva Rahmani.

Thank you to Yermiyahu Ahron Taub for sharing Ida Maze's letter from Miriam Karpilove with me, to Zachary Baker for his Miriam Karpilove finds, to Alona Bach for the Raskin cartoon, to Hallel Yadin at YIVO for assistance with copies from Miriam Karpilove's archive, and to Debra Emery at the Jewish Historical Society of Fairfield County, Connecticut, for her help accessing Miriam Karpilove's archive there. Thank you also to Erin Faigin, who spoke with me about her understanding of what "provincial" means in an American Yiddish context.

Thank you to Deb Manion for her enthusiasm for this project, and for her patience; to Emily Shelton for attentive copyediting; to Lynn Wilcox for the beautiful cover (and especially for the roses!); and to the rest of the team at Syracuse University Press. I am appreciative also to the peer reviewers of this volume, whose suggestions vastly improved the book.

I am especially grateful to be part of a community of scholar-translator-activists who are sharing the work of women who wrote in Yiddish with new audiences, including (but not limited to!) Kathryn Hellerstein, Joanna Degler, Karolina Szymaniak, Irena Klepfisz, Anita Norich, Frieda Forman, Eve Jochnowitz, Saul Noam Zaritt, Sonia Gollance, Anastasiya Lyubas, Faith Jones, Hinde Burstin,

Sheva Zucker, Ellen Cassedy, Jordan Finkin, Miryem-Khaye Seigel, Alyssa Quint, Goldie Morgentaler, Miriam Udel, Dalia Wolfson, Julie Sharff, Corbin Allardice, Jonah Lubin, Yermiyahu Ahron Taub, Mindl Cohen, Agnieszka Legutko, Daniel Kennedy, and Naomi Seidman. Thank you for including me in your community, and for your important work.

I am indebted to the Karpilow family, especially David and Miriam Karpilow, for generously and enthusiastically allowing me to share their aunt's work.

Finally, endless gratitude to my family: Sam and Debbie Kirzner, Rebecca Kirzner and Alanna Sklover and Bina and Eitan Kirzner, Joan Kirzner, David and Elyse Crane, and especially Daniel, Jeremiah, and Esther Kirzane, with whom my obsession with Miriam Karpilove has taken up residence. I love you—all three of you—more.

A chapter from *A Provincial Newspaper* previously appeared in the 2019 translation issue of *Pakn Treger*, and an excerpt from "My Three Years in Israel" appeared in the *Jewish Review of Books* in fall 2022.

Translator's Note

When I translated Miriam Karpilove's 1917 novel *Diary of a Lonely Girl* a few years ago, I immediately felt it important that I not stop with the one book. I didn't like the idea of it sitting alone on a shelf, with Karpilove known only as the author of the *Diary*, when the truth of Karpilove's output was much messier: reams and reams of newsprint, sometimes written for the tastes of readers or editors; handwritten manuscripts never published, including self-translations into English that never made it beyond Karpilove's own desk. What was most striking to me about Karpilove was not only the content of her novels and stories but also the sheer volume of them, and the way she had to fight to have her voice heard in each and every one. In a sense, translating only one novel felt like a mistranslation of Karpilove's output: she was no one-hit wonder.

I have chosen to keep some words untranslated, and a glossary at the end of this volume offers translations. Generally, I left these words if I felt they bore a particular cultural connotation difficult to succinctly explain in English, or if they came from languages other than Yiddish, and I felt the need to stress their being disruptive or unusual. Some of these words are translated according to modern Hebrew pronunciation, and some according to Yiddish pronunciation, depending on my sense of how the characters might have been speaking (sometimes an interpretive rather than definitive choice, especially in the case of Yiddish-speaking characters in Palestine).

The works in this volume come from three distinct sources: *A Provincial Newspaper* is available in book form as *A provints tsaytung* (New York, n.p., 1926), which has been digitized and made public by the Steven Spielberg Digital Library of the Yiddish Book Center (no. 09825). "My Three Years in the Land of Israel" exists only as an unpublished, incomplete handwritten manuscript found in Miriam Karpilove's archive: Miriam Karpilow Papers, Box 2, YIVO. The manuscript is undated but was likely written years after the events unfolded, perhaps in the 1940s. The short stories in this volume were all published in the Yiddish daily *Forverts* in the 1930s. Karpilove's archive includes a scrapbook with the label "*geklibene dertseylungen*" (selected stories), that includes a table of contents and newspaper clippings of nineteen stories, presumably of Karpilove's own selection. Rather than choosing from among her short fiction myself, I have followed her wishes and reproduced this selection in my translations. I have, however, made changes to the order of the stories, grouping them roughly thematically, in a way that I felt would make a more comfortable reading experience.

A Provincial Newspaper
and Other Stories

Introduction

Jessica Kirzane

Miriam Karpilove (1888–1956) was a prolific Yiddish writer whose work focused attention on women's lives and the inequality they experienced in the workplace and in romantic relationships.[1] She was born near Minsk in what is now Belarus (then in the Russian Empire), a middle child in a family of ten children. She immigrated to the United States in 1905, settling in Harlem and later in the Seagate neighborhood of Brooklyn, and finally in Bridgeport, Connecticut, which had been a home base for much of her adult life because several of her family members lived there. Karpilove's first published work appeared in 1906, and she continued her publishing career until the mid-1940s.[2] She was among the very few women who made their living as Yiddish writers. Karpilove wrote hundreds of short stories, plays, and novels, most of which were published in New York–based Yiddish newspapers.

Yet, despite her prolific output in the Yiddish press, her obituary in *Der tog* (The Day), a newspaper for which she had served as one

---

1. For biographical information on Miriam Karpilove, see Ellen Kellman, "Miriam Karpilove," in *The Shalvi/Hyman Encyclopedia of Jewish Women*. https://jwa.org/encyclopedia/article/karpilove-miriam (accessed February 8, 2023). See also "Karpilove, Miriam," *Leksikon fun der Nayer Yidisher Literatur* 8 (1981): 147; and Zalmen Reyzen, "Karpilove Miriam," *Leksikon fun der Yidisher Literatur, Prese un Filologye* 3 (1929): 575–76.

2. Miriam Karpilove, "Der forshtayer un zayne droshes," *Idishe Fon*, 1906. The same year she published several pieces in *Rikvorts* (Backward), a parody of the well-known Yiddish newspaper the *Forverts* (Forward).

of the founding writers, is very spare. It describes her as having written "novels for newspapers," without giving titles or the names of the publications, and explains that she "stood close to the Zionist labor movement" without explaining the nature of her political involvement.[3] The sparsity of information available—her work received almost no critical attention either in her lifetime or thereafter—has left me to rely on her personal archive and letters, as well as her published work, including her fiction, to reconstruct her life and career. It is also what makes the present volume of translations something other than a text admired in one language brought to an audience who wishes to access it in another: it is a work of literary recovery that helps to set the record straight about women who wrote in Yiddish, despite their previous erasure. This translation is part of a veritable wave of translations and scholarship that are now making it all but impossible to think of Yiddish literature as a field occupied solely by men, though little more than a decade ago syllabi of Yiddish literature were likely to include only a handful of female-identifying poets if they included women at all.[4] It also joins in a broader effort

3. "Miriam Karpilove nekhtn gebrakht tsu eybiger ru," *Der tog*, May 11, 1956, 10.

4. For observations about the previous exclusion of women and about the current wave of translations, see Faith Jones, "How to Suppress Yiddish Women's Writing," In geveb, May 2022, https://ingeveb.org/blog/how-to-suppress-yiddish -womens-writing; Anita Norich, "Translating and Teaching Yiddish Prose by Women," In geveb, April 2020, https://ingeveb.org/blog/translating-and-teaching -yiddish-prose-by-women; and Irena Klepfisz, "The 2087th Question, or When Silence Is the Only Answer," In geveb, January 2020, https://ingeveb.org/blog/the -2087th-question-or-when-silence-is-the-only-answer (accessed February 8, 2023). See also Joseph Berger, "How Yiddish Scholars Are Rescuing Women's Novels from Obscurity," *New York Times*, February 6, 2022, https://www.nytimes.com/2022 /02/06/books/yiddish-women-novels-fiction.html. For analysis of women's writing in Yiddish, see Allison Schachter, *Women Writing Jewish Modernity, 1919–1939* (Evanston, IL: Northwestern Univ. Press, 2021); Rosemary Horowiz, ed., *Women Writers of Yiddish Literature* (Jefferson, NC: McFarland, 2015); Kathryn Hellerstein, *A Question of Tradition: Women Poets in Yiddish, 1586–1987* (Stanford, CA: Stanford Univ. Press, 2014); Joanna Lisek, *Kol isze—głos kobiet w*

toward feminist literary recovery beyond Yiddish, the strength of which lies, as literary critic Joanna Scutts explains, "not with the return of a single neglected voice, but with a chorus."[5]

Miriam Karpilove's Writing Life

Miriam Karpilove started her career by publishing a handful of pieces—short stories and humorous sketches—in newspapers. Her first major success was her 1909 play *In di shturem teg* (In Stormy

---

poezji jidysz (od XVI w. do 1939 r.) [*Kol ishe: the voice of women in Yiddish poetry (from the Sixteenth century to 1939)*] (Sejny: Pogranicze, 2018); Carole B. Balin, *To Reveal Our Hearts: Jewish Women Writers in Tsarist Russia* (Cincinnati, OH: Hebrew Union College Press, 2000); *Di Froyen (Conference Proceedings): Women and Yiddish—Tribute to the Past, Directions for the Future* (New York: National Council of Jewish Women, 1997). For a bibliography of women's Yiddish writing translated into English—including many works that have been published in the past several years—see "Yiddish Women in Translation," Dorot Jewish Division Staff, New York Public Library, August 17, 2020, https://www .nypl.org/blog/2020/08/17/other-words-yiddish-women-translation-month. Among the recent translations that have brought women's prose writing in Yiddish to the forefront are Blume Lempel, *Oedipus in Brooklyn and Other Stories*, trans. Ellen Cassedy and Yermiyahu Ahron Taub (Simsbury, CT: Mandel Vilar, 2016); Yente Mash, *On the Landing: Stories*, trans. Ellen Cassedy (DeKalb: Northern Illinois Univ. Press, 2018); Kadya Molodowsky, *A Jewish Refugee in New York: Rivke Zilberg's Journal*, trans. Anita Norich (Bloomington: Indiana Univ. Press, 2019); Salomea Perl, *The Canvas and Other Stories*, trans. Ruth Murphy (Teaneck, NJ: Ben Yehuda, 2021); Fradel Shtok, *From the Jewish Provinces: Selected Stories*, trans. Jordan D. Finkin and Allison Schacher (Evanston, IL: Northwestern Univ. Press, 2022); Chana Blankshteyn, *Fear and Other Stories*, trans. Anita Norich (Detroit, MI: Wayne State Univ. Press, 2022); Ida Maze, *Dineh*, trans. Yermiyahu Ahron Taub (Amherst, MA: White Goat, 2022); and Shira Gorshman, *Meant to Be and Other Stories*, trans. Faith Jones (Amherst, MA: White Goat, forthcoming). Even this long list does not fully capture the momentum of the moment, which includes even more forthcoming works, as well as anthologized literature.

5. "Joanna Scutts on How We Find—and Lose—Women Writers," LitHub, May 13, 2019, https://lithub.com/joanna-scutts-on-how-we-find-and-lose-women -writers/.

Days), about a Jewish family during the Russian Revolution of 1905.[6] That play was performed by the Yidishe Folks–Bihne in New York in 1912, bringing new attention to Karpilove and her work.[7] In 1911 she published her debut novel, *Yudis* (Judith).[8]

In 1914 her writing career appears to have taken off. She started publishing short stories and sketches in the newly founded literary-oriented newspaper *Der tog*, among other leading newspapers such as the *Fraye arbeter shtime* (Free Voice of the Worker) and the *Forverts* (Forward). It was grueling but exhilarating work. As newspaperman Joseph Margoshes describes, Karpilove and fellow novelist Sarah Smith would wait in the cold lobby of *Der tog* early in the morning, eager for the doors to open so they could begin their long workday.[9] When Karpilove began serializing *Tage-bukh fun a elende meydl* (*Diary of a Lonely Girl*), her novel about the travails of a single woman in New York, in the newspaper *Di varhayt* (The Truth) in 1916, she gained broader recognition and the stability of a regular income.[10] The novel itself was widely popular, and as a result she became a regular contributor to *Di varhayt*, the *Ladies Garment Worker*, and other New York papers. This was her first foray into writing serialized novels, which became a specialty of hers. As early as 1917, before *Tage-bukh fun a elende meydl* appeared in book form, Karpilove had already begun her second serialized novel, *Di farfirte* (The Woman Who Was Led Astray), also published in *Di varhayt*.

6. Miriam Karpilove, *In di shturem teg* (New York: s.n., 1909).

7. "Fayer Funken," *Der Kibitser*, February 16, 1912, 8.

8. Miriam Karpilove, *Yudis: a geshikhte fun liebe un leyden* (New York: Mayzel et ko, 1911). This is available in an English translation by Jessica Kirzane as *Judith* (Tours: Farlag, 2022).

9. Joseph Margoshes, "In di ershte teg fun tog," *Tog-Morgn zhurnal*, November 14, 1954, 7.

10. This novel was published in book form as Miriam Karpilove, *Tage-bukh fun a elende meydel, oder der kampf gegen fraye liebe* (New York: S. Kantrowitz, n.d.). It appeared in an English translation by Jessica Kirzane as *Diary of a Lonely Girl, or The Battle against Free Love* (Syracuse, NY: Syracuse Univ. Press, 2020).

Karpilove continued publishing short stories, reportage, and serialized novels in *Di varhayt* until 1920, when her situation appears to have become more tenuous as the newspaper was absorbed by *Der tog*. In 1922 she published her melodramatic novel *Brokhe*, about an ill-fated shtetl romance.[11] There is a gap of several years in her newspaper publishing at this time, and, although she was at his point a well-known entity in the world of Yiddish letters, it seems that it was difficult for her to find regular work.

In 1925 she left New York for Boston in search of work. There she published about fifty editorials for a newspaper, *Der Idisher firer* (The Jewish Leader), which she considered exasperatingly provincial. Although she kept meticulous records of everything she ever wrote, she did not individually list these pieces in her bibliography, suggesting that she did not find them important or notable.[12] She did list by name one serialized novel she wrote for the newspaper: *Mener un froyen* (Men and Women). Inspired by her work for the *Idisher firer* in this period she published a slapstick novel *A provints tsaytung* (A Provincial Newspaper), included in this volume, about a woman writer-editor who is hired as a staff writer for a poorly managed provincial newspaper, where she is exploited and ill treated; one might assume there is some autobiographical content in the novel, though it was likely exaggerated for comic effect. When she returned to New York, two of her serialized novels were published in *Der tog*.

With no opportunities for stable employment on the immediate horizon, Karpilove left Boston for Palestine, hoping she could write about her experiences for the American Yiddish press. A devoted Zionist, she wanted to remain in Tel Aviv, but she faced financial difficulties there and returned to the United States in 1929. She later

11. Miriam Karpilove, *Brokheh: a kleyn-shtedteldige* (New York: Gothic Art Book Store, 1922).

12. Karpilove wrote by hand two meticulous lists of all her publications, listed by month, year, and publication. They can be found in the Miriam Karpilow Papers, box 5, YIVO.

wrote about this experience in a manuscript, published for the first time in this English translation.

Back in New York, without a sustained source of income, Karpilove managed to publish several novels and short stories in newspapers. She also tried to break into English-language publishing, translating her own work to seek out new audiences, but with no success. In 1934 she was hired as a staff writer for the Yiddish daily newspaper the *Forverts*, and for several years she published her short stories there. A selection of these stories is included in the present volume.

In 1938 Karpilove left New York for Bridgeport, Connecticut, to live with her brother Jacob and to help care for him and her ailing sister-in-law, Rebecca, although her letters to friends demonstrate that she disliked living there and felt removed from the lively world of Yiddish letters.[13] Still, a 1952 letter from famed Yiddish poet Yankev Glatshteyn to Karpilove suggests that she continued to be in touch with the world of Yiddish letters and was eager to share her work and ideas.[14] In a 1949 letter to Yiddish author Sarah Hammer Jacklin, she writes, with some resentment, "It would be good if we could see each other and talk about your, mine, and others' literary creations. I mean the work of those who are forced to stand outside while other, talentless people get the well-paid positions."[15] Until her death in 1956, Karpilove maintained correspondence with many friends in the Yiddish literary circles and planned to publish her selected stories (included in this volume), to revise and publish several novels, and to write her own life story, but her poor health made it difficult for her to realize these projects.[16]

13. See Jessica Kirzane, "Miriam Karpilove's FOMO," Yiddish Book Center, https://www.yiddishbookcenter.org/language-literature-culture/bronx-bohemians/miriam-karpilove-s-fomo (accessed February 8, 2023).

14. Yankev Glatshteyn to Miriam Karpilove, October 22, 1952, Miriam Karpilove Papers, Folder 6, Jewish Historical Society of Fairfield, Connecticut.

15. Miriam Karpilove to Sarah Jacklin, February 3, 1949, Sarah Hammer Jacklin Papers, box 1, folder 2, YIVO.

16. Some of these plans are detailed in a letter to Rose Shomer Bachelis, dated September 6, 1955. Rose Bachelis-Shomer Papers, RG 519, box 3, YIVO.

In some ways, Karpilove's story is one of remarkable success: she was a tenacious woman who used her sharp, sarcastic pen to win fame and financial independence despite the lack of opportunities for women in the Yiddish press. But Karpilove's story is also one of a constant need to hustle as well as concern and anger about the public's lack of interest in her writing, which remained largely unread and unexamined until recent years. I am fortunate to be working on Karpilove at a moment when activist scholars and translators have reshaped our understanding of Yiddish literature by recovering the work of women authors, and my translations of Karpilove have contributed to this effort.

The more I read of Karpilove, the more I understand her work to be strikingly creative within the constraints, and opportunities, of gender and genre, which is why it is so important that her writing is joined by that of other women's voices in translation. Her writing displays conformity to expectations of "women's literature" and popular fiction, while also making room for her unique voice. She wrote diary novels, epistolary novels, romance novels, stories and sketches, fragments of thinly veiled memoir, jokes and satire. The present collection of her narratives, many of which peek behind the curtains of her career in Yiddish letters, might ask us to reexamine what it means to place great books of literature by women on a shelf next to their male counterparts, and what such methods of inclusion might tend to exclude about literary history in a hunt for conventionally "great books" by women writers. Though it would be a mistake to overstress the divide between high and mass culture, perhaps what characterizes Karpilove's writing as something other than a work of high literature is its immediacy. As Saul Noam Zaritt explains, "Less invested in institutional longevity or even in the possibility of historical survival, popular fiction is oriented, explicitly, toward the present without much consideration for how the text will be retrospectively judged." Zaritt also discusses the gendered dimensions of popular fiction, noting that the demand for immediacy within popular writing requires such work to be responsive to the experiences of its readers, especially women, in a way that other genres do not.[17] Karpilove's writing—uncelebrated (sometimes, in the case of this volume, unpublished), immediate, and popular in orientation—asks us to break apart our allegiance to polished, and well received works, and to honor the hastily scribbled, half-finished writing that captures the demanding nature of Karpilove's writing life. Even if this writing was never geared toward "retrospective judgment," still it can be our task as readers to enjoy and value it.[18]

This volume offers a peek behind the scenes in the life of an important, if overlooked, Yiddish newspaper writer, in the form of memoir and fictionalized semiautobiographical writing, as well as a selection of Karpilove's short stories that appeared in the *Forverts* and were never published in book form. Together they create a portrait of an author who took her own humorous writing seriously and men in power with a grain of salt, and who always looked at the world through rolled eyes.

A Provincial Newspaper

In 1934, in the column "Tsvishn undz geshmuest" (Between Us), in which the editorial staff of the anarchist newspaper *Fraye arbeter shtime* publicly exchanged notes with those who had written to them, one editor addressed Miriam Karpilove, thanking her for submitting her writing and encouraging her to advertise her novella from several years prior so that the *Fraye arbeter shtime* might purchase and read it. He proclaims, "*A Provincial Newspaper* is a very successful portrait not only of a provincial newspaper, but of all Yiddish newspapers, even those in New York. Those who haven't read the novella

17. Saul Noam Zaritt, "'Yiddish Trash,' A Taytsh Manifesto: Yiddish, Translation, and the Making of Modern Jewish Culture" (unpublished manuscript).

18. Zaritt argues for the examining popular Yiddish American fiction because, in its relationship to American popular fiction it "reflects the importance of translationality to the entire corpus of Yiddish." See Saul Noam Zaritt, "Sarah Smith: Yiddish, Translation, and Popular American Fiction," MELUS, 2023; mlad009, https://doi.org/10.1093/melus/mlad009.

before won't regret reading it now."[19] This assertion remains true for today's readers, who will find the novella to be a fascinating window into the world of Yiddish journalism in the early twentieth century.

Although applicable to the newspapers in New York, Karpilove's account sheds light specifically on the Yiddish literary sphere geographically peripheral to, and relying on, New York as the prestige center of American Yiddish publishing. Locations outside of New York depended on the city as a center for publishing and literary life.[20] New York Yiddish newspapers, such as the *Forverts*, sustained by advertising dollars, played an important role in linking Russian Jewish intellectuals and driving the tenor of political and cultural ideology.[21] Karpilove criticized the way that the clout of Yiddish culture in New York, and its export to satellite areas such as Detroit, Montreal, Chicago, and Boston, crowded out local Yiddish cultural production.[22] In Karpilove's *A Provincial Newspaper*, we see the provincial newspaper as a poorly resourced institution lacking in a viable readership because any potential readers either turn to other languages or to the more prestigious newspapers emerging from New York.

Still, the aforementioned editor wasn't alone in this assessment that the absurdities and frustrations experienced by the novella's protagonist as a "lady journalist" in a ragtag editorial staff of a newly established Yiddish newspaper were relevant to the entire state of Yiddish publishing, even in New York. In the front matter to the novella, which was first serialized in *Gerekhtikayt* (Justice), the Yiddish organ of the International Ladies Garment Workers Union, between August 7 and November 13, 1925, and later published in

19. "Tsvishn undz geshmuest," *Fraye arbeter shtime*, July 13, 1924, 7.

20. See, for example, Rebecca Margolis, "Ale Brider: Yiddish Culture in Montreal and New York City," *European Journal of Jewish Studies* 4, no. 1 (2010): 137–63.

21. See Gennady Estraikh, *Transatlantic Russian Jewishness: Ideological Voyages of the Yiddish Daily* Forverts *in the First Half of the Twentieth Century* (Boston: Academic Studies Press, 2020).

22. See Miriam Karpilove, "Chicago," trans. Jessica Kirzane, in *Another Chicago Magazine*, April 21, 2020, https://anotherchicagomagazine.net/2020/04/21/chicago-by-miriam-karpilov-translated-from-the-yiddish-by-jessica-kirzane/.

book form in 1926, M. Goldstein, one of the newspaper's editors, writes that the novella "describes, in essence, how Yiddish news-papers conduct themselves" through "comical scenes" that are still "very much in earnest" in their critiques.[23] He pointed especially to the commercial aspect of the newspapers, which ran in contradiction to high-quality prose. Saul Yanovsky, editor of *Gerekhtikayt*, hailed the novella as "original, one-of-a-kind, unique" for its honest, true-to-life portrayal of Yiddish journalism.[24]

Karpilove's novella gives a back-stage tour of the Yiddish news-paper industry, from the English-speaking office girls who can't read the Yiddish newspaper they're working for to the publisher who views the newspaper as a business for profit and not an outlet for thinking or art. It is a farcical portrait of a mismanaged, haphazard, fly-by-night operation in which all the writers are unhappy. But what the editors of *Fraye arbeter shtime* and *Gerekhtikayt* fail to capture in their comments about the work, and much of what makes the work so fascinating, are the ways it illuminates in particular the tri-als of the newspaper's sole woman journalist.

Karpilove's novella is a first-person account of a woman writer, already a well-known author of novels for the Yiddish press when she is hired to work as the editor for the women's pages of a start-up provincial newspaper. It appears that, despite her previous success, the invitation finds her between engagements, as she is waiting for a new New York newspaper, whose staff she plans to join, to begin publication. This situation points to the precarity of Yiddish publish-ing at the time, even among the more successful. Having accepted the position with wages so low she is embarrassed to say the sum out loud, Karpilove's protagonist packs her bags and foots the bill for her own train ticket from New York to a city she coyly refers to as "B--n" (as if to preserve anonymity, though presumably anyone who knew

23. This letter is included in the paratextual material of Miriam Karpilove, *A Provitns Tsaytung* (New York: o.fg., 1926).
24. This letter is included in the paratextual material of Miriam Karpilove, *A Provitns Tsaytung* (New York: o.fg., 1926).

the author would have also known the city) to work for a newly established newspaper. There she finds editors who care more about sales than the quality of their writing, working conditions so demeaning that she is not even offered her own desk, and a community of Americanizing potential readers who want nothing to do with Yiddish.

According to her own record-keeping, in 1925 Karpilove published around twenty short stories and fifty editorials, as well as one serialized novel, in the short-lived Boston Yiddish newspaper *Idisher firer*, upon which the fictional *Pathfinder* of her novella *A Provincial Newspaper* is presumably based. Publishing *A Provincial Newspaper* in *Gerekhtikayt* concomitantly with her Boston writing work, Karpilove slyly reconstitutes the exasperating, often demeaning experiences of being a woman working for a publication with an all-male editorial staff into a screwball send-off of the world of Yiddish journalism. The protagonist winks at the audience about the novella's drawn-from-life quality, intimating, "I learned something from my experience at the *Pathfinder*. It'll come in handy," while knowing full well that she is recycling the experience to present it to her readership. This practice of fictionalizing real-life events into dramatic tales was common in the era of the newspaper novel, in which the boundaries between journalism and fictional narratives were often fungible.[25]

Yiddish newspapers at this time were eager to hire a select few women writers for their otherwise entirely male staffs in order to draw

25. Karen Roggenkamp, *Narrating the News: New Journalism and Literary Genre in Late Nineteenth-Century American Newspapers and Fiction* (Kent, OH: Kent State Univ. Press, 2015). One must, of course, be careful when assuming that writing that is ostensibly fiction is actually about an author's life, the close correspondence between Karpilove's life events and her novels notwithstanding. Insisting that a fictional character is a version of the female novelist may imply that the woman writer is not capable of creating believable characters outside herself, or may force her into a genre—memoir—often perceived as having lower literary status. For more on the thorny issues of gender and literary status as it relates to memoir and autofiction, see Rebecca Van Laer, "Just Admit It, You Wrote a Memoir," Electric Literature, May 25, 2018, https://electricliterature.com /just-admit-it-you-wrote-a-memoir/.

in women readers and a broader popular audience, and they promi-
nently displayed the names of women writers as an attractive feature of
a fresh, modern newspaper. Yet, as historian Ayelet Brinn has detailed,
women who worked for Yiddish newspapers in the early twentieth
century often found that the scope of their writing was limited to
"women's features"—advice columns, human interest pieces, poetry,
and short stories focusing on women's lives and their presumed interests—or took on behind-the-scenes roles as secretaries, office workers,
and translators, amounting to what Brinn calls "the hidden history of
unattributed work that women performed for the Yiddish press."[26]

Such experiences were analogous to women's professional lives in
the English-language press in the United States. In her 1887 article
"Women in Journalism," famed muckraker Ida Tarbell writes:

> The woman who would become a journalist must fit into the orga-
> nization wherever she is needed. She may be asked to read articles
> and prepare them for the printer, to condense a paper of five thou-
> sand words into one thousand without omitting a point or weaken-
> ing an argument, read proof, hold copy for the proof-reader, write
> advertising paragraphs, attend to editorial correspondence, look
> after the make-up of the "forms," prepare advertising circulars,
> review books, write obituaries, report events, write headlines,
> answer questions, look after the exchanges, make clippings, com-
> pile articles, write editorials, or do a hundred other things. If she
> earns a permanent place she must do some one of these things bet-
> ter than any other available person, and before she rises to an edi-
> torial position she ought to know how to do them all, and what is
> more know when others are dong them right.[27]

26. Ayelet Brinn, "Beyond the Women's Section: Rosa Lebensboym, Female
Journalists, and the American Yiddish Press," *American Jewish History* 104, nos.
2–3 (April–July 2020): 347–69, 349.

27. Robin L. Cadwallader, "Ida M. Tarbell's 'Women in Journalism,'" *Legacy*
27, no. 2 (2010): 412–15. For further context, see Alice Fahs, *Out on Assignment:
Newspaper Women and the Making of Modern Public Space* (Chapel Hill: Univ.
of North Carolina Press, 2011).

Here, Tarbell notes not only the enormous and varied scope of a woman journalist's role but also the double standard she worked under in order to prove her worth on the job.

All of this is reflected in Karpilove's novella, in her signature ironic tone, and from her perspective as a woman with extensive newspaper experience. Karpilove's protagonist is required to take on tasks far beyond what is officially in her contract: "Six days a week, one day off. Writing articles and editing the women's section. That's all" (p. 100, in this volume). In actuality, she is called upon not only to edit but also to write all of the content for the women's pages—writing that will largely be uncredited. While her well-known name, plastered across the pages of the journal, is meant to attract readers, still, much of her work for the newspaper is unacknowledged and uncompensated: conducting interviews, writing advice columns, translating fashion notices from the English newspapers, penning jokes, aphorisms, and musings, reportage, and composing gossip-oriented articles. It is more than a reasonable workload, and new assignments keep piling up at the editors' whims. Meanwhile, her boss treats her outrageously, at one point even measuring her columns with a ruler in order to prove that her work is insufficient and insisting that her novels don't "count" as work. He dictates the subject and style of her writing, insisting that she make her novels more scandalous, and that her articles double as advertisements for the newspaper itself. His arguments and demands are so vociferous and unpleasant that at times she gives in for the sake of escaping him: "So instead of refusing more work, I end up promising to do even more," she recounts (p. 67).

All the while, despite acquiescing to these unreasonable demands, Karpilove's protagonist remains refreshingly confident about the merit of her writing. From the first moment she sits down with an editor, we know we are in the hands of a woman who can hold her own. When her editor suggests that the newspaper might reprint one of her earlier novels, and that "no one will know" because they will have forgotten some of her earlier work, she retorts that "They'll know. . . . It is hard for me to believe that people outside the city could have forgotten even the first of my novels" (p. 34). In arguments over the content of the novels, the protagonist questions her editor's demands before dryly remarking, "If I understand correctly, you don't want me to write a novel, you want an advertisement" (p. 59). She refuses to write the kind of novel he describes, insisting that he "leave that to the people who know how," because she simply "can't" write the kind of pulp he desires (p. 60). She knows what she is capable of and tries to do her best work, and she is resistant to critiques she doesn't agree with. Throughout the novella she conveys a strong sense of herself as an author who should be valued and treated with respect, who is above the kind of work she is being asked to do, and who can and will find work elsewhere. Her self-confidence is the impetus behind her ultimately leaving the newspaper and advocating for herself when the newspaper continues to monetize her name in her absence. Her exploitation, despite her resilient self-regard, speaks to the extent to which misogyny was an inescapable feature of the workplace in the early twentieth century, in the world of Yiddish journalism and far beyond.

Though it serves as a record of the unequal workplace, Karpilove's novella is also a victory for the capable woman who endures those conditions, excels within them, and manages to escape from them. Making fun of the world of Yiddish newspapers was particularly audacious when women writers were more likely than not to be the target of sexist humor. Karpilove herself was lampooned in caricatures that made fun of her height and exaggerated her bodily features while downplaying the quality of her work.[28] In contrast to these misogynistic portrayals, her protagonist's certainty of her value comes through in her tone. She believes herself to be a better and more important writer than her bosses, so she can take on a stance of a bemused, urbane, cosmopolitan observer pointing out and poking

---

28. See, for example, the cartoon by Sh. Raskin, "Literatur un teater afn zamdign breg fun Seagate geblayshtift fun lebedign un bamolt fun Sh. Raskin," *Der groyser kundes*, July 31, 1925, 9; and A. Fotograf, "Vayberikum talantikum aynlaytigungs," *Der kibetser*, May 15, 1914, 4. See also Elyash, "Father of the Whole World," trans. Jessica Kirzane, Jewish Currents, January 10, 2020, https://jewish currents.org/father-of-the-whole-world.

fun at the foibles of the provincial newspaper's small-time staff. In conversations with her boss, she barely masks her satirical detestation, which is fully clear to her readers if not to the boss himself. Karpilove's ironic tone and the exaggerated qualities of her blustering boss allow her to raise a lighthearted critique that even newspaper editors like Yanovsky can enjoy—and publish. As psychoanalyst Joan Riviere argued in her influential 1929 essay "Womanliness as a Masquerade," a professional woman could navigate a hostile workplace through performative humor, becoming "flippant and joking" to deflect male aggression toward her controversial ambition while also "enabl[ing] some of her sadism to escape" under the guise of humor.[29] By sneaking her ambition and sense of superiority into humorous writing, Karpilove makes it palatable to the editors, writers, and readers who are the very target of her critique.

My Three Years in the Land of Israel

On September 1, 1926, Miriam Karpilove set sail from the Brooklyn harbor on the Fabre line steamship *Canada* headed to Palestine. An active Labor Zionist since her youth in Minsk, where she and her siblings had been founding members of the local Poale-Tsiyon chapter, Karpilove had decided to travel with her brother Jacob; his wife, Rebecca (Becky); and several members of her extended family to settle in Palestine and participate in the Zionist project.[30] The family

29. Joan Riviere, "Womanliness as a Masquerade," in *Female Sexuality: The Early Psychoanalytic Controversies*, ed. Russell Grigg, Dominique Hecq, and Craig Smith (London: Karnac, 2015), 172–82. See, especially, the discussion of this text in Catherine Keyser, *Playing Smart: New York Women Writers and Modern Magazine Culture* (New Brunswick, NJ: Rutgers Univ. Press, 2010), 4.

30. The Labor Zionist Poale Tsiyon (Workers of Zion) organization evolved from various groups in Eastern Europe and sought to base Zionism on the Jewish proletariat. It straddled the boundaries of revolutionary socialism and Jewish nationalism. See Samuel Kassow, "Po'ale Tsiyon," YIVO Encyclopedia of Jews in Eastern Europe, October 11, 2010, https://yivoencyclopedia.org/article.aspx/Poale_Tsiyon.

were not strangers to the idea of settling in Palestine—several of their extended family members and friends had previously settled there.

In a letter to Chaim Liberman, secretary of the I. L. Peretz Writers' Union, Karpilove wrote about the upcoming journey and made it clear that it was precipitated at least in part by her frustrations working for Yiddish newspapers, as described in her novella *A Provincial Newspaper*. The Writers' Union, she complains in an ironic, roundabout turn of phrase, "always helped me not to forget to remember that I must understand that writing is an art, and not a job . . . and left me free to enjoy my freedom so I could depend on being independent." In other words, Karpilove did not have steady employment despite her many years writing for Yiddish papers, which, as she points out, "I have so honorably served for more than twenty years (I've earned a jubilee celebration, right?)"[31] Instead, the literary establishment has patronizingly insisted that she write for art's sake rather than earn wages for labor.[32] Feeling slighted and undervalued, and with the promise of sharing in her brother's passion for the Zionist settler movement on the horizon, she left her beloved New York behind.

The chapters of her memoirs published in this volume are the first seven chapters of what presumably was a much longer manuscript detailing her time in Palestine. Unfortunately, only part of this handwritten manuscript remains in her archive at YIVO.[33] They focus largely on her arrival in Palestine and first impressions, as well as Karpilove's observations of her travel companions. They are an intriguing historical record told with Karpilove's signature attention to humorous detail.

31. Karpilove to Chaim Liberman, July 18, 1926, I. L. Peretz Yiddish Writers' Union, 1903–73 (RG 701), series 3 (Correspondence), box 9, folder 176, YIVO.

32. For one example of writers publishing in newspapers without pay, see Joseph Rolnik, *With Rake in Hand: Memoirs of a Yiddish Poet*, trans. Gerald Marcus (Syracuse, NY: Syracuse Univ. Press, 2016), 186.

33. The manuscript can be found in the Miriam Karpilow Papers, box 2, YIVO.

Among the most significant achievements of this memoir, and among the most challenging to translate, are its attention to multilingualism and to the humor that ensues in the interaction between the languages themselves (Yiddish, Hebrew, English, and, occasionally, Russian and Arabic) and the competing cultural and national identities held by those who use them. Karpilove's extended family of Yiddish-speaking immigrants from Minsk, some of whom settled in Palestine, and some of whom are newly arriving there after decades in the United States, express themselves through their names (Moyshe has become Mosheh, according to modern Hebrew pronunciation), their exclamations ("No, sir!"), and their assertions ("I am an American") in Karpilove's careful representation of their multilingual speech patterns. Their colorful use of language is essential to Karpilove's dialogue-heavy characterization as she at times mocks her characters for their linguistic pretensions and at other times shows them to be out of place or overwhelmed.[34]

When Karpilove and her family disembark from their steamship in the Jaffa port, they are immediately confronted with discussion of the financial and economic crisis in British Mandatory Palestine in 1926, which led to large unemployment, social discontent, and growing tensions between Jewish and Arab communities. As the owners of the Tel Aviv hotel where Karpilove stays later explain to her, the crisis had come directly on the heels of a time of prosperity, particularly for the Jewish population in Tel Aviv, the city that characters in her memoirs regularly compare to its older, neighboring,

34. Karpilove published a version of the first chapter of this memoir as "A Jewish Huckleberry Finn: 'Landing' in the Deep Mediterranean," in the *New Palestine*, the English-language organ of the Zionist Organization of the United States on October 19, 1928. In this version, told with a focus on Izzie, the young US-born boy who was among Karpilove's party, the multilingualism of the encounter is flattened, but Karpilove emphasizes the cultural differences between Izzie and his relative Moshe, who has been living in Palestine for decades, with Moshe praising Palestine's climate, and Izzie declaring that he wants to leave because "I'm an American, ain't I?"

primarily Arab port city of Jaffa.[35] An economic downturn in Poland in 1926, coupled with British restrictions on immigration beginning in 1922, resulted in a slowing-down of the flow of Jewish migrants and capital to Palestine, precipitating the economic crisis in Palestine and dealing a blow to the morale of Zionist organizations.[36] During this period, many Jews emigrated from Palestine in search of better financial conditions, a pattern Karpilove represents in her memoir with her hotel owner's daughter and her fiancé's plans to settle in America. In her memoir Karpilove brings to life this decline in new immigration as she describes how the owner of the hotel where she is staying climbs to the roof of his hotel each morning to look out over the docks in hope of seeing new immigrants arriving on steamships and is routinely disappointed. Karpilove details how she and her family are treated with incredulity for arriving during the crisis, even as the Jewish settlers they encounter in Palestine are desperate to receive more immigrants. "[The British immigration officers] were surprised that American citizens with money had come to settle in Palestine: Is it so bad in America, or so good in Eretz Yisrael, that the Jews would want to settle here? Especially during the present crisis?" (p. 126).

In addition to the financial crisis, the events of Karpilove's memoir unfold at a time of shifting strategies for settlement and investment in Palestine, and, through her various family members, Karpilove represents competing ideological commitments vis-á-vis settlement.[37]

35. The differential development of the two economies—Jaffa and Tel Aviv—was the result of British mandate policy, which favored the Jewish over the Arab economy. See Sreemati Mitter on how the financial structures of colonization resulted in Palestinians' dispossession: Sreemati Mitter, "Pensioners, Orphans, and Widows versus Banks: Palestinian Financial History," *Journal of Palestine Studies* 50, no. 3 (2021): 39–42.

36. See Jacob Hen-Tov, *Communism and Zionism in Palestine during the British Mandate* (New York: Routledge, 2017), 11.

37. For a discussion of intra-Zionist struggles during this period between private enterprise and centralized national models of land acquisition and management, see Liora Halperin, *The Oldest Guard: Forgetting the Zionist Settler Past* (San Francisco: Stanford University Press, 2021).

Karpilove's uncle Shmuel sees his pilgrimage to the land of Israel as a religious one: he plans to take part in the study of sacred texts in Jerusalem, and he looks down on modern Zionist accomplishments such as the building of Tel Aviv. He understands his aspirations to be traditional, in contradistinction to secular Zionism; his goal is to increase his merit in the afterlife through acts of piety and charity in Jerusalem. The rest of Karpilove's family, however, do not have religious aspirations and hardly set foot in Jerusalem, setting their sights on new areas of settlement, such as Tel Aviv and the Karmel neighborhood of Haifa, and the modern, apparently secularized Zionism that they represent.[38]

As Jewish immigrants coming from the relative prosperity of the United States, the Karpiloves have the potential to participate in the furtherance of a model of Zionism grounded in private enterprise, but, as Labor Zionists they are wary of such schemes. As Karpilove's brother Jacob says in her memoir, he didn't immigrate "to become a moneylender" (p. 158). Both Karpilove and her brother are solicited to invest in a new suburb of Haifa, Bat-galim, with the promise that the return on the investment would result in their personal gain.[39] Karpilove is not only uninterested in the project because the loan lacks guarantors and seems like an unsafe investment but is also repulsed by it for cultural and philosophical reasons. She deplores the mannerisms of the agent sent to persuade her, who, according to Polish or German custom, bows and kisses her hand; such behavior marks him as politically and culturally old-fashioned. Karpilove remarks, "If he thought he might win me over that way, that was a

38. Karpilove's continued references to Hebrew phrases lifted from religious contexts is one indication of the way Zionists, presenting themselves as secular, mobilized religious texts and traditions on behalf of their nationalist project. See Suzanne Schneider, *Mandatory Separation: Religion, Education, and Mass Politics in Palestine* (Stanford, CA: Stanford Univ. Press, 2018).

39. Bat-galim, now a coastal neighborhood of Haifa, was part of the Garden City movement, a forerunner of modern urban planning. See Miki Zaidman and Ruth Kark, "Garden Cities in the Jewish Yishuv of Palestine: Zionist Ideology and Practice, 1905–1945," *Planning Perspectives* 31 (2016): 55–82.

mistake. He lost me." Karpilove does not object to the idea of investment itself so much as the cultural trappings of what she sees as an
old-guard outlook that is anathema to the radical social circles in
which she has been engaged. Indeed, the Karpiloves would be among
the first investors in the Gan Hadar Corporation, a group of American Zionist investors organized in 1928 that purchased land south of
Tel Aviv for agricultural development.[40]

While the capitalist model for Zionist settlement offends the cultural sensibilities of Karpilove, who is ever-sensitive to pretentious
self-presentations, she is also skeptical of the socialist Labor Zionist
culture, as represented by her cousin Mosheh. Karpilove herself is
devoted to Zionism, but, as with all of her ideological commitments,
she approaches politics warily. When Mosheh takes her on a tour of
Tel Aviv, she does not wax ecstatic about the newly erected buildings; rather, she sees the flaws in a city that is only half built, and,
in pointing them out, she takes the wind out of the sails of Mosheh's
self-congratulatory, triumphalist Zionism. As she allows Mosheh to
bloviate on his racist attitudes toward Arab workers or his certainty
of Jewish success, Karpilove gives him the opportunity to demonstrate that his enthusiasm for the cause has pushed him ad absurdum,
until he discredits himself and exposes the chauvinism of the Zionism he espouses.

Karpilove herself is certainly not exempt from such chauvinism
and racism, and entire passages of the text deal in troubling racist
and Orientalist representations, comparing Arabs to animals with
preverbal tongue clicking and repeatedly depicting them as lazy,
slovenly, and unsanitary. She describes Arabs as a curious and pic-
turesque component of the Palestinian landscape, hardly allocating
them a single line of dialogue so that they could speak in "their own"
voices. She blames their poverty on their own habits—for instance,

40. "Karpilov familie lozt iber farmegen far national fond," *Der tog*, March
25, 1958, 9. On Gan Hadar, see Joseph B. Glass, *From New Zion to Old Zion:
American Jewish Immigration and Settlement in Palestine, 1917–1939* (Detroit,
MI: Wayne State Univ. Press, 2002), 239–42.

she claims that Arab children have cataracts because they wipe their eyes with dirty hands—and brushes aside the discriminatory nature of life in Palestine. There is nothing excusable about her straightforward assertions that Arabs are "lazy. They even look lazy" (p. 137). It is important to note Karpilove's racism in the text particularly because she sees herself as outside of the ideologically strident voices calling for the exclusive use of Jewish labor over Arab labor, as in the incident in which the Karpilove family is browbeaten into using Jewish porters to carry them to their hotel. Yet, as a Westerner settling in the "Orient," she succumbs all too easily to prevalent Orientalist sentiment and expresses it bluntly and unapologetically.

Although Karpilove can be a cynical audience for her characters and is especially skeptical of any ideological purity, she can also be a sympathetic conveyor of her characters' travails, especially when it comes to her cousin, sister-in-law, and dear friend, Rebecca Karpilow. Karpilove describes Rebecca's hard life in service of her ailing mother, demanding father, and many younger siblings and later to her husband. She dedicates substantial space in her memoir to her brother Jacob's first and second wives' obstetrical tragedies and shows that Jacob's dedication to Zionism is a passion built on a foundation of personal loss. In so doing she deftly integrates her family's intimate story into the broader geopolitical landscape they traverse and act within and lifts up the struggles of women, as daughters, wives, and mothers, as of equal significance to the building of cities and colonies.

Three years after her arrival in Palestine, having failed to make ends meet, Karpilove returned to the United States. As she describes it, her "diplomatic relations" with the Yiddish newspaper *Der tog*, which had offered a verbal assurance that they would print the Yiddish writing she sent them from Palestine, "suffered a disruption as soon as I stood on the gangplank connecting the ship to dry land." While Solomon Dingol, one of the editors, "declared *Der tog*'s love for the colonization project in Israel," he explained to her that they already had "an overproduction" of material about Eretz Yisrael and needed to save space to cover agricultural colonies in Crimea.

"I said to him, 'So you plan on exiling Zionism to Siberia?'" Karpilove recalled, suggesting that the newspaper's reduced coverage of Zionists in Palestine amounted to condemning the movement to oblivion. Reflecting on her financial situation, she concluded: "With such people you should never enter verbal contracts, only written ones."[41] Over the course of the next few years she sent her writing to *Der tog*, *Forverts*, and elsewhere, with the help of her friends in the United States, only to mostly receive rejections. She continued to express her love for Eretz Yisrael, where there was everything—flowers, good climate, culture—"except milk and honey, in the sense of prosperity."[42] This statement, with its barbed criticism, encapsulates her sharp-tongued, wary worldview, as well as her lifelong support for the Zionist project. In 1949, in a letter to famed poet Ida Maze, Karpilove confided that she hoped her health would allow her to return to Eretz Yisrael, though, as far as the archival record shows, that hope was never realized.[43] Upon their deaths, Karpilove and her brother Jacob both left their estates to the Jewish National Fund.[44]

Other Stories

Miriam Karpilove's archive at YIVO contains several scrapbooks of newspaper clippings of her writings, embellished with montages of photographs and magazine clippings of bright and varied illustrations.

41. Karpilove to Rose Shomer Bachelis, May 8, 1928, Rose Bachelis-Shomer Papers, box 3, YIVO; Karpilove to the Y. L. Peretz Writer's Union, April 10, 1928, Records of the I. L. Peretz Yiddish Writers' Union, 1903–73, series 3 (Correspondence), box 9, folder 176, YIVO.

42. Karpilove to Rose Shomer Bachelis, May 8, 1928, Rose Bachelis-Shomer Papers, box 3, YIVO.

43. Karpilove to Ida Maze, May 15, 1949, Ida Maze Collection, Group 3, Correspondence, box 8 (Letters: Tsadi-Kuf), Folder: קארפילאוו, מרים, Jewish Public Library Archives, Montreal, courtesy of Yermiyahu Ahron Taub.

44. "Karpilov familie lozt iber farmegen far national fond," *Der tog*, March 25, 1958, 9.

Among these is a scrapbook that begins with a title page, "Selected Stories," with a table of contents, listing nineteen of the many stories she published in the *Forverts* in the 1930s.[45] The present volume honors Karpilove's wishes by reproducing all nineteen of what seem to have been her favorites from this period.

All of these stories are attentive to lively dialogue and end with tight, tidy resolutions. Many of them are attuned to the experiences and love lives of older women, divorcees and widows, whose romantic decisions are also pragmatic ones about the kind of domestic labor and living situations they want to pursue. Although Karpilove may be familiar to some readers as the author of *Diary of a Lonely Girl* who brought her audience into the mind of a single young woman, here we see her as a more mature writer, taking us into the perspective of the mother of a married woman, or a woman who has been placed in a nursing home.

Two of these stories stand out as exceptions for not depicting Jews' lives in New York, and I have rearranged the stories from Karpilove's table of contents to place them at the start. "A Marriage and a Divorce" centers on a woman in a Yemenite Jewish community in Palestine, a community that Karpilove racializes as having traditions similar to "the primitive Arabs" (p. 179) and whose phenotypical difference she accentuates through reference to "full lips and white teeth," (p. 179) a description typical of Yiddish representations of racial difference. Although Karpilove expresses some admiration for the level of scholarship she believes Yemenite Jews possess and also acknowledges the discrimination the community faces in a racially hierarchical labor market in Palestine, this racializing characterization frames her narrative as mediated by Karpilove's exoticizing and paternalistic gaze.

"A Marriage and a Divorce," which is about a young woman forced into marriage, bears close resemblances to the other story in the collection that is set outside of the United States, "In a Country Town," which is about an East European bride hiding in an effort to escape from an arranged marriage she has been sold into like livestock.[46] In both cases, a woman subjugated to a patriarchal marriage system is denied choice and freedom during a wedding, a moment of communal celebration that overrides their individual desires. In the case of "A Marriage and a Divorce," however, the bride escapes her marriage and plans to obtain a divorce. With sparkling eyes, she declares her control over her own fate. She speaks of her independence to the "American lady," presumably a stand-in for Karpilove herself, who comes from a world in which arranged marriage is aberrant—though, as we can see in "In a Country Town," it was commonplace for Ashkenazi Jews only a generation prior. The contrast between old country (European country town and Yemenite settlement) and the perspective of Karpilove's "American lady" and the world of Karpilove's American characters in the other stories in this collection, foregrounds the notion that, for all the hypocrisies that the women in Karpilove's New York–based stories face, they are operating in what Karpilove might characterize as a modern and somewhat more liberated environment for women.

Still, the choices of Karpilove's women characters in America are constrained. In "Just Like the Old Folks Do," a fifty-nine-year-old widow is dismayed that the women in her social circles are still driven by their desire to find the perfect match, although they know that men only pursue them for their money or for their domestic labor. In "A Clever Mother," a mother saves her daughter's marriage by guiding her to leverage the possibility of her pregnancy in order to manipulate her husband; in this way she negotiates soft power for her daughter within the confines of traditional marital expectations. In "Man and Radio," a woman who dotes on her radio as one would a child decides whether to marry a man whose habits are

---

46. This story has been previously translated: "In a Friendly Hamlet," in *Have I Got a Story for You*, trans. Myra Mniewski (New York: W. W. Norton, 2016), 310–15.

antithetical to society. In contrast to the stories of arranged marriage the choice is left entirely in her hands. Yet both society's power to make demands and her lack of control over the man's habits seem to limit the horizons of her opportunity and render the choice a difficult one.

Several of the stories continue themes Karpilove explores in *A Provincial Newspaper.* "For a Bit of Respect" and "The Invitation" are send-ups of, on the one hand, a hapless Yiddish writer who yearns for an audience to celebrate his work, and, on the other hand, the Yiddish reading public who have no interest in proper literature. "A Kosher Swimming Pool" and "The *Shadkhn*" hinge on the mutual incomprehensibility between young seagoers—like the English-speaking office girls of the novella—who don't know or respect Yiddish language and customs, and a traditionally observant Jewish man who is out of touch with the culture of the younger generation.

"From the Same *Yikhes*" deserves particular mention because of the way it seamlessly integrates Karpilove's frequent subjects (tensions between parents and children, romances and marriages) with the political atmosphere. The story's reference to the rise of Hitlerism in Germany as a relevant backdrop lends urgency to its message against intra-Jewish prejudices.

Karpilove's stories, written to be read around kitchen tables, reflect the daily lives and interests of Yiddish newspaper readers in the 1930s. They showcase a broad range of themes, from internal classism and racism within the Jewish community ("From the Same *Yikhes*") to the performative hysterics of an overbearing wife ("Good News—and Bad"). Some offer predictable structures in which confusion is introduced and then resolved, while others end ambiguously. Each features the assertive voice that readers knew to expect every time they saw Karpilove's byline on the printed page.

It is my hope that this collection will demonstrate Karpilove's range as a writer of fiction and shed light on the conditions of her labor as well as its results. Most of all, I am thrilled that a new generation of readers will now have the opportunity to laugh along with Karpilove.

Bibliography

Works by Miriam Karpilove Translated in This Volume

A Provints tsaytung. New York: o.fg., 1926.

"A roman mit 'Yisroel': Mayne dray yor in Erets Yisroel." Unpublished manuscript.

"A koshere sviming pul." *Forverts*, August 5, 1930, 3.

"Der shadkhn." *Forverts*, February 14, 1934, 3.

"In a heymishn dorf." *Forverts*, June 14, 1934, 3.

"Gehaltn vort." *Forverts*, August 7, 1934, 3.

"Fun eyn yikhes." *Forverts*, September 18, 1934, 3.

"A kluge mame." *Forverts*, October 18, 1934, 3.

"Di aynladung," *Forverts*, March 28, 1935, 3.

"M'iz dokh epes menshn." *Forverts*, May 16, 1935, 3.

"Basherte." *Forverts*, June 17, 1935, 3.

"Tsvishn man un radio." *Forverts*, July 15, 1936, 3.

"Far a kleyn bisele koved." *Forverts*, July 30, 1936, 3.

"Un zey hobn beyde khasene gehat." *Forverts*, August 24, 1936, 3.

"S'iz gut un nit gut." *Forverts*, September 4, 1936, 3.

"Azoy vi bay di yunge." *Forverts*, October 28, 1936, 3.

"Di alte Sore." *Forverts*, July 4, 1937, 3.

"Der alter iz antlofen." *Forverts*, August 9, 1937, 3.

"Zi iz geven in Pariz." *Forverts*, October 19, 1937, 3.

"Korbones fun libe." *Forverts*, November 16, 1937, 3.

"A khasene un a get." *Forverts*, January 5, 1938, 3.

Other Works Cited by Miriam Karpilove

"A Jewish Huckleberry Finn: 'Landing' in the Deep Mediterranean." *New Palestine*, October 19, 1928.

"Chicago." *Di varhayt*, June 12, 1918, trans. Jessica Kirzane, in *Another Chicago Magazine*, April 21, 2020, (https://anotherchicagomagazine.net /2020/04/21/chicago-by-miriam-karpilov-translated-from-the-yiddish -by-jessica-kirzane/), 5.

"Der forshtayer un zayne droshes." *Idishe Fon*, 1906.

"In a Friendly Hamlet." In *Have I Got a Story for You*, trans. Myra Mniewski, 310–15. New York: W. W. Norton, 2016.

Brokheh: a kleyn-shtedteldige. New York: Gothic Art Book Store, 1922.

In di shturem teg. New York: s.n., 1909.

Tage-bukh fun a elende meydel, oder der kampf gegen fraye liebe. New York: S. Kantrowitz, n.d. *Diary of a Lonely Girl, or The Battle against Free Love*. Translated into English by Jessica Kirzane. Syracuse, NY: Syracuse Univ. Press, 2020.

Yudis: a geshikhte fun liebe un leyden. New York: Mayzel et ko, 1911. *Judith*. Translated into English by Jessica Kirzane. Tours: Farlag, 2022.

Archival Materials

Miriam Karpilove Papers, Jewish Historical Society of Fairfield, Connecticut.

Miriam Karpilow Papers, YIVO, New York, New York.

Sarah Hammer Jacklin Papers, YIVO.

Rose Bachelis-Shomer papers, YIVO.

I. L. Peretz Yiddish Writers' Union papers, YIVO.

Ida Maze Collection, Jewish Public Library Archives, Montreal.

Other Sources

A. Fotograf. "Vayberikum talantikum aynlaytigungs." *Der kibetser*, May 15, 1914, 4.

Balin, Carole B. *To Reveal Our Hearts: Jewish Women Writers in Tsarist Russia*. Cincinnati, OH: Hebrew Union College Press, 2000.

Berger, Joseph. "How Yiddish Scholars Are Rescuing Women's Novels from Obscurity." *New York Times*, February 6, 2022. https://www.nytimes .com/2022/02/06/books/yiddish-women-novels-fiction.html.

Blankshteyn, Chana. *Fear and Other Stories*. Translated by Anita Norich. Detroit, MI: Wayne State Univ. Press, 2022.

Brinn, Ayelet. *A Revolution in Type Gender and the Making of the American Yiddish Press*. New York: New York Univ. Press, 2023.

———. "Beyond the Women's Section: Rosa Lebensboym, Female Journalists, and the American Yiddish Press." *American Jewish History* 104, nos. 2–3 (April–July 2020): 347–69.

Cadwallader, Robin L. "Ida M. Tarbell's 'Women in Journalism.'" *Legacy* 27, no. 2 (2010): 412–15.

Di Froyen (Conference Proceedings): Women and Yiddish—Tribute to the Past, Directions for the Future. New York: National Council of Jewish Women, 1997.

Dorot Jewish Division Staff. "Yiddish Women in Translation." New York Public Library, August 17, 2020. https://www.nypl.org/blog/2020/08/17/other-words-yiddish-women-translation-month.

Elyash. "Father of the Whole World." Translated by Jessica Kirzane. Jewish Currents, January 10, 2020. https://jewishcurrents.org/father-of-the-whole-world.

Estraikh, Gennady. *Transatlantic Russian Jewishness: Ideological Voyages of the Yiddish Daily* Forverts *in the First Half of the Twentieth Century.* Boston: Academic Studies Press, 2020.

Fahs, Alice. *Out on Assignment: Newspaper Women and the Making of Modern Public Space.* Chapel Hill: Univ. of North Carolina Press, 2011.

"Fayer Funken." *Der Kibitser*, February 16, 1912, 8.

Glass, Joseph B. *From New Zion to Old Zion: American Jewish Immigration and Settlement in Palestine, 1917–1939.* Detroit, MI: Wayne State Univ. Press, 2002.

Gorshman, Shira. *Meant to Be and Other Stories.* Translated by Faith Jones. Amherst, MA: White Goat, forthcoming.

Halperin, Liora. *The Oldest Guard: Forging the Zionist Settler Past.* Stanford, CA: Stanford Univ. Press, 2021.

Hellerstein, Kathryn. *A Question of Tradition: Women Poets in Yiddish, 1586–1987.* Stanford, CA: Stanford Univ. Press, 2014.

Hen-Tov, Jacob. *Communism and Zionism in Palestine during the British Mandate.* New York: Routledge, 2017.

Horowiz, Rosemary, ed. *Women Writers of Yiddish Literature.* Jefferson, NC: McFarland, 2015.

Jones, Faith. "How to Suppress Yiddish Women's Writing." In geveb, May 2022. https://ingeveb.org/blog/how-to-suppress-yiddish-womens-writing (accessed February 9, 2023).

"Karpilov familie lozt iber farmegen far national fond." *Der tog*, March 25, 1958, 9.

Kassow, Samuel. "Po'ale Tsiyon." YIVO Encyclopedia of Jews in Eastern Europe, October 11, 2010. https://yivoencyclopedia.org/article.aspx /Poale_Tsiyon.

Kellman, Ellen. "Miriam Karpilove." In *The Shalvi/Hyman Encyclopedia of Jewish Women.* https://jwa.org/encyclopedia/article/karpilove -miriam (accessed February 9, 2023).

Kirzane, Jessica. "Miriam Karpilove's FOMO." Yiddish Book Center. https://www.yiddishbookcenter.org/language-literature-culture/bronx -bohemians/miriam-karpilove-s-fomo (accessed February 9, 2023).

Klepfisz, Irena. "The 2087th Question, or When Silence Is the Only Answer." In geveb, January 2020. https://ingeveb.org/blog/the-2087th -question-or-when-silence-is-the-only-answer (accessed February 9, 2023).

Leksikon fun der Nayer Yidisher Literatur 8 (1981).

Lempel, Blume. *Oedipus in Brooklyn and Other Stories.* Translated by Ellen Cassedy and Yermiyahu Ahron Taub. Simsbury, CT: Mandel Vilar / Dryad, 2016.

Lisek, Joanna. *Kol isze—głos kobiet w poezji jidysz (od XVI w. do 1939 r.) [Kol ishe: The Voice of Women in Yiddish Poetry (from the 16th Century to 1939)].* Sejny: Pogranicze, 2018.

Margolis, Rebecca. "Ale Brider: Yiddish Culture in Montreal and New York City." *European Journal of Jewish Studies* 4, no. 1 (2010): 137–63.

Margoshes, Joseph. "In di ershte teg fun tog." *Tog-Morgn zhurnal,* November 14, 1954, 7.

Mash, Yente. *On the Landing: Stories.* Translated by Ellen Cassedy. DeKalb: Northern Illinois Univ. Press, 2018.

Maze, Ida. *Dineh.* Translated by Yermiyahu Ahron Taub. Amherst, MA: White Goat, 2022.

"Miriam Karpilove nekhtn gebrakht tsu eybiger ru." *Der tog,* May 11, 1956, 10.

Mitter, Sreemati. "Pensioners, Orphans, and Widows versus Banks: Palestinian Financial History." *Journal of Palestine Studies* 50, no. 3 (2021): 39–42.

Molodowsky, Kadya. *A Jewish Refugee in New York: Rivke Zilberg's Journal.* Translated by Anita Norich. Bloomington: Indiana Univ. Press, 2019.

Norich, Anita. "Translating and Teaching Yiddish Prose by Women." In geveb, April 2020. https://ingeveb.org/blog/translating-and-teaching-yiddish-prose-by-women (accessed February 9, 2023).

Perl, Salomea. *The Canvas and Other Stories.* Translated by Ruth Murphy. Teaneck, NJ: Ben Yehuda, 2021.

Raskin, Sh. "Literatur un teater afn zamdign breg fun Seagate geblayshtift fun lebedign un bamolt fun Sh. Raskin." *Der groyser kundes,* July 31, 1925, 9.

Reyzen, Zalmen. *Leksikon fun der Yidisher Literatur, Prese un Filologye* 3 (1929).

Roggenkamp, Karen. *Narrating the News: New Journalism and Literary Genre in Late Nineteenth-Century American Newspapers and Fiction.* Kent, OH: Kent State Univ. Press, 2015.

Rolnik, Joseph. *With Rake in Hand: Memoirs of a Yiddish Poet.* Translated by Gerald Marcus. Syracuse, NY: Syracuse Univ. Press, 2016.

Schachter, Allison. *Women Writing Jewish Modernity, 1919–1939.* Evanston, IL: Northwestern Univ. Press, 2021.

Schneider, Suzanne. *Mandatory Separation: Religion, Education, and Mass Politics in Palestine.* Stanford, CA: Stanford Univ. Press, 2018.

Scutts, Johanna. "Joanna Scutts on How We Find—and Lose—Women Writers." LitHub, May 13, 2019. https://lithub.com/joanna-scutts-on-how-we-find-and-lose-women-writers/.

Shtok, Fradel. *From the Jewish Provinces: Selected Stories.* Translated by Jordan D. Finkin and Allison Schacher. Evanston, IL: Northwestern Univ. Press, 2022.

"Tsvishn undz geshmuest." *Fraye arbeter shtime,* July 13, 1924, 7.

Van Laer, Rebecca. "Just Admit It, You Wrote a Memoir." Electric Literature, May 25, 2018. https://electricliterature.com/just-admit-it-you-wrote-a-memoir/.

Zaidman, Miki, and Ruth Kark. "Garden Cities in the Jewish Yishuv of Palestine: Zionist Ideology and Practice, 1905–1945." *Planning Perspectives* 31 (2016): 55–82.

Zaritt, Saul Noam. "Yiddish Trash." In "A Taytsh Manifesto: Yiddish, Translation, and the Making of Modern Jewish Culture." Unpublished manuscript.

———. "Sarah Smith: Yiddish, Translation, and Popular American Fiction," *MELUS,* 2023; mlad009, https://doi.org/10.1093/melus/mlad009.

Part 1
A Provincial Newspaper

1

The telephone: "Hello?"

"Hello! Is that you? I just got you on the wire. Listen, I made you an appointment at the Café Royale. He is—"

"May I first know who *you* are?" I asked.

"Sure! I am Danchenko!"

"Oh, Danchenko-"

"Yes, as I was saying, he is a Mr. Sohn, from B--n, Mass. He wants to see you about some kind of newspaper. Be at the Royale tonight. He'll be waiting for you."

"How will I know who he is?"

"You'll know. He's a thin, pale man with large eyes and—he knows you! Will you be there?"

"Yes, I will. Thank you for calling."

"You're welcome. Goodbye!"

"Goodbye!"

I hung up the receiver and thought that it's very nice of this Danchenko, someone I barely knew through professional connections as a writer, to take an interest and call me like this, and to make an appointment for me. Very nice of him.

In the café. Mr. Sohn. We sat together at a table and he said:

"I want to start a daily Yiddish newspaper in B--n, Mass. A man there, Mr. Rat, will be the publisher, Mr. Kahm will be the chief editor, and I'll be the managing editor. I came here to commission a novel and to talk to writers about coming to work for us. So, how much would you ask for a novel?"

"For a new one, a translation, or a reprint?"

"It doesn't matter if it's a reprint. No one will know."

"They'll know," I say. "My novels are widely read, even outside the city."

"Maybe they've already forgotten one already? I mean, one of the earlier ones."

It was hard for me to believe that people outside the city could have forgotten even the first of my novels, but, if he wants to think so, that's his business. So I said, "Maybe!"

"So, about a fee. I must tell you from the outset that we can't pay very much. We just can't."

I didn't know what price to name, so we agreed that he'd take a few of my novels and read them first. He'd write to me about them and then we'd come to an agreement.

I didn't hear from Mr. Sohn for some time. I kept on waiting and then I received a letter from Mr. Kahm, the chief editor.

He wrote to tell me he'd spoken with Mr. Sohn about me. They wanted to hire me to work with them. Their new newspaper, which would be called the *Yiddish Pathfinder*, would have a women's section, and they wanted me to be the editor of this section. So, what were my conditions?

I asked for more information about the newspaper and about my novels that Mr. Sohn had read: How many times a week would the women's section be published, and how much compensation could they offer? Here, in New York, there is a certain amount that is considered the minimum wage for this kind of work: $55 a week. I wouldn't ask too large an amount from them, but I wouldn't accept an offer for too little either. They should write and tell me more candidly about everything, and then I could give an informed response.

A few days later I received an answer to my letter. Here it is, word for word, just as it was written:

The *Yiddish Pathfinder*
Mr. Rat, publisher.   Mr. Kahm, editor.
Telephone: Mass 9999
123 Being Street, B--n, Mass

To the esteemed _____ (my name),

It is not possible to explain in a letter all that we have in mind for our *Pathfinder.*

Therefore, I can only answer these few questions.

First: a women's page will be published every day, except for Saturday.

Second: you would be expected to edit the page, and also to write something, from a column to a column-and-a-half in length, every day.

Third: it is necessary for the *Pathfinder* that you be located *here*: you would be our full-time employee.

Fourth: we are unable to offer you the New York minimum wage. All of those who work for the *Pathfinder* will receive only minimal compensation so that they can help the newspaper establish itself. If it is successful, they will receive raises.

With these explanations, it would be our pleasure if you would become part of our team. We can offer you, for the time being, only $25 a week. *We cannot afford more!*

The *Pathfinder* will begin publishing in a few days. If our offer appeals to you, come to us no later than next Saturday morning.

With regard to your novels, that remains to be seen. It is a great shame that they have already been published. But we will see.

      Please let us know soon whether you will come.
      Respectfully,
      S. Kahm
      Editor of the *Daily Yiddish Pathfinder*

I read over the letter and thought about how to respond. I had to respond quickly, I knew. It was already Friday afternoon.

I thought about going: another city, different people, a new newspaper and—a position as an editor. I'd never held such a position. But the wages! I couldn't even bring myself to say out loud how little it was.

But what's money? Nothing! The main thing is the work, the free rein that I'd have with the newspaper, the influence I could have. And if I didn't like it, I could always come back.

I'd have to come back eventually. The new newspaper that had been in the works here for the past few years would need me. I was supposedly an employee there, or at least a future employee.

I called the future publisher of this new newspaper, and asked his advice about whether I should take a position outside of the city or stay here and wait until his newspaper would come out. He advised me to go. Maybe if I worked in the provincial city for four or five months I could earn a thousand dollars. It would be a shame to let this go. And the position he was offering would not change. When I returned I could have it, or when he finally was ready to publish the paper he would see to it that he called me back.

I wrote right away to the *Pathfinder.* Having weighed the options of going or staying, I decided to go, for my own peace of mind. I'd get used to the small stipend because my excitement about building a new newspaper was stronger than my desire to make more money.

So I told them I had resolved to come on Saturday. I'd call the newspaper from the train station.

I sent the letter. I looked around the room where I lived and I thought about the people in the building who'd grown so familiar to me. It would be hard to leave such people.

As I was thinking, Mrs. S., my landlady, a cheerful woman with a bright smile, came to speak to me. She had heard of this business with the *Pathfinder* and wanted to know how I felt about it.

I gave her their letter: she has a quick grasp of things, a strong mind. I wanted to know her thoughts.

She said she didn't want to see me go, but she was sure it wouldn't be for long. My room would be waiting for me. In the meantime it would be good for me to go. I would see a new city, new people, work for a new paper. She wished she could go with me; it's boring to stay in one place for too long.

"But the wages!" I said. "It's too awful even to say the amount out loud."

"Who do you need to say it to?" she asked. "Who needs to know? The main thing is not the wages, or the job, but the journey itself."

She spoke about it like a pleasure trip. It made me feel like packing my things right away and setting off for the small town to show it how excited I was to see it. I wouldn't be dismissive of it, like those who say that small towns are backward, have no taste, and will gobble up anything indiscriminately. If you just give the small town something good, how well it takes to it! The small town has so much time, more time than the big cities, to take in the most gourmet intellectual fare. I pledged to the town, and to myself, that I would see to it that the gourmet fare of the *Pathfinder* would be of a quality that would not leave its belly wanting.

2

I sat on a train that carried me to the *Pathfinder* and thought about what kinds of columns I'd create for the women's page. One after the other, ideas crammed into my mind. Each idea came too fast for me to consider, each idea was too new, too fresh. They formed a line, waiting to see which of them would be chosen to help me to fill the women's world with something exceptional.

I looked them over like a foreman, considered them, then put them aside for later, when I would return to them. I would see if I could use them once I got there. Maybe new ideas would come to me there, too. Why should I worry about that now?

I told myself to put aside this line of thought. In the meantime I'd better look out the window of the train at the green fields.

They stirred a sense of longing within me. I thought like a proletarian: the rich were traveling to their summer homes to rest in the lap of nature, while I was traveling to work, to sweat.

The poor newspaper! A rich newspaper would not come out in the summertime, in the heat. It would wait until winter.

But surely they knew what they were doing. A provincial newspaper must know who its readers are and when to find them. Maybe the best time for a small-town newspaper to bloom is the summer, growing on the farms or by the sea's edge.

I decided then and there that I would rent a room somewhere by the sea. I would rise early, go for a swim, and then go to work. I wouldn't allow even one good idea to go by untried, not one interesting picture to go unseen; I'd use everything for the newspaper that would bring meaning to my life.

I watched the woods and fields of Connecticut, Rhode Island, Maine, and New Hampshire rush by. I read in them pieces of history from the revolution against England's rule. An interesting story: settlers, pioneers, Quakers, Puritans, Indians . . . and suddenly there were clouds. Big, heavy clouds. It began to rain. It was a downpour!

I arrived in B--n in the midst of this rain. I looked around the empty station cloaked in clouds, hoping there was someone here from the *Pathfinder* to meet me.

There was no one.

I called the *Pathfinder* on the telephone:

"Hello! I'm here! Should I wait for someone to meet me or come on my own? It's pouring. How far away are you? Very far?"

A voice from the other side of the wire said, "It's not far. Take a taxi and come straight here, to the office of the *Pathfinder*."

I said alright, I would be there right away.

I called a taxi, rode, arrived, paid, tipped, and climbed with my baggage to the fourth floor of an old, worn-down, darkened building.

A bright office. Noisy. The publisher, Mr. Rat, and the chief editor, Mr. Kahm, greeted me with a "Sholem aleykhem." They introduced me to Mr. Frost, a music professor. He was so fat that it seemed like he would burst out of his clothing. Next to him stood another man, Mr. Stein, who was very thin. The publisher himself was a small man, and the editor, who was certainly not small, was young and not at all unattractive.

"Such a young man!" I said with wonder. "And *already* an editor!"

"Yes," Mr. Kahm smiled a bit sheepishly. "And what do you think of the rain?"

"I don't like it at all, but that doesn't matter," I said. "It'll pass. And where is Mr. Sohn?" I asked.

"I don't know," he said, looking around. "He should be here. He'll probably be back soon. How was your trip? How is New York?"

"New York is what it is—incomparable. What's it like here, in B--n?" I asked and turned, probably too soon, to the *Pathfinder*. "When do you start publishing?"

"In a few days. We've had to delay because of technical difficulties. If you want, we can go into my office and talk more about it."

All we had to do was go through the doorway we'd been standing right next to. He sat on the editor's chair. I sat on the other side of the desk.

"What did you bring with you?" he asked, looking at my baggage. "I mean, for the *Pathfinder*." He smiled.

"Kind regards," I smiled and then answered with seriousness, "Several things that could be of use to the newspaper. But first I want to know more about what your plans are."

"Did you bring a novel?"

"You have my novels here."

"But these have already been published. I mean have you written anything new? Something that will . . . that will be quite . . . you know, quite interesting. The success of the newspaper depends on novels. So, what are you thinking of giving us for the women's page?"

The publisher, Mr. Rat, came in during that question and asked, "Well, how's it going?" He turned to the editor. "Did you explain to her what we need?"

I looked at him. How loud he talked! Such a small man—where did he get such a loud voice? But his swift, beady eyes laughed with optimism so that I could not help but smile.

I asked him what kind of mission his *Pathfinder* would have. He answered:

"The mission of the paper is that it will change all other papers! It will supply everything that the city, the state, and all of the surrounding states need! It will be a living paper! Full of the most current events and everything that will make it successful! The women's page must be so, so . . . round and pointed! It should attract both men and women! A novel must attract the reader from the first issue, so that he cannot tear himself away. I am in favor of pulp fiction. You may laugh at me, but I don't believe in highfalutin literature! That's what the library is for, that's all! The paper must be a success that everyone will envy. I'll show them that I can publish a daily newspaper without them. I can be the boss myself!"

I waited until he finished speaking and asked the editor what I needed to do.

"You should write an editorial every day," he said, "and—"

"And—?"

"That's it. An editorial and edit the page. After that, we would like—a novel."

"A *good* novel!" the publisher cried. "The kind of novel that will grab the reader by his right—"

Telephone: "Wrong number!"

The editor hung up the receiver and continued to talk. "It must be the kind of novel that—"

"It must snap!" Mr. Rat clicked his tongue and quickly snapped his fingers. "Something like *The Secrets of the Imperial Court*, about Catherine the Great with her—you know! Or like the *Iron Woman*. That's a good one, too."

"I am afraid that I can't write something like that," I said.

"What do you mean, you *can't*? What do you need to know to do it?"

"You don't have to know something, you have to *be able* to do it."

"It's nothing! You just take any old novel and change it around a little, here and there, and the readers will lap it up!"

I'd initially been sympathetic to Mr. Kahm, but this wasn't helping. I looked out into the street. It was still pouring. My head began to ache. I remembered that I needed to eat something. And where could I do this? I needed to find myself a room to rent.

Aside from these things I also thought about a novel: if they refused to publish one of my novels, who knows what kind of trash they'd publish instead? What kind of image would this newspaper have, with a novel like that?

Soon, Mr. Sohn would arrive. He'd read my novels. I'd wait to hear what he had to say. But he seemed to be in no hurry. Where could he have disappeared to? Without him, they said, they didn't know where I could rent a room. He knows about such things. In the meantime, did I want to take a look around the editorial offices?

"Oh, yes, very much!"

Mr. Rat, the boss himself, showed me around. "This is the general office, this is Mr. Sohn's office, this is Mr. Kahm's office, this is the printing area, and this is the business office!"

"And where," I asked, "is *my* office?"

"What do you need an office for? You have a desk. Does it make a difference to you?"

"Yes, I believe so—"

"That's alright. It will be alright. Don't worry!"

But I did worry. I'd pictured a separate office with a desk and instead I had nothing: it seemed I'd have to write my pieces in my own room, once I'd managed to rent one.

In the meantime I still had no room, and the managing editor, Mr. Sohn, still had not shown up. I decided to try to find myself something to eat.

3

The managing editor finally arrived and took it upon himself to ask someone over the telephone whether they could possibly find a room for me. They searched, asked around, and found one.

Baggage in hand, I summoned a taxi, and Mr. Sohn accompanied me to my new residence. Mr. Rat, the publisher, joked in his bossy way about my taking a taxi and invited me to his home for dinner on Sunday.

Mr. Sohn was outraged that they hadn't come to meet me at the station or prepared a proper reception for me. It's a good thing he came and asked his acquaintance to arrange for a room for me. If not, where would they have put me? In the editorial offices overnight? What a load of nonsense! What imbeciles! And they left it all for *him* to deal with!

I begged him not to get so worked up on my account. I'd much prefer for him to tell me a little more about Mr. Rat.

"What is he like? He has no character at all!" he said, waving his thin hand dismissively. "I'd much rather know, has he paid you anything yet?"

"Pay me? Already? For what? I haven't earned anything yet," I responded.

"Who cares? You should ask for it in advance," he insisted.

"No. How could I do that?"

"Well, what about your travel costs? He told me expressly that he was bringing you here on his own dime."

"Well, if he told you so, then I believe he'll reimburse me for them. I wouldn't want to ask," I demurred.

"Why not?" he blustered. "With what you're getting paid, how would you even consider coming here out of your own pocket? It's an expensive business! Say, you must have money spilling out of your pockets like woodchips."

"That's right. I have as much money as I have woodchips—none at all," I replied, laughing.

"Go on and laugh," he said. "Once you've been here as long as I have, you'll even forget how to smile, never mind laughing."

"You give me such high hopes! Is it really so bad?" I asked.

"You'll see. This place will make you crazy!"

"Why?"

"Why? Because it's *here*," he sighed. "Oh, New York! New York! Long live New York! Where you can go to the café and see who you want to see, and talk to the people you want to talk to—what a joy! How good it is!"

"It's not so good. If that's the only reason this place could make me crazy, I'll be in the clear."

"You won't stay here for long," he asserted. "Not for long, whatever you say. You'll see."

"That may be, but not because I'll be pining for New York cafés. Maybe I won't find myself suited to the work at the newspaper. Perhaps Mr. Rat will ask me to do things I can't or won't want to do. If they don't give me a free rein here, if they don't let me write the way I want to, then—"

"Back to New York? Is that it?"

"Well . . . how about my novels? Did you read them?" I asked, changing the subject.

"Yes, but your novels are too good for what they want. Too literary. They need something more popular. I told them—"

"What did you say?"

"I told them that your novels are *very* good. Quite literary."

"You didn't have to say that," I responded dryly.

"They would've figured it out on their own eventually and they would've blamed me for fooling them and not telling the truth. I would've lost my job over it, and you wouldn't have gotten anything out of it either."

He was disaffected with his town and yearned for the New York cafés. How he longed for them! I was almost jealous of his passion. I also wondered: How can a weak person like him long for something that saps away the health of others?

We set a time when we would meet to go see our publisher. I went into my new room to get settled.

It was a large room with a very long table, well suited for an engineer to draft his plans. There was a rocking chair, a dresser and a large, wide bed—a horrible thing! You could get lost falling into such a bed. Once you got in it, no one would ever be able to find you!

The landlords were intellectuals. He was a doctor of something that had nothing to do with health. He was American born, and she was from Germany. They were well suited to their large house with many rooms, most of which were rented to strangers. They had no children. When they were lonely, they went out to concerts, to the library, to the movies, and sometimes to their Jewish neighbors, who led very full social lives.

The Jewish family was disappointed that they didn't have a spare room they could rent to me, since I was someone they felt certain they could talk to. But, since they lived so close by, they promised they would take advantage of the opportunity as best they could.

They were kind, dear people, if a little needy. To befriend them a person would have to have a lot of free time at their disposal, and I anticipated that my time would be entirely occupied with the *Path-finder*. I was already racking my brain over how to write my first editorial. What should I write about, and who?

On Sunday it stopped raining and it was only cloudy. Mr. Sohn, the managing editor, came to go with me to see Mr. Rat, the publisher, grumbling, "Why should I go there? Who needs this? And why today, of all days?"

"If we don't go there today, maybe we'll never go. As soon as we start publishing the *Pathfinder*, we'll be too busy. So we might as well go today and see what kind of a castle our boss lives in. Today is as good a day as any to tread on the carpeted floors of his palace," I urged.

It wasn't easy to get to Mr. Rat's home. We had to take a streetcar to a subway, to another little stretch of subway, to another streetcar, and then a walk to an elevated line, then a ferry, to a train, and then a taxi! It's not that it was so far away, but it was a circuitous journey, a kind of merry-go-round. In order to complete the picture, we should have also taken a bicycle, a horse, and a hot air balloon! And everywhere we went, it cost ten cents carfare. New York is truly, just as Mr. Sohn says, a blessed city. In New York you can ride from 242nd Street, Van Cortlandt Park, New York, all the way to Pennsylvania Avenue, Brooklyn, or to Bronx Park, New York, for the cost of one nickel. That's nothing!

The Rat family had prepared a generous meal for us. The house had been cleaned, the children bathed and dressed in their holiday best.

The whole newspaper staff was there: Mr. Rat, Mr. Kahm, Mr. Sohn, myself, and someone called Mr. Bleck, a boy from the boy's club who had been hired as our circulation manager. He was comically foolish.

They started to talk. Of course, the conversation centered on the *Pathfinder*, the new newspaper that would soon be published in order to show the world how a paper should truly look. Mr. Rat spoke with angry pleasure about how his enemies would faint when they saw that he, of all people, was publishing such a paper. They would all collapse with the shock of it.

"There will be a fainting epidemic!" he boasted.

"Do you really have so many enemies?" I asked.

"Plenty!" He nodded energetically.

"But why? What did you do to them?"

"What? Nothing! They're my enemies because I won't let them do anything to me, that's all! I am not one of those men who lets other people go around and spit in their soup. Not me! They want to take over everything, they want to be the bosses of this city, they want others to close their eyes and refuse to see what they're doing. I won't have it! If I'd have let them, they would've bought me out.

I'll be damned if I let them! I don't care how much it costs. I'll show them that no one leads me around by the nose. No, sirree!"

"But," I started cheerfully, "can't you establish an amicable relationship with them, make friends with them, and then together you can all—"

"Make friends with them? Never!" Mr. Rat cried. "Making friends with them would mean handing over the reins and letting them drive!" He spoke like he was talking about horses, not a newspaper. The only thing left for me to do was ask again whether his enemies were really so large in number. He assured me again that he had "plenty!" and added that, however many there were, he'd break them down. He'll show them that he's not playing around. When he sets out to do something, he does it. He's not afraid of anyone. They'd like to drown him in a spoonful of water if they could, but he won't let them! The power won't be in their hands, but in his! He'll show them what he's made of.

"Don't you think," I asked, "that it's a bit of a risk, to publish a newspaper when you have so many enemies?"

His wife turned her anxious gaze on him with curiosity. She put down the serving trays and waited for his answer. He replied, "Sure, it's a risky business, I'll betcha! But I'll take the risk. And I'll win! That's business. In business you have to put it all on the table. If you don't risk anything, you won't get anything. That's the game. I'm not afraid of them. I'm taking a risk, and I'll take even more!"

What a bully!

I was beginning to understand that the *Pathfinder* was not founded to fight for ideals. It was clear that the paper was Mr. Rat's alone. It was his personal business, a curse or a blessing for him and his household, a colossal failure for those he'd borrowed money from to set out on the venture. He would've been better off opening a grocery, or a butcher shop, or even a shoe store. Why would someone like him attempt to go into the newspaper business?

I couldn't imagine what I could possibly do for such a newspaper. I could hardly believe that I had agreed to come here as a hired member of the staff, a full time editor! I was trying to convince myself that this was the truth when Mr. Sohn asked, "What do you think we should write in our newspaper?"

"Who cares? My job isn't to fuss about the newspaper. I'm only concerned with the wages!" exclaimed Mr. Kahm, the chief editor.

"How long, do you think, will we—" another began to ask.

"As long as it takes to earn enough money to make it to New York, that's all!" Mr. Sohn interjected.

The chief editor didn't understand why Mr. Sohn said this, or why I laughed.

Mr. Sohn gestured dismissively. "Never mind."

Mr. Kahm, the chief editor, asked me about the status of my novel. He must have a new novel. We can reprint my old novels later. He must have a few chapters of a novel and an editorial for the women's pages right away, for the first issue.

"An editorial about what?"

"Who cares!" The subject didn't matter to him. He'd leave that to me. And the novel, too. "As long as it's suspenseful—that's what the readers want. The worst novels have the most readers. There's no need for it to be literary, as long as it's interesting."

I wanted to talk more about it so that I could understand all the details of what he wanted, but the editor felt full after his heavy meal and decided to put off further conversation until tomorrow, Monday, in the editorial office of the *Pathfinder*.

He'd leave it to an hour before Shabes candle-lighting, as they say. Right up to the last minute.

As for me, I was in a hurry to ride back into town and think about the novel, the editorial, and everything else. I didn't want to leave it all for later, although I couldn't begin anything without seeing what sort of a paper I was working for, what kind of a perspective it would have. And who knows how a paper in a provincial city like this was supposed to start out? Maybe all of the institutions in the Jewish community emerge out of arguments like this?

Mr. Rat asked me to wait for a while. The man with the black hair, Mr. White, our staff photographer, wanted to take our picture.

He lined us up in a row on the sunny side of the street. "Look over here and smile. Very nice. Don't move. Look at the sun, but don't squint."

I didn't want to be photographed with the rest of the bunch. I didn't want to appear in the same picture as the rest of them. Who are they? What are they? But it wasn't appropriate to refuse, so we were all photographed together "for posterity."

Mr. Sohn accompanied me part of the way home. He wasn't concerned with how the chief editor talked about the work of the paper. He was preoccupied with thoughts of New York.

"The best place in B--n is the station, where you can take the train to New York," he said. How he would lift his arms to the heavens in praise on the day he would finally travel to the big city!

"And you? What are you going to do until tomorrow?" he asked me.

"I'll get to work."

"On the novel, or on the editorial?"

"Both."

"Good luck with it! Let's hope God is on your side!"

"You, too."

"Thank you. As for me, I plan on helping myself," he said.

"You're placing yourself at the mercy of your own weak powers," I said teasingly.

"For a newspaper like this one you don't need a lot of strength. You'll write the best you can, and the worse it is the better off you are. The main thing is not to take up such vaunted subjects, nothing too fancy. You saw Mr. Rat and his family? Everyone here is like that. There are a few exceptions, of course, but I'm afraid they won't read our paper. They'll just ignore it."

"Maybe they'll write for us," I ventured.

He said that he doubted it. It wouldn't be worth their trouble. But who cares, let them do what they like. We won't take it too seriously. We'll just work to earn enough money to go to New York so we can live it up for a few nights!

"As weak as he is, what a strong passion he has for living!" I thought as I watched Mr. Sohn go. Little by little, he'd pull things together and then . . . But maybe that's the way it is. A strong man gets what he wants, so he doesn't want it as much.

In any event, that didn't have anything to do with the work I had to do right now for the *Pathfinder*. It was rapidly approaching the moment of its birth, but it had nothing at all. It would be ugly, naked, and vulnerable for the world to see. I had to take to my work with gusto to give it something to wear.

4

I locked myself in my room and got to work, writing what I needed to for the *Pathfinder*.

Out of the corner of my eyes I could see Jacob Wasserman's *The World's Illusion* lying on the table. I was deeply tempted by it, but instead of reading a good book I had to force myself to write a bad one.

I told myself that if I wanted to, I had every right to refuse to write a novel entirely. Let them publish one of my previously published works, or let them buy a novel from somebody else! But just as I was thinking this, the inspiration for a novel struck me, so I took hold of the moment. I sat down to write.

As I wrote the novel, I thought to myself that I would be better off polishing off an editorial. As an editor, that's what I was obligated to do. But I prefer writing novels, so I wrote the novel. I'm like the person who wrote once to his friend, "I wrote you a long letter because I didn't have the time to write a short one." I wrote the novel because it comes more easily. I asked myself, "What's the logic?" but the answer was that there's no logic to it. "If logic was involved, I probably wouldn't write anything at all," I told myself. In writing, as in love, it's much healthier not to ask too many questions. You have to follow your passions.

So I wrote the novel and promised the editorial that I would write it soon enough. I will put off my must to satisfy my muse. He's stronger, she has to give in to him because he'll always win in the end.

I sat up all night, writing my novel, and in the morning I wrote my first editorial.

When I came to the editorial office with my writings in tow, everything there was in disarray. Things that should have been ready long ago weren't done yet. The editors were scrambling to assemble the first issue so they could publish.

"Did you bring copy?" demanded Mr. Kahm, the chief editor, in place of a greeting. "Give it to me right away! We have to give it to the typesetters."

"Don't you want to read it first?" I asked.

"What for? We're leaving it up to you."

That was very nice of him to say. I'd handed him several chapters of the novel and I was hoping that at least he would read over the editorial. I wanted to know his opinion of it—after all, it was the first time I'd ever written one!

He looked it over, and he liked it. He was very pleased! The managing editor, Mr. Sohn, was enraptured: it was such fresh, free, lighthearted and original writing! It was just what he was hoping I could do!

Mr. Kahm diplomatically held his enthusiasm at bay. He said that the editorial was all right, and he had anticipated that I would be good at writing editorials. If not, he wouldn't have hired me. He would have just bought existing editorials from somewhere, "ready made," so to speak.

At these words, Mr. Rat flung open the doors to the editorial office and came in, saying, "Sure, nowadays it's a world of prepre- pared things. Ready made to order! But I want everything to be writ- ten by our own editorial staff, and I want everything to be about our own city, B--n! That's what I'm after!"

"That's a laudable goal, but this is such a tiny office. Where am I supposed to write?" I asked.

"Oh, if you know how to write, then you can write anywhere. You can even write standing up!" Mr. Rat assured me.

"I need someplace to sit. Not only that, I have to have my own place. If not, I'll have to write in the room where I'm boarding," I insisted.

"Well, we'll see about that." As he searched for a place where I could sit in the meantime, he changed the subject, asking what I'd written about. I told him.

"Is it good?! Is it what I wanted?" Mr. Rat asked.

"Ask the editor . . . the editors."

Mr. Rat looked at the two editors questioningly, and they told him that it was good, very good, extraordinary.

"Alright then!" he exclaimed and went off to the side to speak with Mr. Kahm.

Mr. Sohn took me aside and reminded me, "Ask him for your travel expenses. Don't put it off. Say something now, while it's fresh."

I gathered my courage and asked, as politely as I could, and Mr. Rat said he would have a meeting about it. That is to say, he'd bring it up at the next executive meeting. He'd make sure it was taken care of, sure thing!

When Mr. Sohn heard that answer he laughed out loud. "What meeting? When do we ever meet? He just wants to put it off so that nothing ever comes of it. It's just a clever excuse."

I didn't want to believe that. A publisher wouldn't trick someone out of ten dollars with clever excuses. How could that be?

I got the material for the women's section in order and then I went back to my rented room to continue with the novel and write another editorial. I also worked on other items for the newspaper. I wanted to make sure nothing was missing from the first issue.

I spent part of the evening with the Russian-Jewish intellectual neighbor. She categorically refused to recognize the *Pathfinder.* "What kind of a *Pathfinder* can it be? Who would publish such a thing? If we want a Yiddish newspaper, we can get one from New York easily enough and if we want to read news about our city we can find it in the English newspapers. *Pathfinder* indeed! What kind of path is he planning on leading us down?"

But inasmuch as the *Pathfinder* brought me here, she was very pleased that I had come to B--n, Massachusetts. Their circles are so small. They have so few intellectual people here; it's a pleasure to see a fresh person. For that reason alone, they hope the newspaper will last a while longer.

Yes, they were willing to forgive my working for such a newspaper because, after all, some people have to make wages! They saw it as a means to make a living, but as a cultural contribution? They'd be damned if they saw it that way. "Quite the opposite—it's an obstacle in the way of everything that has to do with Enlightenment. A stumbling block, a nuisance, a *prepiatstvie*!" she exclaimed in elegant Russian.

In order to cheer myself up after hearing them out, I told myself that this was only the opinion of a handful of intellectuals. A daily Yiddish newspaper is oriented toward and rests largely upon the needs and desires of the masses, the working class—and the advertisers.

The first issue of the *Pathfinder*!

At the top, front and center, in large bold font, were the words:

"Start reading the exciting, wonderful, interesting and realistic novel *Both of the Sexes* by the famous and beloved great authoress and member of the editorial staff of the Yiddish *Pathfinder* (my name followed) today!"

And then—another announcement:

"Read the editorial by our very own great authoress, written especially for the *Pathfinder*."

After that, in bold font, the editorial itself appeared, and then my picture, over and under which were a description of all the marvelous things that the great authoress will write in the future. Then there was an invitation to write to her for advice about family life, children, love—misfortunes with love, of course (no one has questions about happy love)—and anything else! She will answer any question. Write the question clearly and legibly on one-sided paper send it to the address printed below for the women's pages of the newspaper. You won't regret it.

How nice. A substantial advertisement. But it was a bit much. I looked at the newspaper and at the others who were also looking at it. The office girls exchanged meaningful glances and smiled kindly at me. One of them came up to me and asked if I was happy: the whole paper is taken up with me! I am so important. Everyone is talking about me. They say that I must earn a lot of money—why, if I were so famous in an English newspaper, I'd be making a fortune! Why don't I write in English?

I explained to her that English readers have enough writers. We have too few. If the English newspapers like my writing, they can translate it from Yiddish. I feel more at home in Yiddish. Yiddish is the language I love.

"But it doesn't pay!" she retorted.

She is the bookkeeper. She knows what she's talking about. She knows exactly how much money I'm earning. I find that unpleasant. But I said to her, "Money isn't everything. When I write in Yiddish I am helping in the development of the Yiddish language, and that is more important than—"

"Is Yiddish a language?" she asked, and quickly offered her own answer, that she didn't know, since she didn't know any Yiddish. None of the office staff know any Yiddish. The whole newspaper is as incomprehensible as if it were written in Chinese. They brought it home to see if one of their parents could read it for them and tell them what it's all about.

Aside from the Russian-speaking intellectuals, the English-speaking ones, for whom the newspaper should be near to their hearts, are actually far from interested. The former aren't interested in the newspaper because they don't like it, the latter don't like it because they don't understand it—so who will read it? Who are we publishing for?

There wasn't enough time to settle the question of how the newspaper would be read. All of my time had to be devoted to *writing* it. The novel, the editorials, and everything we needed "until the newspaper can stand on its own two feet," all of the editorial tasks, large and small, that were needed to fill its empty columns.

A new daily newspaper, with few advertisements, needs a lot of material for publishing, and when the entire editorial staff consists of three people, not only do they have to edit their sections, they have to write the whole thing themselves!

5

The newspaper goes down like butter. Thanks to the terrible heat, there's no reason to fear that anyone will have the patience to read it through and notice all the mistakes.

So many mistakes! Every day I have to read over the proofs of my novel and editorials and other things twice. And then, when the final version is printed, there are still more mistakes. The number of mistakes rises like yeast.

The typesetters say that it's not their fault. The machine has a tendency to mistake one type for another. And just try to pick a fight with a machine!

Mr. Rat runs around like he's been poisoned. Nothing works as it should, and he's ready to poke his own eyes out. So he says. So he *screams*.

I want to escape from his hollering. His hard, piercing voice grates on my ears. I hand over everything I've written to the editors. I look over the newspapers, Yiddish and English, local B--n news and the New York papers, and then I read the proofs, correct the mistakes, clip a few items that I think I should write about from the papers, and gather my things so I can go back to my own room, make myself comfortable, and get to work.

Mr. Rat stops me, yelling, "Are you leaving already? You just got here!"

"Do you need me here?" I ask.

"Sure, I need you! If I didn't need you I wouldn't have brought you here. Tell me, where's the logic in your not working here, in the editorial office, like everyone else? What's the problem—are you ashamed to be with us? You want to be a stranger?"

"I don't have any room here."

"Oh, you want your own office?" he asked accusingly.

"Yes, an office would be nice. I don't even have a desk here."

"You can sit at whatever desk you like. And if someone tells you to move, I'll have something to say about it. It's all right, you could write here just as well as you can in your own room, if you wanted to."

I explained to him that I wouldn't be able to and had no desire to. I need quiet, I can't write amid chaos, and I don't want to sit at anyone else's desk. I don't want to wait until someone else tells me to leave and I don't want to come to him to complain about it. If he wants me to stop asking for my own office, he should leave me alone about working at home. I bring all my work in on time, I stay up late at night writing the novel.

Ah, yes, the novel! That reminded him. He'd actually been meaning to talk to me about the novel. Would I kindly step into his office to speak to him about it?

I agreed to be kind.

I entered, sat down, and waited to hear what he had to say about my novel. I was interested in his opinion not just as a publisher, but also as a reader. He was quiet for a while, and then he placed a few pages down on his desk and began, "Tell me, please, what kind of a novel is this? What are you writing for me—I mean, for the *Pathfinder*?"

"Didn't you read it?"

"Yes, I read it. A little, not the whole thing. I want to know what will happen next."

"You mean you're curious. Well that's a good sign . . ." I teased, smiling.

"Sign—nothing! I want to know what's going to happen next, not for my own sake, but for the readers! I want to know if it's something we should publish. What is there—a wedding? A divorce? A bastard child? Or what?"

"You want a bastard child?"

"Why do you keep asking what *I* want? It's not what I want, but what the *reader* wants that counts! Do you have a bastard child or not?"

"Yes, almost . . ."

"What do you mean almost? Either you have one or you don't!"

"But—I was trying not to laugh—*you* want a bastard child. Very good. So when? And who do you want to have the child—the mother or the daughter?"

"Who? How should I know who? The mother or the daughter— what do I have to do with it? I can't dictate it. The main thing is that one or the other of them has one. But it should happen soon. The bastard child should already have appeared in the first chapter. A novel in a daily newspaper should start off right away in the right direction. Your story starts with a party where they meet each other. Even if they fall in love at first glance, it still takes nine whole months until they can have the bastard child. Let me ask you, how is the reader expected to have the patience to wait that long?

"Now, one more thing," Mr. Rat continued, seeing that I had nothing to say. "In a novel there should be heroes and villains. There should be fine, upstanding moral people and there should be scoundrels. But in your novel the heroes are somewhat bad and the villains are somewhat good. It'll take too much time to figure out what they really are. And one more thing—why did you make your hero a writer, a poet? Have you ever heard of a hero who is a Yiddish writer? I certainly haven't! For the same money you could make him a lawyer or a doctor or a manufacturer. Can you spare it? What kind of a fate can the bastard child have if the woman who carried him is fooled into her mistake, or ravaged, by a poet? What can she demand from him? What could she possibly get out of it? I'm asking you, what?"

I responded calmly, "What would she get from a lawyer, or a doctor, or a manufacturer?"

"What?!" he cried in astonishment. "How can you even ask? She could get money from them. Alimony, how should I know? What can she get from them? What *can't* she get? The main thing is not what she'll get but the fight, the trials she has to undergo. You could write about the case just like they do in the papers. Just clip something from the paper with a hero and a judge and lawyers, and let them read it in the Yiddish *Pathfinder*. Do you understand?"

"If I understand correctly, you don't want me to write a novel, you want an advertisement," I responded dryly.

"If only you could do that! That would be good for me!"

"Why don't you write the novel, then?" I countered.

"Why? What do you think I'm paying you for?"

"You're paying me to write editorials. Just editorials and editing."

"I'm paying you for everything!"

"No. Ask the editor, Mr. Kahm, if you like. He'll tell you that you're not paying for everything."

"There's nothing to ask him. I know who I pay for what. And if you don't think I'm paying you enough, go ahead and ask for more."

"Would it help if I begged?"

"Once the newspaper gets off the ground, if you help it stand on its own feet—" he reassured me.

"Which feet? How many feet does it need to have?"

"You're making fun of my paper?" he challenged.

"If you tear apart my writing . . ."

"I have a right to tell you what to write. I pay your wages, and no one else does. Don't you know that if I wanted to I could get along just fine without any writers at all?"

"How?" I rejoined.

"I can reprint a paper from another provincial town, and it would only cost me ten to twelve dollars a week!"

"Really?" I responded with mock astonishment.

"Yes, yes, that's all it takes for the whole paper," Mr. Rat reassured me.

"What a sale, what a bargain!"

"I'll make you a bet that it's true. Believe me!"

"So why don't you just do that?" I asked.

Mr. Rat didn't have an answer. After a pause he gathered his words and explained, "Why don't I do it? Because. Because I want to give others a chance, you see?" He cheered up a little. "I believe in live and let live."

"That's very good of you. Truly."

"Yes, it is! And I just want to be appreciated for how good I am. People should listen to what I say. When I say something, I know what I'm saying. And I say, never mind literature. That's what the library is for. There's a huge library. What I want is a suspenseful novel. A *shund* novel, a piece of pulp fiction. A novel like they have in the New York papers. With millionaires, bastard children, trials and alimony, detectives and gangsters! How long do you think your novel will take you?" Mr. Rat demanded.

"If you want, I can end it right now," I responded.

"You can do that, and write one like I told you about?"

"No, leave that to the people who know how," I said curtly.

"You expect me to pay another expense? No, thank you," he replied.

"If it costs money, it's worth money," I advised.

"Why won't you write one like I asked you to?" He scowled.

"I can't."

"Yes, you can, you just don't want to."

"Fine, if you say so."

"But it shouldn't be that way. You work for me at the *Pathfinder* and you are supposed to do what I say. It's for your sake as much as mine. I want you to be a part of the paper. The paper wouldn't be able to go out without you," he cajoled.

"Why do you make your paper so dependent on me? It would be better for you if your paper could go out without me. That would be better for you, in case I left and went back to New York."

"Are you planning on going back?" he demanded.

"If you ask me to do things I can't do—"

"I see. You miss New York. You feel it drawing you back. Fine, if that's so, if you are here but your soul is there, it won't work out. You have to be here entirely," he insisted.

"I'm here."

"No, ma'am, you're not. No, sirree!"

I swore that I was here and Mr. Rat swore that I wasn't until they started to close the building. Everyone went home and only Mr. Kahm stayed behind to wait for Mr. Rat so he could accompany him home.

6

I stared at my novel and told myself it was time to put an end to it: I'd refuse to write it how Mr. Rat wanted!

I was annoyed at myself for having started it in the first place. The *Pathfinder* is not one of those newspapers created out of love for literature. It's business. Nothing more than business! It's a simple shop that belongs to the sort of man who has nothing at all to do with art. All he wants is merchandise: cheap, sensational, something that will attract the attention of popular audiences.

He needs a drum, not a violin. He wants garlic, radishes, and onions, not a fruit compote.

The compote analogy actually comes from him. "You're serving compote," he accused me. "The reader wants fish with horseradish, he wants *meat* and you're serving him poultry!"

I glanced over my novel and was overtaken by pity for my heroines. Where have I dragged them to? My God! How did they end up in the *Pathfinder*? What did I have against them, against myself? My God! I was so riled up I was practically steaming. I'd be better off lounging by the seashore reading *The World's Illusion* and writing something worthwhile myself. Next to me were a stack of ideas begging for me to put them onto paper. Why do I keep putting off writing them? My God, I could die waiting for myself.

I'm not afraid of death. That's what I tell myself. I think it's because they say that writers are immortal. Yes, in a certain sense they are dead even while they're alive, and they live on after their deaths. In any case the world has a better opinion of a dead writer than a living one, and so do newspapers and the whole literary establishment. They come out right away with articles in tribute to dead writers. They pour out whole columns of inky tears. In short, if you want to receive your full due, all you have to do is lie down and die.

I lay down, but I didn't die. I buried myself in *The World's Illusion*, a novel full of conflicts between good and evil. Evil spirits rule over the faithful and lead them to ruin. It's a book full of revolt and protest against false ideas and beliefs. His pessimism (Jakob Wassermann's) robs the reader of any hope. His characters are symbols of the mysterious forces that make it impossible for individuals to be simple human creatures. They have such power that you can't help but be infected with them. It was hard to put the book down (the two books, actually, it's two volumes long) until you read them in their entirety.

Having satisfactorily taken my rest with *The World's Illusion*, I decided to finish my novel for the *Pathfinder* as quickly as possible, and let Mr. Rat decide for himself if he wanted to print it or not. If not—all the better. I'll have a written manuscript that I can sell to someone else.

The Jewish, Russian-speaking colony from B—n had left the city to escape the summer heat and they invited me to join them, but I had to excuse myself and couldn't travel to share in their enjoyment. I doubted how long I would be staying at the *Pathfinder*.

The intellectuals were not at all surprised that I might be leaving the *Pathfinder*. They were surprised that I had come to work for such a scandal sheet in the first place. How did I end up at that rag? If it weren't for my own writing, there would be nothing of worth to read in it at all. "You fill up the whole newspaper," they said. "If it weren't for you . . . and what are they paying you? Is it really worth it to you to write for them?"

Of course I didn't tell them how much I was making, and I didn't even ask if they actually read what I write. I was almost certain they didn't. In such heat it's hardly possible to think, never mind to read.

On Sunday I turned down an invitation to "go out" and stayed home to write copy for my novel instead.

This is how I got ready to write. I sat in a light, summery dress that was so thin that the breeze passing between the door and the window came right to me. I felt comfortable, I felt prepared to accomplish a lot of work. But then—the telephone!

Who was it? What did he want? It was Mr. Rat, and he wanted me to come into the editorial office. What? On a Sunday?

"So what if it's Sunday? Do you have to go to church?"

I wanted to know why he needed me there, and he grew furious when I asked. "What do you mean, why? For writing, of course." What kind of writing? I'd find out when I got there. Why was I asking so many questions? When he said to come, I should just come without asking anything. And right away. If I didn't come soon I'd be too late.

It was impossible to get anywhere as fast as I wanted to in this city. However much you manage to catch a ride, you always have to do a lot of walking, too. Winding streets made of crooked stones that animals used to tread on. The animals were the ones who trampled out the original plan for the city, and since then the people have walked on their paths.

I walked, I rode, I walked again, and I arrived, cooked through from the insane heat. I crawled up the tall staircase of the old building and paused at every floor to catch my breath. I had to cool down somehow or I would faint. I was dying!

"Oh, you're here!" Mr. Rat met me with a wry smile. "I had to beg you, but you came in the end."

"What do you need me for?" I asked.

"I'll tell you in a minute," he snapped, and walked into the printing room.

I figured that something must be wrong with the editorial we were printing for tomorrow. I thought it was good, but that's not all that I thought . . . In the meantime I spied Mr. Kahm and asked him about the editorial. "Is it coming out in the next issue?"

"Sure!" he said, looking puzzled that I would ask him such a question.

"So why did you ask me to come here?"

"I didn't ask you here." He smiled weakly. "It was Mr. Rat who asked for you. He wants you to work here in the editorial office like the rest of us. He says no one is better than anyone else here—we're all equal."

"That's the ticket!" said Mr. Rat, carrying a sack full of fashion plates on paper and in boxes. "You just separate these and write down in Yiddish how to make these styles and paste it over the English and that's all! A child could do it!"

I was furious at the task he'd come up with for me.

"Go ahead, do it!" he handed the fashion plates to me. "I need it every week and you should make enough that we can put out two or three a day."

I didn't rush to do his bidding. I needed to cool down, and to calm down a little because I was furious. How could he have the audacity to pull me from my work (which is also for him)! Just tear me away for nothing and sit me down to a task like this!

"I should give him a talking to," I thought, all the while cursing myself for not speaking up. Like Wilson said about America (before he went on to help the Allies quash German militarism), I was "too proud to fight!"

I saw Mr. Rat watching me and I grabbed my fan and plopped myself down, to my boss's annoyance. He saw that I was not the kind of girl who jumped to follow his orders. I took my time.

"What's the matter?" He approached me. "Are you hot?"

"Very."

"Then why aren't I hot?"

"I don't know."

"If you didn't fan yourself so furiously you wouldn't be so hot, and you'd be able to work. Why are you doing that?"

"I feel better if I do it."

Dismissively, he responded, "You don't belong in an editorial office. You belong at the seashore, with the millionaires."

"I think so, too," I replied.

"Then why don't you go there? To the seashore?"

"I'll go."

"When will you go?"

"Oh, when I can."

"You can't go now? Who's stopping you?"

"I promised to help get the *Pathfinder* on its feet, all four of them . . ."

Mr. Rat cried, "Are you making fun of the *Pathfinder*? Of your own paper? Very nice. What don't you like about it? And if you see something you don't like, why don't you make it better? You just sit here fanning yourself while the work doesn't get done."

"Whose work?" I asked.

"Your work!" he shouted.

"This is not my work."

"It's what you came here to do, isn't it?"

"I came because you called. If I did the work, it would only be as a favor and because I'm already here."

"Oh, is that all, as a favor?"

"Yes, Mr. Rat, a favor."

"And what am I paying you for?" he asked.

"For editorials and for editing the women's section," I responded coolly.

"This *is* for the women's section! It's fashion!"

"Is that so? But I shouldn't have to write it all myself. You could give this to that schoolboy who's busy reading the proofs and learning how to make mistakes."

"Then he'd make mistakes on it!"

"Then I'll edit it and correct them."

"Oh, is that so!" he responded in a huff.

I expected him to say that he didn't want me to do him any favors, but he didn't say anything.

"Well, so be it," I thought. "I'll work. I give in. But I won't come into the editorial office for a job like this again."

Before I left the editorial office, Mr. Rat stopped me so he could pour out his heart to me about the New York papers and how they hardly pay any attention at all to the provincial press. They don't care! But he wants to get even with them. He'll publish things that have to do with B--n's everyday life, he'll send me out into the streets of B--n and the surrounding summer resorts to gather material for the *Pathfinder*. I'll find the juiciest content. He's sure I can do it. If I can't, no one can!

He talked about this for so long that in order to pry myself away from him I had to promise to go out into the city and its surroundings to get some tasty morsels for the *Pathfinder*. So instead of refusing work, I ended up promising to do even more.

7

The city was wrapped in a blanket of fire and I paced its poorly paved streets looking for material for the *Pathfinder*. As I walked, I thought I must be crazy for doing this. Why did I take on such a task? I should have flatly refused. Let Mr. Rat hire someone else to do it if he wants it so badly.

B--n is a city in which no one knows precisely where they are going. Even those who were born here are always getting lost. So I walk, and I get lost. I promise myself I won't get lost. I know my own address, and I'll make it back, eventually.

Sickly sweet odors, boiling in the heat, attack my nose. I'm in the poor neighborhood. The Jewish ghetto.

I stumble over the burning, crooked stones while in my thoughts I compose an editorial:

"We pride ourselves on things that are beautiful. We are embarrassed about ugly things. That's natural. It's also natural that those things that are not so pretty, but are close by, are dear to us. We're pained, and instead of hating them we have pity on them. It bothers us that they're not up to our standards."

That's the introduction—the first foray. Then it continues:

"It's a shame and a pity to be cramped, packed like jarred herrings when the world has so much harmony and freedom. The people who live in the ghetto suffocate in narrow, unclean alleys. And their children, smeared with mud, play in the streets, inured to the dangers of the wagons, trucks, automobiles, and streetcars that threaten to run them over. In these terrible conditions, in air polluted by dirt, our Jews of the ghetto live and conduct their business. The food in the grocery stores is besieged by flies, clothing hangs over shop doors, drooping tiredly as though their souls were yearning for better sellers. When you see the same merchandise in better surroundings you pay higher prices, and that means that it's worth more to you. Here, you buy it out of pity for the seller, and however much you pay you feel that you've overpaid.

"'Maybe that's not the right way to display your wares?' I suggest. When I ask a ghetto businessman why he doesn't make his store look prettier and cleaner, he responds, 'Why? I don't want to drive away my customers. If they see the material laid out like it is in the fancy stores they'll think that I'm expecting higher prices and will be afraid to open the door and come in.' That is to say, the mud, the disarray, makes them feel at home. These people, you can haggle, you can bargain with them, you can beat down their prices, but just try giving them something to read . . ."

In the end, I thought about writing something about the pretty, good-looking types of people that you meet in the ghetto: the Jew with the perfect face, the simple but graceful Jewish woman sitting at the window with her child, like a Madonna, and the old motherly Jewish woman worrying over her sickly neighbor's children. Yes, they're filthy and poor, but they're ours. They're ours, just like one of them was singing:

> "I wasn't invited, I came here myself
> Though I'm poor, I'm still your aunt
> It's no good to be poor, no good
> But don't be ashamed of your own blood!"

As soon as I returned from the ghetto to the editorial office I started writing my editorial.

The editor, Mr. Kahm, who should have been used to the heat, was almost out of his mind with it. I thought he looked like he was going to fall asleep, just standing up.

Mr. Sohn, his brow dripping feverishly, quickly looked over the errors on the front page. He handed me the *Pathfinder* and gestured. "Do you see how many mistakes there are? Just count them!"

"Who has time to count?"

"It'll drive me crazy! It's horrible! Scandalous!"

"It's too hot to get so excited, Mr. Sohn. Try to stay cool."

"I can't. Try to imagine. Until the age of thirty-six, I was a Mama's boy. I spent my summers sitting with her at her farm. When I turned thirty-seven, I finally went to work, and all I got out of it was this—these mistakes! I can't stand it anymore. I'll go crazy! My mother cries and begs me, 'Why are you killing yourself like this? Why do you choose such a death sentence for yourself?'"

I suggested that he could choose an easier death if he wanted to.

"How was I to know it would be like this? Mr. Rat told me to edit the front page, alright. So now I'm something of an editor. And that was an easy enough job. I used to get free passes to any theater I wanted to go to, and I could even bring a guest. I thought it would be like that here, too. But first of all, it's summer so there's no theater. Second, even if it were winter, where would I find the time to go when I have so many papers to read and I have to write out all the new articles and read over all the proofs, and then in the end I see all these mistakes! Couldn't a man go crazy from it? I'm asking you!"

"You could."

"You could die from it!"

"You could do that too, if you wanted."

"What do I care? As far as I'm concerned, maybe I'd be better off dead," he declared.

"Well, if it doesn't bother you . . ."

"Then why should anyone else care?" he finished for me.

From these few cut off words, I understood that Mr. Sohn was doing so much work because he was trying to forget something. Probably a misfortune in love. Since he didn't have the will to kill himself by other means, he was killing himself through the press. Seeing how he tortured himself with the *Pathfinder*, it seemed to me that he had chosen the most difficult, but surest, form of suicide.

"Then what do you say," he asked. "Can a man die from this?"

"You can."

"And no one cares? Not even you?"

"No. If you want to die like this, then die in good health. That's your business," I said.

He laughed and said, "You also won't last long either with so much work. Why do you write so much? How do they manage to throw so much work onto your shoulders? What a swindle! They called you, they hired you for one thing, and you do so much more! Take a look at Mr. Stein. What's he doing? I'm asking you—what does he do? He just wanders among the office girls and bothers them. He says he wants to teach them Yiddish! And he does it all with his hands . . . What a load of rubbish! And they're not even interested. They're happy not to know it. Here they are, working for a Yiddish *Pathfinder* without knowing any Yiddish! Is it his job to teach them? Hardly! Girls! He's interested in *them*. He's looking for a bride."

"That's hardly a sin."

"But he doesn't know how or where to look."

"I heard he already found a new one in the Bronx, in New York."

"In the Bronx? I heard she was from Bronxville."

"What's the difference?"

"Nothing. But if he already found a bride, why's he looking for one here?"

"Maybe he's having second thoughts."

"No, he'll always be the way he is—an old bachelor."

"I hope you don't suffer any more than he does."

"It doesn't bother me. But I can't see how he can just play around, while I sit here and work so hard. I know he doesn't get much for his work. He gives us reports for the society columns. But he shouldn't behave like that."

Mr. Rat glared at Mr. Sohn just standing there and talking. Mr. Sohn returned to his desk. Mr. Rat came up to me and asked, "Is the editorial about ghetto Jews ready yet?"

"Yes, it's ready."

"Good! Now go to the seashore and write about life there. The sea has many different kinds of fish, and if you're there maybe you can catch us some. The *Pathfinder* needs them. Can I take a peek at your editorial?"

"Yes, you may," I replied.

He nodded to himself as he read. "It's all right. Good! It's actually a little too good. I think you could write here about their rags, their washing lines, how they argue with their neighbors and throw bags of garbage out their windows. And how they holler, 'Women! Women! Two for a nickel! Fresh, juicy women!' And about how they sit by their doors and read the *Pathfinder*—nothing but the *Pathfinder*! Do you get it? You should write all that and—"

"And what else?"

"You should write about how the women go to the milk store or the grocery store or the butcher shop, and ask 'Moyshe, Berl, Chayim, or Shmerl, why are you reading the paper?' and they answer, 'It's a wonderful paper. There's no other paper like it in America. You've never seen a paper like it!' The woman gets interested and asks, 'What's the paper called?' And he tells her, 'The *Pathfinder*!' All the customers want to take a look. They gather around in a circle and they look and they tear it out of the man's hands. But he refuses to give it to them and he says that for three pennies they can buy it at the newsstands!"

"At all the newsstands? The *Pathfinder* isn't on the newsstands. I didn't see it there."

"Then the newsboy will have it! I'm sending out plenty of boys with papers. Let them buy it from their own poor boys who are out there helping their parents make a living! They run around with the papers and wave them in the air and shout. Who cares how they buy them, they won't regret it. The boys need to make a living, too. Let's give them a show."

"One of them was run over," I told him.

"Yes, that's not my fault. He should have been looking where he was going. The paper may be a *Pathfinder*, but you still need to use your eyes if you don't want to get run over. It's an ugly business that they ran over him. Now the other boys will be afraid to take the papers. But they should just watch out."

Meanwhile, Mr. Rat used the death of the boy who was run over to advertise the *Pathfinder*, taking up half a column with an article about the death of the young boy, who was robbed of his young life during the noble work that he did after school, namely, selling thousands of Jews in B--n the only local Yiddish newspaper, the *Pathfinder*.

Under the obituary were instructions for the boys who weren't run over about how to watch out for themselves: they should look both ways, and when they see that no vehicles are coming then they can sell the *Pathfinder*. And one more thing: they should make sure to have enough petty cash and change to make sure that they won't take too long bothering the readers. And they should make sure to take enough *Pathfinders* so they don't have to keep coming back to the *Pathfinder* office when they need more.

8

Not so much for the *Pathfinder* as for my own sake, I agreed to travel one time, on a Sunday, to see the seagoers.

In order to avoid wasting too much time getting lost, I brought along a girl from B--n. She was a nice girl, a homemaking type but also up-to-date in her attitudes. She was both of these things at once. She could read Yiddish letters and make her way through a Yiddish newspaper, and she was also a passionate reader of women's fiction. She believed in love and also in matchmaking. She loved New York and lived in B--n.

She eagerly agreed to go with me to the seaside and to introduce me to a family there. A family of means with their own house, a phonograph, a piano, a telephone, a car, and a radio. In short, a family with all of the latest *improvements*.

She was sure, she told me, that they would be happy to meet an editor of a Yiddish newspaper. And they would be a windfall for me, too. I would find plenty to write about them. They love to talk.

And one more thing. Since they have a lot of room, they would certainly want me to stay with them. They would drive me to and from the editorial office in their car. They would be happy to do anything for me!

Based on the girl's conversation I formed an opinion of her acquaintances as Yiddish lovers. And if they weren't entirely, they were probably half- or quarter-patrons. So you can imagine my surprise when I met them and heard what they had to say.

The lady, a heavy woman with a powdered and painted face, soon let me know that she had no use for the Yiddish papers. She didn't even care for Yiddish books. What she likes are Russian and "Heynglyish" books. She likes Artsybashev's *Sanin* and Emil Zola's work. She's always after her husband for reading Yiddish newspapers like a greenhorn.

The husband added that he, too, didn't care for the Yiddish papers, but he liked to glance at them from time to time because it reminded him of his childhood days when he went to *kheyder*. That's all! As for their children, their own boys and girls, it's alright with him if they can't read a word of it. He doesn't want to "aggravate" with them (he used the word "aggravate" every time he should have said the word "argue"). It's their America and they can do what they like. He can be "interesting" (he meant "interested") in one thing, and they in another. Everyone should mind their own business, don'tcha think?

When they heard about the publication of a daily Yiddish news-paper in B--n, they threw up their hands. "Who needs a Yiddish paper here?" they cried, explaining that you can read all the news that such a paper would write about B--n in the "Heynglyish" papers two days before a Yiddish paper would ever write about it, and it certainly wouldn't be able to carry better literature than any other papers. It hardly even matters to the few people who have jobs there. They won't have their jobs for long because the paper is bound to fold soon. No one will read it.

"What did you think of them?" the girl asked me as we left their home. "They have mouths and they love to talk, right?"

I responded with my own question. "Are there many others like them?"

"Like them? What do you mean?"

"Yiddish lovers, like them?"

"Oh, now I see what you mean. Well, yes, they don't really care for it."

"What *do* they care for?"

"They like a good time. They like to enjoy themselves. Would you like to stay with them?"

"I don't think so. I'd end up 'aggravating' with them too much. Anyway, they said they didn't have any more rooms that we could use, and that they don't like to drive their car because people are always asking them to drive them to and fro."

"What pigs! What swine! What *alrightniks*! And I thought that they were intellectuals, so well read. It was my mistake."

"They are simple, happy people who live for pleasure and are raising one-hundred-percent American children. That's what America likes to see. They are 'all right'!"

The girl soon cheered up. Since I had such low regard for her acquaintances, she knew that by way of comparison I couldn't think so lowly of her. So with more bounce in her step she led me to the seaside to acquaint me with their Coney Island.

It was an ocean like any other. The water democratically rushed and flowed for everyone, equally.

But those who let themselves be rocked by the waves were divided into classes and cliques.

There were those familiar fat seagoing women in their bathing suits with their noses smeared with zinc oxide paste, accompanied by their children, bags, and whole meals laid out on the beach. They ate their filling food, they and their husbands. Both cheeks were full with the large bites they took. They peeled oranges in their hands and squirted juice in the eyes of the people walking by. They left food scraps scattered around them, fish skeletons, herring and chicken bones, empty bottles, paper, and who knows what else? Around them mosquitoes and flies buzzed and bit the children, who shooed them away and cried noisily. This was the segment composed of married couples with children.

Beyond them, at the sea's edge, were the freewheeling, strolling, good-time-seeking masses. An unregulated crowd of men and women, disorganized, butting against one another, pushing, glaring at one another as though they were all in each other's way. Girls walking with girls, boys walking with boys (or hoodlums), and between them many single, lonely people who didn't find anyone to go with and couldn't quite blend in with the crowd. They got swallowed up with the others and then spat out with them. It seemed to be like some kind of game of blind-man's-bluff, or even a *broygez-tants*, a wedding dance between quarreling in-laws, groups of children broken apart and thrown together at the sea's edge.

"What do you think of the people?" asked my companion.

"The people that the sea spat out?"

"Yes, them!"

"People! They seem to be running but don't know what they're chasing, like they're running away from themselves!"

She told me that she also feels like running away from herself. She feels that way all the time, dissatisfied with her life. She's afraid people will be disappointed in her. She's no more than a person, but she wants more than this everyday monotony. She wants to live, and how can she live the way she wants to when there are so many rules? When you don't know who is the right person to be with, who will make you happy? And everyone is only looking out for themselves. They're only superficially attracted to you, while deep inside their souls are uninterested and don't care about you. There are so many simple, foolish, worthless girls who get everything they want, while the fine, worthy, young people don't get anything at all. Why does it have to be this way? Where's the wisdom in it?

"Where foolishness flourishes, who needs wisdom?" I joked.

"You can say that again," she agreed. "All you need is a little luck, that's all."

When we got back to the city it was late and we were worn out. She went home still philosophizing about life, and when I got back to my room I plopped myself down to write an editorial, a few little stories, and an article.

I tore myself from sleep and set myself to writing the next installment of my novel. It was so hot that it was more comfortable to use the nights for writing. The sun wasn't shining, and no one could see me in my nightdress as I sat alone in my room in the dim shine of the electric lamp under a green lampshade. I decided not to sleep all night. When I got tired of the novel, I would write letters to my friends in New York. I could sleep late the next day and show up late at the editorial office to scribble whatever giblets the press wanted from me.

9

When I arrived the next day at the editorial office there were two new things waiting for me there: an assistant from New York and a clock at which all the assistants had to punch in to record their comings and goings, like at a shop or a factory.

I didn't even get close to the clock. But I approached the new assistant right away to shake his hand.

"Welcome!"

"Can you please tell me," he asked (the new assistant was a man), "what kind of a newspaper this is, and whether you think it's good to work here or not?"

". . . It's good!"

"It is?" he asked incredulously. "How is it good?"

"Because . . . it's not so bad."

"It could be worse?"

"No!"

"No?" he asked, laughing, as his pale, poetic face creased with worried wrinkles. "How's the pay here? And how long do you think the newspaper will last?"

"It's impossible to say. Maybe you'll be the one who helps the newspaper last longer."

"You're joking. What could I do for it?"

"Mr. Rat will tell you. And Mr. Kahm."

"They're both strange people. They talk and talk, but I still don't know what they want from me. They seem to want me to write about everything that's happening in the city. But how am I supposed to know about B--n when I just got here? I don't even know how to get to the editorial office. Mr. Rat wants me to illustrate what goes on in the streets. To describe everyone and everything. But walking around the streets in such heat is no mean task!"

"He won't make you do it by yourself."

"Yes, at least for the first time he'll ask a photographer or a cartoonist to go along with me. He told me he wanted to send them along with you, but you didn't want to go. Why not?"

"Because I have enough to do already."

"So I'm taking away some of your work?

"Yes, and I wish you luck with it!"

"Thank you."

"It's nothing."

Mr. Rat glared angrily at me for talking to my new coworker and walked over to stand at the side of the room. The new man studied him, puzzled.

"A strange little man!"

"So you're already calling him a 'little' man. He's lost some stature with you."

"Yes, a little man, but I like him well enough. I find the way he talks amusing. Have you heard it?"

"Yes, I've had the pleasure."

"He talks so fast. Quick and loud! What a racket. I like him! And that editor, Mr. Kahm? I like him too. He doesn't talk much, but he seems like a nice enough man. Well, *ládno*, that's fine! I'll see to it that I make a big hit. Anyway, I didn't have anything better to do in New York. All of the assistants there refused to die and leave their jobs for me. So I guess we in the provincial newspapers will just have to show them what we've got. I'll have a free hand here, right? That's what I want. I want to practice, to get some experience!"

The new assistant (Mr. Barg), left, and Mr. Rat came up to me. Glowering, he asked me accusingly, "Do you know what time it is? I'll betcha you don't even know how late you are!"

"I know."

"And you just got here! Just now, mind you!"

"Was I late for something?" I asked cheekily.

"Because you didn't agree to my request, I had to bring in a new assistant. Since you won't give me depictions of life on the street, I'm sending him after them instead! You don't care what I want. I told you to get here early, just like everyone else who works in this office, but you show up so late it's almost time for everyone else to leave! How could you show up after four o'clock in the afternoon?"

"Because yesterday, on a Sunday, I went to the seaside for the *Pathfinder*, and I was up all night writing and I knew that I wouldn't be missing anything if I got here late and anyway there's nowhere for me to work. Not only do I not have my own office, I don't even have a desk."

"Excuses! If you cared about the paper you wouldn't talk like that. That's what I think."

"Fine, you can think whatever you want. I can't be held responsible for your thoughts."

"So? Did you write something about the seagoers?"

"Yes. Here are a few things. And here's my novel."

"How many installments will it take up?"

"It depends how many columns you give it per day. If you give it a lot of space, it will end quickly. If not, it'll last longer."

"I'll talk to you about the novel later. For now, give me everything you wrote."

I gave it to him and he took them into Mr. Kahm's office. Meanwhile, I sat down in front of the only electric fan in the office to cool down a little, and looked over the daily newspaper. My sleepless night was catching up with me. My eyes grew droopy from heat and exhaustion. My head throbbed.

The office girls peppered me with questions. Where did I go on Sunday and who did I see? Did I have a good time? How late did I get home? Did someone drive me in a car? What did people say to me about the *Pathfinder*? Did they know about my writing? When they see friends whose old folks read the Yiddish newspaper they always want to know about the lady editor of the women's section. They like my writing, it's better than everyone else's, in fact they say that it's the only thing worth reading in the paper. And Mr. Rat resents that people are only talking about the women's section. He's jealous. He's mad that I don't come into the office like everyone else. He's always asking, "She's not here yet?" He brought in a clock so now the girls have to punch in. He'd be better off using the few hundred dollars that cost to put in a toilet. Does he think the girls aren't human? If the board of health knew what was going on here . . .

In the meantime, Mr. Rat emerged from Mr. Kahm's office and went into his own office. He saw that I was looking at him and could have invited me into his office with nothing more than a wink or a gesture. But he wanted to make an impression, so he picked up his telephone and called the office girl and asked her to send me in.

We rolled our eyes about it and laughed. Wanting to make an impression, too, I walked to his office with grandiose, measured steps, like I was processing in a parade.

"Sit down!" He gestured to the chair across from his desk. "Please."

I sat.

"I have to speak with you."

"How can I be of service?"

"I read what you wrote yesterday with the editor. It's all right. But it could be better. It absolutely wouldn't hurt to have less literature, and a little more 'pop.' You were there until after dark, didn't you see any boys and girls embracing in their bathing suits and doing who knows what else? Why didn't you write about that? That's what our readers love to read. That's what tickles them. That's what grabs their attention. What do you have to say about that?"

". . . Well, you can't write about everything at once."

"Alright, so you'll have to write about it another time. Now, as for the household that doesn't care for Yiddish newspapers—can you make it so that they don't care for any Yiddish papers but the *Pathfinder*? They *have* to like our paper! Don't you see? They have to!"

"Unless you forced them to with a policeman, I don't think—"

"Forget about your policemen! They have to enjoy it without needing to be convinced."

"But what if they don't like it?" I asked.

"You have to make them like it."

"How do I do that?"

"You talk to them, you make it clear to them that the *Pathfinder* is something every Jewish home needs. You keep on talking until they're convinced and agree to become subscribers. That's what you do!"

"What do you want me to do, write articles or advertisements?" I retorted.

"Well—advertisements, if you want to call it that! That's what a newspaper's all about. Yes, ma'am! The more we advertise ourselves, the more publicity we have. That's what a newspaper needs. Do you get me?"

"But what if I don't have any talent for writing advertisements?"

"Who cares? If you wanted to, you could write them well enough. You could do it if you wanted to. Mr. Kahm thinks so, too. You can do anything you set your mind to, but you're not willing. I'm afraid that you won't last long here. You'd rather be in New York. You don't want to settle down here. Now, a few words about the novel . . ."

"What's wrong with the novel?" I asked, and I was actually curious to hear what he had to say. I told myself that I would promise to take his remarks about my novel under consideration, and write about them someday, so that someone aside from me might be able to amuse themselves reading his absurd opinions.

"I was looking for the bastard child, and I didn't find one. Where was it? Did she throw it away somewhere? Did she kill it? Strangle it?"

"No," I responded coolly. "She didn't have one."

"She hasn't had it yet? How long will it take her to have a baby already?" he shouted. "What the hell!"

"How should I know? It takes as long as it takes. According to the laws of nature it takes as long to have a bastard child as it does to have a legal one."

"The laws of nature! She should have had the bastard long ago! And you didn't make the man who got her into trouble a manufacturer like I told you to. You made him a poet, of all things! So, let me ask you, how is it going to end? What will she get out of him for her love, for the bastard and everything else? Where's the satisfaction? How can she take him to court? What's the point in finding a lawyer if he has nothing she can take from him? I'm asking you!"

"I haven't thought about it yet."

"That's the trouble with you. You aren't thinking about it, or about so many other important things. And you didn't take any of my advice."

"What is your advice? I could take it now."

"Now? It's too late!"

"I do apologize."

"Unless maybe your miserable poet could inherit a fortune? What do you say to that?"

"From whom?" I asked.

"From whom? Not from me! From a rich uncle in America, or something. No, wait! From the widow who followed him here. She could die suddenly—you hear?—suddenly, not after some long, drawn-out disease, and leave him everything she has."

"But she doesn't have anything!" I responded.

"Make her have something!" he demanded.

"Where would she get it from?"

"Make her steal it! Make her kill someone for it! Make her become a bootlegger! What do I care? Let her come into some money and leave it to him in her will!"

"Why should she leave it to him?" I asked.

"Why? Because she still loves him, doesn't she?"

"Yes, but she wants him to marry her and he doesn't want to. He doesn't want to marry someone who was married before."

He bellowed, "Then she should take it all out on him. She should shoot him!"

"Will that make him a manufacturer?" I asked.

My question threw him for a loop. He was flummoxed and I tried to dig him out of the hole he'd fallen into.

"Maybe I'll make the poet win a prize for his writing. Some kind of patron, maybe someone who will publish all of his work?"

"A prize? A patron? What are you talking about? Who gives prizes for writing in Yiddish? And if they did, how much could it possibly be worth, and how could the patron have enough money to publish all of his work, and even if he did, who would read it? He'd just be throwing it away!"

"And you think she should throw the bastard away?"

"Who? What?" he cried.

I continued, "Maybe she should abandon him in the editorial office where he writes. I'll make it an editorial office just like at the *Pathfinder*. What do you think?"

He actually liked that plan. But I'd need to do it artfully. I shouldn't drag the newspaper into this mess. It could be like this: "The woman and her bastard child come with a complaint to the *Pathfinder*—I mean to the newspaper where the poet who got her into trouble works—and his boss at the newspaper is furious and makes the poet marry her or he'll be sacked. He gets scared and he marries her and—"

He remembered that he had to meet with someone else and put off the discussing the novel until later.

10

Mr. Barg, the new assistant, can barely stand on his own two feet. All this running the streets of B--n in the heat makes him hardly a person at all. Nevertheless, he seems to be happy that he, a café regular, a writer of little poems, is suited for a newspaper like the *Pathfinder* and that his boss approves of his work.

His descriptions are illustrated with drawings.

One drawing shows a pack of Jews with crooked noses and goatish beards, the kind of image that antisemites propagate. The group sits on a bench in a park, looking at the *Pathfinder*. They appear to be surprised and excited by what they see.

Another drawing shows a group of news boys holding out the *Pathfinder* as though they were passionate about the paper. Barefoot boys, ragamuffins without a penny to their names, but they look happy. Why? Because they're selling the *Pathfinder*! "How fortunate they are," reads the caption to the cartoon in the *Pathfinder*, "to have survived their poverty long enough to have their very own newspaper!"

And, supposedly for the sake of these ragamuffins, these dear rowdy youths, they started publishing some things in the *Pathfinder* in English, too. The youths should be able to appreciate something in their own paper!

Another group (they all seem to come in groups) was of storekeepers, "businessmen" of the ghetto. They look around with approval at the results of their advertisements in the *Pathfinder*.

Mr. Rat is pleased with himself for the instructions he gave to Mr. Barg to write these descriptions. It's not just pictures, it's more than that. Every description has an advertisement for the *Pathfinder* embedded in it. A city full of people scrambling in their groups to get the *Pathfinder*. They want nothing more than the *Pathfinder*.

But, in the end, hiring an assistant and paying weekly wages for daily descriptions was a little too much for Mr. Rat. He decided to break the man in by having him come every morning to help write the news. Mr. Sohn was hardly able to accomplish anything on his own, so let the new man help him. It's no big deal.

Mr. Barg was used to sleeping in. But he wanted to gain experience and "work on the staff" of a newspaper, so he pushed himself to wake up early. He had to prove to himself that he was able. He had discovered that he had a talent for street scenes, for descriptions. Now he wanted to discover his own talent for writing done indoors, as well. He hoped that over time he might get a promotion. In the meantime, he wouldn't refuse them, no matter how much work they gave him. He was embarrassed they gave him so little. He even once sat in an editor's chair when he was on vacation. Mr. Stein was very jealous. He was more qualified to be the editor's substitute. But this is how Mr. Rat wanted it, and he was the boss, after all. He can do whatever he wants.

The boss's bossiness filled the editorial office with noise. He let it be known and heard at every moment. He used every opportunity to tell me off for coming into work so late.

"You're late again. What can I say? I'm asking you—what?"

"Nothing," I answered.

"Do you still want to write in your own room?"

"Of course. There's nowhere for me to do it here."

"There's room for everyone else, but that's not good enough for you."

"That's what I told you."

"That's just an excuse. If you can work at one desk or another for three or four hours in the afternoon, then you can work there in the morning, too!"

"The work I do in the afternoon are the lighter assignments—notes about daily happenings, fashion, remarks, anecdotes, jokes. I can do that while I'm looking over the proofs. But even then, working at these desks bothers me. Anyone who comes into the editorial office comes right to me to ask for information. Anyone who wanders in stands next to my desk and talks. They sit on the desk."

"Send them away!" he cried. "They should all go to hell."

"If I sent them away, others would come."

"Then send the others away, too!"

"I can't force them to leave. If you don't want them to bother me, give me my own office. If you don't want to do that, then don't tell me off for doing my work in a place I find more comfortable."

"Do you know what?" he asked, as though he'd had a revelation. "There's no need for you to live in B--n to write what you're writing. You could even live in New York and send it to us. How much would your writing from New York cost me? Would you send it to me for fifteen, or maybe ten dollars a week?"

"Would it hurt to pay twenty-five?" I asked.

"Who cares if it hurts or not? Of course it's easier for me to pay less than more. You understand. It's business. Saving is earning. The material I buy from the New York offices and the other provincial newspapers costs me next to nothing. I could get plenty of material, if I wanted to. I could fill a whole paper without hiring writers! But I can't get anything like what you write that way. So I want to order it from you. And if you don't want to come into the editorial offices, and if you don't like B--n as much as New York, so be it. When you write to me from New York I will know that you're not here, and I won't have to have a fit every day that you have the gall to come in so late. You know that I want all the people I employ to be right here before my eyes. I want to see them working. And if outside guests want to come in and see the business, I want them to have something to see! They need something to look at."

"Now you're talking about something different. If we, the hired staff, are here to be on display, then it's important that we are here the whole time the show goes on."

"So are you willing to work here the whole day?"

"No, not that. There's the same problem. Nowhere to work. But when I've finished my novel and I don't want to start another one, and when the heat relents a little, and if I had my own desk with a clock on it, then . . ."

"How long will it take you to finish the novel?"

"A few weeks."

"That reminds me to ask you—the hero in your novel has yet to work his way up. He hasn't caught any fish yet?"

"Yes, he's still poor," I informed him.

"Very interesting! Did he commit a crime? What will be the end? What will be her compensation? What will she do with her bastard child? How will she mourn him?"

"She will raise him," I explained.

"A bastard? What are you thinking?!" he asked incredulously.

"Well, the bastard will become a legitimate child."

"How? How do you do it?" he interrogated me.

"He'll marry her."

"And what about her husband? Is he no more than a dog?"

"He'll divorce her."

"That's not bad . . . And what about the widow?"

"Nothing."

"And the patron's daughter? Also nothing?"

"Also nothing."

"They both loved him, didn't they?"

"Yes, but a man can't marry all the women who love him, can he?"

"No, I guess not. Unless he divorces the woman he married and runs off with someone else."

"Then what would happen with the third woman, or the fourth, and so on?"

"What would happen? That's what I want to know! *You* tell *me!* You're the one who writes the novels, not me. If I were in charge of this novel, you would write it the way I told you to, and believe me, it would be a peach! You'd have to tear the *Pathfinder* out of their hands. The whole city would be talking about it! They'd eat it up!"

"Why don't you just write a novel yourself?" I asked him.

"I'm not a writer, I'm a publisher!" he pompously proclaimed. "I give orders to the writers, and they do the writing. Of course, that is, the ones who listen to me. Not those with their own ideas . . ."

"Tell me, what does your wife think of the novel?" I inquired.

"My wife? She says she likes it. But I'm not publishing the paper for my wife. So what do you have to say about writing from New York? Give me an answer by next week. I told you that I want you— you especially—for this paper. If I wanted to, I could publish the whole newspaper without needing any writers at all. Yes, ma'am! Writers are the last thing I need. You know—"

I wanted to tell him I was leaving him then and there for New York, and that I wouldn't send him anything from there. But I told myself to wait a week. Not to get too riled up. I'd learn more about the *Pathfinder* and its publishers. I'd find out more about the status of the Yiddish press in this town and get a better sense of the city of B--n, which people think of as an educated, historical city but so far seems to be just the opposite.

Later—after my conversation with Mr. Rat—Mr. Sohn, Mr. Barg, Mr. Stein, and the others came and asked me what my conversation with the boss was about. I told them he wants me to leave B--n. He thinks he can publish the *Pathfinder* without writers.

"Without writers? How?" they asked.

When they heard how he planned to do it, they just looked at each other and agreed, "He really could do it." They were sad and happy. Sad, because they wouldn't have jobs, but happy because they wouldn't have *these* jobs. They'd be able to breathe more freely away from B--n. They'd go to New York.

"I'm leaving next week," Mr. Sohn declared.

"And I'll leave the week after that!" cried Mr. Stein.

"And I don't know what to do," Mr. Barg equivocated. "I work like a horse and can't get a raise. I'm afraid I won't last long here, either. It's no good. This job is nothing but misery. Even so—"

Even so, it seemed he was going to let the misery go on a little longer.

11

I finished the novel and gave it to the typesetter. He looked at it and said, "That's all?"

"It's not enough?" I asked.

"Sure, it's not enough! The novel should go on and on. We just started reading it. It's interesting. So give us more! Don't be stingy!" the typesetter demanded.

"I can't give you any more. This is the end. I'm leaving the newspaper soon," I told him.

"What? *You're* leaving? You'll kill the newspaper. You have to be here. Without you—"

"It will go on without me." I reassured him. "But if *you* left, that would be another thing. It would be impossible to publish the *Pathfinder* without a typesetter. But without a writer—"

"It can't be published without a writer either!" he cried.

"Mr. Rat thinks he can do without," I told him.

The typesetter was beside himself. "How can that Mr. Rat say such a thing? He's out of his mind! He's a lunatic!"

And the typesetter, who was the one and only, and his own boss, poured out his bitter heart about Mr. Rat. Mr. Rat was always throwing all of the work onto his shoulders, and he's only one man! Every day he promises to hire helpers, but nothing changes. And when he does find someone, it's quite a find. To hell with him. The other printer, who is also the one and only man working in his section of the printing room, is on his last legs. He doesn't know what he's doing. No wonder the paper has so many errors. How could it not, when the boy who does the copy editing doesn't know any

Yiddish? An American schoolboy who Mr. Rat found, promised to teach Yiddish, and brought onto the staff for three dollars a week! It's unbearable to see how the schoolboy reads over the proofs. And as for his role as a writer, that schoolboy should earn a medal for it—it's so absurd! The typesetter could sell tickets for people to come and watch him work. The schoolboy writes advertisements or studies Yiddish by translating things from English. He takes large sheets of paper and writes along the whole breadth of them, starting all the way to the right and ending at the leftmost edge. One thick line followed tightly by another until it looks like a fishing net. And no matter how much he tells the boy to write on narrower paper, and to write in thinner lines, without so many curly flourishes, nothing helps. Mr. Rat says it's all right, it'll all be all right, but the typesetter doesn't think much of Mr. Rat's opinion.

Now that the novel was over and done with, I could spend more time writing about contemporary events, the questions of the day that were preoccupying the press. I wrote editorials, articles about what people with good taste can do to maintain pretty, orderly, well decorated homes; I wrote about the Prince of Wales, Queen Maria of Romania, young Schildkraut and his wife, about whether or not girls should bob their hair, the dangers of being beautiful, about tramps, vagabonds, and hitchhikers, and the difference between them, about equal rights, jealousy, vengeance, curiosity, family life, love, marriage, baldness, beards, operations, accidents, murders, and who knows what else!

I had a little trouble writing about the Prince of Wales, the Queen of Romania, and Joseph Schildkraut. They weren't from B--n, so Mr. Rat didn't easily let me get away with having them in the *Pathfinder*. But the editor applauded them and suppressed the authority who threatened to keep them from freely emigrating to our paper. With them, our quota was filled and now there was only room for items that pertained strictly to the city of B--n.

B--n's inhabitants über alles!

But the God of all the news didn't want one single incident in B--n to occur. All of the news about hold-ups, murders, fires, divorces, and scandals, seemed to happen in New York, the Bronx, or Brooklyn. Sometimes in other cities, but not in B--n. There was not a single misfortune here. Such a damned upstanding city! Everyone keeps to themselves. They keep the traditions of the first settlers: don't do anything that might make anyone talk. Take care of your name, protect your reputation.

The *Pathfinder* suffered from B--n's good reputation. A local newspaper is like a neighbor, a gossip, a fussbudget. And if there's nothing to talk about, that's really a tragedy.

So, as Mr. Rat explained, the *Pathfinder* suffered from B--n's good reputation, and Mr. Rat took out that suffering on his assistants. He yelled at the circulation manager because the mountain of returned *Pathfinder*s kept growing. Why didn't he send them out to be sold? Why was he always just standing there next to the office girls and talking? What did he think would come of talking to them?

He yelled at Mr. Stein for just standing there and not understanding what people said to him.

Mr. Stein got insulted and left. He's gone. He's not part of the *Pathfinder* anymore. He'd be better off going to the Bronx, he said.

Mr. Rat yelled at the people who brought in advertisements, because they weren't bringing any in. Why did they let the advertisers go to other papers and advertise among strangers in other languages or other cities? Why didn't the assistant in charge of advertising grab their business before it got away? What was he waiting for? Did he expect them to come to him and beg?

He yelled at the "city editor," Mr. Sohn, for writing *apelsin* instead of *orendzsh*, *untererdishe bahn* instead of *subvey*, *fenster* instead of *vinde*, or *gas* instead of *strit*.

Mr. Sohn said he would use whatever words he liked, as long as Mr. Rat stopped making so much noise about it. But if Mr. Rat's going to keep on yelling, Mr. Sohn will just leave. He's sick to death, and one person can't do the work of ten. He feels like he might just die.

Mr. Rat yelled at the typesetters, and the typesetters yelled back, and it almost came to blows. They threatened that there was no one who would stop them from pummeling him. But they put it off for another time.

Since I didn't have to write the novel anymore I wrote more and more articles for the women's page. Mr. Rat thought this was what was due him, and he demanded even more. More articles and more material, and all about B--n. Because everything that I write, he said, could be published in any newspaper, and had nothing to do with B--n's interests in particular. For instance, "Home decor? You can decorate your home in other cities too! You didn't say in the article that you intended the advice for B--n's Jews."

And as for the Prince of Wales, the Queen of Romania, Schild-kraut, and all that other nonsense, they have nothing at all to do with B--n. As for the hairstyle piece, it's a little "ahead of the times" for B--n. B--n wouldn't like it. B--n women keep their hair long and their minds small. As for love, marriage, jealousy, baldness, beards, murders, and so forth—these are just general things that exist in the whole world. The *Pathfinder* needs things that are about people who live in B--n itself, people who everyone knows and has shaken hands with!

He paused for a moment and then cried, "Interviews! Yes, ma'am! Interviews! Descriptions of the lives of leading Jewish figures in our city—businessmen, community leaders!"

"Politicians . . ."

"Yes, ma'am! You got me!"

"Cheap politicians," I added.

"Cheap is fine. Cheap can make us money. Everyone will want to read about them. Yes, ma'am! That's what I want you to do. And if you do it, you'll really be a part of the *Pathfinder*, you'll be essential. You'll stay here in B--n. You'll earn thirty, maybe even thirty-five dollars a week! Go ask the telephone girl for the addresses of the most prominent people we can afford. People who like publicity. Then start looking for them. Head over to one today, another tomorrow."

"You should say *drive* over to one today. Take an automobile and drive, since it's so hot outside."

"An automobile!" He laughed out loud. "The streetcar, the subway, the el aren't good enough for you? There's so many options you don't have time to get sick of them."

"You expect me to walk and to take all those things you mentioned? I'll waste all my time just trying to get from place to place."

"I will not give you an automobile. A car! Ha! Who wouldn't laugh at that! What do you think, girls? What do you think of that? Ha!"

The girls didn't say anything and he left to tell the editor and the typesetter, so they could laugh with him.

12

When the Jewish Russian-speaking intellectuals of B--n learned that I was leaving the *Pathfinder*, they said with some regret, "That's B--n for you—whenever people venture here, they always run back to where they came from. Few people are willing to settle here. There's nothing and no one here to recommend it. Summers are so hot you can barely stand them and you spend your days searching for somewhere to cool down. But when you finally reach the short days with long dark evenings, there's nothing to do."

They were jealous of anyone who had the good fortune to live in New York, a city where you can see all the wonders of the world, and when you don't have anything to do, you can go to the literary cafés and nurse a cup of tea all night long, just sitting and talking. There are people worth talking to there.

Mr. N., the darling of the intellectuals, takes down those literary folks until they're little more than mud. In his opinion, the people that gather there are full of pretensions, but without any real talent. He points out deficiencies in every writer he's heard of. Speaking of some writers he knows personally, he asks with glee, "Who are they? What are they? Back when I knew them, I didn't see a speck of talent in them. The only reason they left B--n for New York was that they were looking for high-paying jobs, and because they thought they were something special. And now they're literary critics, politicians, and who knows what else! Now, as for their personal lives . . ."

He has a whole trove of secrets about them, which he insisted aren't secrets anymore. Everyone knows. He heard these stories from traveling literary agents, speakers, actors, and so forth, from whom a clever person can learn a lot. He told me about this one's husband with that one's wife, this one's daughter with that one's son. He told me about so-and-so's past and so-and-so's missteps.

I wondered, "How is it that I didn't know any of this, even though I've known these people so long and so well?"

"Even if you knew it, you'd never divulge because no matter how much one writer hates another, in the end they're as close as family. They don't tell secrets about each other. That's some *yikhes*."

I told him, "You were misinformed about them. Some fool enjoyed shooting his mouth off at you about them because he could tell that you liked it. And since he didn't have any real dirt to dish, he came up with lies. I can tell you have a particular hatred for writers. You're angry at them for not recognizing your talent. Tell the truth—you must have tried your hand at writing once, and been unsuccessful."

I immediately regretted what I had said to him because he turned beet red and looked around as though he didn't know what to do with himself. The others, avoiding eye contact with him, looked at each other and smirked.

I was inclined to believe that actually he loved writers because there was so much to criticize about them. More than once at a gathering he spent almost the entire time talking about them. Certainly he wasn't indifferent to them. It wasn't enough for him to hate them as intellectuals, who he didn't think were so intelligent; he also hated them for being what he thought was low class. Maybe he was interested in them because he wanted to have the luxury of taking such "missteps," the possibility of permitting himself to "sin," to a certain degree, like the writers.

I said as much to him, and he bit his lips as though he was trying to punish them for letting such talk fall out of his mouth. He gave a vexed smile and said he would have to be careful about who he talked to about these things from now on. He'd better not let anything slip in front of a member of the writer's family.

He said this and then explained to me that I'm the only writer who isn't interested in hearing nasty rumors. The others are happy to hear their colleagues' reputations torn to shreds. But he doesn't believe I'm so much better than them. It only goes to show that I'm more secretive, that I keep things to myself, *in zikh*—that is to say. I'm an introspectivist!

Fine. If he wants to think so, let him.

As for the *Pathfinder*, the intellectuals weren't interested in discussing it. That rag, they said, isn't even worth talking about. It's trash! With the exception of what I write there, of course. But soon I won't be writing there either, and then its only use will be as kindling. Why should they pay any attention to the newspaper, given its publisher? Who is he, what is he, where and from whom does he get the money to publish? We know where. We can guess well enough. Politics, campaigns, votes. But who cares? It's not worth getting upset about the *Pathfinder*. We don't even need to lift a finger, it'll die on its own. It'll self-destruct!

"That's good to hear!" I said, laughing.

They didn't understand why I thought this was a problem. Since I didn't have anything to do with the political side of the newspaper, and since I was about to leave my position at the newspaper, what could be the matter? I'd be better off writing in New York than in B--n at the *Pathfinder*, and I'd be better off leaving sooner than later. If it were a question of making money, as one of them said, "if you eat pork, let it drip down your chin." But not only is there no honor in it, there's also no money. How much were they paying me, anyway?

They wanted to know. But I said I didn't feel comfortable telling. Money isn't everything.

"Yes, if you're working for an ideal. But if you're working for a small-time politician who takes money from everyone, not worrying about how he'll be able to pay it back, that's foolishness. Not just foolishness, it's a sin."

They talked about Mr. Sohn. It's a pity, the way he looks. The *Pathfinder* will kill him. He's wasting away. It's a shame. He had so much more life in him. They mourned him as if he were already dead.

And the new editor who came from New York seems like a fine young man, he seems intelligent. But he must be crazy. Certainly. No one in their right mind would come to work in an editorial position like that, in a city like this, at this time of year! Running through the streets looking for things to write about that no one will read! Who has the strength to read in this heat?

They wanted to know where I will go when I leave B--n. Will I go straight back to New York, or somewhere else, a summer resort near B--n with them, or near them? I didn't know what to say. First I had to say my goodbyes at the *Pathfinder* and then . . .

It seemed to me that I'd already borne the brunt of the hard work, and now my work didn't seem so bad. Maybe I could keep working there week after week, as long as Mr. Rat didn't ask me to write him a new novel, or twist my hand with interviews with politicians. He'd be happy to see me come into the editorial office earlier, like I did the first two weeks. I found that it's better to go in earlier. It isn't as hot. You can even walk on the shady side of the street. And the desk that I usually sit at is almost as good as my desk at home.

Every day when I looked at my page, I could hardly believe my eyes that I'd filled it with writing! Even though I thought I couldn't possibly fill it. I was wrong about myself. I was wrong, too, about getting up early in the morning, and I was easily able to get by without coffee. Everyone back home wouldn't believe it. They must have imagined I'd die of loneliness for them.

As soon as I began to think I was over with the whole thing, in order not to let my feelings get the better of me, I said, "Tfu! It doesn't bother me!" I'd grit my teeth and bear it. After all, I was lonely. Everything in and around my house was unfamiliar and cold. It seemed like there was no one in the world who was close to me. But I had myself.

Day by day, things got better for me at the editorial office. It got better in part because being there forced me to work, and the more I wrote the less I thought or felt.

Apart from my work and life, the atmosphere around the *Pathfinder* got busy from time to time. Half-baked, thinly written romances happened between the office girls and office boys. Odd individuals came to offer their services to the *Pathfinder* for money, and Mr. Rat kept on searching for goings-on to narrate from the standpoint of B--n. He kept on chasing after business from those who put their advertisements in other newspapers, and not the *Pathfinder*. He kept on screaming and hollering and laughing. And the circulation manager, who wanted to agree with whatever his boss said, kept on getting more and more confused. And in the middle of all of this some well-to-do Jews would come to visit and get a look at the business.

With great pleasure Mr. Rat would take the visitors to see how the place was run. He was boastful that he knew every aspect from the inside out and he wanted to demonstrate to the Jews of B--n who and what he was, so that they would request to invest their money in his business, even though he would refuse it in no uncertain terms. If they hadn't been willing to give money before, he wasn't about to take it now! He didn't care for those who wouldn't care for him. Yes, sir! That's what he's all about.

As soon as visitors like these left, Mr. Rat would get more ambitious about innovative news items. He came to ask me what I was up to. He wanted to talk to me. He said, "I want you to write articles on Monday based on what the Saturday and Sunday newspapers publish in English. As many as you can. There are many excellent articles. I want them. You'll wait on Friday for the Saturday paper, and on Saturday at about eleven o'clock at night you can get the Sunday papers downtown. You'll read through them thoroughly and get everything read by Sunday afternoon so we can publish on Monday!"

I asked, "Where will you find room for all this? The *Pathfinder* only has so many pages!"

He told me to let him worry about the room. My job was to write the articles.

I didn't like the way he spoke to me in commands, like a boss ruling them over me, and I swore to myself that I wasn't going to listen to him.

"Will you do it?" he wanted to know.

"I'll see if I have enough time for it," I responded laconically.

"What do you mean, 'enough time'?"

"Enough time means enough time."

"Would you talk that way to a New York editor if he told you to do something?"

"A New York editor wouldn't tell me what to do. Knowing how much else I had to do, he would give the work to one of my colleagues, or he would offer to pay for the work separately from my wages."

"Is that so? You want to be paid separately for each thing you do? I see what you're trying to do," he accused me.

I told him I was happy for him to see it. I have to do almost everything for free, and, anyway, he's not even really my editor. The editor is Mr. Kahm, who wrote me a contract explaining how much work he was expecting from me each day. Six days a week, one day off. Writing articles and editing the women's section. That's all. Writing a novel in addition, and not only editing but also writing the women's pages—is that still not enough for you? Excuse me, but I can't do any more than I already do!

"You don't want to do it! You are perfectly capable, you just don't want to!"

"Fine, I don't want to," I agreed.

I don't care what he thinks. It's clear that I won't be able to stay here much longer.

13

Something newsworthy happened in the city of B--n. An important philanthropist passed away.

The English newspapers were filled with the news. Mr. Rat scolded me, saying that if only I'd listened to him and done interviews as he said, I would've snagged an interview with the philanthropist for the *Pathfinder*. I kept putting it off, and now it's too late—she's dead!

"There's nothing to be done," I consoled him.

But he refused to be consoled. He hollered that by the time I choose which important figures of B--n to interview, they'll all be dead! "And you see? All of the English newspapers are full of her."

"I don't see why they shouldn't be full of her. She's one of theirs. An American. A Christian."

"She was good to everyone. She was good to the Jews, too. She gave charity. And she left us without giving an interview to the *Pathfinder*! Whose fault is that?"

He wanted me to say it was my fault. But I didn't say anything. Finally, he said it. "It's your fault. You didn't go to get one."

"How could I have known she was going to die so fast?"

"So fast? She was almost a hundred years old! That's hardly fast."

"Almost a hundred years old?"

He didn't know whether I was more amazed that she lived so long or that she died so fast. He sputtered, "What? What are you asking me? Are you interviewing me? Huh? That's easy enough, I'm right here in the office. You don't have to go anywhere to do it."

The chief editor, Mr. Kahm, appeared like a ghost in the door of his office and seemed to inquire, without speaking, why there was so much shouting. Mr. Rat told him why, and he didn't say anything. It was easy to see that he thought Mr. Rat was right. Mr. Rat was pleased and went into the editor's office. They closed the door behind them.

The office girls asked me what he wanted and I told them, "He wants me to interview the woman who just died."

They laughed. "An interview with a corpse? You should send him. Let him do it himself. The nerve of him! To send an author-ess, an editor, to search out interviews for the *Pathfinder*, as though anyone would read them. Say, how large is the circulation of the newspaper, anyhow?"

No one knew the answer to that question. No one even knows how many copies we print. Those who know won't say. Probably they were told not to.

The girlish laughter was cut short. Mr. Rat came back. He entered in a huff. He started toward us, hopped as though on a spring, and barked, "What's today?"

"Tuesday," answered his secretary, and glanced at a calendar to supply the date.

He turned to me. "Do you have today's *Pathfinder*?"

"Yes. Here it is."

"And an evening paper?"

"Here's the evening paper."

"Let me see Monday's evening paper. What is there from the Eng-lish-language weekend papers? Nothing! And I told you to include it. Why didn't you do it?" he barked.

I could see that he was picking a fight with me and was just wait-ing for me to give him a chance to yell at me so that everyone could hear. I made myself very calm and composed, though inside I was screaming bloody murder and I wanted to hit him over the head with a telephone book, especially since his head was the weakest part of his body and a blow to it might kill him. I said, "I had so much other work to do . . ."

"What kind of work? Where is it?"

I showed him the evening *Pathfinder*, the women's section: the editorials, fashion notices, notices about women's issues, a short story, jokes, aphorisms, musings, an article about the Broadway girls who had been choked to death.

"Where were they choked?"

I know he would prefer for them to have been choked in B--n, but I told him anyway, "In New York!"

"Is this everything that you thought it was important to include?"

"Yes."

"And I can tell that this isn't what you found in the Sunday papers. This is—fruit compote! You gave me a whole page of fruit compote!"

"Very well, then," I said, resigned. "Fruit compote. Now if you want the rest of the meal, take a look at the other pages."

"We're not talking about the other pages right now. We're talking about what's on your page! Yes, ma'am! How many pages did you give us last week? I mean, how much of it was yours, that you wrote yourself?"

"How many pages should it have been? I'm asking because we've never talked about a mandatory page count before. So, how much? I'd be very interested to know."

"Six pages!" he shouted. "And I'll betcha you didn't write that much. Let's see! Let's count them up. Give me a whole week of *Pathfinders*."

"Ask the circulation manager to give you some copies."

He asked, and the man handed them to him. He spread them out on the table in order according to date. He took out a carpenter's pencil and rolled up his right shirtsleeve (he'd already removed his jacket because of the heat).

"Which of these are yours?" he asked.

As I told him which ones were mine (since I didn't sign my name to everything I wrote), he marked them with his pencil. The ones I told him were pieces from other provincial newspapers he left alone. Once he'd marked up all the *Pathfinders*, he started measuring the articles with a yardstick. Once he'd finished his measurements, he shook his head vigorously, and explained that the reprinted articles, which don't come without a price, took up more than half of the pages. So I wrote less than six pages!

"Does it have to be a full page each day?" I asked.

"Yes, ma'am! And if not, you have to supplement with articles that you summarize from the Sunday papers. You get me?"

"Wait," I said. "You forgot to measure the columns of my novel."

"The novel doesn't count!"

"Why not?"

"It's nothing!"

"Nothing? My novel is nothing?" (I said all this calmly, without a trace of anger.)

"No." (He said it with anger.) "Nothing!" And then he even translated it into English for me. "*Nothing!*"

"Is that so?" I said with surprise. "Nothing at all?"

"Yes, nothing, *nothing*! I could buy the best novel by the best author for thirty dollars!"

"For thirty dollars! So little!"

"Even less—for twenty-five dollars!"

"For twenty-five dollars?" I asked, amazed.

"Yes, even for twenty!"

I stopped acting incredulous and said, calmly, "That's a lie. You can't buy it for those prices."

"I'll make a bet with you that I can! I'll show you letters from famous New York writers begging me to buy their novels. And because we're a new paper, they offered to give their work to us for whatever I was willing to pay. One of them wrote that we'll talk about the price later, that I can pay him after the *Pathfinder* gets off the ground. If our situation doesn't improve he won't expect payment from me. He's doing it out of love for the Yiddish language and he is willing to sacrifice what he can for the sake of Yiddish!"

"You have an active imagination," I said.

"Is that what you think? I have a letter from a writer with a novel, who wants me to—"

"Pay him!" I interrupted.

"Yes, ma'am. He was born in B--n, he's a window cleaner, but he's written a fine novel that he wants to see published. It might be as well written as the novels of the New York writers. Who knows?"

"Who knows?" I replied. "It could be good, or it could be—"

"—better!" he interrupted.

"Aha!" I scoffed.

"You see?" he asked.

"I see. But I can't see why you haven't published the window cleaner's novel . . ."

"Maybe I will!"

"You should. Maybe he'll clean your windows for you, too. You could use it."

Realizing that I was joking, he became as angry as he had been before and told me to *never mind* about the windows, he'd see to them himself! What he wants to know is whether I'll do what he asked of me or not.

I declared that I would not.

"If not—" he began.

"Then we'll go our separate ways," I finished for him.

"That's all!" he consented gruffly. He stomped away to the editor's office and slammed the fragile door.

The office girls clamored around me. Am I going to leave them? Oh, I can't do that! They'll miss me. They like me. They're sorry to see me go. But that Mr. Rat is a rat! Yes he is! The nerve! Demanding so much. He should thank me for letting him print my name in his paper, and he—

The telephone rang. Mr. Kahm called, inviting me into his office.

14

The editor greeted me with a nod, and started in with the weather.

"It's very hot."

"It's terrible!" I agreed.

"It's probably not as hot by the sea."

"Naturally."

"The weatherman says that it will get even hotter."

"Yes." A pause. "Was there something you wanted to say to me?"

"I wanted to say that I was surprised to hear that you're leaving us."

"You'd be better off being surprised that I ever came at all," I rebuffed. "You must remember the stipulations under which I agreed to come here to work. You wrote to me yourself explaining everything I'd be expected to do here—write a column every day and edit the women's section. Do you deny it?"

"No. But you understand. You know how it is. You can't be stingy with the work you have to do to get a new newspaper going."

"I didn't hold back. I gave generously. And then he said that my novel was nothing."

Mr. Kahm tried to calm me down. "He didn't mean it. He was acting rashly, in the heat of the moment. He has a temper. Things heat up so quickly with him."

"Then let him burn," I wanted to say, but I held back. I hate cursing.

The editor continued. "You have to know how to talk to Mr. Rat. Do you want to talk to him again?"

"No, I've had enough. We've said everything we need to say."

"So you've made your decision?"

"I'm leaving."

"I'm sorry to hear it. Why can't you come to an agreement?"

"There's nothing to agree about," I retorted.

"If you wanted to come to an agreement, you could."

"Then I guess I don't want to."

"I hope you don't hold me responsible for this?"

"No, you're irresponsible."

"Why would you say that?" he asked.

"Because you're not an editor. He won't let you edit. He edits you instead. He can make you do whatever he wants. You won't say a word in protest."

He didn't say a word. He was just a tired, weak man sitting in the editor's chair staring wearily through the dirty window into the street.

"I'm thinking . . ." he said.

"Yes? What are you thinking?"

"Where will I get the next novel?"

"From the window cleaner."

He looked at me, confused. I told him about all the people Mr. Rat said he could get novels from. He said he didn't know if those novels would be suitable for the *Pathfinder*, and asked me not to just up and leave in the middle of everything. He asked me to leave him with a few editorials and other things to last at least a few days.

I agreed to do that much.

There are editors that you have to feel pity for. This editor must have fallen into his job. He couldn't help it. Mr. Sohn told me that he'd invested his life's savings into the *Pathfinder*, that he'd never been an editor before. He was bound to it now, an unfortunate partner in the lamentable business.

Mr. Sohn also reminded me about the travel expenses. I shouldn't let Mr. Rat get away without paying. I should write an invoice and give it to the accounting secretary to have it "okayed"—tell her to send it to him.

The accounting secretary went into his office with a sour expression, showed him the invoice and he refused to okay it. She returned it to me. "He refused to okay it," she told me. "He yelled, 'Give it back to her!'"

Mr. Sohn was very upset about it. He said he would speak to Mr. Rat about it himself and demand that my travel expenses be paid.

The accounting secretary was also disgusted. She called Mr. Rat a "cheapskate" and a "mean thing."

In short, I didn't get the money. The truth is, I had accounted for that already. It wasn't a surprise and it didn't bother me.

Mr. Rat emerged from his office, incensed, and turned off the electric fan that I was standing next to. "Whoever is hot can sit next to the window," he announced. He yelled at the circulation manager for forgetting to turn off the electric lights that weren't in use. Then he went into the printing room to argue with the typesetters. He was in a towering rage.

While Mr. Rat was busy bossing everyone around, I sat next to the open window and read a letter I had just received from New York. Among other things, the letter said that "the new newspaper that has taken so long to get up and going will soon be ready for publication, in time for Labor Day. I hardly need to tell you that you should come back to New York. You were one of the first people they wanted to hire. So, you may wish to leave B--n with its—begging your pardon—'city' newspaper. There's no need for you to waste your time in the province, when you can write in New York. It's a wonder that you held out there so long. We wonder if you're having a love affair there (not just writing about them). That's the only reason we can come up with for your still being there . . ."

I let Mr. Sohn read these lines and he begged me to look for a place for him at the new newspaper. "Put in a good word for me. You see that I can work like—"

"—a horse!" I agreed.

"Like ten horses! Help me tear myself away from here. If I don't die from it I'll go crazy. Please understand and forgive me for helping to bring you here. Believe me that if I had known that they would treat you like this I wouldn't have asked you to come. They threw just as much work at me, too."

"Who is the 'they'?" I asked. "It's just him, Mr. Rat."

"It's not just Mr. Rat. It's Mr. Kahm, too, and the people who stand behind them and egg them on. It's the whole band of exploiters, each of whom hold positions above the lowly writer. What do they care about our misfortunes? Promise me that you'll put in a good word for me in New York?"

I promised him.

When the office girls heard about my good fortune in New York, they were happy for me and also a bit jealous. One of them, Miss Geyer, whose job was to canvas for advertisers for the *Pathfinder* by telephone, constantly saying "Thank you very much!," promised that she would write to me if I would answer her letters. Would I answer them?

I promised that I would. We parted as friends.

Mr. Sohn and Mr. Barg went with me one last time to Child's Restaurant, where we laughed about the mistakes in the *Pathfinder* more than we ate. Mr. Barg did a very good impression of the three-dollar boy who stuck out his tongue and pushed it from one side of his mouth to the other, following his pen as it made its way across the wide sheet of paper. Today, Mr. Rat had watched him work with authoritative self-importance and clapped him on the back, saying, "That's all right!"

Mr. Sohn did an impression of Mr. Rat criticizing the front page. "The headline is too big. The headline is too small. You should get rid of the headline. This piece of news should be in a textbox. We can get rid of this textbox, don't you think? We already have plenty! And what's the point of all this Yiddish? Who uses the word *antoyshte* when there's a word like *disapointedte*, and why would you use the word *iberrasht*? Where did the word *suprayzd* go? Was it eaten by wolves? And why use the word *umophengike* when there's a perfectly good word, *independete*? And so forth, and so on."

15

I left the *Pathfinder* and said goodbye to everyone and wished them all good luck, even Mr. Rat, and I headed to the seashore. By the sea I could think all of my thoughts and let them get washed away.

A week passed. I wanted to see the *Pathfinder*. I wanted to know what it looked like without me. It wasn't easy to get a copy, but when I got it I saw that they were still running my novel. I'm not kidding. It was printed in small letters, but there it was. And under the editorials that I didn't write—they printed *my name*!

Am I still working for the *Pathfinder* even though I'm not there anymore? What is the meaning of this? How can this be right?

I started to read the editorials that weren't mine, but that the whole world might assume were mine. I was curious to see what "I" wrote, when I wasn't writing. And I read there about "those poor souls who are so misguided, and what is happening to Jewish modesty, when girls go fifty-fifty with men?" The editorial asked why we Jewish girls have such loose morals. Why do we destroy family purity for all Jews by lowering the high standards of modesty? Why?!

"I read a letter from a reader," the editorial continued, "who is no longer a spring chicken. She wants to exchange her husband for another, a lover."

The letter from the reader was included, as though it was a real letter, and the editorial writer, who was supposed to be *me*, continued:

"This is what a woman writes, a Jewish girl, about her own husband, whom she shares her life with! They are raising their children together, they share their joys and sorrows, and so much more, that if we tried to add it all up it couldn't be calculated on paper. Just the thought of such a woman would be enough to make any person of honor blush!"

The editorial bemoaned a newspaper that gave such letters a prominent place, and explained that the *Pathfinder* responded to this horrible woman by saying that "her parents should not try to forbid the life she chooses. Quite the opposite. Our opinion is that everyone is entitled to the pleasures of happiness and love. We applaud your strength and wish you success in turning your life around!"

"This is the advice, the *tsenerene,* that a certain paper (not in B--n) gave to the misguided woman with her poor soul," the editorial went on. "It's no wonder that our standards of modesty are dragged through the mud! The *Pathfinder* would *never* answer such a letter from an older wife with children! Because the *Pathfinder* observes the traditions of family purity and would never encourage such behavior from a married woman!"

Another editorial was about a woman who is often forgetful. What was she forgetful of? Instead of running to the doctors, she'd be better off taking a bath! And the editorial explained the importance of water for—women. Medical science around the world says so. "By washing their bodies she kills two birds with one stone: she gets the dirt off her body and she doesn't need to run to a doctor. The ancient Greeks also believed this. Whenever a guest came, they would offer him a bath. So did Moses and Mohammed. After all, there are stylish ladies who sit all summer by the sea and never go for a swim! They live in palaces with servants, but they don't bathe!"

After that came a "scientific explanation" about the skin and the organs and how bathing keeps it elastic and fresh, and opens the pores and at what temperature the bath should be—ninety-five degrees is all right!

In short, the more baths you take, the better your health will be, and you won't need to go to the doctors. It's the best remedy for all of the sicknesses one hears of in the modern world!

The third editorial evaluated the statement "Women are just as good as men!" It compared them physically and mentally. One sign that women are not just as good as men is that women don't have the same capacity for memory!

After that came a list of all of the advantages and disadvantages of women, showing that they are not at all different—no higher and no lower, no better and no worse—than men.

"Nevertheless," the editorial continued, "men still give their seats to women on the streetcars. Why? Surely the war should have destroyed this custom. A woman can sit in Congress and can make a good governor or even a conductor or a policeman!

"Men have better heads, but women have better hearts. Men are physically strong, but women are morally strong. A true hero is someone who is in control, so the Jewish sages have said since ancient days ('Who is strong? He who suppresses his evil inclination.') So why do the men say the blessing thanking God for not making them women? Because men are the ones who composed the blessings and they can interpret them as they like. Women are more open-minded and tolerant than men, and that's why, for this and for other reasons, they would never even think of composing a prayer thanking God for not making them men!

"Wives, if your husbands don't read the *Pathfinder*, make sure they at least read this editorial. At least make sure they read this article so they'll learn that the whole idea that men are better than women is nothing but a myth, nothing but a gut reaction that has no legs to stand on. It's made-up nonsense! It's all just a bluff!"

That's what "I" wrote in the editorial? I didn't like it at all! I wanted to go right back to B--n and go into the *Pathfinder* office and curse them all and forbid them from using my name as a byline for anything at all! My name is mine alone—it doesn't belong to them or to their readers.

"What a fool you are!" I said to myself. "You should have published something in the Yiddish press saying that you're no longer associated with the *Pathfinder*! You shouldn't have left yourself vulnerable to that Mr. Rat!"

But what good is talking to yourself? I called the editor of the *Pathfinder* and told him to take my name off of the editorials.

"You don't like the editorials?" asked Mr. Kahm.

"Whether or not I like them, I don't want my name on anything that I didn't write. How dare you do such a thing? You—"

"I thought that—"

"Will you take my name away right this minute, so you don't forget?" I demanded.

"Yes, I'll tell the typesetter right away," he assured me.

"Don't forget!" I admonished him.

"Alright. How are you? What are you up to these days?" he asked.

"I'm at the seashore. How long will you keep publishing my novel? Why are you crumbling it into little bits and stretching it out like that?"

"So it will last longer. It will end one of these days, unfortunately. Maybe you'll come back to us?"

I told him I would not. It's too hot, and I have nothing to do there. I told him not to forget to remove my name from the editorial, and goodbye.

Now that I felt a bit calmer, I took a look at the rest of the *Pathfinder*. All of it was translated versions of items from the local English papers and reprints from other provincial Yiddish newspapers. Above all, there were advertisements in the *Pathfinder* for the *Pathfinder* itself. The advertisements targeted the Jewish residents of B--n, telling them to support their only Yiddish newspaper, which was devoted to them because what is in their interest is also in the interest of the *Pathfinder*. It needs them and they need it. They're linked together. What's more, the Jews of B--n should conduct their business through the *Pathfinder*, whose address is located right in the center of B--n, which is a city unlike any other because it has its own newspaper ready to be at your service.

And you wouldn't believe how many mistakes were in the newspaper. Good grief! The machine jumped around and jumbled up the type. It wasn't just letters here and there, or even words, but whole lines of text that came out like:

"The jury deliiiibbbbbbbberrrattttsss for a long time until it rrrreeeeeeakhschtedahb:!ed that the accused was innnooookkljnatented;: -

!eeeeiiieeaaaklhggggggssssggggrrrr page 3 rrrrvvvffkdts ""'"""""'"!!!!
--- --- rrr

There were cut-off titles, missing bylines, continuations from the front page that were missing from inside the paper, and so forth.

These things didn't bother me. My name wasn't printed under them. But those editorials!

The only way I could comfort myself was to trust that the editor of the *Pathfinder* had already removed my name and I wouldn't have to think about it anymore. I shouldn't ruin my short vacation with it.

16

Back in New York in a café, I saw Mr. Sohn. I wondered how and when he left the *Pathfinder*.

"How?" he replied. "Plain and simple. I edited the city pages until I completely fell apart, and I fainted away, though as you can see I lived through it. They took me to the hospital. I rested up. It was breezy and nice, and pretty nurses fussed around me. After the hospital, they told me to go away to a farm. I went away. I couldn't stand the boredom and the fresh air and the rest. I took the first express train and here I am in a New York café!"

"Are you happy now?" I asked.

"Thank God, things are looking up. And what about you?"

"Thank God, so far so good. So, tell me, who took over your job?"

"How should I know? Mr. Stein and that man Mr. Bein, and the three-dollar boy and—isn't that enough? Mr. Rat is enough on his own!"

"And Mr. Barg?"

"Mr. Barg? You haven't seen him? He's here, too. He'll probably come through the door any minute now. As soon as you left, everything began to change. Mr. Stein was prepared to do everything Mr. Rat asked him to do—interview people, write a series of articles, biographies of B--n businessmen and how they began their businesses, and how they worked their way up thanks to their own virtue, and that if one of them should run, people should vote for him because he will bring prosperity and everything will be good!"

"Why did Mr. Barg leave?"

"Mr. Barg? He—why don't you ask him yourself? Hello, Mr. Barg! We were just talking about you!"

Mr. Barg had a similar story to Mr. Sohn's, but he told it a bit differently.

"I got tired of writing street descriptions and getting up early to help write the news, and he didn't want to give me a raise. He talked about lowering the wages of anyone who complained or refusing to pay them at all. That is to say, he expected me to work for a bargain. My name may be Barg, but I have no intention of working for one. I didn't want to wait until I collapsed, like Mr. Sohn. I took the train to New York. Whatever God gives me next, I'll take. I'd rather swallow a shark than be gnawed by a Rat!"

"Nicely put!"

"Did you see how they sneak fancy Hebrew words into the B--n editorials that they're still publishing under your name?" he asked me. "When I think of how they mixed up your style . . ."

I gathered that the *Pathfinder* editors hadn't removed my name from the damned editorials.

"What do they think they're doing?" I cried.

A lawyer friend of mine told me I should take the *Pathfinder* to court. I could win a lot of money. It's a good case and I'd win it. But I don't want to get mixed up with lawyers and cases. I sent a letter to the *Pathfinder* with a final warning that if they didn't stop using my name, it'll cost them a pretty penny. I have a lawyer . . .

I think that did the trick. When the *Pathfinder* thinks they might have to pay for something, they don't want it anymore. Let alone something expensive!

The telephone rang. "Hello? Who is this?"

"It's me, don'tcha know? I'm calling to apologize."

"For what?"

"For the appointment I made for you at the Café Royal with the editor of the B--n newspaper. He just told me what a 'terrific' job you ended up with there. I feel responsible. Forgive me. It wasn't my fault. I didn't know what kind of newspaper it was. Mr. Sohn told me about the punishing work you were subjected to there and I felt guilty, although I assure you that it wasn't my fault! Was it?"

"Of course you're not responsible!"

"So you don't blame me at all?"

"Absolutely not. Actually, I should thank you for it. I don't regret going to B--n. I learned something from my experience at the *Pathfinder*. It'll come in handy."

The End.

Part 2
My Three Years
in the Land
of Israel

Written by Myself, in *Goles*

Author's Note: This novel is drawn from real life, from events that happened to people who carried on a quiet love affair with the land of their ancestors their entire lives. They lived and strove to realize the wondrous dream: to fight for a home for the nation of Israel.

The individual recounting these facts is a writer who was born in Minsk, Belarus; emigrated to America; became an American citizen; and traveled to settle permanently in Eretz Yisrael.

1

Once the *Canada* left the Brooklyn harbor with her passengers, she ferried us with ardent devotion for an entire month until she reached the harbor in Jaffa, Palestine. The *Canada* was a small, very old ship on her final journey. It was a miracle that she didn't sink.

We disembarked from the *Canada* onto narrow, flat boats captained by two Arabs, one with wide brown trousers that fluttered in the wind and a blood-red Turkish fez on his ponytailed head, and the other in a striped robe that looked like a nightshirt, with an old rag on his head and a rope for a belt. They were both barefoot, their splayed toes crowned with mud. The narrow, flat boats rose and fell, limping as they crashed against the large stones that stood in their way.

Into such a boat, which looked like a giant bread trough, stepped my brother; his wife; his wife's sister, with her husband Aaron and their "boychik" Izzy; Izzy's grandfather, our uncle Shmuel; Moyshe, Aaron's brother—that is, Izzy's uncle; and I.

Moyshe—Mosheh, as he's known, according to Sephardic Hebrew pronunciation—had come to "take us" from the ship and bring us to the Nordau Hotel, where he'd already booked us a room, and to take his brother Aaron and his family home to their mother, who was waiting for them.

Mosheh was pleased to see his brother, sister-in-law, and especially his young nephew, whose head was bathed in freckles that complemented a thin-lipped mouth with a row of white teeth that stretched widely across his narrow young face. He made an effort to speak in English to show off for his American nephew. He warned us, Americans, about the Orient: no more not knowing many languages.

Here they speak every language there is. People come here from all corners of the world. Oh, ho, Eretz Yisrael!

Young Izzy didn't like the way his uncle was lording it over them with his Palestine, and he tried to get a leg up. America! Oh, ho, America! "What do you know about America?"

Izzy pointed at the stones that the boats were crashing against and, almost falling overboard, asked, "Who put those here? Why don't they get rid of them?"

Mosheh answered, "Pirates," and then again in English, "you know, *pie-rats*, placed them here. They would hide behind the stones and shoot at the ships! Do you see that big building by the shore? That was once a monastery, and the pirates turned it into their fortress. The walls of the fortress are strong and thick so no artillery can take them down."

"Do the pirates still hide there?"

"Oh, no!" Mosheh's laughter was loud and vivacious. "The pirates are long dead. The building belongs to the government now. You know, the British government."

"Does the government shoot at the ships? No? Anyway . . . the government should remove the stones. In America they would certainly have already gotten rid of them. Yes, sir, I know, because I'm an American, see?"

"You are a Jew!" Izzy's grandfather corrected him.

"No, sir! *You* are a Jew!"

"You'll be a Jew soon enough. A good Jew in Eretz Yisrael."

"Will I?" Izzy asked his mother, and when she answered with a "Yes," he gestured to her father. "A Jew . . . like *him*?"

" . . . Yes," she responded hesitantly.

"Never!" he cried. "I don't want to be here! No! I want to go back to America. I am an American!"

"Alright, then go. You're here now, so try to be a good boy," she chided in Yiddish-infused English. "Yes, dear?"

"Well . . . yes." He heaved a sigh at his mother like an old man.

The mother was worried about the child. She felt guilty for taking him away from America. Since he'd already had the good fortune to be born in America, maybe she should have raised him there. But what kind of an upbringing does a child get in America, where most of the children are raised in the street, under unsavory influences? In Eretz Yisrael he will be under the supervision of good teachers. He will not become estranged from his own.

She often spoke about her only son's upbringing. Aaron, her husband, was a bit jealous that she poured so much attention over the child and had so little love left for him. He had to compete with the child for her love. He used to pretend not to be bothered by it, but ever since he was a victim of a hold-up in America, he had become another man. All his previous jollity vanished. He was often caught up by the feeling that there would be an attack, and he feared for his life.

He'd liked America. He'd passed the state pharmacy exams with flying colors and had found a good position. Bit by bit, he'd stopped yearning for Eretz Yisrael, where he was born and raised. He'd decided to put off returning there until he had more money. Enough to make a comfortable home for himself and his family in Eretz Yisrael. All had gone according to plan. Then one day, all of a sudden, a few hold-upniks broke into the pharmacy when he was there alone, took all the money out of the cash register, beat him, and locked him in a bathroom in the back. He banged on the walls that bordered a dark alley, but no one heard him. It wasn't until the next morning that a postman heard his pounding and freed him. He was never the same after that night. He was returning to Eretz Yisrael with his tail between his legs. He'd left it to her, his wife, to arrange everything. She was energetic and devoted, and she was too crazy for her child. She didn't want to have another. The more dedicated she was to her son, the more she distanced herself from her son's father . . . But they were both united in their love for Eretz Yisrael and their desire to cement their family life there.

As soon as we reached the shore, Arab porters fell on us like locusts. They tore our baggage from our arms and shouted at the other porters who tried to grab it from them. Mosheh shouted over them, telling them to bring our baggage where we were going and not to confuse it with others' belongings. We continued on to the Palestinian "Ellis Island."

Our way forward was difficult because of the sharp heat of the thick dust and the path paved with sharp stones. Uncle Shmuel could hardly keep up with the others. Old age hobbled his tired legs.

"He's too old, isn't he?" Izzy asked his mother, glancing over at his grandfather.

"He's tired," said his mother, trying to help her father walk as he waved her away with his hand. He didn't need any help, he wasn't a cripple. He could walk fine on his own.

He and Mosheh went over to the side of the government building where a hand reached out through a window, like at a bank, to take passports from the new arrivals.

The government official wanted to hear an explanation for why the words "Born in Russia" were on the passport. "How old are you?"

Moshe pointed to the passport. "It's all written right there."

Once we had finished with the governmental hand, we went to the Zionist Organization's office, where we had to pay a head tax: three pounds (five dollars) for each of us, including Izzy, the child, for a total of thirty-five dollars, plus an additional sum for our eight trunks and for the two visas that were delayed in coming from America. Mosheh complained to the Zionist Organization for taking so much money, but they said they weren't taking it for themselves but for the British government, the Mandatory power that makes you pay more and more.

Shmuel was angry at my brother for paying so much money (for everyone's head tax and the trunks). But my brother smiled good-naturedly. "Don't worry, uncle. It costs money because it's worth money."

Mosheh smiled broadly and called us all over to the medical department to get our smallpox vaccines. Entry into the country was strictly forbidden without the vaccine.

A guard stood by the open door to the medical department. He was a tall young man in shorts. My uncle Shmuel asked him a question: How long will *that thing* have to take? Was it possible to exempt him? He wanted to travel to Jerusalem as quickly as possible . . .

"Zeydenyu," said the guard, "find a chair and take a seat until they call you. You came from America, right?"

"Yes, from America."

"Over there they're always in a hurry, but here, Zeyde, we take our time. *Shwaye shwaye.*"

We waited to hear the word "Next!" The old doctor and the not-so-young nurses grabbed an arm. They cleaned a small area, cut a small incision, gave a squirt, and it was done. Most people bit their lips but didn't make a noise. They accepted the pain of the stab like it was something they deserved.

But not the girl who we nicknamed "the Goat" on the ship because she leapt from third class to second and from second to first, where she even had the privilege of dancing with the captain. She made a fuss: Who asked them to stab her? If someone is healthy, why should they make her sick? This is the "pleasure" you get when you arrive in the Orient, which they advertise in such beautiful colors. It's bad enough that it's so hot and dusty and muddy—they also force unnecessary pain on you. "Some country," she said in English. "Gee!" She looked longingly through the window toward the *Canada*, the old ship where she'd had such a lovely time.

Mosheh couldn't stand to hear the girl criticizing Eretz Yisrael and said to her, "Miss, if you don't like 'the Orient' then go back to your America. Your ship is still here."

She didn't like how Mosheh spoke to her. She retorted, "Fresh!" and turned her back to him.

Our uncle spoke to the girl. "Whether you need it or not, they'll grab you and stab you. One law for everyone!" It was a pity about the pain from the stab of the needle. As for him, he'd experienced much greater pain in his life. What bothered him was the waste of time. The doctor didn't care about anyone's time. He said that everyone had to come back to him in three days. Anyone who didn't return would be severely punished. So, unwillingly, the old man had to postpone his travel to Jerusalem. He'd have to go with us to Tel Aviv.

We had to make one more stop. We had to show a group of British government officers all our documents so they could see that our coming here to Eretz Yisrael was kosher and we'd followed all the legal requirements they set out for us.

These government officials sat at a long table in the middle of a large room. We had to stand. Stand and wait in line until someone looked over our papers and gave them to another official, who gave them to a third official, and so forth.

More than anything, they noticed the stamp on our papers with the word "settler." They were surprised that American citizens with money had come to settle in Palestine: Is it so bad in America, or so good in Eretz Yisrael, that the Jews would want to settle here? Especially during the present crisis? One of the officials asked my brother why he wanted to settle in Palestine. Isn't it good to be an American citizen?

"Oh, very good!" Jacob said. "But I think Palestine has more for us."

"Remarkable . . ." The official shrugged his shoulders and asked *me* what compelled me to settle in Palestine. I looked him straight in his squinty eyes and said, "Historical connections, you know . . ."

"So, so . . ."

They didn't like us. I could tell. But *why?* It seemed to me they should be grateful to have immigrants like us who came with a desire to help build up the land under their Mandate. We'd come to enrich it and they puffed themselves up like smalltown in-laws on the groom's side.

We told ourselves to forget the cold reception. "Forget it!" said the girl, the "Goat," waving off the deputy's prim posture. "He's nothing but a boring old law enforcer." She smiled at them with the same smile she'd made at the ship's captain, flirting with them. But it didn't help. They looked at her coldly, not paying any particular attention to her.

"Sourpusses! Who the devil do they think they are?" she protested to us after we left them. "They take our money like regular racketeers and do nothing for us. Why doesn't anyone do anything about it? America should tell them a thing or two about treating us, her citizens, so . . . so . . . *impolitely*." She would have a word with the American consul!

"*Tov*, good," said Mosheh, and asked her to be quiet in the meantime. She should save her clamoring until after we hire carriages to take us to the Nordau Hotel in Tel Aviv.

2

There was quite a hubbub among the carriage drivers. They glommed on to us and the other newcomers, clamoring to drive us to Tel Aviv. Each one wanted to take us and the others to "their" hotel.

Mosheh's telling them we already had a hotel that we'd reserved long ago fell on deaf ears. None of them believed him: it was just an excuse for him to grab up a bunch of guests all at once and leave none for the rest. Where's the justice in that?

The drivers who didn't represent a hotel and would drive you wherever you asked grabbed all our luggage and put it in their *droshkies*, which were cushioned with colorful rugs in Russian and Oriental designs.

Mosheh scolded, "Don't grab like that! We haven't hired you yet!"

One of them shouted back, "It's none of your business." They could negotiate with the newcomers without him. He was nothing but a bourgeois, aristocratic swell, and they'd like to liquidate the likes of him!

Mosheh was ready to exchange blows at this. "That bully! That dog!" Mosheh shouted at the angry man, hoping to cause a scene by letting him know that there were plenty of other drivers we could choose from. He told us to stay put and wait for him while he went to fetch some others.

We saw Arab shopkeepers lounging with legs up in their stores' doorways, smoking their hookahs. Other Arabs sat with their backs against the walls, in the mud, on the sand, biting rock candy and idly chatting. They looked at us and clicked their tongues. Across from them sat Arab women and children covered with flies, eating crusts of bread that looked like shiny fly-covered flypaper. When Izzy cried, "Gee! They're eating flypaper!," his father corrected him that those were actually berries, not flies.

The Arab mothers broke off little pieces of the bread and put them in the children's mouths. The children blinked their eyes, which were also covered with flies. From a distance the flies looked like the dark rims of eyeglasses.

Larger children approached us with their dirty hands outstretched and begged us for *bakshish*.

Izzy wanted to know what the white spots on the children's eyes were. His mother told him that those were cataracts. "They get them from wiping their eyes with dirty hands," she said, warning him not to do so himself.

Mosheh returned with a driver, frustrated that he moved so carefully and slowly, taking his time. We took our places. We were on our way to Tel Aviv!

The horses kicked up a thick cloud of dust under their feet. The dust practically covered our heads. Mosheh pointed out to us where Jaffa ended and Tel Aviv began. We were impatient to get to the hotel.

As soon as the quiet, peaceful drivers reached the hotel, they asked us for more money. Mosheh argued that he'd already paid them. They didn't deny it. It was the truth. They had been willing to drive the guests for the amount they'd agreed on with Mosheh. But they'd been sure that they would get an extra tip. Americans are generous.

My brother gave the drivers what they asked and added a little extra for "tea money" or what they call *bakshish*. The drivers were grateful, thanked and blessed him and hoped to serve other such fine Jews from America. Mosheh was angry. Why on earth would my brother agree to their price? They had some *khutspe*! What a nerve!

Mosheh's brother said he was lucky to have hired them at all. They hadn't wanted to pick up any customers and so they had simply demanded their due later. You can't fool a businessman.

The owner of the hotel met us, his *esteemed* guests, at the front door with a warm *"barukh haba."* He told "his people" to bring in our things and took it upon himself to show us the rooms he had prepared for us. Lofty guests like ourselves, he said, deserved the best that he had! Now his guests should brush off the dust, wash up, and change out of their travel clothes, and he'd prepare a fine meal for them. It would be a taste of paradise to travelers who'd come such a long way, by land and sea!

I was hoping to lie down and rest until the meal was ready, but this proved impossible because of the noise in the hotel and outside. The telephone rang as though it was trying to show the whole Orient how loud it could ring. Outside, bicycle drivers dinged their bells. In the overzealous hands of the drivers, the clacking clappers of the bells resounded loud as clanging iron. Horns of automobiles hiccupped, castigating the pedestrians for walking in the middle of the streets instead of on the sidewalks. Arab men and women shouted out the names of the wares they carried on their heads. A donkey's sudden braying occasionally pierced through all the noise. Amid all this was the tinkling of bells and the murmur of camels.

Oh! A clang was coming from the hotel itself! Its tones summoned people from throughout the hotel's dispersed corridors. Since it was calling them to one place, it had to be able to be heard everywhere. Amid the sound of the Asian gong you could also hear calls for Malka and Yasha, the hotel's staff. Answering the gong, Malka shouted that she heard, she heard. She was coming, right away. Yasha's tall Russian boots spoke for him with their stomping.

If you measured Tel Aviv by its noise alone, it would seem like a big city. Bigger than New York.

I remembered how quiet, how peaceful New York could seem on a Sunday morning, with its fantastic, grand buildings majestically illuminated in the hours outside the workday. How many times have I strolled there to take in the beauty of those silhouettes at night! I parted regretfully with those giants, the sky scrapers, begging their forgiveness for my leaving . . .

I grasped at the last bit of quiet that was banished from the hotel. I heard some movements and chatter in the next room over. My brother and his wife were sharing their opinions about the hotel: an attractive establishment with modern improvements, and such friendly people! The hotel owner's wife came to beg our pardon because she was busy in the kitchen and unable to greet her guests as she should. The cook was away. She saw that they could get on without her, and she left. The hotel owner's wife told us that, thank God, her daughter, she should live and be well, was engaged. She was busy getting ready for her wedding. Her fiancé was here with her right now, in the hotel. Where else should he be if not here? After the wedding they were going to America. He, the fiancé, had well-off relatives there. They said they'd give him *protektsiye*. He was a singer. They were sure he'd get a position there as a *khazn*. Then, remembering that she had something cooking in the kitchen that might burn, the hotel owner's wife left her guests in the middle of the conversation with the promise to visit with them later, when dinner was served.

We were ready to go to dinner, but we still had to wait. So, we spoke about the hotel, its owner, his wife, and their workers—Malka with her wooden shoes, and Yasha with his Russian boots—and so forth. My brother was excited about everything he saw and heard. He was even more infatuated with Eretz Yisrael than he'd imagined he would be and even the disadvantages seemed like advantages in his eyes. His wife (and cousin) was not at all excited. She was tired from the journey, nervous because of the vaccination and jealous of her husband's great love of Eretz Yisrael and everything in it. Still, she always agreed with everything he said, even now. He didn't smoke or drink or show interest in other women, and he never begrudged her any money. He was in every way a perfect gentleman, so she could forgive him for his love of the Zionist ideal.

She complained about the doctor for giving her *two* vaccinations. One wasn't enough for him. Her arm burned painfully. Her nerves were on edge. She didn't have any strength, she was fatigued. Too tired to eat. She was worried about her father. Our uncle. He was counting the minutes until he could go to Jerusalem, but he had to sit here in Tel Aviv for longer than necessary just so he could go back for more vaccinations! And what would happen when he got to Jerusalem? Who would keep an eye out for him? What would he do there, all on his own?

"He won't be the only person there," Jacob reassured her. "There are many Jews there who sit and study. They'll be only too glad to welcome someone so respectable, who has so many holy books with him, into their community. He won't want for anything."

The table was set for us outside in a sukkah: a large terrace covered with green branches and flowers.

Our uncle sat at the head of the table. Next to him sat his daughter and her husband (that is, my brother and his wife), and I sat opposite them (Aaron, Minnie, and Izzy were with Aaron's family). After spending a month on the ship and eating fish every day, the food tasted very good. We reveled in the large, plump grapes, the sweet butter and the Jewish dishes, and the sukkah and its green leaves, red, white, and pink blossoms. And what service! The owner of the hotel regarded us with eyes as watchful as though he had borrowed them from a loving mother. He fussed over the dishes that his *eyshes-khayil* made. She had studied under the professional chef who had worked at the hotel during the time of great prosperity.

"They talk a big talk about productivity and land, but the truth is, things are stalling a little and you have to improvise," he explained. "Take this butter, for example. It comes from Australia. Why? Because it's cheaper to import butter from Australia than to purchase butter churned in the colonies in Eretz Yisrael." Still, he did sometimes purchase the Eretz Yisrael butter. "Why? Because it's purer, tastier. And it's made by our own."

The hotel owner changed the subject from the butter, the grapes, and other items on the table to Jews who do not immigrate to Eretz Yisrael: Don't they know that just as much as the Jews need a land of their own, the land needs Jews? Now, when there's a crisis in the land, is the time when they should come. We shouldn't allow Jewish possessions, won at great risk, to fall into the hands of Arabs who are already wealthy enough. They buy out, for very little money, property that we purchased from them for a fortune. "Between us," he said, "I think the Arabs are better at business than the Jews. They are very clever. And they are excellent at hiring themselves out!"

Our uncle finished the blessing after the meal and slowly rose from his chair, holding onto the table for support. The hotel owner told his employees to help him to his room, but our uncle refused. He could find it himself. Thank you and good night.

Only after our uncle had already left the table did the hotel owner's wife, her daughter (the bride), and her daughter's fiancé join us. They weren't quite as talkative as the hotel owner. They behaved very properly. They were very circumspect. They asked about America, marveling at people who would leave the "Golden Land" and come to settle in Palestine. Where was the logic in that? But they quickly realized they shouldn't talk like that to people like us. If we were duped into coming here without knowing, while we were still in America, about the critical situation in Eretz Yisrael, we'd find out soon enough. It would cost us a pretty penny. But, after all, we were always free to go back. What wouldn't those in Palestine give to become American citizens!

We didn't like the way they spoke about Eretz Yisrael: Did we come all this way to listen to such talk? So we took Aaron and Mosheh's suggestion—Mosheh had come to check in on us—to go for a stroll and take a gander at Tel Aviv. Minnie and Izzy would join us tomorrow.

Mosheh pointed at the buildings: "It's like they grew here overnight! Look at them! Nice, right?"

My brother and his wife nodded in agreement. Very nice. But I wanted to know why they—the buildings, that is—were so exposed to the outside, without any awnings or front yards. They looked rather prosaic.

Mosheh had a ready excuse: the land was so expensive that they couldn't afford any more space than was needed to erect a building. Prices were rising every day.

And why did some of the buildings look unfinished?

Because, Mosheh explained, there wasn't enough money to complete the whole building all at once. They'd add more floors over time. "Like a bookshelf—one shelf on top of another. First, we start with the buildings' width, and eventually we'll establish their height. We'll grow them. Someday you won't even be able to recognize them!"

"Not enough stores and too many little storefronts here. It makes the whole thing look cheap . . ."

I didn't need to say anything more. Mosheh, and, with him, Aaron were furious at me.

"Those storefronts, which we call *kiosks*, sell drinks to refresh thirsty passers-by. It's hot here, people need to drink."

"Orange juice costs ten cents for a small glass in New York," Aaron added. "And I'd wager it's usually watered down. Here, a much larger glass costs less than two cents. You can buy four oranges for five cents."

"And as for the stores," continued Mosheh, "we have plenty here. Maybe too many. Land, earth, that's what we need. We did enough merchandising in *golus*. Eretz Yisrael doesn't want people to come here to speculate, profiteer, or put their interests ahead of others'. Those who flocked to Eretz Yisrael just to make easy money were badly burned. They ran back to *golus* with their tails between their legs. Good riddance. Those who follow will know better what Eretz Yisrael expects from them."

3

It was time to see the doctor to put an end to our quarantine.

Once again, we sat in the local *droshkies* with their Asian bells. The driver held his whip high over the horses and cried out to the pedestrians, "*Hatsadah*! Get out of the way! Giddy-up, and *yalla*!"

The whole way our uncle was staring at his old golden watch, its face warped from the years that had passed since he'd received it as a groom. The watch was still set to American time. He planned to set it once he arrived in Jerusalem.

We had asked Mosheh to travel with us. We managed to mitigate his annoyance at our giving too large a tip to the drivers upon our arrival in Tel Aviv after he'd already negotiated a price by promising not to be too generous this time. He said it ruins their morale. There's enough corruption in *golus*, but we don't want any part of it here in Eretz Yisrael. Here, a promise is a promise.

"*Nu*," our uncle replied, "enough talking, more action." He urged us to go faster, so we could be over with the business of the vaccinations. He wanted to be in Jerusalem as soon as possible.

Mosheh tried to tell him that if we showed up there too early we'd just have to wait. But our uncle didn't want to hear it. If we had to wait, we'd wait. Better to wait than to be late.

As we drove, clattering over the cobble stones, Mosheh instructed us to look each way and notice the contrast between Tel Aviv on the one side, and Jaffa on the other. "Look at what our Jewish hands have wrought! Wait and see what they have yet to accomplish! Oh, our *bachurim*! And our *bachurot*, too! They're good helpers. They know how to hold a hammer and how to hew stones. They aren't made up or gussied up like the girls in *golus*. Not on your life." He went on like this until we reached our destination.

The quarantine guard was rather surprised to see us. "What are you doing here so early?" he asked. "There are no doctors or nurses here yet."

"When will the doctor be here?"

"When? When he wants to."

"But . . . he's coming?"

"He's coming."

"*Nu*, as long as he's coming. We'll wait," asserted our uncle.

"*Ken*. Good things come to those who wait."

So we waited. In the meantime, more passengers arrived who had traveled with us on the *Canada*. They embraced us. "Shalom, sha-lom! How's Eretz Yisrael treating you? It's grand, isn't it? If it weren't for the tremendous heat and the dust, it would be quite something."

"And if it weren't for the crisis . . ." I added.

"*Nu*, the crisis will pass. People just have to take the plunge and immigrate in large numbers, and the crisis will be over soon enough. They have to come *with money* and get busy buying land and build-ing on it."

We spotted the girl from Patterson, New Jersey, whom we called "the Goat" when we were on the ship. She was fired up and speaking a mile a minute. She'd gone to our hotel hoping to travel here with us, but they told her we'd already left. So, it was good that the young man who accompanied her from "mikve" (she meant Mikveh Israel) brought her here. Oh, is he a *gentleman*! He treated her like a prin-cess! Neither her own relatives nor strangers could treat her so well. But she, oh, she didn't know. She liked America. She was used to America. They say she'll get used to Palestine. Maybe so, maybe not. "But it's alright for now . . ." she sighed, speaking a Yiddish overrun with Americanisms. "I mean it."

"Say," the Goat continued, "Baron Rothschild knew my grandpa. I mean, Grandpa knew Baron Rothschild. He's a big millionaire who believes in Zionism. Maybe Grandpa can put in a word with him about me. Say, where is the doc anyway? They told us all to come here but he didn't show! The nerve! Why doesn't anybody say something?"

Our uncle was the most impatient of all, but he kept quiet. His silence spoke louder than words.

When we'd practically given up hope that the doctor would ever come, he stumbled in, short of breath and sweaty. He glanced at all the waiting patients and told us we could go home. Having said this, he stole out of the large room into his little office and closed the door behind him.

We all, or as many of us as were still there, were astonished. We asked each other, "Is *this* what we waited all this time for?"

The Goat adjusted her little red hat so it was tilted to the side, and clapped her hands against her cheeks, crying, in English, in the most American of sing-song voices, "Did you *ever*? Can you beat *that*? Gee whiz, it's awful! Would such a thing ever happen in America? *Neeeevvver*!"

Our uncle breathed freely now. He could finally go to Jerusalem, at long last! After packing up, sitting, and waiting, he was finally ready.

But there was one more thing. In order to travel to Jerusalem he would need his books, his two Torah scrolls, and many other things—clothes that he brought to distribute to the poor. He had to retrieve all of these things from the custom house at the Jaffa harbor.

It was a "job for a policeman," but my brother, Aaron, Mosheh and I took on this difficult task and soon completed it. We figured we'd better take care of the business while we were already there. We sent the rest of our party back to Tel Aviv.

It was Friday, the Arab Shabes. Arabs wander around the fort doing nothing. Lazy Arabs. They're lazy, they even look lazy. Whatever Mosheh asks them (in Arabic) they respond with a lazy look and a click of their tongues.

The click of the tongue carries a lot of meaning. It can mean, "Who knows?," "Yes," "No," and "Don't ask."

A policeman was standing on the way to and from the fort, whose job it was to check the Arabs and make sure they hadn't stolen anything. He placed his hands under their armpits and groped to the end of their wide sleeves. Then he patted them down, front and back. He rummaged around under their wide sashes, which were long and wrapped several times around their waists.

The men being searched stood quiet and still, uncomplaining. They showed no sign of being insulted, or of trying to hide a theft.

After much bell ringing, Mosheh realized that we would have to wait quite a while until the top custom house officer would see us. He would come. We had to wait outside because the door to the custom house was locked.

We waited outside, under the hot sun, near walls that looked like they were smeared with mud. We tried not to step in holes or ditches that were full of yellow refuse from horses and Arabs. The sewer, like their tongue clicking, served them for most things. You had to hold your nose and your breath.

Good things come to those who wait. Soon enough, he was there, the custom house officer. An Englishman with two Arab guards. They got right to work: as soon as they opened the trunks and the boxes they started to sniff around. The officer set aside a few items that struck his fancy: a pair of scissors, a file, a carving set, and so forth. Mosheh whispered to us that we should bribe the officer and his aides with a gift so they wouldn't charge us such a hefty duty or cause us further delays by requiring additional searches. Once they get going, you never know how far they'll take things!

If it hadn't been for a certain Jewish man who had often had legal run-ins with the custom house, we would've needed to keep returning and returning just to rescue our baggage from the English official with his Arab adjutants. They found too many of our things to their taste and wanted to bring them home. The Jewish man managed to get us our trunks with the boxes of books so we could send them on to Tel Aviv. He showed us where we could hire Arabs with horses.

Mosheh took it upon himself to do the hiring. They agreed to a price. Though of course we'd have to give them *bakshish*.

Suddenly several Jewish drivers descended upon us, demanding that we hire them for the work.

Them? How, when they didn't have any horses? They said that if we would just wait a while they would go fetch their horses. We'd be doing a mitzvah. We should just hand over our baggage and let them do the work on Shabes. If they didn't manage to get a horse, they'd carry the trunks themselves. They were used to carrying heavy loads.

What was wrong with them? They wouldn't leave us alone, they insisted that we pay them for nothing, just so they wouldn't be insulted that we were doing business with the Arabs.

"Mosheh, this is no good!" my brother said.

Mosheh waved him off. "What's taking so long? Hire the ones who have horses and get on with it!"

One of the Jewish drivers—a Yemenite Jew—muttered angrily: "Arab horses . . ."

"Do you have any Jewish horses?" Mosheh asked him.

Another Jewish driver retorted, "*You're* a Jewish horse!"

"Ha!" cried Mosheh. "You're nothing but a dog, you bastard. People like you are everywhere you look. Even where you don't see them, they come out of the woodwork."

Since we didn't want it to come to blows, we decided to wait for the Jewish drivers to get horses and drive us, but to send our baggage to the hotel in Tel Aviv with the Arab drivers.

So Jacob, Mosheh, and I traveled with the Jewish drivers in front of the procession of trunks in a colorful *droshky* covered in strips of Oriental carpet and strung with bells. White dust like steam accompanied us all the way to our hotel where our uncle Shmuel was impatiently waiting for his baggage so he could make his way to Jerusalem. I realized, sadly, that his hurry to get to Jerusalem was because he was impatient to cushion his grave with good deeds. He wanted to pass his inheritance directly to his inheritors who were sitting and studying sacred texts. Torah scholars who study and beg the Eternal to have mercy on the People of Israel and help them rebuild the Beys Hamikdesh.

"A fine Jew with a handsome face," the hotel owner remarked to me about my uncle when we returned from the Jaffa port with our baggage.

"He's also a fine scholar," I told the hotel owner. "At one time he ran a large lumber business. He raised a large family. All his children are married and in his old age he's become very pious . . ."

"Fanatically pious," I should have said. I'd spoken with my uncle about Eretz Yisrael. I'd explained to him that Tel Aviv is as important as Jerusalem and wanted to show him what Jewish hands accomplished in the land when they are dedicated and set their minds to it.

But he said dismissively, "Sure, what they did is tremendous! They erected buildings so they could raise prices and collect rent. They chase fame, deal in politics. They speculate on the markets and earn high dividends. They carry on like children, always running off to Paris or Berlin on vacations. I heard enough on the ship about love of the Holy Land. Don't tell me any more!"

The hotel owner was beside himself hearing such talk about Eretz Yisrael. He could personally vouch that Shmuel had better not rush off to Jerusalem. He should spend time in Tel Aviv and get to know the city and its inhabitants better.

Perhaps, the hotel owner suggested, I could have a word with him. If it came from me, my uncle wouldn't suspect that I wanted him to stay in Tel Aviv for business motives, "you understand?"

"I understand." I said, promising that I would speak to my uncle and try to convince him to put off his travel to Jerusalem. But the hotel owner would never know if I didn't say anything, and I resolved not to. He's very stubborn, my honorable, wise old uncle.

4

When I saw that I would have no success trying to convince my uncle to stay in Tel Aviv, I turned to my sister-in-law/cousin to ask her father not to travel to Jerusalem so soon. Here in the hotel, he was getting the best possible treatment. In Jerusalem, he'd be all on his own and would surely languish.

She agreed with me and spoke to him, saying, "Father, maybe you should put off traveling to Jerusalem for a little while. You didn't have a chance yet to rest up after the journey. And Jerusalem's not going anywhere."

"*Dvorim btelim*!" he cried, interrupting her. "Not another word. I've been delayed here in Tel Aviv long enough. I should have gone already. I intend to go to Jerusalem, and, for as long fortune allows me to live, I will stay there among my peers. In a Jewish environment. Near a study house with Jews who know how to learn."

The hotel owner inserted himself into the conversation. "There are plenty of Jewish scholars in the cities, towns, and even in the settlements. It would be a mistake to think that the entirety of the Torah only belongs among those who are in Jerusalem. After all, Jerusalem has its share of *ameratsim*, but *tsadikim* are few and far between. At best, you'll find there a mishmash of different kinds of people and animals. The place is swarming with Arabs, donkeys, camels, flies, dust, and mud. You can't find a single street without a beggar. They all ask for more and more *bakshish*! The great and holy Jerusalem of yore was destroyed long ago. All that remains of it is the wall that people come to wail beside. It is besieged by dirty Arabs and 'protected' by gun-toting English soldiers. Gazing upon what has become of our former greatness is enough to make you faint, at least until the day comes when the ones who ruined it are doing the fainting themselves!" The hotel owner's tone shifted entirely when he spoke of Tel Aviv, the "one-hundred-percent Jewish city. Before, it was nothing but bare soil. Sand. And it became a city. A little Paris. A model city for other cities in other lands. And what it is now is nothing compared to what it *will be*. Over time it will grow in breadth and height—they'll add more and more floors with verandas and balconies to all the buildings that now look short and stocky. There'll be more boulevards like Rothschild Boulevard. In the place of kiosks for seltzer sellers there will be grand businesses."

I wanted to point out to him that the settlement of the city was not going very well and ask him when *that* would improve. But I didn't want to interrupt him, and, anyway, his words had the opposite effect on my uncle than what was intended. He dismissed them with a wave of his hands. "So? It's just *shtus, dvorim btelim*." He didn't travel all the way to Eretz Yisrael to visit a "little Paris" and wait for it to grow into a big Paris. Of course, he's glad to hear that they're building more settlements and *kibbutzim*. Each to his own taste. But, as for him, he'll live out the rest of the time he's allotted in Jerusalem. If they want to help him arrange for the journey there, then good. If not, he'll help himself. He's already made his way from Minsk to America and from America to Eretz Yisrael, and he'll make his own way from little Paris, or Tel Aviv, or what have you, to—forgive the comparison—Jerusalem. All he's asking was that no one get in his way. Better they should come with him on the journey and help him find a room among respectable people, near a *shul*.

My brother and Aaron, both sons-in-law of my uncle, were prepared to travel with him. His daughters cleaned and packed up his clothes tidily. He seemed pleased and spoke more freely and jokingly with the hotel owner. "So, who won out in the end? The young folks and their Tel Aviv—your little Paris—or the old folks with their Holy Jerusalem?"

When the time came to make the journey, he was in quite a hurry, but he parted warmly with everyone. We all wished him safe travels and a long life in the holy city of Jerusalem. We even promised to visit often so we could see him. "*Lehitraot BiYerushalayim!*"

I watched the automobile drive away and thought about how hard it always is to say goodbye, especially when elders leave young people behind. Shakespeare says, "Parting is such sweet sorrow." Maybe that's so for lovers who will see each other again soon. For lovers, but not for those who have reached old age. All of those promises to see each other again sound weak.

My heart told me I'd never see him again. My uncle, my departed father's brother. Yet another old tree from our family's forest, falling away.

Upstairs in the hotel, my sister-in-law was teary eyed. She blamed herself for not insisting that her father stay with us in Tel Aviv. How would he manage in Jerusalem all on his own? All his life he was used to others taking care of him and showing him respect. People stood up when he walked in the room, like he was a king. Children spoke to him in hushed tones. When people came into the house—lumber merchants and even, often, landowners themselves—his whole army of children would hide in the corners and they wouldn't make a peep. Only her mother, until her illness and death, spoke to him as an equal. His children couldn't leave the house without his permission. When he gave his permission, it was with the understanding that they would return at the time he had imposed. And they weren't allowed to make friends with just anyone, either . . .

"Yes," I said, moved by her recollections of the past when, as she recalled, he was in his "seven fat years" and was something of a despot.[1] He ruled over the family with an iron fist. But then came the revolution and the war, and if the children hadn't acted upon their own will and dispersed, some to America and some to Eretz Yisrael, he would have starved to death in Minsk. He should be grateful that he had, *barukh hashem*, lived long enough to spend however much of his life might be left in Jerusalem. There's no reason to pity him

1. A reference to Genesis 41.

or feel bad, other than the pity you might feel for all elderly people, though old age is inevitable for all those who don't die young.

And I reminded her of all the ways she'd suffered under her father's (my uncle's) dictatorship. How, for example, he forbade her to marry the teacher who tutored students in the small rural village (before they moved from the village to Minsk). He was in love with her, and she wasn't indifferent to him, but her father refused, saying that she was too young to marry. She should wait. She should marry a lumber merchant's son and not some poor small-town tutor. And when her father said "No" then "No" it was. He had the tutor fired. His daughter, who was the eldest of eight children and had a mother who was infirm, had to take on the heaviest housework. She aged under the burden. She wilted before she had a chance to bloom. Her mother sighed in pity that nothing could be done for her daughter, but only from time to time. Most of the time she sighed and moaned only for herself. She went to doctors, took medicines, and lay in bed more than she stood up. She felt sorry for herself and demanded that her husband and nine children take pity on her. They were the ones who made her ill, and they should help her get well again so she could live to take pride in them.

The sickly mother didn't hurry her husband to marry off her daughter. She was afraid of how they would get by without her. You'd have to search the whole world to find a girl as hardworking as their eldest daughter. Once their younger girls grew up, and once they moved from the village to the city, then the eldest daughter wouldn't have to work so hard and could go out among people. People would come to visit them in their home, as well.

But once they moved to the big city, to Minsk, nothing changed, and they didn't enter into a more leisurely existence. Society was only worthwhile if it helped them get a doctor or more medicines. The younger daughters helped their older sister even less in the city than they had in the village. They made friends with children of wealthier parents than their own and learned big-city pretensions from them.

The younger children stood out from their family with its rural ways. Their demands exceeded their father's wages, despite his being in a more privileged position. They doubted that their situation would improve if their older sister were to marry, and they started to talk about America. "Everyone's going to America, so why shouldn't we?"

Talk is talk. But their father was earning less and less, and the children were getting older, bigger. None of them had learned a trade. It was beneath fine, important, upstanding people to teach their children a trade. They talked over the question of going to America until they decided to let the eldest daughter go with three of the girls. She could take care of them and make sure they behaved.

The eldest daughter would have liked to travel alone to seek her fortune, but her parents and sisters told her that they wouldn't let her leave unless she took her sisters with her, so she agreed. She and three of her sisters prepared to leave their parents' home. Two of the middle sisters and the very youngest stayed with their parents and brothers in Minsk. Some time later, after her mother had passed away, her father and the younger children came to America.

All of the girls, all five of them, found their mates and were married. They recognized from seeing their older sister wait for marriage that when you're pretty, uneducated, and poor, you shouldn't hold off until you're also old, on top of everything else.

Only the eldest sister can say what she felt when her five younger sisters (and a brother) were married before her. But she didn't say anything. She didn't give up. She held on to the idea that it was better to stay as she was, all alone, in sacred solitude.

Her five younger sisters all had children. Their older sister gave them gifts. Her sisters offered their wishes that she would marry someday, like them, and soon have her own child. She thanked them for their kind wishes and went on as she was, alone. Eventually she gave up all hope of ever being married. She made her peace with becoming an old maid. She comforted herself with the fact that she was not alone in the world; there were hundreds, thousands of women who for one reason or another never married. Back in the little villages in the Old Country it was scandalous to remain unmarried, to settle for such a life. But in America there was nothing to be embarrassed about. Unmarried women had a lot to contribute to society. They excelled in many areas.

"Those are just words. Fine sounding phrases," one of her relatives said, urging her to marry. The relative had found her a widower with only two children. His wife had recently passed away and he didn't know what to do. His children needed a home and a mother. "Listen to me, Becky. Pursue this one. This is a good match for you. He's a fine man. He has a steady job. He earns well. He has a home and well behaved, quiet children. Say yes."

Her answer was "No." She didn't want to be a stepmother.

Her relative was quite irritated, after she'd taken such pains on her behalf. She wanted to see the eldest daughter happily married. How could she so cold-bloodedly refuse? "Wait, wait," the relative warned her. "You'll see how foolish you're being. You'll realize later when you end up married to someone who has twice as many children!"

"Alright, then, that's how it will be," Becky answered. "Why should it bother me if another woman bears a few more children for me?"

"You'll never get married! Never!"

"Alright. Maybe I won't."

"Alright," the relative echoed in annoyance. "You made your bed and now you can lie in it. When a woman is old enough to decide for herself then you have to let her go her own way, even when she stumbles into a pit like a blind horse."

Her words fell on deaf ears. She would stay as she was, "old and cold," as another relative described her. "What a pity, when she would have made a loyal wife and a good homemaker. I suppose this is just her fate. And she won't do anything to help herself. *Meyle*, that's just how it'll have to be, God help her."

When it seemed God had forgotten all about her, my brother Jacob's wife died in childbirth. After a year of mourning, he was still in despair over the loss. He gave up his home because everything reminded him of her. He gave away all their household goods to his wife's sister. He became a boarder and avoided society, even loyal friends who used to visit him often in his home when his wife was still living, and who had found their home comfortable and joyful.

We tried everything to bring him back to life. We encouraged him to volunteer more in organizations. He had always been deeply involved in Poale-Tsiyon and took part in the movement as much as he could. Now he devoted most of his time to it. And much of his money. But this did not fulfill him. He needed a person he could be close to: a friend, a companion, a woman who would fill the empty place in his life and relieve him of his unrelenting loneliness.

His family turned his attention to Becky. She was the right woman for him. This woman he'd known since childhood, and whom he'd previously overlooked. Perhaps he was fated to lose his first wife because his true *basherte* was this very woman. She had been waiting for him . . . Her heart must have told her to wait, to wait for her *bashert*.

And so, in the name of fate, the match was made. Two worthy partners united as one to lead a quiet, unassuming life together.

She changed, grew more animated. Her eyes flashed triumphantly at those who had sentenced her to stay an old maid forever. It's true, she had waited a long time, but now the wait was over. Her own married sisters could not be more proud of their husbands than she was of hers!

"You don't know, sister," she crowed to me once, "what a gentleman your brother is!"

I was happy to hear this and waited to hear what else she had to say. "There's something strange about all this, it feels like a made-up story. I can't believe I'm the same woman. Me? I'm married? Me? So strange, so odd."

The relatives of the wife who had died also said the same thing, though in a different way. "It's strange, very strange! How could he marry a woman like Becky after he had such a beautiful, lovely wife? Usually, a man looks for a prettier woman for his second wife than he even had for his first, not an older and uglier one! So much older!"

"A woman can possess qualities that you can't see from the outside," I told the first wife's sister when she spoke to me about the uneven match. "It's true, his first wife was pretty, lovely, and younger than his second. But, to all of our sorrow, she died. He will never forget her. She was his only love. His second relationship is founded on the basis of friendship. Two lonely people who need a home and are building one together."

With explanations like these, I convinced his first wife's sister to approve of the match. She understood that this was how it had to be, and even expressed a wish to not end the friendship that had existed for years between her deceased sister and her sister's husband's cousin, Becky. Her deceased sister had loved Becky more than anyone. Becky had always made herself useful in their home when she was living there as a boarder. She had always teased her about what a fine housewife Becky would make and told her husband that if she ever were to die, he should marry his cousin. She would see to it that he wanted for nothing.

At the time Becky stayed with them, the first wife had been preparing to undergo an operation to treat her prolapsed umbilical cord, but the fetus was strangled inside of her before the procedure could be done. She had lost two other babies this way and had decided not to give up. "He loves children. I must give him at least one child!" she responded when she was encouraged to go under the knife and be sterilized. "He says that as much as he wants me to give birth to a living child, he loves me and doesn't want me to risk my life. But what is life without children? I *must* have a baby. If I can, I want two, three, four, five babies!"

5

"Say, where are you?" cried Becky. "You're so lost in thought that you can't hear what I'm saying to you. Tell me, where are you?"

"In Eretz Yisrael, now. But in my thoughts, I am long ago and far away."

"So am I," she sighed. "It's not what we imagined when we spoke about coming here. Take this hotel—why does there have to be so much noise? And the faucet above the sink is too high. The electric lamp is in the ceiling, so if you want to read a bit before you go to sleep it's too dark. When you want to turn it off you have to get out of bed and feel around on the wall until you hit the right button. The balcony hangs over five dusty streets. There's noise everywhere. It bothers my nerves. It gives me a headache. My arm aches and is swollen like a mountain from the vaccination. It's hot. Who knows if they'll manage to set things up the way they should be for my father in Jerusalem? He's exhausted from the journey. I hope he doesn't get sick. You have to mind an elderly person like you do a child. That's what a woman should do. But he doesn't have any of his six daughters nearby. That's how it is with children. You're better off not having them. They cause more misery than joy, more worry than pride. If only my mother had lived long enough to make it here. She could have lived out her final years here, with him. When you get older it's better for a husband and wife to leave the world at the same time . . ."

She was lying across the bed and thinking out loud, something she rarely did. She usually chose her words carefully and was withdrawn and terse. The difficulties must have been weighing down on her until they all came spilling out. As she kept talking about them, it was hard to tell if she was happy or displeased that her husband had gone with her father to Jerusalem.

Since she'd been married there hadn't been a single day or night that she'd been alone. He always came home right after work, and not a minute later. If he was delayed because of business, she would telephone or stare out the window to see if he was coming. She waited by the door to greet him and tell him how worried she was. When he came home, dinner was always ready. Everything on the white table-cloth was sparkling clean. She asked how good each dish was. Does something not smell right? She would try to make it better. After he ate, she would give him his dressing gown and slippers. She turned on the radio. She showed him where the newspapers were (Yiddish and English), although he'd seen them already: near his arm, on the cof-fee table next to his chair. She drew him a bath, maybe he wanted to wash up. She laid out clean, pressed, colorful pajamas. She warmed a glass of milk for him to drink before bed. She waited until he fell asleep so she could be sure that he didn't need her anymore, and then she washed up, put on a fresh nightgown, and went to sleep.

That's how it had been every day for years in America. But since they left their home to travel to Eretz Yisrael, all their routines were broken. She didn't have her carefully planned out work, but she was prepared for everything. She looked after everyone like they were paying guests.

At first, she'd liked it on the ship. It broke the monotony of every-day life. It gave her time to fantasize about the idyllic life she would lead in Eretz Yisrael, where she would have her husband back under her wing and her care.

But now they were in Eretz Yisrael, in a hotel in Tel Aviv that was like a ship anchored in place, and who knew how long she would live there until they found a suitable home. In the meantime, the hotel wasn't cheap, and she didn't even enjoy it. All that she could do here to take care of her husband was to make sure he didn't take too many bites of new kinds of food that he wasn't used to, because they might bother him. It wasn't good for his digestion. The heat interfered with his appetite. It also made him dissatisfied with the new Eretz Yisrael dishes which were actually delectable. The vegetables here were best of all for those who suffered from digestive issues. Natural foods, not processed foods like they serve you in America. Americans should come to Eretz Yisrael to learn how to cook.

She lay there across the bed thinking about all the disadvantages of Eretz Yisrael while I sat by the door with its window that looked out onto the five streets and listened. I had to add that, as she seemed determined not to enjoy Eretz Yisrael at all, perhaps it wasn't such a good plan after all for a middle-aged woman without children to start a new life.

"You could adopt a child," I suggested.

"Yes, we could . . . if we wanted to. But why would I want to? I don't think I could love a strange child the way I would love my own. And, anyway, to raise a child you need energy, patience, and experience. And to top it all off, the wife becomes more restricted than her husband. He's free to leave the house while she has to stay home and watch the child. It's a huge responsibility."

She was speaking from experience. She knew from her life in the Old Country, in the village and the city, how much work it takes to raise children: Hadn't she given away her youth to housework before her time? As the eldest she bore the heaviest burden in the family, like her mother. Her mother's body was weak from all her pregnancies and births, so she, the eldest daughter, had to raise and care for them. And some thanks she got for it! They blamed her for not giving them everything they wanted, and they wanted more than she could give. The sisters who came with her to America wanted to use their precious few rubles to see the city and go shopping for pretty things. They wanted to treat their journey of desperation like a pleasure trip. She hadn't wanted to give in to them and refused to do so. She knew the circumstances she had left her parents in and as soon as they arrived in America she sent back to them all the money that remained from their journey. It took a long time for her sisters to forgive her for it. That money belonged to them just as much as it did to her, so what right did she have to send it away? Their parents wouldn't die from hunger in the Old Country if she didn't send it. Their sister was only doing it to prove what a good daughter she was. She wanted their parents to think she was the best of all their children!

Was she a good daughter, after all? she asked herself now. She answered that she was *not*. If she were a good daughter, she wouldn't leave her father alone. If he didn't want to be in Tel Aviv, she should settle in Jerusalem for him. But did she have a say in it? Hardly. Back in America she and Jacob already decided that they would settle in Tel Aviv, where there were better prospects and they would be able to manage things better than they could anywhere outside of the city. Jacob believed all the fine things that were said about Eretz Yisrael. If anyone detracted from Eretz Yisrael even a jot, he would get angry. He had been devoted to the Zionist ideal since he was in the Old Country. His love for it had only grown through the years. And when you're in love, you see through rose-colored glasses. Not that she had anything against being in love. But she prayed to God that he wouldn't be too disappointed.

It wasn't hard to tell that she, herself, was already disappointed in Eretz Yisrael. She shouted her disappointment even when she didn't put it into words. Instead of saying what she felt, she probed me to find out what I thought of the "holy" land, unless I was afraid to sin against it by saying too much . . .

I didn't know what to say. So I told her it was too early to form an opinion. But, since I hadn't expected to find personal happiness in Eretz Yisrael, I wouldn't be surprised if I never did. I was willing to serve the land with my whole heart. I intended to give more than I received. And Tel Aviv is not everything—there are other cities, towns, *yishuvim*, and *kibbutzim* where you are expected to appreciate the important work that "we" have accomplished. It's a shame we didn't come from Minsk directly to Eretz Yisrael, rather than going to America first. We could have already been established here long ago and we would have been happier if we didn't have the American life to compare it to. Of course, there were plenty of negative things about Eretz Yisrael, and they were easier to see than the positive ones. Eretz Yisrael is not known for what it is, but for what it will be. Besides, no one forced us to come to Eretz Yisrael and no one was forcing us to stay there if we didn't like it. After five years of living in America we had become American citizens. Once we'd been in Eretz Yisrael for five years we'd know better whether we like it here or not than we knew now, after only five days.

My sister-in-law sighed. "Five years is a long time when you're not young anymore. A very long time. But that's how it goes. I suppose we're fated to live our lives this way. If you're too self-sacrificing once, you end up sacrificing yourself again and again, giving in. First you give in to your parents and later to your husband. And you always give in to *society*, which clamors after you to get married and then is forever asking why you don't have children. In America you aren't so tirelessly confronted with society's expectations. But in Eretz Yisrael, that's another story. 'How big is your family? How many children do you have?' Just try to tell them you don't have any children. Such a *travesty*! Try to tell them that you were meant to have a child shortly after your wedding but you lost it during an operation on a tumor that they removed, together with the fetus, and it ruined your chances to ever get pregnant again . . .

"You know well enough. You were there with me when I had the operation. You spoke with the professor about it and he told you that they couldn't save the baby because of the tumor in my uterus, and they had to remove everything—tumor, fetus, and uterus together!"

She went on speaking to me with deep regret. "You saved my life that day. Maybe it would have been better if you hadn't. You came to stay with us in Bridgeport. You were supposed to go on a vacation in the country. But you saw how I was buckled over and groaning, and you broke your date and brought me to New York to see a doctor, a fancy professor at Lincoln Hospital. I remember how you came to the hospital every day after the surgery to take care of me and helped prevent a lung inflammation after the operation by closing the windows when they opened them before they were supposed to. I remember everything. Don't think that I've forgotten it. I think about that time and remember it all as if it were yesterday, even though it was more than ten years ago."

She recalled even more details from that time. But there was one thing she didn't speak at all about. Was she waiting for me to bring it up? It was an important detail. Without it the course of her life would have taken a very different turn.

After the operation she told me that she wanted to speak candidly with her husband. She would tell him he was free to divorce her. He was entitled to have a family. He loved children. He should leave her and take another wife. Someone who could bear him children. According to Jewish law, he was allowed—required, even—to divorce a wife who couldn't bear children. She would tell him he was free, she was prepared to receive a *get*. They could remain good friends. They would never be total strangers: they were cousins, after all. Yes, she had determined that this is what she must say to him. If not, she would feel guilty for the rest of her life.

Had she said it to him after all? As far as I could tell from their life together that followed, she never actually said it. Maybe she kept putting it off for later, when his behavior toward her would lead her to say something. But he kept on being a gentleman, as he was before. She was grateful and tried to repay him for her guilt for not giving him a child by acting as tenderly toward him as if *he* were her child. He wouldn't lack a single comfort. She would care for him, serve him, so that he couldn't do without her.

It's easy to forgive yourself for a sin. Especially a sin that isn't truly your fault: Hadn't she desired the child? Of course she wanted it, but she lost it. That's what happened, and there's nothing left to be said. And when something happens outside of your own will, it doesn't matter what you want.

That's how it is with tragedy, and you either accept it or you're done in by it.

So, she accepted the tragedy. She didn't give up on herself because she didn't have any children. She wasn't the only woman in the world without children. She occupied herself with keeping her home clean and tidy, pleasing her husband, and caring for his health. She didn't refuse him anything. He gave plenty of money to *tsedoke*, sent money home to his family in Minsk, supported a nephew who was studying at London's finest college. He volunteered and sent plenty of money to Eretz Yisrael. And she agreed to it all. He could do whatever he wanted. He could do what he liked. He was the boss.

I told her that I didn't think it was such a good idea to be so good to one's husband (even if he was my brother). She shouldn't say yes to everything he said and did. She should raise a little opposition to keep things interesting. Having her agree to everything could get a bit tiresome.

She laughed at me. "You of all people know what sort of a man he is!" He was an ideal husband and so she would be an ideal wife. She could understand why other women take pleasure in arguing with their husbands. But she would prefer, as she said before, for him to be the boss over everything that he wanted. "Do you see?"

"Yes, I see."

That's how they carried on their happily married life until they tore apart their comfortable, well-ordered home in America to realize the promise he had once sworn to himself to make the journey to Eretz Yisrael.

Here, in the ancient land, they were trying to build a new life. Those who had settled here already didn't know any better and didn't complain about all the ways life here was primitive and inhospitable. Like having an icebox instead of a refrigerator. The stove, called a Primus, was powered by a hand crank like an old-fashioned Ford automobile. You poured water, like from a pump. You filled the Primus with kerosene, and it hissed more than it burned. She took one look at it and she knew she would be unhappy here. She could hardly believe, she said, that she would ever get used to such a nuisance. This and other things like it simply weren't for her. True, for a few pounds (ten dollars), you could hire a servant . . .

Meanwhile, while she was in the hotel, she was being taken care of and sat with idle hands like a noblewoman. She didn't have to lift a finger. After our long journey here, she still had a long time to wait in the hotel. It was quite expensive and she was eager to have her own place as soon as possible. Somewhere she could call *her* home, like she had in the city not far from New York . . .

For the time being she wasn't able to do anything tangible, so she wanted to talk. She wanted to provoke me to speak ill of Eretz Yisrael. Did I really mean to stay there forever? How could I expect to be happy here? Wouldn't it be too hard after spending over a decade in America's freedom? Could I really settle down in a backward land controlled by the English? She was afraid that Eretz Yisrael was not for . . . us.

"Maybe we're not good enough for Eretz Yisrael," I replied.

"Maybe so," she answered. "We're too old to build up the land with the young people, but too young to hold back from the work. It's a country for youths who haven't yet grown up or for the very old who come here to die, like my father."

Remembering her father, she said, "Who knows how long it will take Jacob to get my father settled. It's not easy to find an apartment in a foreign city . . ."

"Jerusalem? A foreign city?"

"Alright, maybe it's our city. But he's still unfamiliar with it."

"Aaron will acquaint him with it. He grew up in Eretz Yisrael."

"Yes, that makes it easier for Aaron. He's used to the climate in Eretz Yisrael and to the food here. Jacob is used to my preparing suitable food for him. It all has to be fresh, tasty, and on time. It's not as simple as you think, keeping house. It takes a lot of time and organization to be a good homemaker."

She talked and I listened. If I had conflicting opinions, I kept them to myself. In order to lighten her heavy mood, I made myself agreeable, more with my silence than with my words.

As soon as Uncle Shmuel's two sons-in-law returned from Jerusalem to Tel Aviv, their wives, my sister-in-law, and her sister were much happier and more content. Everyone was in good spirits. The old man had gotten what he wanted: a room in the home of a pious family, a few steps away from the shul with a community of Jews around his age who spent their days studying Torah. In addition to the price that the pious family asked for the room, my brother gave them several additional pounds without my uncle's knowledge, hoping that would convince them to be good to him. If he was happy with how he was treated, my brother would give them more money. The family was very happy with the arrangement. They said that if it were up to them the old man would live and be healthy for one hundred and twenty years!

6

"We've been in Eretz Yisrael for a whole week and we haven't accomplished anything yet . . ."

When the hotel owner heard me say these words he laughed out loud. "What a good joke, a terrific joke! There are people who have been in Eretz Yisrael for years and haven't accomplished anything yet. In Eretz Yisrael we take our time. We do everything in its own time, slow and steady. It's not like in America where everything is business. There's none of that hustle and bustle here. Before you do anything, you have to rest up from your journey. Then you can travel around and get a look at the land. That way you'll get to know some people. It's a shame that those who come to Eretz Yisrael for just a short visit have to rush through these things. But those who come to settle in Eretz Yisrael can take their time and scope out what they want to do here. Nothing good comes from haste."

As we spoke a man approached who had already interrupted the Americans (us) several times with his eagerness for us to build a colony. It would be called Bat-galim (daughter of the waves) because it was located on the shore. If we didn't want to take it upon ourselves alone to build the entire colony, perhaps we could lend some money to those who were building it. At nine percent. The greater the sum, the higher the percentage, of course. The colony's certain success would serve as a guarantee for the loan. Bat-galim was sure to have a grand future.

No matter how many times my brother tried to tell him that he didn't come to Eretz Yisrael to become a moneylender it was no use. The man wouldn't let him be. He tried to get the hotel owner to talk to us for him, to explain, to persuade. It's kind to convince people of a good thing. It's a mitzvah. Didn't he want to perform a mitzvah?

What Jew doesn't want to perform a mitzvah? The hotel owner promised to put in a good word for the Bat-galim colony.

There was no one to guarantee the loan. The handful of gentlemen who were looking for a loan for the great undertaking didn't want to sign their names to it. The secretary, as the man who approached us with the project called himself, wouldn't give his own name either.

Nothing came of the business.

In order to soften the blow to the secretary, we told him not to lose hope. He might yet convince us to finance his Bat-galim, even though the wealthy owners of the not-yet-built settlement weren't willing to take responsibility for it. He cheered up. "*Ken?* Yes? When?"

"After we've explored the country we'll make a decision about what we're going to do here."

Good. He expressed his wishes for us to explore soon in order to hasten our return.

For the time being, he decided to spend the night in "our" hotel so he could continue to discuss the matter of Bat-galim with us. He tried to convince me to persuade my brother not to give up on the grand plan he laid out for him: to materially support the construction of Bat-galim.

He politely requested an opportunity to visit me in my room. He wanted particularly to speak to me, alone. I gave him my permission and he shook my hand vigorously: "*Todah rabah, giveret.* Thank you very much for being willing to hear me out." From what he'd heard and surmised, he told me, sitting on the chair I'd offered him, the *giveret* (me) is independent from her brother. The *giveret* has her own capital and can invest it as she wishes. Wouldn't it be appropriate that if the *adon*, the *giveret*'s brother, should set his sights on Bat-galim, the *giveret* might lend her own money as well—as much as she is able? Any small amount is better than nothing. He would be ashamed to return empty handed. He would give the *giveret* some time to consider it and she could answer tomorrow morning. They say that morning is wiser than evening. Perhaps the *giveret soferet* would realize by morning what a good idea had been presented to her this evening.

Having said this, he stood, bowed, and kissed my hand.

His kiss made me uncomfortable. To think that a Jew in Eretz Yisrael would practice such Polish or German *zamashki*! If he thought he might win me over that way, that was a mistake. He lost me. I opened the door for him and said goodbye. He responded with his own goodbye and added, "'Til morning."

My brother, his wife, and I went to see one of the Anglo-Palestine bank directors to inquire about the Bat-galim business before we would meet the man again the next day. Perhaps he could give us some advice. He listened to what we had to say and advised us to stay away: investing would be like a healthy person crawling into a sick-bed. So long as the owners—he knew them personally—would not change their position about their refusal to guarantee the loan, we'd better not take it on. "You didn't come to Eretz Yisrael to speculate and live off the interest. Your goal is to build a comfortable home for yourself and for the family that you'll bring over. So hold onto your money. First, take some time to get the lay of Eretz Yisrael and then you can see about 'business.'"

The next day I somewhat shamefacedly refused to loan the money and asked the man from Bat-galim to forgive me. We were still greenhorns here, and we needed to take our time, get our bearings, and then decide what we'd do. He would have to wait. Maybe he'd manage to find other investors with more capital than we possess, and he would be happy that he hadn't settled for so little . . . We parted with the assurance that we would remain good friends. *Shalom! Shalom uvracha*!

"If I were a rich man . . ." my brother said after the man from Bat-galim had left. "I would give him all the money he needed. Him and others like him besides. He seemed so disappointed that he didn't get anything from us."

"He was too overconfident that we should give it to him," my sister-in-law said. "He was a nudge. They think anyone who comes here from America is rolling in cash. Someone should tell them we made our hard-earned money through honest labor in America so we could support ourselves in our old age. We didn't just scoop up money off the streets. Some reception we get here! The shopkeeper at the spice store asked me, 'Did you come from America?' and when I said yes, she exclaimed, 'What, are you crazy?'"

I asked her how she responded to the shopkeeper.

"What did I say? Nothing. What could I say?"

"You should have told her that *she's* the one who's crazy," my brother said.

But his wife said she wasn't so certain about that . . . The shop-keeper must know what she's talking about.

My brother wasn't pleased with what she said. They disagreed over his stance toward Eretz Yisrael. In his indescribable love for the land, he couldn't stand her cold feelings toward it. "Crazy? Anyone who says we're crazy to come to Eretz Yisrael is crazy themselves!"

Just as my brother was getting overcome about those who would detract from Eretz Yisrael, the hotel owner came to us to ask if we wanted to see some visitors who would like to meet us.

"Visitors? What visitors?"

"Good people. Eretz Yisrael people. They say that they are your *landslayt*. They come from America."

They were waiting in the guest room. We went to see them. We greeted each other with a "Shalom!," shook their hands, and thanked them for coming.

The woman who took it upon herself to act as the "leading lady" introduced the other woman and the two men (I don't remember their names). They had read in the Palestinian newspapers that the writer (me), along with her companions, had come from America to settle in Palestine, and they were curious to see them (us) and . . . if possible, to give us advice about what we should do here. Of course, a writer doesn't need any advice. She has an occupation from before that she can continue with here: writing. She'll find plenty of material! As far as she, the leading lady, could tell, a person could not only write a whole book about it but ten books or even more. She could write whole volumes! But she was no "writer" (she said this word in English). She didn't have the patience to put pen to paper.

To give others the "chance" to speak, she would leave aside things that didn't "directly" have to do with the "subject of Palestine" for another time. What they wanted to know was why rational people, American citizens with money, "I am sure," had come to settle in Palestine. What can be the logic in that, the *sachal hayashar*, the "common sense"? "Excuse the question," but many people left Palestine due to the crisis. Everything has gone bankrupt. If they would let them in America, everyone would go there. And, "for instance," take this woman, her brother, and her sister-in-law. They were in America, they had a fine life for themselves there. They had a good business, saved some money, had a few dollars to call their own, and then all of a sudden they up and moved to Palestine! One of the men got rich here. He built some apartment buildings and went into real estate. He was living easy! That's how it was at first, "you know, prosperity." They didn't anticipate that the crisis was on the horizon. They can't "complain" too much. Others are "worse off." But if they had been "American citizens" she's sure they would go back to America.

Now a man took over speaking (from his wife). "It's true, there's a crisis and things aren't as grand as they used to be, but if you think about it, it's not so 'perfect' in America either!" After all, could his wife get "help" as "cheap" there as she could in Palestine? And what about going to the country? Here, you're in the country all year long. "We may not make as much money here as in America, but we also don't spend as much. And once the crisis is over . . ."

His wife interrupted: "You mean 'if' or 'maybe.' You can't be sure that the crisis will end for a very long time. More people will leave, and no one will come to replace them . . ."

"Stop your doomsaying!" her sister-in-law snapped. "We don't need any evil prophecies." She turned to the leading lady's husband, saying, "The way she talks, you'd think the whole world was ending. It's alright. We didn't lose money on Ertsroel. If you don't expect much you can be happy with what you get. We're not the only ones who don't have much. And in America there are poor people too."

"*Dotsrayt!*" she affirmed in accented English.

When they realized it was time to say goodbye—the chauffeur was waiting outside with their automobile to take them somewhere else—they asked what we Americans were planning to do here.

"To become Israelis!" my brother responded sharply. "We came here to help build up the Jewish homeland. Not to exploit and not to speculate. If we end up having to return to America, it won't be because Eretz Yisrael is not good for us, but because we weren't good for Eretz Yisrael."

"And what are *your* plans?" the leading lady questioned me. "What are *your* 'opinions'?" She snuck English words into almost every sentence to demonstrate that she was still American. "I'm sure you'll describe us in your writing, and we'll read all about it. We get the American papers. They bring back fond memories. Will you?"

"I will try . . ." I responded in English.

The hotel owner hurried to us as soon as the others left. "Rich folks," he told us. "They made a lot of money in Eretz Yisrael when there was money to make. People like that will go on making money. Maybe even more than before. They'll buy up cheap real estate and sell it later when the prices rise."

"*Nu*, you already have plenty to write about!" My sister-in-law laughed. "That was our welcome number two, a fine how-do-you-do!"

My brother was solemn. It troubled him that there were such people in Eretz Yisrael. They discredited Zionism. They made a bad impression for other Jews who gave up the best they had for Eretz Yisrael. No, it wouldn't do to write about such people. It's better to ignore them. If he were a writer, he would write about people who love Eretz Yisrael with all their hearts. People who would go against their own interests for the sake of others, for the sake of everyone! But, he conceded, he was no writer. He didn't like the literary profession. There's neither honor nor money in it. Only a person who is her own worst enemy would choose such a profession. And if you're going to write, you should at least do it in Ivrit! "I'm telling you, you should try to learn some Ivrit and become a Hebrew writer!"

He went on in this vein and his wife agreed. "Too true. When you're in America, close to the editorial offices of all those Yiddish newspapers, that's one thing, but here, in Palestine, I mean in Eretz Yisrael, where they call Yiddish *zhargon*, there's no use in writing in Yiddish. There's no honor in it and no money either. It's a . . . a sin!"

I didn't even have a good place in which to commit the sin. I asked the hotel owner to give me a different room because my room was connected to another by a door that was always shut. In the other room resided some kind of magnificent Effendi who snored like he was sawing a board, talked in his sleep, and all the while spun the door handle noisily. I was at my wit's end.

The hotel owner gave me a little room of my own without a connecting door, far from the offending Effendi, and close to . . . the toilet. Every time someone pulled the chain the water tank made a tremendous clatter and water gushed out, roaring, roiling, whistling, and squealing until it got tired of making a ruckus and finally shut itself up. These long "concerts" with their all-too-short intermissions disturbed and offended me. At first the hotel owner told me to "pretend you can't hear it." He blamed it on the sewer system in Eretz Yisrael. "You should be grateful, this is top of the line," he told me. "You should see what they have in other hotels . . ." He spoke about buildings that have their so-called amenities—their restrooms—outside. They say they'll put in a good sewer system, but talk is cheap, and nothing ever comes of it. Why? It would cost the state a tidy sum, and even in better days there wasn't a whole lot of money, never mind during the crisis.

All of a sudden, as we were speaking of the crisis, which is the most repulsive of all things, the hotel owner slapped his forehead. "I have it!"

"What?"

"I know exactly what you need. I do have a room—what a room! Where? Right here in the hotel, or, rather, *on* the hotel, on the roof!

A circular palace." All he had to do was give it a bit of a clean first and then he'd show it to me. He was sure I'd like it.

I was curious to see the palace. I was impatient and didn't want to wait for it to be cleaned. We went up the stairs and onto the roof. "Here it is!"

So, how did I like it? He wanted to know. Isn't it fine! Bathed in sun, with a view of the sea. You could see the Jaffa harbor and the arriving ships. If you had binoculars, you could see the people. It truly was the finest room in the hotel!

"How is it that the finest room is unoccupied?"

"It used to be occupied," he told me, "but then its tenant left due to the crisis." Actually, the room hadn't been empty for long. A woman, a writer, had lived there for a long time. She'd departed Tel Aviv saying that when she returned she'd rent the room again. She'd left her bed there without a mattress. He gestured to it, saying that he'd have someone carry a mattress up and clean the room for me.

I offered to help. I wanted to get settled as fast as possible into the room that I jokingly called the hotel's *yarmulke*.

My brother didn't like the *yarmulke*. The heat was unbearable. The two windows and door didn't face the sea.

The hotel owner said that it was designed that way to keep out the wind from the sea. And if you don't want to be inside you can go outside, there's enough air outside the room to satisfy anyone. If he'd had the money, he would have made the space into a roof garden with little tables and chairs and flowers and so on. That would have ultimately brought in more than the one and a half pounds (seven and a half dollars) that he was charging for the room . . .

"That's cheap, practically free," the hotel owner's wife told him, which is why she never wanted to furnish the room. Let the American lady buy her own furniture. Her husband told her that no one comes to live in a hotel with their own furniture, and if she didn't want to put first-class furniture in the room, the least she could do was send up a mattress. A bed, a table, and a chair would be enough. He charged me a month's rent in advance and gave it to his wife. She took the money and agreed to send up a mattress.

I hired a few porters to carry up my luggage: two large trunks, a steamer trunk, a suitcase, and some smaller items. I was eager to get to work cleaning up the little "palace" and sit down to write, write, and write!

As soon as my trunks and suitcases were brought up to the roof, next to the domed room, it started to pour. The first rain we'd seen in Eretz Yisrael, a sure harbinger of the Eretz Yisrael winter, pouring like diamonds under the hot Eretz Yisrael sun.

I watched as my things got wet and the hotel owner said it was nothing, the first rain never lasts long. It'll only take a minute for my things to dry out. I should be pleased: the rain was a sign that I moved up here at a fortuitous time. Thank you very much, I told him, but all the same I'd like to bring my things into the *yarmulke*. The hotel worker, my brother, the hotel owner, and even my sister-in-law all lent a hand in the job that the porters who carried up my luggage should have done themselves.

Inside the dome, soaked through, I got to work.

"Look how she's taken to the *yarmulke*!" My sister-in-law laughed to my brother. "We'll just get in her way here, let's go." They left.

I looked around at where I was and what I had to do. I had to admit that it was prettier and brighter around the dome than inside of it. Its walls were dirty and gray and had gaping holes where nails had been pulled out. There was a patina of dust over everything and stains everywhere.

I liked the curvature of the walls. They felt like arms embracing me. The floor was plastered with gray asphalt with cracks in it.

I wiped the walls, removing a layer of who knows what, and covered the holes by hanging soft needlework landscapes. I put hand-made rugs down on the stony floor. I opened my trunks to take out everything I needed to beautify my tower. Every object made me feel closer to Eretz Yisrael. I felt I had a personal relationship with the land. The two little windows on either side of the door seemed like eyes. I hung them with light green curtains, and the "eyes" now had "brows." I set flowers down on their ledges, carnations. They smelled like sour almonds.

I pushed my half-open steam trunk against the wall. It would serve as my wardrobe. I hung my cow needlework above the trunk. The cross-stitching was so artistic that it looked like it was alive. It was very precious to me. I brought it with me from Minsk. It was a present from my sister. The cow's dreamy eyes looked gentle and kind, as though she were pleased to have survived long enough to hang on a wall in Eretz Yisrael. I also hung my oil paintings: *Yom Kippur in Shul* by the talented painter Lyubovski, a painting of a sunset, a large print of a portrait of Dr. Herzl, and smaller portraits of other important figures. In this way I covered over the holes that the nails had left. The walls came to life. They had soul!

I also covered over the holes on the hard floor with a tiger pelt from the Catskill Mountains and a bear pelt from the Wild West, as well as some hand-woven rugs. And now for the bed! I made it up with snow-white linens and covered it with a colorful bedspread and decorated it with cushions embroidered with birds and flowers. On the little round table in the middle of the tower I placed a hand-sewn tablecloth, and I draped the electric lamp with a green silk lampshade decorated with red, white, and pink flowers.

When I finished the work, I left the dome and went onto the roof to admire the beautiful panorama before my eyes: a bright blue sky over the buildings of Tel Aviv with their golden cupolas, like crowns. I saw the sea, with its white waves rushing to the shore and back again, like snow. In the long baskets on the little fence around the roof, flowers, refreshed from the first rain, smiled to me, as though saying "Nu, how do you like Eretz Yisrael now?" and I answered them with a *zeyer* and a "very *tov!*" I went back into my tower and stood in the doorway, contentedly contemplating my own little corner, my *makom menuchah* in Eretz Yisrael. I was tired but happy.

I heard footsteps. My brother, sister-in-law, her sister, her sister's husband, and her sister's husband's sister all were coming up the stairs. They were taken by what they found in the *yarmulke*. "Such lovely decorations! How long will you be here? A month? It doesn't make sense to stay longer when you could rent an apartment. Maybe a month is already too much. What will happen when it rains? Will you take an umbrella to go from your dome to the rooftop door? And what about water and . . . plumbing? It's too far away from everything. It's no good putting so much work into settling into a temporary place."

Their talk went in one ear and out the other. I liked my tower and I felt pleased with it. I felt, as I told them in English, "on top of the world!" and I didn't want to hear a peep out of them about my *yarmulke*, understand?

"*Meshuge!*" They laughed at me, and I laughed with them.

7

It's wonderful after a day of physical labor to lay yourself down on a bed made up with white linens, with your own pillow under your head, and a light bedspread, with the silver-white shine of the Eretz Yisrael moon above you. The Eretz Yisrael moon is different from the moon that you see in *goles*. It shines as though it is closer to the earth, you feel like you could reach out and touch it!

I wouldn't let myself fall asleep. It's a shame that you can't sleep with your eyes open. The flowers in the two little eye-windows swayed in the breeze that wafted from the Judean Hills, and the shine of the moon silvered over their green stems so their leaves also looked like flowers, white flowers. It was peaceful, quiet, the noise of the street was far from the heights where I found myself now. It mingled with the rhythmic rush of the waves.

Night fell quickly over Eretz Yisrael, and the night was like the day. It was bright even in the darkness. Couples strolled hand in hand. They formed larger groups, singing a song that was carried into the distance, "*Mi yivne hagalil?*" Who will build the Galilee? The response followed right after, "*Lanu yivne hagalil!*" We will build the Galilee! I quietly joined in the song. I thought to myself, How good it is to be young! How beautiful it is to want to build a home for the homeless. Dear children of Israel, of Eretz Yisrael.

I thought about my brother and sister-in-law. They had no children. A land, I thought, is like a lover who wants to be married and have children. I thought about myself as well. "What can *I* do to build up the land? Create paper children, spiritual children . . . and send them to America to be published. No, that's not enough. I must see to it that I do something more substantial for Eretz Yisrael. And I will!"

I fell asleep with that resolve, a deep but not restful sleep. I dreamt I was crawling across sandy mountains. One of my legs almost got swept away in the sand before the other was buried in it. Before my eyes the mounds of sand formed into strange creatures veiled in white with cataracts that shone like phosphorus. The creatures took handfuls of sand and poured it over me. The sand was seething and burned my skin, stabbed me like needles and bit me. I tried to protect myself with my hands, and then I tumbled down from the tall mountain and woke up.

All around me it was dark. The moon was no longer peeking into the dome. It was on its way to the sea. But even in the darkness I saw red flecks on my white nightshirt, sheet, and pillow. I cautiously climbed out of bed and went to the door to turn on the light switch and saw that the red flecks were none other than . . . bugs.

A little red army scuttled away under the light. I stood, startled, not knowing what to do. Then I grabbed my bedsheets and threw them outside on the wooden bench that was on the roof. I quickly closed my steam trunk so nothing could climb in, and I took down everything I'd hung on the wall. I carried the mattress out of the dome, and then I saw where the red army came from. Bedbugs lined up under and around the buttons of the mattress and at its seams. A fine mattress the hotel owner gave me! She must have bought it for a bargain.

Incensed, tired, and powerless against the attack of the little creatures that I was afraid to touch, I resolved to leave the hotel. In the meantime, I sat on an overturned box, covered in my cloak, and waited for daylight. A raw wind was blowing from the sea. A heavy nighttime dew ran from the roof and landed on the grey asphalt in round droplets, like tears from the night. The day began to break. The sun rose from behind the Judean hills, slowly, like it was just waking up and stretching out its rays.

I asked myself why I was sitting there. Why didn't I go down and give the hotel owners a piece of my mind over my horrible night? But

I kept myself from waking everyone up so early. When I decided that it was finally time to go down, I found that the door that led downstairs to the hotel's rooms was locked. I banged on the door, at first quietly and then with more and more force. I felt a powerful urge to shatter the door to pieces, but I didn't act on it. I didn't have the strength. And even if I could break the door in, what would come of it? Let it be. It would only strengthen my case for leaving the hotel.

Finally, I heard footsteps. The door opened and the hotel owner himself came through it. I remembered that he told me yesterday that he regularly came up here to see if a ship had come into the Jaffa port, so he could send someone to find passengers to bring here as guests.

He took one look at me and with my things strewn in disarray on the roof and stared in bewilderment. "Wh . . . what happened?"

I told him and he held his head in his hands. He swore, as he lived and breathed, that he'd never seen such a thing happen in his hotel before. Why, he asked, didn't I come fetch him? He would have let me sleep in his own bed. I asked how I was supposed to fetch him when he'd locked the door.

"*I* locked the door?" he asked incredulously.

"If not you, then who? Me?"

"No, that couldn't be. The door locks from the other side. My worker must have done it, that idiot. He must've forgotten to leave it open for you and locked it out of habit. He's going to get it from me, and she, my *eyshes khayil*, will also get a piece of my mind. I told her to buy you a new mattress, not an old one stuffed with bedbugs. She should sleep on that mattress herself, that *kushenirke*!"

"It's no use casting blame when the thing is already over and done. Instead of ruining your *sholem bayis*, simply allow me to move out."

"Where? Back downstairs? Certainly, with pleasure!"

"No, entirely. I wish to leave here."

"God forbid! You mustn't do that! I'll go out right now, myself, and buy you a new mattress and a bed, too! Everything you need! Only the finest and the best!"

The hotel owner hurried toward the stairs, but then, realizing that he'd forgotten to take a look at the port to see if a ship had arrived, he sighed. There was no ship. No one was coming. There was a crisis. Everyone knew about it, and so no one was coming. Why should they fool themselves? There was no reason for them to come. They could hardly expect to have good fortune here in Eretz Yisrael!

His wife came up to see why her husband hadn't returned downstairs. She worried after him with his youngish appearance. He seemed younger than she did. He was careful about his looks. She was no longer attractive, she was aged and embittered by having to do all the cooking herself while her daughter, the bride, took care of her hands so they wouldn't become calloused from housework. Her daughter was forever busy with her fiancé. She stared into his eyes. She waited on him at the table. She sat with him and listened to everything he said. He painted a picture for her of their future happy domestic life in America. As soon as they got the tickets from their wealthy relatives, they'd set sail. In the meantime, while they waited, they'd live on her father's dime. They were the center of their own universe; her parents were only peripheral.

Seeing the mess outside on the roof, the hotel owner's wife asked what was going on. She heard that last night the *giveret* had already completely settled into her new room, so how did her belongings come to be strewn outside?

"It's your fault, with your bargain hunting!" her husband said, showing her the mattress. "Go on, see what you so expertly purchased! A sea of bedbugs! If we had other guests here too, I bet you'd drive them off as well. An experienced housekeeper should know better. Don't you have eyes in your head to see what you bought?"

She cursed the man who sold her an old mattress and passed it off as a new one! She'd chase after him and tell him a thing or two, mark her words!

She swore to me that it wasn't her fault. But she'd make it up to me however she could. She was mortified that there were bedbugs at *her* establishment! She could hardly bring herself to say it out loud.

She was always so careful to ensure that everything was quite clean. You wouldn't find a single bedbug in her home, not even to use in a home remedy. And then, all of a sudden, to have an infestation! She would send the mattress back to the "nobleman" who sold it to her and let him deal with it. With the bedbugs.

They both stormed off, and I was left alone with my destroyed Temple, my fallen tower, like a Magen David made out of toothpicks. I stood on the rooftop and looked out at the sea, toward Jaffa harbor. There were no ships of Jews, none at all. It was the crisis. How long would it last? It was hard to say.

I was in a foul mood. I hadn't gotten any sleep. I sat, and sighed, and waited. What was I waiting for? I didn't know. If I were at home right now, I'd take a bath. But here, before you took a bath you had to prepare the water. You couldn't even wash yourself here comfortably. You had to carry the water up. But I had to do *something.* Not just sit here and bemoan the *khurbn.* What was there to do?

The roof of the golden dome gleamed under the hot Eretz Yisrael sun, and its rays also shone on the unfortunate mattress. More of the red army hatched from its eggs. I wondered how long it took for the hatchlings to mature.

I couldn't just sit and do nothing. I needed something to do. I went over to the pretty objects I had used to decorate the walls. I comforted them, telling them I was looking for a better place for them, though I didn't know when I would find it. I put them aside, in a clean place, together with the wall hangings. I didn't have anywhere to set them up.

My brother and sister-in-law came up to the roof to tell me it was almost time for breakfast. I told them what a fine night I'd spent in the *yarmulke.* My brother said, "It serves you right!" And my sister-in-law added, "You reap what you sow!"

"How was I supposed to know that they would sic pests on me?" I asked.

My brother said that even without the pests, the room was not suitable. It was too small, too high up, without any modern comforts, far away from everyone, lonely. "I'm telling you, it's no good!

We need to see about finding an apartment. A nice apartment with modern improvements. *Then* we'll feel like we've made it to Eretz Yisrael."

His wife agreed with him one hundred percent. She hated hotels. There's too much noise. They cost too much, and you have to deal with all sorts of nuisances, like that Effendi who walks around the hotel in his pajamas and peeks into all the rooms.

"You could always close your door . . ."

"It's too hot. You can hardly breathe. And what about the guests who come exactly when it's time to eat? You have to invite them in, right? After all, we come from America where money is cheaper than dirt. So, our doors should be open to everyone, like the hotel itself. You can't have a smidge of privacy here!"

Her sister was having quite a time with her husband, she told me. His mother and sister wanted them to stay with them in their apartment. Her sister didn't want to crowd them, and, anyway, she would prefer to be the mistress of her own home, like she was in America. And her son, young as he was, criticized everything that was going on, just like a grown-up.

A porter climbed up the stairs to take the mattress away. I breathed more freely now that I was rid of the pests. Though, truth be told, I found it hard to believe that not even a few of them hadn't managed to hide out in the *yarmulke* and stay there. I didn't want to talk about it. I didn't even want to think about it. I got ready to go down to eat, though all I wanted to do was sleep.

Downstairs, in the dining room, everyone sitting at the table had agreed not to talk about what happened in the *yarmulke* with the old mattress. The hotel owner tried to keep up a banter about worldly matters: the future of Eretz Yisrael would be grand. If only the English would let us bring in raw materials without imposing such a large tariff on everything we imported or exported, then we could get to work. For now, though, the situation was grim.

As he went on talking it became clear that Eretz Yisrael had a magnificent past and a promising future.

Now he had to pay a bill. He owed fifty pounds. He asked his American guests to consider performing this small *gemilut chesed*.

Fifty pounds was two hundred and fifty dollars. That was a lot of money. My brother was in an awkward situation. He couldn't avoid the hotel owner's begging gaze or his words about not being afraid. In the worst-case scenario, the hotel owner said, he would pay the piper and swallow his losses.

Just yesterday my brother and I had paid in advance for the entire week. Twenty-five dollars each. And we had paid for several meals as well . . . As though he were reading our thoughts, the hotel owner kept on trying to persuade us to loan him more money on top of what we'd paid. "Of course when you are staying long-term in a hotel it's reasonable to expect that the price will be reduced. I took that into consideration when I quoted you a price, but if you're leaving so soon, my dear friends . . ."

And that's how he received his loan, that is to say, *gemilut chesed*.

Our bags were already packed. My sister-in-law told us as were leaving the table that she didn't expect he would ever return even a cent of the money.

"If so, it's not so terrible," my brother answered. "We'll manage."

I had a separate bill to settle with the hotel owner, over a month's room and board for the *yarmulke*, where I would continue to stay, with two meals a day, rather than three, as I didn't want breakfasts. Breakfasts take too much time and make you gain weight. An orange every morning is enough for me. I wanted to have mornings to myself for writing.

I gave up a whole day to clean the *yarmulke* and put everything back in order. I didn't fuss over it as much as I had done before the attack of the "red army." I put the bed and new mattress (the bed had been scrubbed with boiling water) in the middle of the room. That way if there was still a little "red army soldier" hiding out, it wouldn't get to the bed. I tried to forget what I lived through and assume it wouldn't happen again.

Part 3
Short Stories

A Marriage and a Divorce

Forverts, *January 5, 1938*

Author's Note: This story concerns a girl from a Yemenite family. For those who aren't familiar with the subject matter, the following explanation may be helpful. In Palestine there is a large community of Jews from Yemen, a country that is very different from Palestine. It's an Arabic country. The native language of the Jews there is Arabic, and also partly Hebrew. They are very pious, and many of them are learned. In Palestine they often perform the hardest labor, as porters and servants. It's very common to encounter a porter who looks like a learned man.

Some of their traditions are the same as the primitive Arabs. For example, when a man marries, he gives a bride price to the bride's parents. The Yemenite Jews in Palestine have their own neighborhoods, but they are also mixed with other Jews. Some of them have already worked their way up. They speak Arabic with one another and Hebrew with other Jews, and they are learning to speak some Yiddish to the Polish and Lithuanian Jews.

She was already eighteen years old, which means that she wasn't young anymore, although she still had a childish look about her: small and thin with wide eyes, a short little nose, full lips, and white teeth. She spoke Hebrew, Arabic, and, when she was with her acquaintance, the American lady, a broken Yiddish.

She was fatherless. Her mother was remarried to a man who carried heavy goods. She bore him a child every year. The children did not survive long. Only three remained of the ten she had borne. Their windowless one-room home, constructed out of sheet metal and old boards, was no place for the three children to live. The young woman (her name was Osnas, or, in Sephardic pronunciation, Osnat) slept in her friends' homes, or if there was room to sleep in the homes where she worked as a servant, she slept there.

Osnat had already been engaged for two years. The groom, who was more than twice her age, was a widower who lived in Jerusalem. She lived in Tel Aviv. The groom would come from Jerusalem to visit with his bride, her mother, her uncles, and her stepfather. But the bride hid from him. Her mother would search for her at the home where she worked as a servant and at her friends' homes, but she never found her and eventually she would give up. When the daughter appeared, the mother couldn't stand the cries and wails as she hollered that she didn't want to marry that man! She didn't want him at all!

The nerve of the girl! Her mother tried to talk sense into her, cajoled her, scolded her, and, when speech wouldn't convince her, took to beating her. But even a beating did nothing. She didn't want the groom, and nothing could be done about it!

Her mother wept and ululated as though she were in mourning. Why did the daughter want to hurt her this way? Why would she cause her such misery? The groom had already paid twenty pounds (a hundred dollars) for his bride. The mother had already spent it on the family, and had even used it to pay for a dress, shoes, and a coat for her daughter, the bride. Even if she'd wanted to repay him the money, she had no way of getting such a large sum. So her daughter would simply have to go to the *khupe* with him to be married. If not, people would start to talk. They would say that the girl must be rebellious and wanton. No one would want her after a thing like that. She would hang like a curse over her mother's head, an outcast, damned.

If her mother's words had no effect on Osnat, her mother's tears took their toll. She wavered. She gave in. She would marry her groom.

One of Osnat's friends had a brother, a fine young man around twenty years old who worked in a pharmacy. Osnat was infatuated with him, and he wasn't at all indifferent to her. He had to keep his distance because she was engaged, and because he came from a higher-status family than hers. The two of them, Osnat and her friend's brother, often strolled on the beach in Tel Aviv and talked. Most of the time they spoke of inconsequential things, like his position in the career ladder at the pharmacy, or the easy housekeeping work she had now as a servant in the home of an American lady and the gifts that the lady gave her. Maybe the American lady would take her to America. Would he like to go to America someday? It's a large country, and a wealthy one. There are many other Yemenite Jews there. They write that it's good for them there, very good!

As long as she was talking to him, things were good for her, too. But that goodness could only last so long. The short holiday gave way to the never-ending workaday week. Reality prodded her toward the *khupe* with the man who bought and paid for her. She would belong to him, even if she ran away to America with her beloved . . .

A dream!

The reality was that she didn't have the fortitude to stand up to her poor mother, or the strict uncles who had supported her and held up the honor of the family, or the entire Yemenite community in Palestine.

Her wedding was held at the home of a "rich" uncle. It was a two-room house with a separate front room with a long bench in the yard. There were more neighbors spilling outdoors than there were inside, and inside the home it was tremendously crowded and noisy. Between the two families it appeared that not a single person was without children. Almost every woman was carrying a child in her arms, with the rest of her brood hanging onto her skirt.

In one of the two rooms stood a long table (made of boards that had been hammered together), and on the "table" were refreshments: bottles of seltzer, and a bottle of rose-tinged wine, the color of beets. Cheap sweets were spread on the plates: chocolates, grapes, and oranges.

The bride, Osnat, was dressed in white with a veil that trailed after her. She was overheated, and her friends fussed over her. She glanced often at one of them in particular (the young pharmacist's sister), and they locked eyes in silent understanding.

The groom was dressed up in a cheap suit. A tall hat towered over his head. He looked like a man in a hurry to get somewhere. Like he had no time to spare. He appeared to be perhaps three times the age of his bride. He was dark, stooped, and full of desire.

The ceremonies of *bazetsn*, leading the bride to the *khupe*, and the *khupe* ceremony itself were all slow and monotone. The groom sang in a high, ornamented style and recited psalms until he, himself, lost all patience for it.

Osnat had invited the American lady who employed her so that she could have a chance to see how the Yemenite Jews conduct a wedding. The lady came and brought a wedding present. The bride thanked her. She (the bride) didn't seem despondent, as the American lady had expected her to be. She greeted her guests, beckoned them to the table and smiled.

"Are you happy?" the American lady asked Osnat, taking her to the side.

"Happy?" asked Osnat. "I don't know."

"He looks like a fine, respectable man, and not unattractive . . ." the lady supplied.

Osnat glanced over at the groom and saw that he was looking at her. She flashed him a smile and said, "Yes, ma'am, he is a good man. He bought many lovely things and paid for the whole wedding."

They weren't able to speak any further. It was already time for the couple to catch the train to Jerusalem. The groom couldn't afford to miss more than a day of work, so he had to take the bride home with him as soon as possible.

About six weeks after Osnat's wedding, the American lady saw her on Rothschild Street with a baby in her arms. She sat with the baby on one of the long benches that line the boulevard, near a tree in front of which stood a baby carriage.

"Ma'am!" Osnat cried joyfully. "*Ma shlomech?*" (How are you?) Look, I already have a baby, a *yeled tov, nechmad* (a good, lovely child)." And she laughed out loud.

The lady smiled. She sat down on the bench next to Osnat and asked, "What are you doing here in Tel Aviv? Where is your husband? Where did the child come from?"

Osnat explained: After the wedding her husband brought her to his home in Jerusalem. He led her through narrow streets into a one-room home, dark and small. The only furniture was an old bed, a little table, and two chairs. To her it seemed like a grave where she was to be buried alive. He told her that if she was a good wife, and did as she was told, he'd rent a larger apartment and buy nicer furniture for it. Then he told her to get undressed and lie in his bed. She started to cry. He got angry and asked why she was crying. She told him it was because she was unwell . . . she would undress for him when she felt well again. For that night she would sleep with her clothes on. She begged him to forgive her and take pity on her . . . it wasn't her fault.

For a while he grumbled unhappily, but he didn't touch her. He told her to have the bed, and he lay down on the ground. She felt sorry for him, but she also felt sorry for herself. He fell asleep quickly. She wasn't even able to close her eyes. As soon as morning came, she took her bags and snuck out of the room and ran away to Tel Aviv.

She went to live with the friend who was the sister of the man she loved. Her husband had gone to her mother's home looking for her, but she wasn't there. Her mother told him there was nothing she could do for him now. The moment that she was led to the *khupe*, Osnat was no longer in her mother's care. Even if he was able to find her, he couldn't force her to live with him. He could give her a *get*, a divorce contract, and that's what Osnat wanted him to do. It's also what her best friend and his brother wanted. In the meantime, she had a good position. All she had to do was bring this child to the garden and sit with him there and watch as he slept or played. He was a sweet child, and his parents, Americans, wanted to bring her with them to America, but she didn't want to leave Palestine. She especially didn't want to leave her *bachur* (young man). They would stay here. Her husband would give her a *get*. He'd find another girl to marry, and then she'd be able to marry her young man.

This is what Osnat said, and her eyes sparkled like the stars in the sky.

In a Country Town

Forverts, *June 14, 1934*

It was a tremendous shame and disgrace. The country Jew's daughter, the bride, had run away from the groom, his family, and all the guests who had assembled for the wedding, and fled her home as though she were being fired upon.

She fled the house and chose no better place to hide than in the barn! She left the people behind to be with the cows!

She poured out her heart to the cows, as though she thought the dumb beasts could help her. But they turned their heads away. Only one cow, her spotted Hodolya, whom the girl had delivered at birth with her own hands, and with her own fingers had reached into the calf's mouth to hand-feed her mush so she would mistake the fingers for a teat—only this cow looked at her with sorrowful eyes. The bride felt that the cow understood how unfair it all was.

The bride snuggled with the cow and said, "You don't even know how lucky you are to be a cow. If you were in my place, they would try to force you to marry a brute in high boots smeared with dung. That's the kind of boy my father fetched from the market for me! If only my mother were still alive, he wouldn't put me up for sale. He wants sell me off quickly, so that he can get married faster himself. It's miserable to be an orphan!"

The spotted cow bent her head as though in agreement, and the bride nestled against her. "Don't let them take me away from you," she urged. "Kick them, bare your teeth at them if they come close.

I'd rather stay here in the barn with you than stand under the *khupe* with a horse like the boy they're forcing me to marry."

In short order the bride's father rushed from the house into the barn, threatening: "Listen to me, girl. You're a *bride*! You don't want to see how outraged I can get. Go back in the house right this instant!"

"No!" said the girl, clinging tighter to the cow.

"No?" her father repeated, fuming. "Are you asking for a slap in the face?"

"Pummel me, bury me alive, throw me in my mother's grave!" the girl cried.

Her father spat on the cowpat under his feet. "Enough with this bawling. Shut your trap! You should be glad there's someone who's willing to take you, orphan that you are! Look at her—acting like a child! *She* doesn't want to—who cares what she thinks?"

"I'd rather die!" the girl whimpered. "I'd be better off dead."

Her father softened. "Khave-Tsire, don't be a fool. Listen to your father. I know what's best. He is a good groom for you. After the wedding he will make things nice for you. He likes you. He wants you. He's eager to talk to you, he tried to come here in the barn to talk to you and we were barely able to keep him from you. It's not right for a groom to chase after his bride in a barn. It's not respectable. People will laugh."

The father had hardly spoken these words when the groom rushed into the barn brandishing a whip.

"Father-in-law!" he shouted full-throatedly. "Let me speak with the bride alone for a moment. You're not the only man here with a tongue in his mouth. Let me use mine!"

The father considered his future-son-in-law for a moment before nodding his head in agreement. "Go on and talk! Maybe she'll be more willing to listen to you than to her father. I'll wait on the other side of the door as you asked me to." He walked away from the wedding couple.

The groom approached the bride. He cracked his whip and then tentatively smiled at her. "An ox has a long tongue, but it can't talk. Heh . . . It's no use resisting, I mean hesitating. We're bound to be together. Take a look at that cow—she must produce a rich milk. My horse eats plenty of oats. He's a bottomless pit. But he's a good horse. He can make good time and bear a heavy load. I wouldn't sell him for any money. I've had him since he was a foal."

He admired the cow and petted her. The cow's sad eyes looked at him with surprise. "I like her, too!" the groom said, whinnying at the girl and laughing. "She doesn't pull away. A good cow. I have a fine match for her, with God's help, after our wedding."

The bride indignantly cried, "I don't want to get married!"

"You don't? Why not? All girls want to get married."

"*I* don't!" the bride retorted.

"That won't do," the groom said, trampling on the overturned cow dung with his tall boots. "What will people say? They'll laugh and spread all sorts of disgusting rumors. It'll be ugly. I'm an orphan, with no family at all. I spend my nights at different strangers' homes. They take me on as a farm hand. I'm a good man. But I'm nothing without a wife. I'd do anything she wanted, I swear on my life. I'd cherish my wife more than anything. I'm a good worker. I'll work my way up. I'll put money away, I'll become a respectable man. I'm a simple man, I know, but that's why I want a woman who's my better. I'd bow down to her . . ."

He looked down at his boots and flattened the dung with them as he kept on talking and talking until the bride's father returned.

"So?" the father asked, looking at them. "How long will this lecture go on? People are waiting. Who ever heard of a bride and groom standing in a barn? This is a place for cows and horses, not for people!"

"It doesn't matter, father-in-law," said the groom. "What's important is what we say, not where we talk. I'll get to the point." He turned to the bride. "I won't move from this spot if it means that I have to go out in front of all those people alone. I'd rather be hit by lightning! I swear that I'd rather not live to see tomorrow, or my name isn't Moshe."

"Enough already!" the bride's father cried. "Let's put an end to this. Go on and get out of the barn! Go ahead!"

Like cows being driven to the field, the bride and groom walked out of the barn and into the house one by one, following the country Jew.

At the door, the country Jew paused to say a few words to his daughter. "Act like a respectable person now. Do what you're told. If not, your groom will leave you. After the wedding you can walk all over him, but not right now. Go on, that's the way! May you have good fortune!"

The bride hung her head as she entered the house. Women and girls, her friends, flocked to her. They led her into a side room and danced around her, combed her hair, patted her, gussied her up, and gave her their good wishes.

The men busied themselves with the groom. They told him what to do at the *bazetsn*, and at the *khupe*, and afterward. All the while the groom was aware that he wasn't holding his whip and didn't know what to do with his hands. The top hat they'd placed on his head fell over his eyes. He felt uncomfortably hot. Goyim from the village entered the house and gathered along the walls.

Men from the bride's side carried schnapps with bitters to the peasants. The peasants, especially the peasant women, drank it right up, grimaced, and covered their mouths with their hands.

The village girls stole glances at the groom, tittered, and giggled. The musicians readied their instruments. The young girls in colorful rustling dresses began to dance a quadrille, only girls together. The men were separate.

The bride's father negotiated with the *shadkhn*, *badkhn*, and the groom's party. They grappled with him over pennies, telling him that before the *khupe* he should pay what he had promised. But he insisted on waiting until after the *khupe*.

"What do you want from me?" he asked, throwing his hands in the air. "Why are you all coming after me at once? Do you think I'll run away? Didn't I promise you the spotted cow? And I'll give her to you! And the trousseau as well. I'm throwing the wedding, I'm supporting the groom on *kest*, and I'm even giving some cash to boot. What else could you possibly want from me? Wait until the groom's gifts are distributed. There's enough for everyone. Don't disturb the celebration. The groom agrees with everything as long as the bride will agree . . ."

"The bride is seated!" the women announced from the other room. "We've seated the bride!"

The quarreling sides parted to make way for the bride. The *bad-khn* cleared his throat and quietly knelt down next to the groom. He told him what to do.

"Slowly raise the veil and cover her face with it. Do it when I give you the signal."

The groom nodded his shaggy head and buttoned his waistcoat with his thick fingers. He was nervous and impatient. He wanted the wedding to be over quickly so he could be alone with the bride. She was lovely—a fine girl. She wasn't a boorish clod like the girl that had tried to turn his head a year ago. The only trouble was that she was hesitant, that she tried to run away. But that was nothing. He'd break her in. It's just like with a horse, she'd have to get used to her new master. She just needed breaking in . . .

Just Like the Young Folks Do

Forverts, *October 28, 1934*

Fifty-nine-year-old Mrs. Laykin listened to the conversations of other women her age and was astonished at how they asserted the high expectations they still had about men.

These women let matchmakers talk to them about *shidukhim*, went out in public with potential grooms, chose one, rejected him, boasted about the men they rejected, and then kept right on looking for Mr. Right.

Mrs. Laykin looked despondent. She felt beaten back. She felt too old to join the group of aging hopeful brides, with their even older potential grooms. She was embarrassed, especially around her children and her grandchildren, at the thought that she might get married again, so late in life. First God, and then she herself, came to know how lonely she was, living alone in the cottage that her departed husband left her. It was a small cottage on Coney Island, by the sea. In the summer she rented it to a few boarders and took in a few dollars, and since she had nothing else to do she sat for hours on the boardwalk with other women. They all had something, or someone, to talk about. But she didn't say anything. She felt she had to do something to drive away the boredom. But she didn't know what, or how. She told herself that she would have to learn from the other women: they seemed to have a lot of experience. They spoke about their encounters with "young men" with brutal honesty.

One complained, "You should see the fine figure this man cuts. He has no teeth, no bones, no flesh, he's barely alive, he already has one foot in the grave. But he still wants a young, healthy, strong woman. He thinks he deserves it! Isn't that clever!"

"The man that they're trying to set me up with now," said another, "is truly a heroic man. He says he doesn't care if his bride is a few years older than him. As long as she has money. He wants a dowry. He expects me to pay *him* for the privilege of taking care of him. I'll show him a dowry!"

Another woman said, "The men are happy to take me as I am. But I'm not in any rush. If I'm meant to find happiness, it'll come in its own time. If my *bashert* comes, it'll be worth the wait."

"I think," the first one piped in again, "that women our age should find ourselves a man who can give us a nice place to live, someone who makes a decent living. He should be someone we can depend on. Precisely because we're older women, we need to be practical and not let ourselves be fooled into anything. If you're going to take care of someone in their old age, you need to get something out of it yourself. If you're going to be a homemaker, you should have a good home to take care of, isn't that so?"

All the others agreed. All the others, that is, except for Mrs. Laykin. She thought to herself about the someone who might start a new life with her. All she wanted from him was that he be willing to keep her from being alone in her cottage, where it was crowded in the summer and cold and lonely in the winter. Then she wouldn't have to sit on the boardwalk like this all summer long.

When she went to the movies, she saw how people are meant to live, as though they love each other. And then when she turned from the movies and look back at her own life, sitting in her house as alone as a stone, her heart grew heavier. And she thought that she should try to do something about it, and fast. Not wait until summer was over and winter approached . . .

She thought about this and worried that all she would do was go on thinking about it. She couldn't muster the energy, the sense of urgency, that the others had for chasing after one man and then another, searching for "Mr. Right."

The women who talked about their own "joys" barely even looked at Mrs. Laykin. Every now and then one of them would try to draw Mrs. Laykin into the banter between the hopeful brides, but nothing came of it and they gave up on it. She'd stay the way she was, a grandmother clinging to the "fortune" that her late husband left for her. Well, let her! Why should they care?

That evening, Mrs. Laykin felt more than ever that she was completely abandoned. All of the women were out strolling. They all wanted to be seen with a man, a future life roommate. Mrs. Laykin sat alone on a long bench. She had nowhere to go.

As she sat there, she saw that a man was approaching her bench. This man had been trying to get to know her better for some time. But she didn't trust him. There was something off about him. He was too taken by his own cleverness, strength, and pedigree. It was as though he thought it was a gift that he was ever born. The women looked at him skeptically. He seemed to be a great boaster and a meager earner. They didn't believe anything he said. They didn't believe his money or the way he behaved with such gentility toward women. And as soon as anyone showed any interest in him, he'd withdraw his attentions! He didn't think it was worth his trouble!

Any other time, Mrs. Laykin would have gotten up and left the bench before the man reached her. But this time, she thought about how she was sitting alone on the bench while all the other women were out with men. When he asked her, "How are you?," she gave a friendly smile and answered, "I'm fine. How are you?"

"Oh, fine," the man said, sitting down on the bench next to her. "I'm living, I'm healthy, and there's a God to thank for it, so I'm all right. It's warm. Sitting here by the sea, you get very hot."

"When it's warm," said Mrs. Laykin. "It's warm everywhere you go. And in the winter it's cold."

"Do you really live here all year long?"

"Yes, I have my own cottage."

"You must be lonesome, living here all by yourself."

"Solitude is sublime . . ."she quipped.

"But it must get lonely."

"You get used to it."

"I can't get used to being alone," he sighed. "I can't stop wanting someone to be close to, and a home of my own."

"Are you staying with one of your children?"

"I'm not staying with my children. *They* are living with *me*. I have a house, like you do. Mine is a three-family home in Brighton Beach. I have everything I need. Except I need a woman to love."

"Seek and you shall find . . ." she quipped again.

"Have you found someone to love?" he asked.

"No, I haven't even looked."

"Why not? You don't want to be alone for the rest of your life. You're still fairly young. You're an attractive woman, dignified, quiet, not like those other women who are always running around and talking too much."

Mrs. Laykin was pleased with the man's compliments. She blushed and allowed herself a soft, modest, maidenly smile as she said that the modern world requires those women to act that way. Quiet, dignified women are wallflowers. No one notices them, no one cares about them . . .

Her words prompted her interlocutor to speak at length, trying to persuade her that she wasn't entirely correct in what she said. After all, *he* was very happy to speak with her, more than he would be to speak with the others. He would like to get to know her better, and to see whether his heart was fooling him. His heart seemed to be telling him that the two of them could grow closer, much closer. What did she, Mrs. Laykin, have to say about that?

Mrs. Laykin explained that she would need some time to determine what her heart had to say.

He was willing to wait, he told her. She could make inquiries about him. He would give her some references. He had already inquired about her and it seemed to him that the two of them were made for each other. He was very pleased that he had finally found her alone, without the gaggle of women, so that he could speak freely and openly with her. Now that she knew what he thought of her, she could take it into account and give him the answer he was hoping for. She wouldn't regret it.

The news of Mrs. Laykin's marriage to the man they had seen but known so little about exploded like a bomb among the group of women. The women couldn't stop talking about Mrs. Laykin's good fortune. Such luck! Such luck! It seemed that he was a wealthy man with his own house, with money in the bank, and even with his own business.

"You should see the home he fixed for her," one of the older hopeful brides sad to the others. "And did you see how much jewelry she was wearing today?"

"You should have seen how she's blossoming, that unattractive woman who didn't appear to have even two pieces of jewelry to her name!" a second woman responded. "She used to sit here and not say anything. She never had a single thing to say."

"She must have had plenty to say," a third one retorted. "She was just afraid to give away her secret. That must be why she didn't meet *him* when others were around."

"Yes, while all the others were exhausting themselves with their efforts, that quiet Mrs. Laykin would just sit there in her spot and wait for her gentleman."

"She did whatever she wanted. She even managed it without a *shadkhn*, just like the young folks do these days."

"It's *her* America!"

That's how the women, all unhappy about Mrs. Laykin, spoke about her. And when Mrs. Laykin heard about what one or the other of them said, she smiled softly and said, "I don't care what they say. I still don't believe that I did anything wrong by not talking to them, and I'll go on being quiet as long as I can. My husband loves me because I am the way I am. That's enough for me. I don't regret that I listened to what he, and everyone else, said. I learned and gained a lot more from listening than I would have if I had just talked."

Man and Radio

Forverts, *July 15, 1936*

When Molly Shipok was divorcing her husband, she resolved that she would be the one to keep their radio.

The Shipoks had no children, and that's why they decided to take in a radio. They both had grown so accustomed to it that neither felt they could live without it.

Mrs. Molly Shipok was taken with the radio above all else. And what a radio it was! With a tone, a sound, that was truly wonderful! Such a pleasure!

She invited friends in to treat them to her radio. "Just listen to how clearly and crisply it speaks!" she marveled. "Listen to how it sounds, how it works, how it sings and plays! And it never gets sick. Such a dear, devoted radio. And so talented!"

After she divorced her husband, Mrs. Shipok gave up her four-room apartment and rented one room with kitchen privileges. She decided to live there until she could find a good *shidekh*.

She began to concern herself with the matter of *shidukhim*. Not her own *shidukhim*, but those of friends and acquaintances. She was too much of an intellectual, she thought, to go to a *shadkhn* to discuss *shidukhim* for herself. Too intellectual, too sensitive, too refined. The radio would be her *shadkhn*: She would find others who were interested in music, who knew how to talk about music and could appreciate what they were listening to.

It didn't take long for Mrs. Shipok to find a man of that description in Mr. Karkin, an older bachelor who owned a business and an automobile that seated two. He was the kind of man who could find himself a young girl with a lot of money, if he wanted to. But he fell in love with her, a divorcee . . . in her and her radio!

When Mrs. Shipok learned that Mr. Karkin didn't have his own radio, she was astonished. How can it be that someone who is such a music aficionado doesn't have his own radio? Mr. Karkin explained why he had no radio, and she was no longer baffled. He said that he loved radio too much and he'd be too attached to it to do anything else. Furthermore, he'd prefer to share something he loved so much with someone else. He needed someone he could talk to about it, someone who could enjoy it with him. He had long searched for someone who could understand his love of music, but he had never found her. Now he was very happy. Mrs. Shipok was even more than very happy, she was overjoyed. She idolized the radio. Her chair waited with arms wide open for *him* to come. And as soon as he came calling, he'd sit right down in the chair and lean over to turn on the radio. He didn't turn it off until it was time to go. He was constantly turning the dials. He was searching for symphonies. He had a passion for symphonies. He said it was the highest expression of excellent music. There was no higher or better form of music.

Mrs. Shipok had one concern. But she wouldn't mention it. She didn't want the *shidukh* to fall through over such a little thing.

Despite all of his good qualities, Mr. Karkin did have one deficiency. He only controlled the radio dial with one hand. The other hand, which he should have been using to control the volume and tone, was occupied instead with a thick cigar. Until the happy wedding, Mrs. Shipok would simply overlook and pretend not to hear the issue. But there were others in the building who wouldn't suffer his habit: the radio was too loud! It was giving them a headache! It echoed in their ears! Sometimes there were such wild, raucous voices coming out of that radio. Was something wrong with it? She should have it fixed.

She promised to have it repaired. As soon as her beau sat himself down next to the radio, she would hand him the radio program listings so that he could quickly find the station that was scheduled to play symphonies. But he wasn't interested in looking at the listings. He spun the dial from right to left and back again until he landed upon a symphony. Once he found one he would listen to it as though he understood it deeply, winking from time to time at Mrs. Shipok as a comment on how it was going. Occasionally he would hum along under his breath. When Mrs. Shipok wanted to prove to him that she knew the tunes, too, he would wave her away with his hand, shushing her. Embarrassed, she would stop. She didn't want to annoy him. She had decided that for now, until they were married, she would do everything he asked. She didn't want him to think she was as vulgar as other women, who didn't have an appreciation for the highest form of music.

Due to Mrs. Shipok's apparent patience for Mr. Karkin's every whim, Mr. Karkin felt himself growing fonder of her. He even spoke of his future, and hers, and theirs together.

Mrs. Shipok's neighbors began to chatter about breaking plates in celebration of an engagement, about a wedding and a honeymoon, and all manner of things. Mrs. Shipok blushed like a shy bride and responded tentatively. She wasn't in a hurry, she knew what she was getting into. She had only just gotten out of one marriage. There was no need to rush into another. She could wait . . .

The two became so close that she gave him the key to her room, so that if she wasn't home when he came to call he wouldn't have to wait outside.

She wanted to look prettier when she smiled, so she went to a dentist to have her teeth fixed. She felt that the dentist kept her on the chair longer than necessary. She hurried home from the dentist's office, her heart pounding at the thought that Mr. Karkin might be waiting there for her, annoyed at her tardiness. It was lonely and uncomfortable for him to be in her room without her. They'd grown so accustomed to one another! It wouldn't be long until the two would be united as one. Her ex-husband would be green with envy. Well, let him! Serves him right! She'd suffered long enough from his ways, his running after other women, his lies, and everything. She'd show him that now she had someone else—someone better!

Mrs. Shipok rushed home to her future husband with this thought and others like it running through her mind. And she didn't run with empty hands. She had bought some tasty food to share. The kind of treats that *he* liked to have with his tea or coffee. She would tell him that she baked them herself. He would be amazed at what a good housewife she was.

By the time she reached her door she could already hear the shouts from inside. She was afraid to enter. She was terrified of what she would find there. What was going on? She decided she'd better just find out right away. So she put aside her fears and entered the house.

The noise was like thunder in her ears. There was a crowd of people shouting, and when she opened the door they all pointed at her and cried, "It's her! She's responsible for this! If it weren't for her, none of this would have happened! Welcoming a crazy man into her room so he can scare other people!" As they described it, he came into her room and turned on the radio so it called out "Fire!" "Murder!" "Fire!" Everyone ran to see what was going on. And that wild man, that maniac, slammed the door in their faces and went on spinning the radio dial and raising the volume. He scared the children and the elderly to death! What was he thinking? Could they just let him run rampant that way? No, they'd call for the police!

All of their shouts intermingled with the wild voices coming from Mrs. Shipok's radio. As though possessed by the noise and chaos, Mrs. Shipok approached the door to her room. The door was locked. She knocked and shouted, "Open the door!" but Mr. Karkin didn't hear her, or pretended not to hear, and didn't open it. Mrs. Shipok knocked harder. She pounded with both fists. She beat on the door, crying hysterically, "Open the door!" He didn't open it. She couldn't stand it anymore and cried out, "What did I do to deserve this?" The others took pity on her and joined her in pounding on the door, harder and harder. They would help her rescue her radio from the crazed man. Such a dear, good radio!

All things come to an end, and so did Mr. Karkin's refusal to open the door and the nightmare with the radio. Her loud crying finally reached him and moved him. He let her into her room and then quickly shut it behind her to keep out the others. Loudly, so those behind the door would hear him, he shouted to Mrs. Shipok that if she didn't demand that the others apologize to him for the horrible words they said about him, he would leave the house and once and never come back.

"Let him go, let him go!" she heard the others saying from behind the door. "He should leave before we throw him out! Or before we call the police!"

Hearing their outcry, Mrs. Shipok simply couldn't insist that they apologize to him. She begged him to leave. They were too worked up right now, and he should let things calm down.

Mr. Karkin cried, "You have to choose once and for all—them, or me!"

Of course Mrs. Shipok wanted him more than them. After all, she was planning to marry *him*, not them. But she couldn't simply dismiss them with a wave of her hand. They represented all of society, and she didn't want to go against society. What would everyone say?

Society waited for her answer. They waited to see the whole wedding business end with nothing to show for it. Mrs. Shipok didn't know what to do. Mr. Karkin took her wavering as an insult. He stomped out of the house, slamming the door behind him.

"Serves you right!" cried the others after him. Seeing how devastated Mrs. Shipok was, they comforted her, saying that she should be glad to be rid of him. He wasn't such a good bargain after all! They hoped he wouldn't be coming back anytime soon . . .

In the meantime, she hasn't yet decided to refuse the bargain. Who knows what will happen next?

Perfectly Suited

Forverts, *June 17, 1935*

When Mrs. Blum got divorced, she couldn't imagine that it would be difficult to find another husband. She felt sure that as soon as she was free of her husband she'd be surrounded by suitors. Mrs. Blum had a reputation for attracting men.

But three years had gone by since Mrs. Blum divorced her first husband, and she still didn't have a second.

Mrs. Blum was beginning to worry about the situation. She felt that it was time she began a new life, and if she put it off for later it would soon be too late . . . She had to do something about it.

But what should she do? Hire a *shadkhn*? No, she couldn't do that. That turned the whole thing into a business matter. It was beneath her. An intellectual woman like herself should be able to find her own match, without a middleman to intervene.

But how could she find her *bashert*? Where could he be?

Mrs. Blum had often glanced at the personal ads when reading the newspaper. It was interesting to read about a man seeking a woman, or a woman wanting to make the acquaintance of a man. "Goal: Marriage. Write to Box Number . . ." Hilarious. Mrs. Blum laughed at the personals. People are so funny. Sad, too . . . she noted as an afterthought. They don't know what to do about their loneliness, so they keep on searching, searching . . .

Once, as she read one of the articles under the "Personals" heading, a man's ad caught her attention more than any other she'd ever read.

"An intellectual, of means, thirty-eight years old, seeks a bachelorette or young widow of good character from a good family. Only women who meet these specifications need inquire. Write to Box Number . . ."

This is what was written in the ad. Mrs. Blum, at first playfully and flirtatiously, and then more earnestly, asked herself what would happen if she were to respond to the "intellectual man of means." No one would need to know about it. She could give him a fake name. Who knows, maybe she's the right woman for him, and he's the man for her? Maybe this is the happiness that she'd been hoping for when she split up with her unfortunate first husband.

But no matter how many letters she wrote to "Mr. Personal Ad," as she jokingly called him, she tore every one up. She couldn't seem to find the right words to send him. So she decided to send in her own "personal ad" to "his" newspaper that would be particularly attractive so that *he* would write to *her*, and not the other way around.

In her ad, she wrote that a young, pretty, intellectual lady (she figured he could find out later whether she was a bachelorette, a widow, or a divorcee), with a good character, from a fine family, seeks an intellectual man around forty years old. Only men who meet these specifications need inquire. Write to Box Number . . .

Along with several unimportant notes, Mrs. Blum received *his* letter. Her heart told her that it must be from him.

The note was printed from a typewriter and was well written and matter-of-fact. He requested that she accept his invitation to see one another. He hoped and believed they were suitable for one another. He would be delighted to meet her and make her personal acquaintance. If she was comfortable with it, he would invite her to his home for an evening three days from then, and he stated the time and place where they would meet so he could take her there. They would go for a ride in his car and then eat dinner together. He had a new automobile, and he gave her the license plate number and the brand and make of his car. He would be waiting for her at the meeting place, which was right beside a park. That is to say, he'd be sitting in his car, wearing a dark gray suit. Now that she had enough details that she could recognize him, he asked that she write back to him and give him some details about herself, what she would be wearing, and so forth. He signed his letter with "the perfectly suited man for the suitable woman."

Mrs. Blum quickly wrote back to the "perfectly suited man" (also with a typewriter) that she accepted his invitation for the time and place he suggested. She didn't think it was worthwhile to give him details that he would know her by, as she believed that it was enough that she could recognize him. It was hard for her to pick out something to wear several days in advance. It would depend on the weather, which was unpredictable.

That's what she wrote to him, but she had another reason for not giving any details about her appearance. She wanted to see what he looked like first, and then decide whether to make herself known to him. It would be easier to assess him if he wasn't able to recognize her. Of course, she planned on being a little bit late so he would have to wait a while and be anxious that she wasn't coming at all. And when she did make herself known, she wouldn't get in his car. She would say that she preferred to walk. She would talk dismissively about the personal ad she had placed in the newspaper. She would say that a friend of hers had all but forced her to place the ad, a friend who had found her own happiness through such an ad.

Mrs. Blum arrived at the meeting place early, so she couldn't begrudge that *he* wasn't there yet. But when it was already some time after the meeting time and he still hadn't shown up, she was irritated. She felt insulted, like he was playing a joke on her. Her only consolation was that he didn't know who he was insulting. And how could he know? She hadn't given him any details to recognize her by. She wouldn't let on that she'd arrived so much earlier than he had.

Before she arrived, she'd spent a few hours in the beauty parlor. She had her hair, her nails, and her makeup done. When a breeze went through her hair and upset it, her feeling of freshness evaporated. All that she had left to show for it was her nails—but when would she have a chance to show off her nails to him?

She felt anger and hatred rising for him, as it used to do for her ex-husband. She couldn't stand it that her ex-husband never made it on time to any appointment! Their worst arguments were always about this. She would beg him, "Don't make promises, don't fix a time for anything, and that way you won't end up making yourself into a liar. How can anyone believe you if you never live up to your promises? A person could just burst, never knowing what to expect! Who knows what could have happened to you? But what do you care if you leave the other person waiting until their patience runs out, until they lose their temper entirely? There's always something keeping you late, making you break your promises. Tfu, that's what I think of you!" That's what she would say to him, but it was no use. He was, and continued to be, the same old fool. He said, "I won't make it today, I'm coming tomorrow," no matter how many times she told him not to. She felt the same outrage now at the stranger, but she took it out on her ex-husband. In her mind she cursed at him as though he was responsible for the other man's tardiness.

Aside from that one fault, her husband was all right. He did have some good qualities. He was easy to love. And that's what made her so angry at him. He agreed to a divorce too easily. "You want a divorce? Whatever you want . . ." She would never forget the way he did her this "favor."

It was no use waiting. The "perfectly suited man" was never going to come, Mrs. Blum said to herself resignedly. She sat down on the closest bench, since her legs were aching from standing on the corner for so long. She would be able to see from that place as well as any other if an automobile pulled up to wait for her.

She woke with a start as though she had seen a ghost. Standing right next to her was none other than her own ex-husband! He smiled at her good-naturedly and apologized for frightening her. He was also quite surprised to see her here. What a coincidence! He sat down next to her on the bench and explained that he'd had an appointment here with a lady . . . But something delayed him and he wasn't able to make it to the meeting on time. The lady must have left by now. What a pity. It had something to do with his new car. It was as stubborn as an ass and had refused to turn on. He'd had to find someone else with a car who could help drag it to a garage. And they always take more time than they need to fix these things so they can charge more money for it. So he'd only just now managed to drive here. There was his car, parked over there. Did she want to go for a ride with him? Or was she waiting for someone?

No, she wasn't waiting for anyone! Mrs. Blum answered drily. She'd walked here with a friend, and when the friend had hurried off, she stayed here by herself to take in a little more fresh air.

"Very nice!" cried her ex-husband. "Then why don't we both go for a drive and have something to eat? We can go to the theater, like we did in the good old days. Why not? What do you think?"

She didn't know what to say. Her heart was pounding. He looked so elegant, so young, even younger than he used to be, and he had a new car. She admired him as he spoke, he was so energetic. And he looked at her as though the two of them had never met before!

And he admired her: she looked so good! Younger, and prettier than she used to be! Not a day older! How time flies. How long had it been since they last saw each other? What had she been doing this whole time? What was her life like? He had thought about her very often. He was a fool . . . And she had also acted hastily. She'd picked on him too much. Both of them were too quick to quarrel over nothing, like children. And then they got divorced all of a sudden. Why? Over what? Nothing! But it's over now, and what's done is done. What should they do now? Would she accept his invitation?

"Maybe . . ." She didn't know if she should. She hesitated. It was rather unusual . . .

"All good things seem unusual," he said, taking her by the hand. "Come on! Let's go for a drive! We'll take the new car out for a spin and show her off a little, and go get something to eat. I haven't had such an appetite in a long time. Come, take care of me while I eat and tell me when I've had too much, otherwise I won't know when to stop."

She went for a ride with him, ate, went to the movies, and talked. They talked until they came to the conclusion that they should get married again. They agreed that they would have more patience and treat each other better this time.

As he looked through his mail for an envelope of photographs he'd recently had taken, a letter fell out from among the other envelopes. She recognized it. It was *her* letter that she'd written to the "perfectly suited man." He took the letter out of her hand and tore it up. "It's nothing," he muttered. "Some kind of advertisement. It's just taking up space." He had no use for it now.

A Promise Kept

Forverts, *August 7, 1934*

The day of Rosa's wedding had arrived. A great, important day. The bride and her mother both fasted. Neither could wait for the wedding to be over and the happiness they were striving for to begin. Both were anxious that something would prevent the wedding from being carried out, that something might cause the groom and his whole *esteemed* family to decide not to go through with it.

When they'd first started making wedding arrangements, the mother had told the groom's family she was a widow. It's better to be a widow than a woman who doesn't live with her husband. People have more respect for a dead husband than a living one who's a worthless gambler and a bum, a husband who'd landed behind bars, even if, as he claimed, he was innocent. That wasn't exactly good pedigree. You could hardly think of it as an advantage when calculating the dowry. It was an ugly stain on her reputation.

As far as the bride's mother was concerned, her husband might as well be dead. She'd nurtured and supported her daughter alone, with her own two hands. She'd raised a beautiful girl and managed to find her a fine *shidekh*. The groom had a lovely home in Brooklyn. After the wedding he would become a partner in his father's business. His mother played bridge, his sister was married to a lawyer, they owned an automobile. Rozele, the lucky daughter, would soon have her own automobile.

The fortunate mother did feel a tinge of guilt when she thought of the moment in the marriage ceremony when they would honor her daughter's "dead" father by saying his name. She thought of asking the officiant not to do it so he could finish the ceremony as quickly as possible, and of telling him not to ask too many questions. She'd say she didn't like remembering the names of the dead during a happy occasion. She just wanted to celebrate with the living.

But as soon as she crossed the hall to have a word with the officiant about the stipulations of her daughter's wedding, one of her relatives, Rokhl, came up to her and whispered in her ear, "He's here!"

"He's here?" She nearly fainted. "Where? Where is he?"

Rokhl told her. He was in the foyer. He was probably trying to sneak in. He looked like a tramp.

"Sara," Rokhl urged the bride's mother, "you have to do something to keep him from getting in. Save yourself from scandal. Tell him kindly, but firmly, that he has to go away. Where has he been all these years? And who asked him to come now? What bad luck this is! What claim does he have on the girl? What kind of a father is he to her? You're up to your neck in debt because of Rozele's wedding, and he didn't contribute a cent!"

Sara hurried to her misfortune, her husband, accompanied by her relative's admonishments. On her way she smiled at the guests so no one would be suspicious of where she was going and who she was talking to. No one. Not even the bride. What did she know of her father? Nothing. Nothing more than that he disappeared, and that her mother wasn't eager to find him.

Her daughter appeared in her white wedding gown. She smiled brightly and gazed lovingly at the groom.

Sara's husband stood beside the door to the hall and looked exactly like what he was—a bum. A tramp from head to toe! An open collar without a necktie, his strong neck entirely bare. Tousled hair, smoldering eyes. Those same eyes that had once seduced and blinded her at first glance. Now, after all these years of not seeing her, those eyes seemed astonished as they took her in.

With forced composure, Sara showed him the door to the street. He thought she was driving him away and said with a crooked smile, "I didn't come for you. I came to see the bride, just to get a look at her."

Sara shook her head and looked around, not wanting anyone to see her with him. She couldn't stand there with him any longer. She'd take him through a side entrance to the kitchen. She could explain to him there why he had to leave. If he had to see his daughter, at least let it be after the wedding, when the couple was alone.

He refused to wait until after the wedding. He wanted to see his daughter right away. He had something to say to her.

People bustled around the kitchen. It was hard for her to talk to him. She was anxious that they'd erect the *khupe* without her. But she was the bride's mother. They couldn't possibly start the wedding if she wasn't there. They must be looking for her.

"The mother of the bride!" She heard someone calling from behind the kitchen door. "Where is the mother of the bride?"

"I'm here!" Sara shouted. "I'm coming!"

She turned to the tramp and said, "Wait here. I'll be right back."

Sara rushed off, worried that they'd started the wedding. But the groom's side was in no hurry. They were waiting until all of their guests arrived.

Sara took her daughter aside and told her to keep smiling while she listened to what her mother had to say. An unwelcome guest had shown up. He wanted to see the bride. He just wanted to have a look at her, nothing more. She should make some kind of excuse and then go into the kitchen to see him. Just in and out, and nothing bad would happen. It would prevent so much scandal.

The daughter's forced smile faded as she understood. She clasped her mother's hands. "He came! *Today*! A long time ago he promised me he'd come to my wedding! Oh, God, what should I do? They think my father is dead!"

"Shhh . . . Try not to look so upset!" Her mother tried to calm her. "Take a few minutes to think while I smooth the way by talking to him. He's waiting for me. The groom is looking at you, so smile and talk to the guests.

Rokhl, the relative who'd told her, "He's here," was staying with the man in Sara's absence. Sara heard him telling her that he didn't want to ruin his daughter's happiness. He just wanted to show his daughter that he was a man of his word. He'd promised her years ago, when she was a little girl, that he'd come to her wedding. Would they forbid him from wishing her mazel tov? He was her father, after all, no matter what kind of father he was. He'd long imagined coming to her wedding to say "Mazel tov" and give her a present, like a father should.

Sara approached them. "I told Rozele you're here. I whispered it to her and was careful to make sure no one else heard. She nearly fainted . . ."

"Well," he said irritably, "then I'll say 'Mazel tov' later. But let me give her the wedding present now. Here it is." He pulled an envelope of cash out of his breast pocket and handed it to Sara, but she didn't want to accept it.

"It's good money," he said, thrusting it at Sara. "*Kosher* money, so help me God! I saved it for her. I had a special nest egg set aside just for her. I may be a good-for-nothing bum, a gambler, a disgrace, but I have a heart and it's filled with love for my child. She's still my child. It's because of me that she exists at all. And today is her wedding day. May she live with joy and good fortune. May *her* husband be better to her than her father, the bum, was to her mother . . ."

In her heart, Sara felt pity for this no-goodnik, her husband, as he wiped a tear from his eye and, embarrassed, pretended that he was just swatting at a pesky fly.

"Sara," Rokhl said. "Take the gift from him and be done with it. If you don't I'll take it for her. She'll need it. You need it. Just take it. He is her father, after all, and she's his daughter."

Turning to him, she asked, "How much money is in the envelope?"

"More than enough!" he boasted. "If she wants, she can give half to her mother and she'll still have plenty."

Rokhl glanced sharply at Sara and gestured toward the envelope. She needs it. She should take it. But what could she say? "Blood runs deep. He's her father, after all. She's his daughter. You can't deny him that. Let him see what a fine daughter you raised for him, without his help. Maybe from now on he'll behave himself and live a respectable life, if not for his wife's sake, then for his daughter's. Go and fetch the bride and tell her that I'm waiting to see her in the kitchen. Then he can have a chance to see her. It won't cause any harm. He won't give her the evil eye."

She managed to convince Sara, who went and spoke to her daughter without revealing any details. Sara asked her daughter to go see Rokhl, in the kitchen, to tell her that Sara wanted to talk to her. That's all, just in and out.

The bride looked at her shrewdly. "Did he leave yet? You know who I mean."

"Him? Why are you asking? Don't you want to see him?"

"Him? No!"

"Shhh! Not so loud! They'll hear you and figure it out!"

"Figure what out?"

"Figure out that he's alive."

"What a nightmare! I wish he were dead."

Sara's face turned crimson. "Hush! He's your father!"

"I hate him."

"But he loves you. He brought you a wedding present. He wants to have a look at you. Go to him."

"I don't want to see him."

"Do you want him to come out here to see you, and everyone else will see him, too? If you keep him waiting that's what he might do . . ."

That was enough to convince the bride. She went off to the kitchen to see Rokhl, accept the present from her father the bum, and let him take a gander at her. She wouldn't say a single word to him. Just in and out. She didn't know him and didn't want to know him.

In the kitchen she found Rokhl waiting impatiently for the bride to come and summon her to speak to her mother. Good, she'd go talk to the mother. Did Rozele know what her mother wanted? No? Oh, well, she'd soon find out for herself. Had more guests arrived? It's quite the crowd! The groom's side had a nice showing. A large family! A fine family, with good pedigree.

Empty words. The bride understood that the relative was speaking to her to keep her there a little longer so her disgraceful father, who just stood there like a tramp, could get a better look at her. Well, let him look. As long as he kept quiet and didn't try to say anything to her . . .

Suddenly overcome with curiosity, she looked up and met his eyes. He handed her the wedding present and said, "Mazel tov!" She responded, "Thank you."

The bride quickly left the kitchen. The relative was in no rush to leave.

Later, Rokhl told Sara how her husband had cried with joy upon seeing his daughter. Cried and swore to become a better man, to start a new life. Repay his wife in kindness for all the pain he'd caused her. And now that she was living alone, he'd come to her and make her happy again. She was still young and beautiful and she had a right to be happy. He had great respect for her. He loved her, and today he had fallen in love all over again with his wife, the mother of his child.

Sara listened to everything her relative said and smiled sadly. "He talks a good talk . . ."

Even so, the hope of a better life warmed her heart. She blushed girlishly when she caught sight of his shadow outside the hall. She knew that he was watching her and her daughter, and that he loved them. Maybe this love would bring him back. Maybe he would return to her.

Victims of Love

Forverts, *November 16, 1937*

They were both madly in love. She was a married woman, and he a married man. It was pure joy, with an underside of misfortune. Two misfortunes: her husband and his wife. Yet, since love is as strong as death, or even stronger, they couldn't help themselves. They didn't even want to help themselves.

In order not to betray their love, they decided for the time being to keep it hidden. And as long as their spouses didn't know about it, they would have nothing to be ashamed of. So they loved each other and didn't tell. To keep from telling lies, they each suffered romantically in silence.

But, after all, how long can a person keep quiet? How long can you keep hidden something as grand as love? Even if you don't talk about it yourself, surely others are bound to say something, and the beauty of the love will be sullied. They're restless with envy. They can't stand to see others happy.

Keeping their love a secret was often quite uncomfortable. In the middle of passionately expressing their feelings, the clock, like a thief, would sound out the hour that would steal one of the lovers away to go home to their spouse.

They talked and talked about it and tried to figure out what to do: come out with the truth, or wait and see what time would bring. She said that if she were to tell her husband that she wanted to leave him, it would be like a knife to his heart. And if he told his wife, he said, it would be like *two* knives to the heart. She had a weak—one might

212

even say an *infirm*—heart, and she wouldn't be able to survive the blow. Aside from her husband and his wife, it would impact many of their nearest and dearest. They had to take that into account. They didn't want to harm so many victims, just those that they absolutely *had* to harm. So they had to wait for the most opportune moment to let others know about it, and about what they had decided to do.

In the meantime, they came up with an idea to plan their summer vacations by the sea for the same time. When they came back from the country, then they would finally put an end to the lies and build a home together. They'd be done with their families and begin a new life together.

When he saw his wife she seemed concerned, worried, and she avoided his gaze. He was sure she already knew everything . . . Good friends must have informed her of this slap in the face. He came close to her and spoke: he understood how she must be feeling, but, as hard as it was for him to say it, things had to come to an end . . .

His wife lifted her woeful eyes up at him and then looked down again, and, with her head bent in grief, said, "Yes, it must come to an end. We can't go on like this any longer."

"We have to go our separate ways," he said.

"Yes, it's time to part ways," she echoed.

"Better now than later. We can remain good friends," he said.

"Good friends . . . yes, good friends."

He looked at her askance. Why was she repeating his every word? Was she so affected that she had lost the ability to speak in her own words?

"The life we've lived together until now was a mistake," he said to her.

"Yes, a mistake."

"We can correct it. We can be happy."

"How?" she asked.

"We can go our separate ways."

"Do you mean divorce?" she asked.

"Yes, divorce," he replied.

"When?"

"As soon as possible."

"You've always been so good to me." She sighed. "You are a gentleman."

He wondered what was the matter with her. She wasn't even saying anything about the matter at hand. Was it some kind of trick that she was playing to try to keep him somehow? If so, it wouldn't work. He despised such stratagems.

He invited her to talk some more, and she did speak. She had wanted to say something to him many times before, but she hadn't managed to do it. But now she had to say something. She is in love with her young friend, and he loves her too. He is a widower and he wants to marry her, as soon as her husband will release her.

This news should have seemed a blessing to him, but he recoiled from her as though she had slapped him in the face.

At the same time, an even more dramatic scene was occurring between his lover and her husband.

When she saw her husband, he seemed concerned, depressed, as though he had just buried a loved one. She realized that he must already know everything and that's why he looked so terrible. She found it painful even to look at him. She felt guilty. He had sent her to the country so that she would feel better. It was so difficult to try to talk to him about a divorce now. She felt sorry for him because he had suffered without her. She stroked his hair and told him to hold her in his arms like a man. He was touched by her words, very moved, and began to cry.

When she begged him to stop crying, her pleas only made him cry more. She chided him. How can a man have such a weak character? Why can't he just take it like a good sport? After all, it wasn't easy for her either . . . but she's not crying!

"You're not crying, because who do you know that died?"

"Died?" she asked, startled. "Died?"

"Yes, died." And he told her the truth.

He had been in love with a woman, and it was a pure, true love. He didn't want to hurt her, his wife, so he kept it a secret. Certainly, she hadn't been on the up and up with him about everything either . . . She had her own secrets. But the woman that he loved very much, who was so dear and true, had died. So now she knew why he was crying. Now she could forgive him or not. It was up to her.

She couldn't forgive him for it. Just a moment ago she had been so sure that he couldn't live without her, but he was crying all the while about another woman! She felt like a fool, and even felt jealous of the woman he was crying for. She was disappointed, insulted.

She packed her things. She was leaving him for another man. She left over her husband's protests, in a rage.

When the lovers met again, they were embarrassed to look one another in the eyes. Neither of them felt happy to be reunited.

She was the first to ask how his conversation had gone with his wife, and how his wife had taken the news.

After a contemplative pause, he sighed. "It was hard."

He didn't say anything for a while, and then he finally asked how her conversation with her husband had gone, and how he had taken the news.

"It was even harder than yours," she said. "He cried bitter tears."

They looked at each other with uncertainty, each afraid the other would read the lies in their eyes, and then they bowed their heads.

She quietly, sadly, and determinedly said, "But I left him. Love conquers all. Love takes its victims."

"Yes." He struggled to reply. "Love takes its victims. We are victims of love."

They Both Were Married

Forverts, August 24, 1936

He compared falling in love to coming down with an illness when you've never been sick before. It truly was treacherous: a weak sapling bent by the wind will never grow straight and tall. It may get stronger but it will still be crooked until it snaps in two.

He fell in love as only a man who has fallen in love for the first time in thirty years can. He was a well-known painter, dedicated to painting landscapes and still lifes, and now he was eager to paint a portrait. With her as the model, naturally. She let him beg for a little while before agreeing to pose for him. Not exactly the way he had hoped, but halfway. Half naked.

She made him feel like a new man. With a new soul. By nature a quiet man, now all he wanted to do was talk, talk about all his wasted, loveless years. Now it was clear to him why he had never loved before. Now he understood and was glad to have replaced his smaller passions with the tremendous feeling of love. He was happy, now, to be a whole man, with a whole heart. And without any previous experiences with love. Yes, he was full of joy that he had no past to be ashamed of. He had a past and a future, a future!

One day, when she was posing for him in his studio, one of his old friends came to ask him for a favor. She asked him to put in a good word for her brother with a certain businessman he was quite friendly with. His recommendation would surely help her brother get a job. She asked him to give her brother a letter for the businessman, if he didn't have time to talk to the businessman himself. Her brother could come and collect the letter from him. All he had to do was say when. Would he allow her brother to come tomorrow?

"Alright," he said. "Tomorrow would be fine."

In the meantime, until the girl's brother came, he was just happy that she had gone away and he could give himself over entirely, undisturbed, to his model, the girl who meant so much to him! The girl to whom he was devoted with all his heart.

The next day, as he stood in front of his portrait of the girl he loved, the sister and brother came to collect the recommendation letter that he had promised them.

The first moment he saw the girl's brother, the painter's heart skipped a beat. He had not expected to see a young man who was so spectacularly attractive. He was grateful that his heart's desire hadn't yet arrived and wasn't there to see the young man. Jealousy raged in his heart. Ashamed at the seething envy that the young man's appearance provoked in him, he quickly started speaking about his businessman acquaintance. It's true, they were on friendly terms. But it's probably on account of the fact that he had never asked the businessman for a favor. He didn't want to ask for a favor. He hates favors. For his whole life he had never asked anyone for a favor. He had sworn never to ask for one and he was a man who kept his promises. That's why he tries not to make too many promises in the first place.

The girl and her brother thanked him profusely for doing them a favor, especially as it was such a difficult thing to ask of him. They would never forget what he'd done for them. They would return the kindness by serving as his agents and looking for rich people to buy his paintings.

The painter was eager for them to leave so that they would be gone before his beloved arrived. He didn't want her to see the man. She must never see him.

They left before she arrived. Between the time they left and she arrived, the painter had time to look at himself in the mirror and think about how young and handsome the man was, and how old and decrepit he looked in comparison. He had to do something to improve his appearance. What should he do? He worried.

When she arrived her smile chased his worries away, like magic. He told her to hold her smile and began to paint. He soon grew tired from the work and laid his pencil down. He just wanted to sit and look at her in silence . . . She could talk if she wanted to, he told her. He would listen.

Talk? She didn't know what to say. She knew so little about the kinds of things that would interest him. She thought very often about reaching the heights of his achievements, but she knew that she would never be able to. She wasn't intellectual enough. She didn't have what it takes. She was too ordinary.

She gazed at him as though upon an idol.

Then, the thing that the painter was so afraid of happened. The handsome young man came to see him when she, his heart's desire, was with him!

The young man came to thank the painter for the favor and to reassure him that he had already found someone who was interested in purchasing a painting. He would bring the client to see the painter in a few days. The young man didn't stay long, but the painter was sure he made a strong impression on her. He wanted her to say something about it, and he tried to elicit her impression from her. He was suspicious of her silence. When she didn't say anything, she took it as a sign that she was thinking about the young man.

"Didn't you think he was attractive?" the painter asked her.

"Ye-es . . ." she responded. "But . . ."

"What?" he prodded, glaring at her intently.

"He didn't seem very smart. Most attractive people are fools. Anyway, beauty is a matter of taste. And men don't need to be attractive. It's more important for a man to be intelligent!"

"Not a terrible answer," the painter thought. "If only she believes what she says."

He bolstered her response, adding that he read somewhere that intelligent people say that "a man's beauty is in his intelligence, and a woman's wisdom is in her beauty." She agreed completely. Intelligent people know what they are talking about.

It was in his nature to be plagued by troubles of his own invention. His own thoughts always created a web of doubt around everything he wanted to believe in. Now his thoughts wove a net of doubt that he was caught in. The handsome young man seemed to grow into a giant and in comparison the painter saw himself as an insignificant little creature, and he felt overwhelmed and lost. Most of all, he felt he was losing her, the great love he had only just recently found . . .

The young man's appearance bewitched him. Just like the girl had, when he first saw her, now the young man aroused in the painter a longing to immortalize him, to paint his portrait. But he was certain that this would only bring the girl and the young man closer together.

He faced an internal struggle. The painter in him was willing to risk the love of the woman, and the man, the man in love, struggled against him. He didn't know what to do. He was unable to work. He didn't have the patience to listen to his friends or acquaintances when they came to visit him in his studio, even when they were praising his talent. He was rude to them. The young man came time and again to visit him, bringing one art aficionado or another. Friends threw parties in his studio. They brought food and wine, sang, and had a good time. He felt like a guest in his own place. He watched his beloved's every move. He spied on both of them. If he noticed that she seemed to be flirting with him, his blood boiled. When he didn't notice anything at all, he suspected both of them of trying to hide their love for each other from him.

As he watched them, the painter marveled at what a gorgeous couple they made. It was as though they were created just for each other. How could they not see it? They must see it, and they only pretended (for his sake) that they don't. Who knew if they are spending time together outside of his studio? Who knew?

In his dreams he saw them with their guard down. He didn't believe in dreams. But now he had found a way to interpret them and it only made him more miserable.

He bit his lips and gazed at her and at the others with a cold stare. Her unfinished portrait stood in the corner, covered in a black cloth. It seemed she was waiting for him to invite her to pose for him again, and he was waiting for her to mention it first.

She started coming to his studio less often. She told him that she had decided to study nursing. He didn't believe her. He felt it must be an excuse. Surely she was spending all her time with the young man. But, as things with him weren't certain yet, she had to cover for it with this nursing business. Why would she want to be a nurse? What would she want for when she became *his*, when she was married to the young man and the two of them lived happily together? He thought of saying something to her sooner, before the young man had a chance to declare his feelings. But he was sure it was already too late.

Time passed. He went around in bitter silence with a wound in his heart. He was a broken man. His emotional state took a toll on his health and his work. He avoided others. He was afraid to hear them say the names of the object of his affections and the "young Adonis," as they called him at the parties.

Whenever he summoned his strength and took to his work, he soon threw it aside. He saw the young man's face, his profile everywhere. In his shattered thoughts their faces reflected back at him from every angle as in shards of a polished mirror. He never saw them separately, always together, forever together, the two of them in love, building the whole world around themselves.

Due to his cold reception, his friends stopped coming to see him. He disappeared into his studio whole days and evenings.

When he returned to consciousness, he searched for letters, notes, some evidence that someone had written to him, that someone had come to see him. There were some notes and calling cards, but none from *her*. She must be too busy with *him*. Of course she was. It was exactly as he suspected. Even a blind man could see that the two young, beautiful people were created for each other, and he was no blind man. He saw, he knew, that it was too late for him to find such happiness.

By coincidence one day he happened to meet the young man's sister and she asked if he had heard the news—it was so unexpected. Her handsome brother and his beautiful girl model, his muse, had both gotten married on the same day—he to a rich widow from an elite family, and she, the model, to an older doctor from her hospital.

Good News—and Bad

Forverts, *September 4, 1936*

Mr. and Mrs. Hastig have been married for over nineteen years, but no one knows what their married life is like. Everyone thinks they're the happiest couple in the world. Mrs. Hastig is always going on about how well she and her husband get along. It has happened more than once that another woman cast an eye on her husband and tried to tempt him away from her, but he is still hers, hers until death parts them at a ripe old age.

The Hastigs intend to live for a long time. Mrs. Hastig is preparing for when old age will befall them. He is the earner, but she is responsible for their savings.

When no one is around to hear, Mrs. Hastig chides her husband for not being everything she wants him to be. She wishes he made more money. She wishes he would eat everything she cooked for him. She wishes he was more affectionate. She wants many things that he can't or won't give her. But this only comes out when they are alone. When they're with other people, she is the very embodiment of love and devotion.

It's no wonder that Mr. Hastig prefers to be around other people when he is with his wife.

In the summers, the Hastigs leave the city to spend the summer in the densely populated area of Coney Island. They rent a room with kitchen privileges and are happy as clams. Mrs. Hastig spends her days sunning on the beach, going for a dip in the sea, or taking a stroll in the sand.

When it comes time for Mr. Hastig to come home from work, she gets gussied up. She ties a red ribbon around her neck, like a cat, and applies lipstick and blush. Her nose looks like she dipped it in powder. She puts on her pajamas, grabs a cigarette, and hastily lights it up so she can exhale some smoke before Mr. Hastig enters the room, and she affixes the smile on her face that lays him flat. The same smile with which she convinced him to spend the rest of his life with her.

One time, when Mr. Hastig returned from work to find his wife waiting for him this way, she thought something seemed odd about him. When she stretched her arms out to embrace him, he pushed her away, took one wavering step, and fell to the ground in a faint!

Over the course of their marriage, Mrs. Hastig had appeared to faint from time to time. When she fainted, she enjoyed the way Mr. Hastig would fuss over her. But now that *he* was the one who fainted, she was greatly distressed. He had fainted for real!

Because she didn't know how to care for someone who had actually fainted, all Mrs. Hastig could do was scream. She cried out for help. "My husband is dying! Someone come and save him!"

There were plenty of people in the boardinghouse around to hear. They all rushed to her side in great alarm. There was quite a hullabaloo. People pushed and shoved to get a look at the unconscious man. Someone shouted, "A doctor! Quick, someone call a doctor!"

Seeing that she was surrounded by an audience, Mrs. Hastig threw her hands in the air and wept over the great misfortune that had befallen her. She recounted everything that had happened. He never drinks, but he had been stumbling like a drunkard. Why weren't they saying anything! Someone should *do* something!

They told her that they were doing all they could. Someone had called a doctor. In the meantime, someone else seized a tall glass of water and poured it over the man's head.

At any other time, Mrs. Hastig would have knocked out anyone's teeth if they poured water onto her bed. But now she suppressed every protest.

The man who had fainted trembled and opened and closed his mouth like a fish. His eyes even began to open. Mrs. Hastig practically danced with joy. "He's alive! Sweetheart, open your eyes! It's me, your girlie, your . . ."

There was no one to talk to anymore. He had shut his eyes again.

The water pourer dumped freezing cold water on him. In response to the water, the man croaked, "I'm dyyyyyiiiinnnnggggg!"

Hearing this, Mrs. Hastig wailed as though she, too, were dying. But she didn't faint. She didn't want them to pour water on her, too. She just clutched at her heart and begged, "Someone save my husband! Don't worry about me—take care of *him*! Save him!"

The doctor arrived.

"It's the doctor!" Everyone made way for the doctor and his briefcase.

The first thing the doctor did was clear the room to give the man some air. Mrs. Hastig was allowed to stay, but she left with the others because she wasn't feeling well. She didn't want to faint and leave the doctor with two patients on his hands.

When the doctor emerged from the patient's room, he told Mrs. Hastig that her husband was not a well man.

"What's the matter with him?" asked Mrs. Hastig anxiously. "Is it dangerous?"

The doctor told her not to worry. Her husband would be all right. First of all, she'd have to do something for his stomach.

The doctor didn't tell her *what* to do for it, and Mrs. Hastig grimaced and sobbed so that her whole body was trembling. The only thing she was capable of doing was trying not to faint herself! But she would see to it that everything he needed would be done. Good people would come to her aid. She would return the favor in better times.

The doctor left, promising to call again the next day.

As soon as he left, Mrs. Hastig, accompanied by several others, went into her husband's room to see how he was doing.

He was not doing well. He was barely able to tell her that it was hard for him to breathe. Mrs. Hastig once again began to wail. "He is my wall! How can I stand without him to lean on? No, he must get better! They were supposed to live together and love one another, just as they had always done, until they grew old together . . ."

She was so overcome with telling her husband that he had to get better that she forgot to do what the doctor told her to do for him, and, consequently, the illness worsened. Others around her cried out—how can we let a sick man just fade away like a light? Maybe the doctor didn't give the right advice. Maybe Mrs. Hastig should get a second opinion. Who cares about a few dollars at a time like this?

More than anyone else, a few women who often gushed about the Hastigs' loving relationship (or, at least, Mrs. Hastig thought they did) and who envied their happiness were now in an uproar. One of these "jealous" women said that she knew of a man, a doctor, who could heal any sickness with the blink of an eye. It was her own doctor! She stood up to take responsibility for her recommendation and actually called him.

The doctor seemed pessimistic. He examined and listened to the patient's whole body, and when he was finished he seemed reluctant to speak with Mrs. Hastig about the results. Instead he spoke with the woman who had summoned him. Mrs. Hastig would not stand for it. Why wouldn't he speak to the patient's own wife? She wouldn't put up with this sort of behavior. She wouldn't make a fuss now, but, later, when all of this was over, he'd be hearing from her.

Mrs. Hastig gathered that the second doctor didn't like her very much, so she announced that she preferred the *first* doctor anyway. The second doctor didn't know any more than the first. The woman said to her, "When a woman loves her husband the way you love yours, she doesn't call a doctor. She calls a professor!"

Mrs. Hastig fumed. How dare she threaten her with a professor! Fine, then she'd call *two* professors. When it came to saving her husband's life, nothing was too much. Without him, her own life would be no life at all! She ran to her husband's bedside and spoke to him loud enough for all to hear: "I'm here for you! Nothing else matters to me at all—as long as you live! Do you want a professor? Alright, I'll get you a professor. I don't care. Just tell me what you want. Just tell me, my darling . . ."

He didn't say anything. He just moaned and smacked his lips. The doctor, who was speaking to the woman who had called him, came to take another look at the patient before he left. He asked Mrs. Hastig why she was talking to the patient so much, and so loudly. She should let him rest. Didn't she see how unwell he was? How high his fever was? How he . . .

"Save his life for me!" cried Mrs. Hastig.

"My dear woman," the doctor said, "I'm just a doctor. I can treat sick people, but I can't guarantee that I can save them. Please don't talk like that."

"I can't help crying out in my pain and woe!" cried Mrs. Hastig. "Doctor, if you're not capable of helping him, tell me, should I call a professor?"

The doctor said he wouldn't stop anyone from calling whomever they wanted. If she wanted a professor, she could go ahead and call one.

The woman who had called this doctor reassured Mrs. Hastig that if he gave her the name of a professor to call, she could rely on his recommendation. "And," she said, "here's the telephone."

The doctor called one professor, and then another, but neither would agree to come. They were both on vacation. He did manage to reach another professor, but that professor quoted him a very high price—one hundred dollars. He would be willing to make an exception in this case and do it for seventy-five dollars, but no less . . .

When a man's life is at stake, you can't just stand there and hang up the telephone on account of a few dollars. Mrs. Hastig thought to herself that when the professor came and saw their cramped rooms and all the "millionaires" who live there together, he'd lower his fee.

The professor arrived in a sour mood. He'd hardly had time to catch his breath! And it was such a hot day. Unbearable.

He examined the patient and reassured them all that he would have a full report tomorrow about exactly what he was suffering from. In the meantime he'd administer something to help the patient sleep. They should call the professor tomorrow and tell him how the patient was doing. The doctor should be the one to call.

He was ready to leave the house. He was just waiting for his payment. With her heart pounding, Mrs. Hastig turned to the professor and implored him, "Excuse me, but I only have sixty dollars at my disposal right now, and I need at least ten of the sixty for . . ."

The professor took the fifty and the ten dollar bills out of her hands, and said that he hated these kinds of manipulations. Who had ever heard of such behavior? He was very disappointed. To have traveled so far in this heat! Everyone knows what his price is, and those who can't afford it shouldn't call him.

Mrs. Hastig impatiently waited for morning to find out what the report would be. Who knew what kind of illness it was! Just let it be a treatable illness, and not a terminal one!

One of the other residents of the boardinghouse took pity on the poor man and did what the first doctor had told Mrs. Hastig to do for him. And, after that, he did seem to improve. He was finally able to get a little sleep at night.

First thing the next morning, Mrs. Hastig visited the pharmacist, demanding to see her husband's report. In a halting English, Mrs. Hastig asked the pharmacist to read it out loud and explain it to her. The pharmacist read the report and said that everything was "negative."

"Negative? That means . . ."

"It's nothing! Your husband will be just fine."

"You mean that my husband has none of the illnesses on that list?"

"That's what I mean. That's what the report says. He's all right!"

"What a nightmare! You mean to say I gave that professor all that money for *nothing*?"

"Would you have felt any better if after you paid all that money you also had an illness to deal with?"

"I can't believe it!" said Mrs. Hastig, hardly paying attention to what the pharmacist said. "*Nothing*! And I gave him so much money, right out of my own two hands! He snatched it from me and left with it. I hope it makes *him* sick!"

Furious, Mrs. Hastig ran home, carrying the clean bill of health. She was beside herself. She'd wasted a hundred dollars on his fainting. When someone faints, you should just take care of them, and that's it! But instead she'd gone and called not one but two doctors, and a professor to boot!

Mrs. Hastig called the professor and spoke to him about the good report while everyone in the house listened raptly.

When she was alone with her husband, she scolded him. "See what you did? Fainting like that? See how you made me waste so much of our savings? Why didn't you tell me that you didn't need a professor? How was I supposed to know if it was serious or not? Why would you eat so much junk food before supper when it's so hot outside? What could you possibly have been thinking? Are you out of your mind?"

Next time, she swore, she would just leave him there in a faint until he came to on his own. There would be no doctors, and no professors!

Mr. Hastig begged his wife to have pity on him and stop scolding him. He was still feeling weak and she could make him faint again. He couldn't stand it anymore. But she didn't pay attention to him. She just showed him the report with its "negative," its "nothing."

Now, even more than before the fainting incident, Mr. Hastig tries to be around other people when he is with his wife. When she's with others, she's so attentive to him. He doesn't care if she only does it so others will be jealous that the two of them are so much in love, that she is so happy with her "darling." As long as he doesn't have to be alone with her scolding him and always bringing up that report with its "negative" and the money that she wasted on him for nothing.

We're People, After All

Forverts, May 16, 1935

It all began in October of last year, 1934.

Mrs. Berger wanted to rent the room with the porch from Mrs. Sher for herself and her daughter.

Mrs. Sher warned Mrs. Berger that it was a cold room. Mrs. Berger liked that the landlady was willing to be honest about the room's problems. So she focused on its advantages: she liked it very much, and it would be nice if it wasn't too warm, if a bit of breeze was able to get through. Her daughter felt the same way. She hoped to God, and also to Mrs. Sher, that they—mother and daughter—wouldn't freeze to death. In the meantime, perhaps Mrs. Sher could lower the rent a little, considering. If it weren't for them, the room would have stayed empty, so Mrs. Sher should agree to rent it to them for whatever they were willing to pay.

Day after day for a whole week Mrs. Berger came to Mrs. Sher and asked her to lower her price, until they finally came to an agreement. Mrs. Berger and her daughter arrived together with many large pillows, blankets, comforters, pots, dishes, and so forth, filling not only their room but also the bathroom and the kitchen.

"We're people, after all," Mrs. Berger explained when asked why she had so many things. "So we need to have all the things people have. We can't get rid of anything." It might be useful in this house. When her husband was still living and she had a house of her own, she'd had the best of everything. Not just for one room, but for four. It had been several years since her husband died of a fever—a fate she would wish on no one. But these things, these fine things, remained after he was gone. And, she declared, "we're people, after all, so we deserve to have something."

Mrs. Zalkin lived in the room next to Mrs. Berger. She moved in with the expectation that she would have the kitchen all to herself. She couldn't even imagine that someone would move into the cold room during the winter. When she met the aforementioned woman, with a daughter and with her whole host of belongings, she was furious. She threatened to move out. But Mrs. Sher bought her a new oilcloth, hung some new curtains, invited her to have a cup of tea, and spoke to her in Russian, so she stayed.

But Mrs. Zalkin and Mrs. Berger did not live well together. They hated each other at first sight, and their antipathy only grew. They couldn't stand each other.

There was only one instance when the two women got along. It happened in the middle of the night. Mrs. Zalkin was trying to cause a bit of a stir. She knocked against Mrs. Berger's door and Mrs. Berger was frightened and woke up the whole household, crying, "Mrs. Zalkin is dying! We have to save her! We have to do something— we're people, after all! Come quick! Just think of what might become of her!" They saved Mrs. Zalkin. Mrs. Berger threw her hands up and described how her heart had nearly broken when she heard Mrs. Zalkin's knock at the door. She knew right away Mrs. Zalkin must be in danger. It's a good thing that Mrs. Berger was such a light sleeper. Just a bit of indigestion? Think of how many people die from things like that! First you start to shake, then you get a cramp, and a fever, and who knows what else, and soon enough you're dead!

Everything seemed fine, but a few days later, at two in the morning, there was another incident. Mrs. Zalkin forgot to extinguish a cigarette in the kitchen and left it on the stovetop, and Mrs. Berger spoke to her about it, scolding her for leaving a mess for Mrs. Berger to clean up. What was she, a servant?

And Mrs. Zalkin also had complaints. She had a visitor, and she had prepared tea and refreshments for the visitor in the kitchen. But Mrs. Berger just stood there in the kitchen, a third wheel. She didn't leave them alone for a minute. She just kept going on and on about her beloved husband who had died and left her a widow. And she talked about her daughter, such a wonderful girl, and she didn't have a boyfriend yet. There were plenty of boys interested, but she hadn't found the right one yet, she didn't have a "steady." Maybe Mrs. Berger would get married herself, and why not? But she didn't want her daughter to have a stepfather. She wanted her daughter to get married before she did.

Mrs. Zalkin's pleasure was ruined. She didn't try to hide her frustration from Mrs. Berger, and Mrs. Berger retorted that the kitchen was hers as much as it was Mrs. Zalkin's. She pays rent, too, and she has every right to sit in the kitchen. If she wants company to herself, she should invite them into her own room. Anyway, Mrs. Berger's room is cold, and it's warm in the kitchen. So she'll sit here, and just try to stop her!

As for the cold room, that caused problems, too. Mrs. Berger was constantly tapping on the radiator to tell Mrs. Sher to come and see that there was no steam. After each complaint, Mrs. Sher went down into the boiler room to throw a few more coals in the boiler. She was angry. Who did Mrs. Berger think she was, just tapping on the radiator like that? Mrs. Sher had warned her, after all, that the room was hard to heat, and had lowered the rent for her because of it. And now Mrs. Berger was complaining about the heat!

Things were not good. The neighbors were constantly fighting over the kitchen or the bathroom. All that remained was to wait and see how the summer would be and who would stay or move.

Summer arrived. Mrs. Berger had settled into her room, kitchen, and porch, and she would not think of moving out over the summer and finding somewhere else to stay. But she waited to broach the topic with her landlady to see if things would calm down. She would just wait it out. She threw hints here and there, saying that she hadn't frozen all winter for nothing. At least she could get a summer out of it. She would especially enjoy the porch over the summer. Not just for her, but for her daughter, too. The daughter could take up with a boy in fine fashion. Boys like to sit with girls on porches on summer evenings.

She dropped these hints but didn't talk business in any definite terms, although she did mention to Mrs. Sher that, seeing as she had spent all winter living there, it would be appropriate for the landlady to lower her rent by ten or twenty dollars over the summer . . .

Mrs. Sher was not in any hurry to make arrangements with Mrs. Berger to see that she would stay for the summer. When she had an opportunity to rent the room to a single person living alone, some-one who wouldn't make much use of the kitchen and who wouldn't require as much gas, Mrs. Sher went ahead and rented it.

When Mrs. Berger found out she protested to Mrs. Sher, "How can this be? We're people, after all! How could you do this to us?" Then she went on about how she had frozen all winter, only to be thrown out in the summer.

Mrs. Sher said that no one was throwing her out. She would have plenty of time to find a new place to live. There are plenty of rooms for rent. Why pretend it's such a tragedy?

Instead of going out to look for a new room, Mrs. Berger, who was very clever, lay in bed at night and banged on the wall to her neighbor. She reminded her that she had done everything she could for Mrs. Zalkin when she was in trouble, and now she's in trouble herself! Her teeth are chattering, she's shivering, she has a fever, she's at death's doorstep!

Mrs. Zalkin couldn't contain her laughter. She knew it was a trick. She was thrilled that she'd soon be rid of this pain in her side. She called out, pretending to comfort her neighbor, "Don't worry, nothing will happen to you."

And nothing did happen. But Mrs. Berger refused to move, for days on end. She didn't want to go out to look for a room in the rain. She had time, it wasn't an emergency. Let whoever it was who was honing in on her territory wait a while. If she knew who it was, she'd give her a piece of her mind. But she didn't.

The day the new woman was supposed to move in arrived, and Mrs. Berger had not yet found a new room. Mrs. Sher had to ask the new woman to wait another day.

The new woman protested. Mrs. Sher appealed to Mrs. Berger with kind words and stern ones, insisting that she vacate the room. Mrs. Berger made a fuss. "Go ahead and throw me out into the street! Let everyone see what kind of a woman you are! Let them see how a fine upstanding lady conducts herself!"

But Mrs. Sher did not throw her out. Instead, she temporarily rented Mrs. Berger a room in the attic to stay in with her daughter until she found somewhere else to stay.

Seven weeks went by, and Mrs. Berger was still living in the attic room and using the kitchen and bathroom below. Mrs. Zalkin and the new occupant protested that she didn't belong in their kitchen or bathroom, but Mrs. Berger didn't care. She did what she wanted, and when they complained she asked, How dare intellectual, socialist, communist women like them go after a quiet, innocent woman, a widow, who had no one to stand up for her? Has respectful behavior entirely gone out the window? Has the world descended into lawlessness? What do they care if she uses the kitchen to make herself something to eat? It's ugly to behave this way, so petty, so base and brutal, toward a weak woman, at the time of her "deportation." Anyway, someday they might find themselves in the same circumstances. Things might not always go well for them. So they should have compassion for her—we're still people, after all.

This is what Mrs. Berger said, and it seems this is what she'll go on saying all summer.

From the Same *Yikhes*

Forverts, *September 18, 1934*

When the wealthy Robert Gold fell in love with the poor Lower East Side girl Lilly Sher, he didn't hesitate even for a moment to consider her *yikhes*.

He was enraptured by Lilly's chestnut-brown locks, her sky-blue eyes, her wine-red lips, her dimples and beauty marks. From the first time he saw her, he felt that he couldn't live without her. Both of them were enveloped in the flames of a passionate love.

Their meeting was unintentional. They came upon each other at the entrance to a concert hall, when a gust of wind blew her hat off her head and he retrieved it for her. The first time they saw each other, they couldn't look away. He drove her home in his car after the concert, through the dense thicket of the East Side, where she lived with her parents behind a grocery store. She was ashamed to tell the elegant young man where her home was.

Since he kept wanting to see her again and never asked about her family, she decided not to say anything about it. He waited in his car and she would cheerfully approach him and ride around with him as though bewitched, intoxicated with love. It was a love on wheels! From time to time, Robert would park on a side street to embrace and kiss his Lilly, and then he would drive on.

They went on driving all the way to city hall, where they were married in secret. It was only after their wedding that they thought about their parents, and realized that their parents deserved to know about the clandestine wedding.

Lilly told Robert that her parents aren't rich, but they are very proud. Russian intellectuals, enlightened. They vote a straight socialist ticket, and although they run a business they consider themselves part of the working class. They had always hoped that she, their only daughter, would marry a union man, a leader of the worker's movement who gave speeches. But Lilly is not like them. She believes in marrying for love, even if her beloved is a capitalist.

Robert, the son of a capitalist, a ruthless Republican, found Lilly's description quite appealing. In the way she talked, she demonstrated a tendency toward his own class. He would have nothing to be ashamed of when he introduced her to his parents. She was just like them.

Lilly decided they should meet her parents in a downtown restaurant to introduce them to Robert. They could all eat a Jewish meal together.

Robert was very polite to his Lilly's parents. They appeared to be very simple but honorable people. They called him "Son" and gave him advice. They told him to rent rooms to live in, and to be a good husband to their daughter. It was better that they live independently, and not with her parents, like a proper couple. And as for food, there are so many poor families who could silence their hunger with the scraps that the rich people simply throw away. They, Lilly's parents, will provide groceries and even sometimes prepared foods, Jewish foods. The couple won't lack for anything.

Robert was very amused at his poor in-laws' conversation. He didn't understand everything they said. Their Yiddish was mixed with Russian and English. His parents spoke German and English.

Having successfully won over Lilly's parents, Robert promised to return and see them often, and made up his mind to tell his mother and father about his marriage to Lilly. He told Lilly ahead of time not to mention her parents' grocery store. He would say that her family used to be in the *wholesale* grocery business, but they gave it up and were now traveling in Europe. When they returned, his parents could invite them to their home to meet them.

Lilly had to tell her mother and father about all of this, so she could explain to them why they had to wait to meet his parents.

Robert's parents, who were very high-and-mighty about their German culture and the wealth they had accumulated in America, were not overly enthusiastic about their son's choice of marriage partner. They had acquaintances and friends whose daughters they had long had in mind for their Robert. And now, all of a sudden, he married a poor Lithuanian girl, an East Side girl, without much education and without a cent to her name. But there was nothing to be done, as he had already married her. They bit their lips and kept silent about it. And, eventually, they started to come around to their daughter-in-law. Slowly but surely. They welcomed her into their home to teach her, improve her manners, cultivate her taste for high culture, give her some time to get acquainted with better society.

Lilly acquiesced to everything Robert's parents asked of her. She was docile and obedient. She laughed about their pretentiousness behind their backs to her own parents, showing them how they ate, making fun of how they talked, their smiles. But to all appearances she was earnest and refined. Robert repaid her for this with kisses and presents. She was pleased.

Her parents wanted to come and see what her life was like, but Robert kept putting off inviting them. He pretended that they hadn't yet returned from their trip. As far as he was concerned, they were still in Europe.

At first Lilly's parents were amused by this "traveling in Europe" business. But as time went on it began to grate on them until they couldn't take it anymore. Their hearts yearned for their Khaye-Leye (as they called Lilly), but they couldn't go to see her! They had to wait until she deigned to descend from her high society and sneak away for a few minutes to see her humble parents. And she always came when they were busy. She rushed in and out like a stranger, like a customer. If this is what it meant to feel pride in your children, they didn't know what to call it.

"Whatever comes of it," Lilly's father finally said to her mother, "I don't intend to wait anymore for an invitation from our high-and-mighty in-laws. We'll go there ourselves! We'll bring a package of good foods that our Khaye-Leye loves to eat. Let her enjoy it. She's starving from their delicate, poorly prepared meals. She's dying for a piece of herring and a pickle. Last time she saw us she told us that she's bored of their delicacies. She needs something salty or sour, don't you think?"

Lilly's parents, laden with good food to drive away their Khaye-Leye's boredom, took the subway to the West Side.

The prosperous couple were at ease, sitting in their plush chairs, listening to the radio, when the telephone rang and the doorman at the switchboard told them that two individuals, a man and a woman, were asking to come up and see them. Should he let them in? They refused to tell him their names.

This sounded very suspicious. The prosperous couple exchanged worried glances. They were afraid to let just anyone into their home—who knew what kind of a person it could be? They turned off the radio so they could pay better attention to the telephone, and asked for details about the man and woman's appearances. Middle aged? Where did they come from? Oh, from the East Side? Well, then, who did they want to see? The young Mrs. Gold? What did they want from her? Who are they? Oh, the woman wants to say something. Alright, let her talk.

The woman didn't talk, she screamed into the telephone that somebody—two somebodies—had come to visit Lilly.

"Well, alright," Mrs. Gold relented. "Let them come up."

The visitors soon emerged. It was Lilly's parents themselves, full of pride and joy, bearing their package of treats.

They looked around the luxurious apartment with great curiosity. "It's so beautiful!" they cooed. "It takes your breath away! It's like they say, 'I'd sell the shirt off my back if it meant I could live like a prince.' Yes, expensive things are worth plenty of money!"

They quickly turned to Lilly and asked, "Well, daughter, can't you see how your parents have missed you?"

Lilly's mother held out the package to show her daughter all of the precious food she had brought her. The scents of the food intermingled and wafted over the opulent foyer: herring, pickles, borscht. Mrs. Gold's eyes watered and she found it hard to breathe.

Mr. Gold glared at his unusual in-laws over the rims of his lowered glasses. He shook his head and said, *"Ja, so, so!"*

With a playful smile, Lilly's mother answered, *"Azoy . . . So ist es, Lieber Herr!* And this is indeed how they look, and they don't *shprechen* any *Deutsch.* That's how it is in the United States. It's America, ya know. We're just as good as you are. We're not in Hitler's country, after all, so here at least you can acknowledge that you are a Jew like any other. Here, we couldn't care less about a family's pedigree. Our Lilly is just as precious to us as your son is to you. We didn't go out of our way to try to snag him for our family. They found each other and didn't ask anyone what they thought. Now they're both ours as much as they're yours. If you want to share the pride and pleasure of having children with us, then alright, we're in-laws. Neither better than the other—equal in-laws. But if you refuse to treat us well, we'll help ourselves. We won't cut ourselves off from our daughter just because of your high *yikhes.* You can yell at us all you want. It won't change a thing. We won't relent. Not anymore!"

All of the resentment Lilly's mother had built up over being separated from her daughter now poured out of her. Her husband told her, "That's enough," but she didn't stop. She didn't want to stop. She felt compelled to show these hoity-toity Germans how foolish their pretenses were. It all meant nothing!

How dare they lord themselves over other people. Who gave them the right? Wasn't it enough that Jews are beaten down by others, without them bullying their own kind? It was so ugly, so low! It's long past time that they come to see that we're all equal, with the same *yikhes.*

Whether it was her speech or their desire for her to stop talking, something convinced the prosperous couple to welcome their East Side in-laws as guests and invite them to come often to visit them. There was no need, though, to bring packages. They even offered their in-laws a ride home in their spacious automobile.

Overjoyed at their triumph over their wealthy in-laws, the poor East Side couple went home. And the vanquished prosperous couple sank into their plush chairs and sat for a while, thinking about the words that their poor in-law had laid into them. Sharp, piercing words. All people have the same *yikhes*. We're all the same.

A Clever Mother

Forverts, *October 18, 1934*

The mother felt a growing disquiet about her newly married daughter's family life. Her worry that her daughter wouldn't get along with her mother-in-law had not been unfounded. Every time her daughter came to her to unburden herself about her mother-in-law, she decided anew that she had to do something about it.

As in love as her daughter was with her husband, she had as much loathing for her mother-in-law. She spoke of her husband's mother not only as a bad mother-in-law, but also as dangerous competition for her husband's love.

And the daughter had complaints about her own mother as well—for being convinced from the start that she should not set up her own household, but should live with her mother-in-law. Her own mother should have known that no good would come of it. Young people and old people never agree. They are from two different worlds. It would be like mixing fire and water. Mothers should know such things better than their children. But mothers today, her daughter sighed bitterly, only care about what is best for themselves. They're concerned about their own "privacy" but don't care a whit about their children's. Let the children bother their own heads about it!

Hearing her daughter say such things made the mother feel ill. But she was a mother and had to forgive her daughter for what she said. She felt that her daughter wasn't saying it for her own pleasure; she was speaking out of pain. Hers was the wounded pride of a woman in love whose lover refuses to budge. The mother had to admit that no matter how good a couple has it living with parents, they would always be better off living separately. It seemed, and her daughter's comments even bore this out, that the mother-in-law was a good woman, but who can know what goes on in someone else's heart? The mother would have to speak to her daughter's mother-in-law herself.

In order to know how to speak to her daughter's mother-in-law, she decided to ask her daughter for more details about her behavior.

"What does she ask of you? Where does all this unpleasantness come from?"

"What do we fight about?" her daughter scoffed. "Everything. Everything and nothing. Whenever I tune the radio to what I like, she gets annoyed."

"But she doesn't change the station?"

"Of course she does. It's her radio, and she wants it tuned to what she likes. Everything is hers, everything! And as long as she lives she won't release her hold on what's hers! Oh, how I hate her!"

"Does *he* know about it?" asked the mother.

"Who, my Izzy? Of course he knows, but he pretends not to notice. After all, she's his mother."

"She is his mother, and I think you'd do well, daughter, to remember that."

"I remember it all too well! It's not easy to forget. She's forever reminding me. I'll leave and never come back . . ."

"God forbid!" cried her mother, aghast.

"I already did!" said her daughter, casting a defiant look around the room.

"You already did? What do you mean by that? Tell me, what happened between the two of you?"

"Oh, leave me alone with your questions!" the daughter cried. "What do you want from me? You're no better than *she* is. You're even worse! You're not acting like a mother, you're acting like a detective!"

"If you want me to do something about it, you have to tell me everything."

"Tell you everything! You wouldn't believe me anyway . . ."

"I'll believe you. Just tell me the truth. Did you have a fight?"

"Yes," the daughter responded curtly.

"Why? What did you fight over?"

"It was about his mother, that snake, that witch! It's always about her! She's ruining my happiness, she's poisoning my life! He'll have to choose—me or her."

"Did you say that to him?" the mother asked.

"Yes, that's what I said. And that's not all . . ."

"What else?"

"I'll tell you what else! I told him to choose *her*!" cried the daughter defiantly.

"When?"

"Yesterday."

"At night?"

"Yes! That's the only time I have to detail for him all the ways she's insulted me during the day . . ." The daughter sulked.

"I didn't realize you let it get this far." The mother looked at her daughter and shook her head. "You drove him away. You thought he would give up his mother for you. That's a mistake, daughter. A mother isn't something you give up so easily. It's easier to get a new wife than a new mother. You took things too far. Go home and make up with him. Be a good wife. Don't hold back the pleasure you can give to him. You're not the only woman in the world. There are plenty of others like you, and younger and prettier women to boot. If he doesn't know that himself, his mother will tell him so, soon enough, if she hasn't already. Go home as soon as you can."

"I won't go. I'd rather die!"

"If you won't go to him then ask him to come here so you can speak to him," the mother instructed.

"I don't want to talk to him after he hurt me so. He left me alone all night."

"Do you have a right to be upset? You drove him away," the mother chided.

"If he loved me the way he used to, he wouldn't have let me drive him away. He would beg me to let him stay," insisted the daughter.

"Is that the kind of fool you want him to be? You want him to let you treat him no better than a rag? You want him to grovel? If that's how he used to act when you were newlyweds, it's time he started acting with some sense. Now you'll know better than to drive him away from you. He taught you a lesson."

"If it weren't for his mother, none of this would have happened," the daughter grumbled.

"Even if that's true, what would you have him do with his mother? Kill her?"

"Tell her to go away and leave me alone! I can't live in the same house as her. I hate her! I wish she were dead!" the daughter shouted.

"But you love him? You want him to live?"

"He is my husband. He swore he would love me forever. He . . . he . . ." She trailed off and burst into tears.

The mother contemplated her daughter disappointedly and then her hands almost mechanically reached for the telephone. She called her son-in-law and, forgoing all pleasantries, told him right away that his young wife was at her house and wanted to see him. She's crying so hard she could melt a stone, the mother told him. No matter how much the mother asks what the matter is, the daughter won't say. All she does is cry out, "Izzy, my Izzy!" She's crying her eyes out. Her mother can't do anything for her. The mother suspects there might be . . . other circumstances . . . but she can't talk to him about that on the telephone. He'd better come over. She can't talk anymore. She has to go see how her daughter is doing. Maybe she should call a doctor . . . or maybe she'll just wait for her son-in-law to come.

He told her to wait. He would be right there.

The daughter's teary eyes lit up as she looked up at her mother. "He's coming! He's sorry for what he did to me?"

"What *he* did to *you*?" her mother scolded her. "You think I called him to ask him to give in to your whims? I didn't even tell him that I know that you drove him away. It would be better for him not to know. Go ahead, my clever daughter, lie on the bed and moan, sigh, say that your heart is aching. Powder your face so you look pale and he won't guess that he's being set up and will forget what happened last night and forgive you for it. And you shouldn't say a single word against his mother. You should thank her for bearing and raising such a fine son for you. You'll crow over *your* son someday if you have a son who's as good to you. Now go and do what I say!"

"Alright! Stop bossing me around!" her daughter said exasperatedly. "I'll go."

With a worried expression, the mother led her son-in-law into her daughter's room.

Her daughter lay on the bed, pale and suffering, and her lips mouthed his name deliriously. One pale, weak hand seemed to be searching for him. Her forehead was covered with a white cloth. She was a living picture of a martyr.

"Shhh . . ." The mother signaled to the son-in-law without moving from her place. "Let's leave her alone for a while until she comes to herself."

"What's the matter?" the son-in-law asked, worried.

"I can't say for sure, but I think there is something going on with her. It's the start of something, son, and soon I'll be saying a mazel tov to you. As long as it . . . goes well. She's a poor, nervous girl. She's afraid she'll get sick and that you'll feel repulsed by it. She's more worried about you than about herself. And as for your mother—my daughter doesn't want to feel like she's falling behind in your affections. You know how young wives are, my son. And it's hard for women like me and your mother to live with the new generation. Do you want my advice? Take a look at a new house or a two or even one room apartment."

The son-in-law looked at his mother-in-law suspiciously. "Did she tell you want happened last night?"

"No," said the mother innocently. "What happened?"

"Well, it's all right. It's in the past. Let's worry about the present. I want to go in and see her."

"Go to her, my son, and I'll go to the kitchen to make something to eat."

Saying this, she ushered him through the door and closed it behind them. He approached the bed and bent over his teary-eyed wife. "Izzy, my Izzy, my darling . . ." she pleaded. "Sweetheart, where are you?"

"I'm here," he said, bending toward her. "What's wrong, darling?"

A happy smile played upon her lips. Her arms reached out to him and encircled his neck. The mother left the bedroom and closed the door after her.

The mother smiled, pleased that she had sent for him and brought them together. She went to the kitchen to prepare the children's favorite foods so that when they came into the dining room, having made up and become friends once again, they'd find a table laden with good food.

In the meantime, she waited. She had to reheat their favorite foods more than once as they cooled while she waited. Soon, she ran out of patience for warming food. She was about to knock on the door when they emerged, smiling embarrassedly. Seeing the good food on the table, they took to it like a swarm of hungry locusts.

The young wife's face shone with joy and triumph. The mother watched her, pleased that the trouble ended so quickly. One less worry to bear. But in her heart, the experienced mother felt that it was only temporary, that the problems would return. She felt that the two would be torn apart again, and that her daughter and mother-in-law would never get along.

Would Izzy stick with her daughter? She doubted it. But at least for the moment she could stop worrying.

Old Sarah

Forverts, *July 4, 1937*

The whole way from her home to the old age home, Old Sarah couldn't stop crying. Her daughter and grandson, who drove her in their automobile, exchanged worried glances and shared a heavy silence. It pained the daughter to see her mother wipe her old, weepy eyes. But there was nothing she could do to help. She couldn't keep her mother in her house, and neither could her brothers or sisters. She needed someone to take care of her and help her like a child. She couldn't see when she walked and she might fall. She couldn't hear and she was always asking what this or that person had said. When she came to visit, she would lose track of the conversation and say things that people nowadays wouldn't say. When it started to get late at night, she told the girls, her granddaughters (when they stayed up late with boys): "It's not healthy to stay up so late . . ." The young people couldn't stand it. They wanted to stay up as late as they pleased. She should be in an old age home, they said.

The daughter driving her mother to the old age home offered encouragement, saying that her mother would be happier there. She'd have company. She'd like it so much there that she wouldn't want to leave. And if she didn't like it, then the daughter would take her back home . . . But it'd be good for her there. "You'll see," she said. The director of the home had promised to take "special care" of her. She wasn't a charity case, after all. The cost was closer to a hotel than a boardinghouse. And she could have some money all to herself, too, in case she wanted to buy something, or go see a movie. They had parties in the home. They took photographs of the oldest residents, and everyone celebrated them for their long lives.

The daughter told her mother all this, but the cheerful talk only made matters worse. The old lady felt that she was no longer of any use to her children, that they like her better when she's somewhere far away. She was only in their way. They wanted to be rid of her, so they were putting her in an old age home. And it was all because of the money that her husband had left her. Her second husband. The first one, the father of all of her children, had died years ago and left her a widow. For years she was with her children, because her children couldn't get on without her. She helped them raise their children. She was everyone's servant. She never had a moment to herself. But then a widower showed up with his own house, with a store and money in the bank and married children, who needed a woman to run his household. She asked her children what to do and they said that it wasn't such a bad idea to have her own house in her old age. They wouldn't stand in the way of her living her own life.

So she left to run her own household and be a servant to the old man and his grown children. Truth be told, he didn't know what to do with her, and the children were respectful to her. But it was hard for her to work, to cook and bake and clean for a house full of people with large appetites. And she still had to do things for her own children from time to time. They often came to visit her, she wasn't far away. When they were with her they could eat to their heart's content. Yes, they usually brought their own provisions: fish or chicken, but she had to cook it for them. She made them noodles, farfel, cabbage, pickles, and cherry brandy. They couldn't make it as well as she did, so they let her do it.

And she was happy that her children needed her. That she could do something for them. Her husband was pleased, too. He was good to her children, he gave presents to her grandchildren. He was happy that they called him "Uncle" and "Grandpa" and came to visit often.

He was a good man. A kind man. But his age, and his years of hard work, took a toll on his health. Sarah became his nursemaid.

Because she attended to him, he continued on for a long time, a glimmer of his former self. She simply wouldn't allow him to die. She didn't want to be a widow again.

But, in the end, all her desires for him to go on living were of no use. He died. He left a will: a sum of several thousand dollars, from which his wife, Sarah, could draw however much she needed to live on for as long as she would live.

Everyone said it was a generous will. Even Sarah's children said so, even though they would have been more pleased if she had received several thousand dollars all at once and allowed them to invest it in their businesses. But since that might have caused conflict between the children, maybe it was better this way.

The house and the business that the husband left behind went to his children. Sarah could continue to manage the household for them, as she had before, if she wanted to. But she didn't have the energy for that anymore and decided to live out the rest of her life alone, somewhere in a room in one of her children's homes.

She went to live with one child after another, and nothing worked out. The family consulted with one another and decided that the best place for her would be an old age home. So here she was, on the way to the home, with tears streaming down her cheeks. She was embarrassed about her tears. But she couldn't help it, the tears kept on falling of their own accord.

As soon as the daughter and grandson said goodbye to her, promising to visit often, and drove away, the curious residents of the old age home gathered around the newest among them to determine what sort of person she was and to tell her all she needed to know about the institution.

One of the old ladies, a domineering woman, was quite the leading lady. She was grand. All the others were afraid of her sharp tongue. They gossiped that she was looking for a husband. She was always getting gussied up. Her beak-like nose and thin lips, with which she grimaced one way and another, seemed to be laughing and composed at the same time.

She was the first one to approach the new woman, Sarah, and introduce herself.

"I'm Feyge. But most people call me Feygele. What's your name?"

"Sarah."

"You're dressed very nicely, Sarah," Feyge said, touching Sarah's dress with her bony fingers. "That's a fine satin, an expensive one. Is it a new dress?"

"Yes, it's new." Sarah sighed.

"It's a shame to wear a dress like that on an average day like today. You should save it for Shabes and holidays."

"I have better dresses."

"Really! Do you hear, ladies? She has even better dresses. She must have come with a whole trousseau. A wardrobe. Everything that a new husband would want her to have . . ."

Several of the toothless old ladies laughed. "Feygele, you have competition!"

Feyge laughed with them. "Well, I'm not afraid. None of my admirers will defect." She turned to Sarah. "And what's the matter with your eyes?"

"I've been crying."

"Crying? That's nothing. I cried the first few days, too. It's the same with all the women. It'll pass. Once you get to know all the other guests in the hotel, you'll find yourself with plenty to laugh about. Do you see that beautiful woman? She's beautiful, we can agree on that now, but imagine what she used to be like. Once, she was at a ball, and can you guess who she danced with, my dear Sarah? With the governor himself! Yes, she did! Nowadays sometimes she picks up a broom or a mop and dances with it, imagining that the mop is the governor. So that's our dancer . . ."

Then she turned to the dancer and said, "Show us, Masha my dear, how you used to dance with the governor . . . This is a new one. She doesn't know her way around. Let's show her who she'll be sharing her meals with . . ."

"Later," the dancer said, "when she asks me herself. For now, Feygele, show her what you can do. Give her a speech about how you stay looking young when you're as old as you are."

"There are some women here who are older than I am . . . I don't even know which of the two of us is older. How old are you, Sarah? May you live to one hundred twenty." Feygele asked, bending her beak-like nose in Sarah's direction.

"I don't know . . ." said old Sarah embarrassedly, not wanting to tell them the truth, but not wanting to lie. "I've lost track."

"How clever you are!" cried Feyge delightedly. "She's perfect! Sarah, I don't want to be a bookkeeper, I take every day as a gift from God. Each day, each year is a gift. Who needs to count them? Those that have passed are already gone, so why keep track? What matters is those that are yet to come! And God is a father, a good father. Whatever we deserve, he'll give to us!"

When her children came to visit their mother the following week, women flocked to them to tell them all of their mother's witticisms. They praised her to the high heavens: she is so good, and clever, and quiet, and refined! And she's always dressed so nicely, like a real lady, and she tells such good stories. They're so grateful that she has come to live with them.

"So, mother, what do you say now?" asked the daughter who had brought her to the old age home.

"What can I say?" the old lady answered with a lonesome smile. "I passed the test. Things are going well for me. The old ladies like me . . ."

The Old Man Ran Away

Forverts, *August 9, 1937*

A troubled man, all alone after the death of his wife, Sholem moved from his own little home to live in a room in his eldest daughter's house.

"Tate," his oldest daughter had said to him, "when you live with me you won't want for anything. You'll be perfectly at home."

And his son-in-law added, "Shver, I'm very happy that we are together. Now I'll have someone to talk to. These days the children are never at home and most of the time I'm alone and the house feels empty. It'll be homier when we're together. When we have the time, we'll play checkers, chess, or cards. Just as long as you don't pummel me every time, Shver! Take pity on me and let me win every now and then . . ."

Sholem smiled good-naturedly and nodded his head. He appropriately acknowledged how warmly his children received him. Especially his son-in-law, more than anyone else. His eldest son-in-law, his best son-in-law, who also happened to be the poorest one. The son-in-law knew that Sholem had several hundred dollars in the bank, but he'd never even so much as hinted that he should share any of it with him.

The old man didn't want to live with his children like a beggar or a castaway. He was a proud man, and sensitive. He wanted to know that he could stand on his own two feet. So he didn't want to part with his several hundred dollars. He earned interest on them that was enough for his small expenditures. His children wouldn't ask for rent, nor would they ask him to pay for food. Anyway, he earned his keep in helping his daughter around the house.

He didn't want to move out of his house. Whatever he had was good enough. A cup of coffee with bread and butter, a tomato, and a bowl of kasha was enough for a meal. He looked younger than his age. He was almost eighty, but no one would guess he was more than seventy. He moved with ease. He made frequent jokes and laughed. But at night when no one was there to see or hear he quietly groaned. His arms cramped, his legs ached. He felt nauseous and it took all of his strength to get out of bed the several times a night he needed to get up. It was then that he wished he had someone lying next to him who would take care of him. It was then that he longed for his departed wife until his eyes filled with tears. She was such a loyal, devoted wife! She would sacrifice anything to make him happy. Nothing was too difficult, there was nothing she wouldn't do. But she couldn't stay with him, she passed away. She surrendered her soul to God.

Now he lived alone in a room in a house full of sound sleepers.

He didn't begrudge them their restful sleep, but all the same he was plagued with the thought that if, God forbid, he didn't feel well in the middle of the night, not a single member of the family would be there to help him. All he could do was hope that that terrible hour would never come. He could make himself crazy thinking this way . . . But, after all, he's nothing but a man, and an old man at that.

As his thoughts continued through the sleepless nights and wakeful days, Sholem had an idea. Since he believed in taking action, he made a decision to act on it right away.

Sholem's children were very surprised and upset when they didn't find their father in his room, and when the whole day passed and he didn't come home they asked, "What could have happened to him? He always tells us where he's going and how long he'll be gone. But this time he snuck out, like he's running away!"

"Maybe he couldn't stand doing all of those womanly chores around the house," the man's good son-in-law said to his daughter. "You forced him to be a servant."

"That's not true!" the daughter exclaimed. "I always let him do whatever he wanted. He's not someone who can stand just sitting without something to keep his hands occupied. He begged me to give him something to do! He wanted to help."

The son-in-law switched from serious to joking. "Maybe he left to get married?"

"Oh, go on with you! The things you say!"

"It's exactly the kind of thing that a fellow like him could do."

"Aren't you forgetting how old he is?"

"I remember, but maybe he forgot. He looks like a sturdy man. He could pass for younger and find himself a little wife."

"You'd better be quiet. He'd never do something like that!"

"As far as we know, maybe he's already done it."

"No, he wouldn't dishonor my mother's memory that way."

"How long can a person live with a memory?"

When they heard that the "old man," their "grandpa," was missing, the grandchildren all chimed in to tell their father their guesses about his whereabouts.

"Sure. That's the thing! But if . . . if . . . I sure hope he hasn't been run over . . ."

When the daughter and son-in-law told the rest of the old man's children that he had disappeared, they all came running to find out the whens and hows of it. They talked about going to the police or placing a personal ad in the papers. This isn't something you can just let go!

Finally, late, late at night, when they had lost all hope that they would see him, Sholem returned to their home.

The children fell upon him with questions. "Tate, where were you? Tate, what happened to you? Tate, how do you feel? Shver, be reasonable. How can you go off like that from early in the morning until late at night, without even telling us where you were?"

The old man threw his hands up and smiled to them in a new way. Just give him a moment and he'll answer. Just stop asking so many questions. It's good that they're all here. He has something to say to them.

They all stopped talking and listened to him. They were ready to hear anything he had to say.

"Children," the old man said, stroking his beard as though he was daydreaming. "I did something tonight that you might not forgive me for . . . But it's already done!"

"He got married!" the children seemed to say to one another without words as they met each other's eyes. The good son-in-law said jokingly, "Shver, mazel tov! May you be very happy together!"

"Yes, may we live with happiness," answered the father-in-law.

"Tate, you didn't—"

"—get married!" one of his sons completed her sentence.

"Married. Heh, heh . . ."

And seeing how everyone was looking at him with such urgency, waiting for an answer, he sighed and decided to keep it short.

"No, such a thing was far from my thoughts. I didn't get married. But I'm moving out."

"Where are you going?"

"I registered myself to live in an old age home. I will be able to live out my remaining years there with people like me. And don't tell me that I shouldn't do it. I've already paid for it and I am going there. Let's part on good terms. And if you want to see me, you can come and visit. You're invited. Of course, come often! Let them all see what good, fine children I have. Give me something to boast about."

Only a few months after he left, Sholem returned. He looked at his daughter and son-in-law like a shame-faced schoolboy and attempted to speak several times but stopped himself.

His good son-in-law took him to the side and asked, "Shver, you have something to say, don't you? You can tell me. What's wrong? Why do you look so—"

"Humiliated?" the old man supplied with a dispirited laugh. "That's right. I humiliated myself. I'm embarrassed even to tell you the story . . ."

"Go ahead and tell me, Shver. I can keep a secret. I won't tell anyone."

"It's a secret I can't hide. Everyone will know it soon enough. I ran away from the old age home."

"How? Why?"

The old man explained: "At first, when I met all the people living there, life seemed . . . interesting. I thought I had it good there. People respected me, especially because I had registered myself to live there instead of waiting for my children to bring me there. I spent my days with others, sitting at the table or in the courtyard. I sat on benches and talked about this and that. And at night if I needed anything, all I needed to do was ring a bell and a caretaker came. If I wasn't feeling well, there was a doctor on the premises. Everything seemed good there. I couldn't ask for more. But one thing rattled me."

"What was it?"

"It was this—one day I was talking to someone about all sorts of things. We had more to talk about and decided to continue our conversation the next day . . ."

". . . and?"

"The next day when I went looking for him, I couldn't find him. I asked one person and then another where he was. They all looked at me strangely and didn't answer. I told them that I wanted to consult him about a quotation from a book. Someone told me that I should just take a look in the book for myself, and that I should find another friend. I asked: 'Why? How?' And the answer was simply: here today, gone tomorrow . . .

"And so, that's how it is—often, too often, every now and then, someone passes away. You just saw him, you spoke with him, and then, suddenly, he's gone. You look at everyone, and at yourself, and ask, '*Nu*, which one of us will be gone tomorrow?' And then you find yourself caught up in this fear. I know that no one lives forever. But no one wants to be constantly reminded of death. It ruins your life.

I went there to *live* out my remaining years, not *die* them out. And on top of all that, I missed my children and grandchildren. So I ran away. I didn't even tell them why. Some of them will assume that I passed away . . . Let them think so! As long as *I* know that I'm alive, and the people near me are all in good health.

"Now do you understand why I ran away?" Sholem asked his good son-in-law.

"Do I understand?" the good son-in-law responded gleefully. "Hmm . . . Since you told me that you already paid the admission fees, I didn't say anything to you before. But I am very pleased that you came back."

A Kosher Swimming Pool
(*A Scene in Coney Island*)

Forverts, *August 5, 1930*

The four girls were busy cleaning the rooms of their summer apartment when an old man with a beard and *peyes* knocked at their door. One of the girls came to the door.

"Yes?" she asked.

The man bent his head toward her as he took out a pamphlet and readied himself to write out a bill for her. "How much can you afford?" he inquired courteously.

He spoke in Yiddish and she more or less understood him. She attempted to speak the few bungled words of Yiddish that she knew.

"*Vos dos?*" she asked.

"I'm collecting money to support the Mikve Levones Yisroel," he replied in Yiddish.

He understood that his language was too elevated for her, he tried to make it simpler. "It's for a *mikve* . . . where Jewish women go. Right here in Coney Island."

The girl responded in English, "You mean a place where . . ."

"Yes, where they go . . ."

They each spoke in broken words, neither understanding the other. The girl called to her friend, who she thought might know more than she did.

"Oh!" the other, more knowledgeable girl cried. "He's talking about a swimming pool, see, a *kosher* swimming pool!"

"A kosher swimming pool? Gee!"

A third girl approached, asking, "What's the matter?"

When they told her, she waved her hand dismissively. "Who needs it? We don't go to the pool. What use would we have for a *kosher* pool? We go to the beach, that's all." She turned to the man and said, in a hodgepodge of English and broken Yiddish, "Sorry, Mister, but you know *ir'et nit getrofn* the right customers."

"What does 'right' have to do with it?" The man smirked. "You're Jewish daughters . . ."

"*Vos* should we care whose daughters we are when we go to take a swim? We don't need a rabbi to tell us how to do it. Any beach, or any pool, is kosher enough for us, *iznt'it*?"

The man pleaded with the girls submissively. "It's only a *kvarter* a *tiket*," he begged. "And for you, it can be ten cents. A bargain."

"Say!" the third girl called to the fourth in English, "Come here—you're a Zionist, so you must know what he wants from us. Do you think we need a kosher pool?"

"No, I don't think so," the girl answered. She didn't feel comfortable getting close to the man to turn him away herself, especially because he was peddling something she didn't believe in. But the other three girls insisted. After all, she's the Zionist, she's the one who knows all about Jewish things. She should be the one to settle with the old man about the kosher pool. They didn't know what to say to him.

Unwillingly, she approached the man. She told him that they were only girls and they didn't want anything to do with religious institutions.

"But," the man argued, "you can still help the *institushun*. You're girls now, but someday, God willing, you'll get married and you'll have to go to the *mikve* yourself . . . right? Perhaps! And even if you don't go yourself, you could still help others who do go. After all, it's a Jewish thing to do, and you're Jewish girls . . ."

"We're not *religious* Jewish girls, and we don't believe in that sort of thing."

"But other girls believe in it."

"Then let other girls pay for it."

"They don't have the money!"

"That's not our fault . . ."

"Say, Mister! Why don't you trade in boys instead? Honest, I mean it! We're four girls and we want boys, see? Regular guys who will go with us to city hall, or even to a rabbi . . . If you can get us that, we'll pay for your kosher pool, or whatever else you want!"

Another girl added, "That's it! Boys! That's the word! Become a matchmaker! A *shadkhn*—that would be a good business!"

The fourth girl shook her head embarrassedly and watched the man regretfully as he trod away with tired old steps, looking for better Jewish girls for his "kosher pool."

The *Shadkhn*

Forverts, *February 14, 1934*

The four girls who had spent the summer together in Coney Island stayed there for the winter as well. And the same old man who had come to them as soon as they moved in over the summer to ask them to give a contribution to support a "kosher pool" visited them again at the end of winter.

One of the girls came to the door, and when she saw the old man there smiling familiarly at her, she said, "Yes?"

"Don't you remember me?" asked the man, both surprised and insulted.

"No. *Ver* . . . Who are you?"

"I'm the same man who came to see you early this summer."

"What did you say?" asked the girl, and he could see that she didn't have the patience to stand there and talk to him much longer.

"We spoke about a Mikve Levones Yisroel, or, as you called it, a kosher swimming pool."

"Well . . . ?"

"You must remember! Go ask the other girls—I'd like to see them, too."

"Sir, what do you need?" the girl asked the old man, shaking her head at him. "What do you want from the other girls?"

"I want to say something to them. I have something to ask them."

"Ask me, just the same."

"Alright," said the Jew with a tentative smile. "I had planned to start with the oldest girl, but I can do it this way, too."

"Oh, I see. You're a *shadkhn*!"

"Yes," agreed the man.

"Why didn't you say so? *Farvos hostu nit gezogt azoy?*" The girl laughed and called out to the others, "Say, girls, come here!"

Three girls in pajamas with cigarettes between their fingers, nails painted with blood-red polish, emerged from the next room.

"What's the matter?"

"It's a *shadkhn*!" the girl who had called them cried in a playful, sing-songy voice. "He came to help all of us."

"You said something about a *shidukh* . . . A party . . ." the man added.

"That's it!" cried the girl. "You remember the man who came here asking us for a donation to a kosher swimming pool? Well, this is him! The very same!"

"Do you remember what you said to me?" asked the man. "I thought about it and decided that you were right. So instead of asking you for money for a *mikve* . . ."

"A kosher swimming pool," the girl reminded her friends.

"Yes, that's it," the man agreed. "I decided it would be better to act as a *shadkhn* and come to you to talk about *shidukhim*. Such fine girls like you shouldn't sit here like you do . . . I mean . . . it's time you . . . it's better to do these things earlier. It's always better to do it sooner—"

The eldest girl interrupted him. "Why are you so shy about it? Have a seat! When you're sitting down you'll find it easier to tell us what . . ."

The man sat down and the girls stood around him. They winked at each other over his head and started to pepper him with questions about the grooms he had come to suggest to them. Were they American boys? Good sports? They weren't kikes, were they, or rabbis? No? Were they professionals? Did they have cars? Gee! How old were they? Were there enough that the girls could choose from among them?

"One at a time, girls! One at a time!" the man begged. "You're all talking at once."

.

"Well, alright." The girls sat down around him and let their ciga-rettes dangle from their painted lips. "Let him talk. He's got the goods! He's got it all written down in a notebook. No pictures? Too bad!"

The old man nearsightedly peered into his address book. He could hardly see anything. The smoke from the girl's cigarettes made his eyes water and crept into his throat. He started to cough. He felt a strange heat from being in the room with these girls. They were sitting so close to him it made him dizzy. It felt like hammers were pounding against his head. He wanted to wave away the smoke and the heat with his arms. He wanted to say something but couldn't. He barely managed to say one word: "Water . . ."

"Gee!" cried one of the girls. "He looks like he's going to faint! Get some water! This is some luck, when a *shadkhn* comes to call and faints!"

They handed him a glass of water. His hands trembled so much that he spilled more of the water than he drank. He poured some water on himself and that only made him shiver more. He felt hot and cold at the same time.

"How are you feeling?" asked the youngest girl anxiously. "Any better? Are you ready to get down to business?"

"Don't bother him!" said another girl, adjusting her pajama bot-toms. "Leave him alone."

"He needs something warm to drink," fussed the eldest girl. "Should we give him some tea or coffee? Something warm?"

The man nodded obediently. He felt more comfortable with the girls fussing over him. He could take his time, and then he could get to the business. He had a job to do with his address book! He could recite the fine qualities of each of the grooms by heart. And if they weren't satisfied, he could come back some other time to offer them more options.

The hot tea they served him was good. A bit too hot, but good. He blew on it, sipped it slowly, and enjoyed it.

He was ready to start talking business, but more and more girls kept coming into the room. They were all dressed for a pajama party. Girls in trousers, dressed up like boys. They affectionately patted each other's shoulders and legs, smoked, and spoke to each other using words he didn't understand. The newly arriving girls looked down at him insolently. Such brazen girls, laughing at him. He was embarrassed to speak in front of them about the business. He was afraid to finish drinking his tea. They were just waiting for him to finish before they would turn to him again, with renewed energy, to ask him to talk. He looked longingly at the door through which he'd first entered their apartment.

"Well, do you feel better now?" the youngest of the girls asked again.

"Much better, thank you. You've been very kind."

"Oh, that's all right. Do you want to talk business?"

"Maybe we should leave it for another time? You have company, no?"

"Oh, no! It's more fun this way!"

"Fun?" That's what he was afraid of. Fun! He was trying to make a living, and they were in it for fun! They thought they'd caught themselves a poor little Jew and they could make a fool out of him. Well, let them think what they wanted. He'd leave but try to do it politely. He didn't want to pick a fight with them. Who knows, maybe he'd even find that one of them might be interested in what he had to say. He would tell them about the prospective grooms, but first he would insist that they get rid of the trousers and put on skirts, like God intended. And they should stop smoking like chimneys. Jewish girls who wanted *shidukhim* shouldn't behave that way.

He sipped the hot tea, wiped the sweat from his brow, and stood up to leave.

The girls crowded around him asking why he didn't talk to them about his business.

"I'll do it tomorrow," he said.

"Why not today? Why not now?"

"Because . . . I brought the wrong notebook. And I forgot to bring pictures. I'll bring everything with me tomorrow."

"Why don't you bring them along with you—the clients— the boys, you know?" asked one of the girls. "Let us see them for yourselves and then we can tell you what we think of them. You're a *shadkhn*, but we know best about what we want."

■

When the *shadkhn* was on the street, he looked around and sighed.

"Girls!" he said to himself. "Jewish girls in trousers, with cigarettes, talking to a Jew with such intimate disrespect! 'How are you feeling, *shadkhn*?' they ask! 'Bring us the grooms!' They have no shame. Nothing. Anything goes! Ay yai yai! How am I supposed to make a living from girls like those?

"*Feh*! I should go find some other way to make money. There's no money in this. No one wants *shidukhim* anymore. They can find their own matches. What they want is fun. They'll go after fun until the eyes crawl out of their heads!

"Still, maybe I'll go tomorrow to tell them about some potential grooms. Who knows? Maybe girls like that aren't able to find their own grooms. I just have to know how to manage it. Take them to the side and show them who the man is, and let them go and run into him as though it were a coincidence. After all, these girls aren't entirely to blame for running after the latest fashions. And aside from that they may be good, respectable girls . . ."

The farther away he walked from their apartment, the closer he felt them in his thoughts. By the time he was in his home he had decided to go back to visit them as soon as possible, to get to know them better so he could understand what they wanted.

She Was in Paris

Forverts, October 19, 1937

Katherine May, an American public school teacher, was quite popular among her colleagues, friends, and acquaintances because she
had been to Paris.

Before she left for Paris, Katherine gathered the addresses of
people who could show her the city, as one does before travel. One
address was of a family with the last name Baron, former millionaires who were émigrés from the old St. Petersburg high society. They
had fled to France because of the revolution.

The ex-millionaires received the American girl warmly. Such a
guest! She brought them heartfelt greetings from friends they had
known in the good old days. Those were the days! They lived on
country estates with servants and lackeys. True, they didn't leave
with empty pockets. They saved what they could. They brought with
them trunks full of rare and expensive antiques. If only they could
find buyers who understood their worth and were willing to pay the
cost!

After she gave them greetings from their friends in America,
Katherine asked the Paris family to recommend a suitable hotel for
her stay. The Barons were insulted by the very question. Why would
she even ask about some other place to stay? Why would she stay in
the hotel where they lived?

Hotel? They call this a hotel? The girl was astonished. Their
"hotel" seemed worse to her than an old Lower East Side tenement
house. The Barons' home consisted of a cramped bedroom. Three

doors away from their room was a kitchen with an oven, an old table, and a few broken chairs.

The Baron family doggedly pressed Katherine to rent a room in their hotel, and they wouldn't relent until she agreed.

In the gray light, Katherine's shabby little room looked very ugly. There was a single chair with crooked legs tied together with a rope. A pitcher of muddy water stood on a low cabinet.

◌

Katherine began her first day in Paris at the public market, where she accompanied Mrs. Baron to purchase groceries. The Barons were insistent that she eat with them, and she insisted on paying for everything. Mrs. Baron simply replied that if it gave Katherine pleasure to pay, she wouldn't stop her. She would show Katherine how well she had learned to cook in Paris.

In the afternoon, Mrs. Baron stayed at home, and Mr. Baron took the girl out to show her Paris. He agreed to allow her to pay for everything, since he was out of money at the moment. In the old days, in St. Petersburg, hundred-ruble banknotes were as worthless as mud to him, but now the smallest coin was a treasure.

They toured different parts of the city. Mr. Baron was happy to have a chance to see them, thanks to his visitor. Until now he had not allowed himself to spend money on these things. "You know how it is, when you're living off your reserves," he explained to Katherine.

In the evening the Barons and the American girl took a stroll in Montparnasse, an area renowned for its cafés and bistros. Most visitors sat at outside tables. A waiter came to take their order. The Barons hemmed and hawed. "It's all so expensive! But there's nowhere to sit without ordering something. So we'll have to at least have something to drink . . ."

They sipped lemonade and nibbled at dainty sandwiches. Mrs. Baron predicted that when the bill came the cost would be the same as a large meal for themselves and the children. Katherine handed some money to Mr. Baron so that he could play the waiter when the bill arrived. He paid it. They left and went to other cafés, sat at different tables, observed the people, and then decided to go home. To save the car fare, they walked and arrived home exhausted.

And so she spent her first day.

Katherine did not like the hotel. She resolved to find a better one. But she was afraid that the Barons would be insulted. So she stayed in the old, uncomfortable hotel and became a member of the warm and welcoming household with a feeling of responsibility for their daily needs. She showed them how one cleans rooms in America and how to throw away used rags. They showed her how to be economical and not spend too much money on small refreshments when you should cook large nourishing meals instead.

And they took care of her and kept her from coming into contact with people who are always looking to befriend Americans because they're out for their money.

Once, Mrs. Baron opened her trunks and showed Katherine the rare treasures she had: precious embroidered cloths, costly lace, bracelets, glass beads, pearls, and amber. Katherine was amazed. Thinking that Mrs. Baron was showing her these things to interest her in purchasing something, Katherine inquired as to how much she was asking for one of the colorful cloths.

Mrs. Baron smiled scornfully. These Americans think everything is for sale. No, she wasn't willing to part with even a single item. There may yet come a time when she would shine again in these riches . . .

"Won't these things be out of style by then?"

"No, they will only grow more precious with time!"

"Wouldn't it be better to have money?"

"No, money comes and goes but things remain."

Katherine didn't say anything else about buying things from Mrs. Baron. She went with Mrs. Baron to the large Parisian department stores. The prices for quality items were too high. And she didn't want anything cheap or chintzy. She bought a few little things, souvenirs, poor ways to demonstrate that she had once been to Paris.

Whether or not she bought finer items, her money kept disappearing. She spent it on the necessities for the Baron household, on the costs of living, and on seeing historical sites in Paris. She soon realized that if she went on this way she wouldn't have enough money to return home. She decided it was time to leave.

She and her new friends parted in tears.

◌

She was done with Paris. She returned to America. What a relief!

She was the center of attention among her American friends and acquaintances. They wanted to learn the secrets of Paris life from her. Her secrets? She was embarrassed to look them in the eye. She was embarrassed because she had no secrets to tell. They thought she had lived the high life in Paris. They were jealous because she had been to Paris, and she was ashamed to tell them that her experiences were different. Her silence only served to fuel their imaginations, like pouring oil on the flames of their heated fantasies.

She felt that if she told them how she spent her time in Paris, it would be a disappointment to those who already had an idea in their mind about Paris. So she said nothing, or, with a dreamy look in her eyes, she looked into the distance and said it was "wonderful." Yes, yes, Paris is wonderful!

◌

No one failed to notice that Katherine was so circumspect about her time in Paris. It wasn't at all like her. They imagined that perhaps her behavior there was less modest and decorous than it was at home in America, where everything is so *strict* and *conservative*. They could see from her new mannerisms that she must have been taken up in circles with looser morals. She had learned how to smile secretively, and she was constantly dropping French words.

Now, whenever they spoke of Katherine, they added suggestively: "She was in Paris . . ."

Katherine herself, who was cautious by nature, hid her experiences in Paris behind a clever and expressive silence. She knew that those who had a fixed, specific idea of life in Paris would never forgive her if she told them something different from what they believed.

She would fall in their estimation if she didn't take advantage of the good opportunities she'd had.

And so, whenever anyone started talking about life in Paris, they turned to her as an authority. "Ask her, she'll know! After all, she was in Paris!"

The Invitation

Forverts, *March 28, 1935*

Moyshe Marlof, an out-of-work writer, was very pleased when he received an invitation to "Wonder Camp" to do a reading of his work.

He was invited via telephone. The secretary, who was also a member of the committee organizing the program, was the one who called him. The secretary spoke to Marlof on behalf of Wonder Camp.

Marlof listened to her praise Wonder Camp over the telephone and nodded his head. He was eager to get out of the bustle of New York City and go to the mountains, and he was particularly interested in earning a few dollars.

But he soon learned that there would be no talk of payment for his reading. The secretary told him frankly that they were inviting him as a guest. They don't pay literary speakers, although he wouldn't have to worry about travel expenses. A committee would wait for him at the 23rd Street Ferry in New York at a designated time and take him to Wonder Camp. They would give him a return ticket home.

The secretary ended her speech in a curt, businesslike tone. "In light of all of this, will you accept the invitation?"

Marlof suppressed a sigh and said, "Well . . ."

The secretary didn't let him say anything further. She reassured him that he wouldn't regret taking the trip. It would be a delight.

He agreed to go, and she thanked him and promised to be back in touch with him a few days prior to the program, to let him know where and when to meet the committee.

A day before the program, the secretary called Marlof to let him know that the following morning the committee member would call him and tell him when they were to meet. He should wait at home tomorrow morning and not leave his house, so he wouldn't miss the call.

"Are you one of the committee members I'm meeting?" Marlof asked. The secretary told him that she wasn't. The committee consisted of two other women. No one he knew personally.

"Do they know me?" he asked.

"No, they've only heard of you."

"How will they know who I am?"

"I will tell them how to recognize you. I'll give them a sign: you can wear a tie with a Windsor knot, or a flower in your lapel . . ."

"Maybe . . ." Marlof said. "Would it be possible for you to be part of the committee?"

"No, I can't. I'm busy. Anyway, it wouldn't be so easy for me to recognize you, either, without a sign. I've seen you before from a distance at a literary event. You read something, it was quite funny. I thought I would die of laughter. Anyway, Shalom!"

"You speak Hebrew!" he cried.

"Yes, a little. *Shalom Uvrachah!*"

With that, their conversation ended. But that was enough to make him interested in meeting her in person. He painted a picture in his mind: a moonlit night, a stream in a forest, a camp, and the two of them together, him and the *Shalom Uvrachah* girl, the secretary. He would read to her his old poetry that breathed with love. She'd like them. She'd inspire him to write more and more love poetry . . .

The next morning, each time the telephone rang, Marlof jumped up and shouted, "It's for me!" to all the others who lived in the house. He did this all morning until after 10. Eventually, the committee called. They apologized for being so late and asked him to hurry and leave his house, and make sure to bring an umbrella, as it's raining. Oh, and he must not forget to put a white flower in his lapel, so they would recognize him. A white flower! And goodbye.

Marlof hurried out of the house. He would take the subway. At 14th Street he'd take the local to 23rd Street, and from there he'd take the streetcar to the ferry. It was hot and humid, as though rain was coming, and he was sweaty from rushing to meet the committee on time. He was anxious that he might be there too late and would just have to turn around and go home.

When Marlof emerged from the subway it was pouring buckets. It wasn't just rain, it was a deluge! And in the midst of the downpour, he'd have to find somewhere to buy a white flower! He bought a flower and put it in his pocket for the time being. He also purchased a newspaper, his newspaper. He missed the streetcar during the transaction. Perusing the newspaper, he was very pleased to see that something he wrote had been published. His own work! Just as he was about to read in front of an audience. It was a sign that things were going his way. It took up four columns, and in such a prominent place! The whole newspaper seemed dear to him because his writing was there. He carefully folded it back up and put it away to keep it out of the rain, because God forbid it should get wet. He wanted to make sure everyone at the camp knew that he'd been published today. Maybe they'd want him to read it out loud for them.

Marlof ran, out of breath, from the streetcar to the 23rd Street–Erie Ferry terminal. When he got there he affixed the flower to his lapel. He calmed down when he saw that it was only 11:30. He was almost a half hour early! Good. Better than good. In the meantime, he'd soak in the pleasure of reading over his story, and make sure that there were no typos.

He read with unusual pleasure. He was amazed at himself for having written such a fine piece of writing. Yes, he was quite a literary fellow, a talent. He would discuss his story with the secretary. They would confer over whether he should read it out loud. She would be so pleased with it! He was sure of it.

He was so absorbed in reading that he didn't notice people rushing past him and pushing him aside, the bells ringing, or the train's whistle. He heard nothing, he saw nothing. But when he looked around him and saw the time, he was furious. It was after 12 p.m.!

The newspaper was covering the flower, the sign that the committee was supposed to recognize him by! Now when he put down the newspaper and his flower was showing, the committee was nowhere to be found.

He ran around looking for the committee, hoping someone would notice him. No one so much as looked at him. Nothing. As he ran around, he dropped the flower . . . He found it again. It was trampled upon but he put it back in his lapel anyway. He felt wounded. And he hadn't eaten all day. His legs bent underneath his weight. A little ways away there was a bench, but he was afraid to sit down over there because the committee might come looking for him—that is, if the committee had decided to take a later train because they hadn't found him. The committee had called him so late. The least they could do was wait for him if he didn't make it on time.

He didn't let any woman go by who looked to him like they could be part of the committee. He looked into each of their feminine eyes with all of his fainting heart.

Suddenly, a woman looked back at him, and asked him if he was a Jew—she saw that he was holding a Yiddish newspaper.

"Yes, I'm a Jew," he replied. "Why?"

"Can I ask," said the woman, "what station I should buy a ticket for if I want to go to Wonder Camp? I'm afraid I might accidentally go all the way to Camp Boiberik."

"I don't know. I don't know," he answered nervously. He was very upset about waiting for the committee. He felt weak from not eating, and because he was so worked up that it was already after 3 p.m., and from the thought of having to turn around and go home, with his tail between his legs, like some cruel joke from the committee who went to Wonder Camp without him. What an honor! What an insult!

4 p.m. He couldn't wait any longer, or he might collapse together with his crumpled flower into the mud that the rain had left behind. He had to go inside somewhere and have something to eat, no matter what it was or what it cost. And then he'd go back to the noisy city.

He went into a cafeteria, but he couldn't eat. His throat refused to allow him to swallow. He thought about how nice it would have been for him there in Wonder Camp. He thought about meeting the committee, and he wanted to cry.

Worst of all was the sinking feeling that it was all his fault. If he hadn't been so absorbed in his own story, if he hadn't been so busy being proud of his own talent, none of this would have happened. He thought about how women had probably looked for him but he'd been blind and deaf to them. It was probably the committee, but he hadn't noticed. He hadn't seen anyone. He was too busy admiring himself.

For a Bit of Respect

Forverts, *July 30, 1936*

By nature quiet and withdrawn, Marlof had considered declining the invitation to travel to Wonder Camp to read his collected works. But the opportunity to stand in front of an audience, to hear their applause, to receive the appreciation from the readers he deserved, was simply too great a temptation. So Marlof had agreed to contribute something to the success of the evening.

Now he found himself sitting in the audience, looking up at the stage, watching the master of ceremonies and listening to the lead counselors at the children's camp praise the children in front of their parents—such *wonderful children*, who would grow up to be *wonderful people*. We should be very proud of them. Above all, the most praiseworthy thing about them is their interest in learning. Of course, we must thank their teachers for this, and all of those who do everything in their power to raise these children to be good people who will bring us pride. The girl counselor delivered a long speech to the children, and Marlof admired her confidence in speaking before an audience. He imagined asking her to take a stroll with him later. He would declaim his poetry to her under the light of the full moon.

He was next, so, with a nervous smile, Marlof walked onto the stage. He bowed before a hail of applause and proceeded to read without any introductory words.

He had only managed to read for a few minutes when he heard a banging sound from behind the thin curtain. It was the stagehands hammering, preparing the set for the show that the children and many of the adults of Wonder Camp would be participating in. Marlof glanced behind him. The chairman of the evening's event saw this and shouted through the curtain to tell everyone to be quiet. He gestured to Marlof to continue reading.

"Louder, louder!" someone shouted from the audience. "We can't hear a single word!" Marlof raised his voice and read as loud as he could. The hammering behind the curtain subsided, as though lost in his shouting, but then resumed again with new vigor. The chairman hollered again to tell everyone to be quiet, now calling not through the curtain but directly behind it. Several of the audience members who were near the door began to leave. The middle and then the front rows also began to thin out. Marlof saw that his audience was shrinking and decided to try to save the situation with a joke. With a half-smile he quipped that if he was bothering the stagehands with their work, he could stop reading. He could always put it off to tomorrow. It wouldn't spoil. He hoped his esteemed audience wouldn't complain. He understood the sentiments of the parents who sent their precious children to Wonder Camp hoping they would emerge as artists.

Having said his piece, he got off the stage and went out a back door. The scattered applause he heard as he was leaving rang in his ears after him, as though the audience were laughing at him. It was an insult. A better audience would not have laughed when he was forced to stop reading. They would have demanded a stop to the hammering. But it seemed the audience was happy to see him go. Well, fine.

He felt unusually tired and decided to go to his room and go to bed. The next day was going to be a full day, with three concerts: morning, midday, and evening. He would do his duty. He would pay them in talent for the honor of being their guest. Honor! But they weren't even giving him very much of that. Couldn't they have waited to hammer the decorations after he was done speaking?

As he went to the house, he heard some people complaining about these kinds of evenings. "There's too much art. We're trying to get away from all of that in the city. We come to the country for fresh air, but it's the same art again. We can sit through the music well enough, but the readings—who needs it? It's so nice out, there's a lovely fragrance in the air, the moon is bright, and we're supposed to sit inside and hear a story someone wrote in the city! If the story's been published, we could read it ourselves, and if not, if it wasn't worth publishing, why should we want to hear it?"

When he entered the room where he was supposed to be spending the night, he saw a woman and two children lying in one of the two beds. They were fast asleep. The pose in which the woman and two girls were lying was far from modest. Marlof turned toward the door. He was about to leave the room and find another bed when the door smacked him in the nose as the other man who was assigned to this room opened it.

The man, middle-aged and rotund, with a double chin and a cheerful expression in his eyes, lumbered into the room and, seeing the occupied bed, nodded toward Marlof, saying, "How do you like that for a panorama?"

"I don't know, they probably got lost."

"Those girls? We'll show them the right way soon enough . . ."

"How? They're asleep."

"I'll wake them up soon enough! I hate when others take my place. It's *my* bed! And you're supposed to be my roommate, right? So help me clean up this *khomets*. Help me get rid of them."

"How? It'd be a shame to wake them up when they're sleeping so soundly."

"Is that so? Nothing doing. I won't wake them—I'll just make so much noise that they'll wake up on their own."

The man seemed to be quite talented at making noise. He put two fingers in his mouth and whistled as loud as a train. The woman, waking abruptly as though forced out of a dream, clutched her daughters and shouted, "What was that? What are you doing here?"

Marlof's roommate bowed to her mockingly and responded, "A train, Madam. A train went by and woke you. Now, Madam, since you are already awake, allow us to assist you in making your way out of this room. We are weak people, and we need our sleep."

The woman glared at the man and cursed him. He should be ashamed of himself on his high horse barging in on a sleeping woman and her children and then talking to her like that! Only a true rascal could behave that way. A gentleman never would. These weekend guests are all like that, they want everything for themselves! And the regular residents have to suffer on their account. Her poor, innocent little canaries (the girls), must be terrified from being awoken so suddenly. Their father is paying good money to send his family to the country, and what does he get for it? His family is driven from room to room. There are more important people who need the space, they say! Well, no one is more important than her and her two girls. That's all there is to it!

Then she advised the two rascals that they'd better leave *her* room at once, if they knew what was good for them. Or else tomorrow she'd tell everyone about how they barged on a respectable, married woman, a mother with children, and insulted her. Do they realize how bad that sounds?

Marlof's roommate laughed. She can call him a rascal all she likes, but he's just an ordinary man. But that other man over there— he's a writer. A *writer*!

The woman replied that she didn't give a hoot about writers. She has some of them in her husband's family and she knows all about that lot. She doesn't care a whit about them. But she does have respect for a *gentleman*. For a man who knows how to show respect to a lady.

Seeing that he wasn't getting anywhere with the woman, Marlof's roommate went to the camp director. The camp director came and gently tried to persuade the woman to go upstairs to her own room. He would help to carry the children. All of the other rooms were already taken. There were so many guests this weekend, he didn't have enough space for them, so he'd given them her room . . .

The woman argued with the director but eventually she gave in. She couldn't refuse *him*. But if it weren't for *him*, she would have told those two rascals to spend the night outside.

Marlof lay down in bed and tossed and turned. His roommate wouldn't let him sleep. He went on and on about his stomachache, too many sweets, double portions, and bicarbonate of soda. He stood up and went to the sink to heave up what he'd eaten. He criticized the food in these country establishments. The "fresh" food that these farmers import from the cities. Fakers, bluffers! Making money at his stomach's expense.

Finally the man and his stomach fell asleep and began to snore. Marlof felt like he was suffocating. The air in the room was heavy. The room was right over the kitchen and the stench of rotting onions wafted from below, together with the pounding of knives on cutting boards where the kitchen staff were slicing grapefruits and oranges for tomorrow's breakfast, chatting about their experiences in different country resorts. He could hear a coffee mill grinding and a food processor pulsing. Old boards creaking under the feet of guests climbing up to their rooms late at night. Whispers and hushed laugher. The voice of the Wonder Camp counselor, the one he had thought of walking with and declaiming his poetry to . . . Her voice urging, "Shhh . . . Be quiet . . . People are sleeping . . ." and the sound of furtive kisses.

Depressed and dispirited, Marlof arose from his sleepless night and followed the herd to the dining hall to have breakfast, and then to the morning outdoor concert, where several people showed off their talents. It was as if they were trying to prove to the cultural figures who had come to visit from the city that they could do very well without them. Then there was the afternoon concert, also put on with local talent. Marlof decided not to wait for the third concert of the day. He would slip away unnoticed and go home, though he was sorry to miss the third meal.

No, he wouldn't read his work in front of this vapid audience again.

If only he could refuse out loud, so everyone could hear him! Should he wait to be asked? Should he wait to be called on? But what if they never call on him at all? No, he wouldn't stand for such an insult. Let them call on him and then find out that he'd already left!

He went over to the departing automobiles to ask who was headed to New York and found someone who could give him a ride.

The driver was complaining about the speeches and declamations they fed him before lunch and dinner. He'd rather listen to those kinds of things on the radio so he can turn them off whenever he wants to. When he goes to the country all he wants to do is meet new people and sit for a while in the lap of nature. He can be bored at home, where it won't cost him any extra money. There are no attractions for him here. So he's driving back. And if Marlof wants, he can show him a place you can go to laugh and laugh. It's good that Marlof isn't one of those artists. If he was, the man would refuse to drive him. That's what he thinks of those writers, those poets! They'd give anything for a bit of respect. But he's a man who won't give them any respect at all. No one could make him do it.

Marlof was pleased to hear the man say that he had only arrived at the resort this morning. He wasn't at the concert last night, and didn't see Marlof's failure. He probably would have been one of the people to clap mockingly as Marlof stepped off the stage. The man had a vendetta against writers. Marlof didn't need any more insults than he'd already received for trying to get a little respect. Anyway, because he'd been forced to swallow his pride, he'd pay this writer-hater back the best way he knew how: he'd write about him . . .

Glossary

Ameratsim (**Yid, from Heb.**): boorish, uneducated people

Antoyshte (**Yid**): disappointed (with a feminine ending)

Apelsin: nonsense word, derived from English "apples" and a plural suffix

Azoy (**Yid**): so

Bachurim, bachurot: **Heb.**: young men, young women

Badkhn (**Yid/Heb**): wedding jester

Bakshish (**Arabic**): payment, such as a tip

Baron Rothschild: Baron Abraham Edmond Benjamin James de Rothschild (1845–1934), a French member of the Rothschild banking family whose large donations lent significant support to the Zionist movement during its early years

Barukh hashem (**Yid/Heb**): Thank God

Bashert (**Yid**): fated partner (fem: *basherte*; masc: *bashert*)

Bazetsn (**Yid**): to seat (the bride), a reference to the traditional wedding ritual of seating the bride before the wedding ceremony for a moment of personal and communal solemnity

Beys Hamikdesh (**Yid/Heb**): temple, a reference to the desire to build a "Third Temple" in Jerusalem, after the destruction of the First and Second Temples in antiquity, which is said to usher in the Messianic age.

Breaking plates: refers to a tradition of mothers of a wedding couple smashing plates as part of the engagement ceremony

Droshky (**Russian**): carriage, pl: *droshkies*

Dvorim btelim (**Heb**): idle talk that has no benefit

Effendi: an Ottoman title of nobility

Eretz Yisrael (**Heb**): Lit. "Land of Israel," a term referring to the ancient biblical land and the modern geographic region of historic Palestine and the State of Israel

Ertsroel: Yiddish pronunciation of *Eretz Yisrael*

Eyshes khayil (Yid/Heb): Woman of Valor (from Prov. 31: 10–31).

Farvos hostu nit gezogt azoy (Yid): Why didn't you say so?

Feh (Yid): exclamation of disgust

Fenster (Yid): window

Gas (Yid): street

Gemilut chesed (Heb): act of loving-kindness, giving assistance without expecting return.

Get (Yid/Heb): divorce

Giveret (Heb): ma'am

Goles (Yid/Heb): Lit, "exile," often used to refer to diasporic Jewish life outside of the Land of Israel (Eretz Yisrael), and laden with allusions to the destruction of the Second Temple in Jerusalem in 70 CE and the exile and dispersion that followed this event

Goyim (Yid/Heb): non-Jews

Hatsadah (Heb): to the side

Iberrasht (Yid): surprised

In zikh (Yid): inside oneself; beginning in the late 1910s, a group of poets called the *Inzikhistn* or "Introspectivists" formed in New York who wrote in free verse and followed international modernist trends

Ir'et nit getrofn (Yid): you didn't encounter

Ivrit (Heb): modern Hebrew

Kest (Yid): a traditional obligation negotiated in marital agreements, the obligation of the bride or groom's parents to support the new couple for a specified period

Khazn (Yid/Heb): cantor, a synagogue official who sings religious music and leads the congregation in prayer

Kheyder (Yid/Heb): traditional religious school

Khomets: foods with leavening agents that are forbidden on the Jewish holiday of Passover

Khupe (Yid/Heb): wedding canopy

Khutspe (Yid): audacity

Kibbutzim (Heb): collective agricultural settlements in Palestine and modern Israel, owned and administered communally by their members

Kike: a derogatory slur for a Jew, here deployed among Americanized Jews in reference to Jews who are more religiously traditional or more recent immigrants; some believe that the term originated with this intra-Jewish usage, particularly by Central European Jews in America to refer to later-arriving Eastern European Jewish immigrants, although the slur later spread to become a pejorative term for Jews in America, regardless of national origin[1]

Kosher (Heb/Yid): in keeping with Jewish law; here used broadly also to mean legal, legitimate, or virtuous

Kushenirke **(Yid):** haggler (feminine)

Ládno **(Russian):** well, alright, OK

Landslayt **(Yid):** people from the same town

Lehitraot BiYerushalayim **(Heb):** until we meet again in Jerusalem

Lyubovski: Lyubovski was a staff artist at *Der Kibetser*, the satirical Yiddish newspaper in New York to which Karpilove also contributed

Magen David (Heb): Shield of David, a six-pointed star that has been used as a distinctive symbol for the Jewish people and was chosen as the central symbol for a Jewish national flag at the First Zionist Congress in 1897

Makom menuchah **(Heb):** resting place

Mazel tov (Heb/Yid): congratulations

Meshuge **(Heb/Yid):** crazy

Meyle **(Heb/Yid):** well, so be it

Mi yivne hagalil?, Lanu yivne hagalil **(Heb):** the lyrics to "El Yivne HaGalil" (God Will Build the Galilee), a folk song that was popular among the Zionist immigrants to Palestine during the time of the First Aliyah ("Who will build the Galilee? We will build the Galilee!")

Mikve **(Heb/Yid):** pool for ritual immersion

Mikveh Israel (Heb): "Hope of Israel," a youth village, boarding school, and agricultural training school established southeast of Jaffa in 1870

Mitzvah (Heb/Yid): good deed, obligation

Nordau Hotel: the Nordau Hotel in the Tel Aviv neighborhood of Nachalat Binyamin, designed and built by architect Yehuda Megidovich in 1925, had a ground floor that was commercial, with two upper hotel floors and a roof with a silver-domed tower

Nu **(Yid):** well, so, come on

---

1. Eric Wolarsky, "Kike," in *Interactive Dictionary of Racial Language*, ed. Kim Pearson, 2001. http://web.archive.org/web/20080602102925/http://kpearson.faculty.tcnj.edu/Dictionary/kike.htm (accessed February 8, 2023).

Prepiatstvie (**Russian**): obstacle

Protektsiye (**Russian**): influence, pull

Rothschild Boulevard: one of the principal streets in the center of Tel Aviv

Sachal hayashar (**Heb**): common sense

Shabes (**Heb/Yid**): Saturday, the Jewish Sabbath, which begins with candle lighting on Friday at sundown, and ends on Saturday evening; Karpilov uses "Arab Shabes" in reference to the Friday Prayer (*ṣalāt al-jumuʿah*) in Islamic practice. Friday (*jumuʿah*) is considered the holiest day of the week, and many Muslims attend Friday prayers and/or abstain from or shorten their workdays

Shadkhn (**Heb/Yid**): matchmaker

Shalom (**Heb**): literally "peace," used as a greeting or farewell (hello or goodbye)

Shalom uvracha (**Heb**): literally "peace and blessing," used as a farewell

Shidekh (**Heb/Yid**): (wedding) match, pl: *Shidukhim*

Sholem aleykhem (**Heb/Yid**): greetings, peace be upon you

Sholem bayis (**Heb/Yid**): peace in the home

Shprechen . . . Deutsch (**German**): to speak German

Shtus (**Heb**): nonsense

Shver (**Yid**): father-in-law

Shwaye shwaye (**Arabic**): slow down

So ist es, Lieber Herr (**German**): so it is, dear sir

Soferet (**Heb**): writer (female)

Sukkah (**Heb**): A booth or shelter with a roof of branches and leaves, used especially during the holiday of Sukkot

Tate (**Yid**): father

Todah rabah (**Heb**): thank you very much

Tov (**Heb**): good

Tsadikim (**Heb/Yid**): people who do righteous deeds

Tsedoke (**Heb/Yid**): charity

Tsenerene: Yiddish translation of the Pentateuch together with legends and commentaries, traditionally associated with women (first known edition: 1622)

Umophengike (**Yid**): independent (feminine suffix)

Untererdishe bahn (**Yid**): underground trail, subway

Ver (**Yid**): who

Vos dos? (**Yid, broken**): what this?

Yalla (**Arabic**): Hurry up
Yarmulke (**Yid**): skullcap
Yikhes (**Heb/Yid**): ancestry, lineage, importance, pedigree
Yishuvim (**Heb**): community villages, settlements
Zamashki (**Russian**): manners
Zeyde, Zeydenyu (**Yid**): grandfather
Zeyer (**Yid**): very
Zhargon: jargon, a pejorative term for Yiddish

Miriam Karpilove (1888–1956) was a pioneering and prolific author of Yiddish literature whose short stories, serialized novels, and journalistic writing focused on Jewish women's lives in America. Her work appeared in a variety of Yiddish periodicals such as *Forverts*, *Der Tog*, *Fraye Arbeter Shtime*, and *Gerekhtikayt*. Several of her works also appeared in book form, including *Judith* (1911), *Diary of a Lonely Girl, or the Battle against Free Love* (1918), and *A Provincial Newspaper* (1926). Born in a small town outside of Minsk, she immigrated to the United States in 1905 and resided in New York City and in Bridgeport, Connecticut.

Jessica Kirzane is a translator and scholar of American Yiddish literature. She is the assistant instructional professor of Yiddish at the University of Chicago and the editor-in-chief of *In geveb: A Journal of Yiddish Studies*. In addition to the present volume, Kirzane has also translated two other works by Miriam Karpilove: *Diary of a Lonely Girl* (Syracuse UP, 2020) and *Judith* (Farlag Press, 2022).

Printed in the USA
CPSIA information can be obtained
at www.ICGtesting.com
LVHW051137300823
756113LV00007B/2